WILLIAM FORSYTH:

LAND OF HOPES AND DREAMS

CAROLYN NICHOLSON

Cover design: Rebekah Wetmore

Editor: Andrew Wetmore

ISBN: 978-1-990187-22-3
First edition November, 2021

2475 Perotte Road
Annapolis County, NS
B0S 1A0

moosehousepress.com
info@moosehousepress.com

We live and work in Mi'kma'ki, the ancestral and unceded territory of the Mi'kmaw people. This territory is covered by the "Treaties of Peace and Friendship" which Mi'kmaw and Wolastoqiyik (Maliseet) people first signed with the British Crown in 1725. The treaties did not deal with surrender of lands and resources but in fact recognized Mi'kmaq and Wolastoqiyik (Maliseet) title and established the rules for what was to be an ongoing relationship between nations. We are all Treaty people.

William's New England

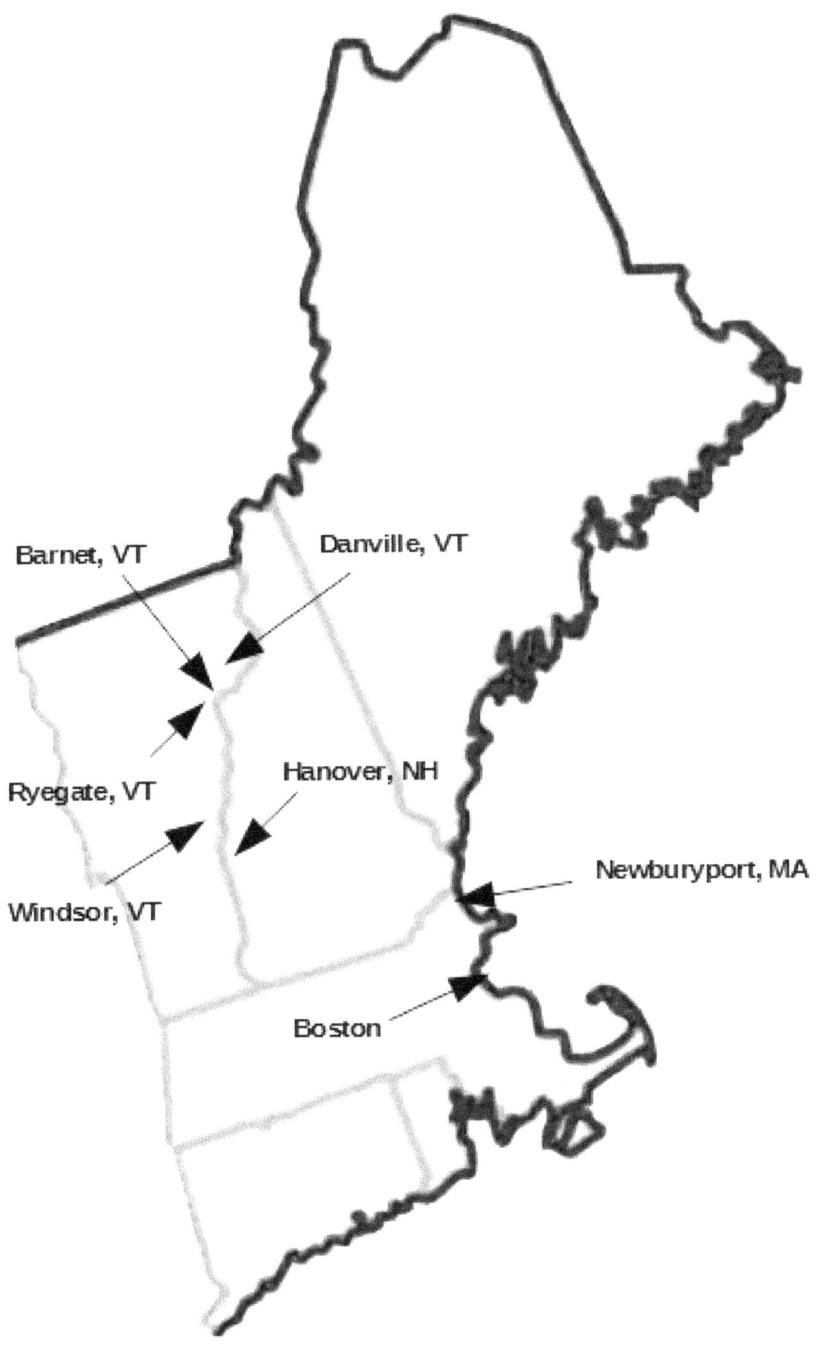

William's Nova Scotia

This book is dedicated to my grandmother,
Elizabeth (Bessie) May (Forsyth) McDonald
and to her daughter, my mother,
Margaret Jean (McDonald) Nicholson,
who inspired my research into our ancestors

This is a work of fiction, based on journals, documents, and painstaking research. The author has created conversations, interactions, and events; her goal is to depict the actions and interactions of a remarkable life in a way that celebrates the best intentions of all involved.

Contents

Carolyn Nicholson

1: Ryegate

It was a bright, brisk day in early May 1798 in Newburyport, Massachusetts. William Forsyth and James Fraser stood amongst the crowd of passengers on the deck of the ship that had brought them from Scotland, watching the sailors finish lashing the furled sails to the spars. Other sailors were readying the gangplank that would join the ship's deck to the dock.

"Will anyone be here to meet you?"

"Nay. I've come on my own, Mr. Fraser."

"Now that still strikes me as a little strange."

"Not at all, sir. Everyone in the Glasgow area knows about the Scotch-American township of Ryegate, Vermont. That's where I'm heading. Settlements on the frontier are in short supply of ministers and teachers and I have heard that Ryegate needs both."

"Still, well, never mind." Fraser shifted on his feet as if he was about to leave.

"It was a pleasure to meet you, Mr. Fraser. Our conversations have helped to make our weeks at sea very interesting and entertaining. I hope the talks with your shareholders go well."

"Thank you and I wish you well in your future in America. I hope Ryegate will appreciate all your abilities."

William was the first to walk down the gangplank onto the dock, excited to set foot for the first time in America—the land of hopes and dreams for his future.

Newburyport Harbour was filled with three-masted sailing ships, their stars and stripes snapping in the brisk breeze that blew in from the ocean and whipped up whitecaps in the harbour. William could see the flag of his own ship, the Union Jack, along with the flags of other European countries on other ships, large and small.

There was the smell of salt water mixed with the aromas of the waterfront—tar, fish, horse dung and other more unsavoury materials. In the distance was the town, closer were the stone buildings used to store materials to be shipped or received. The wharf was bustling with merchants, soldiers, sailors, dock workers, and friends and relatives come to meet a ship. Just thirty-five miles north of Boston, this small port at the mouth of the Merrimack River was known for shipping, shipbuilding and importing molasses to make into rum to be sold far and wide.

As William watched, employees of the taverns that surrounded the harbour scurried to newly-arrived ships, loading the luggage of the passengers on horse-drawn carts. A young man approached him and asked, "Where to, sir?"

"Can you recommend a good place to eat and rent a room for a few days?"

"Well, either the Fancy Nancy or the Wild Turkey has good food and clean rooms."

"Take me to the Wild Turkey, then." William thought the Fancy Nancy was not a name that would suit his profession. "How much?"

"A quarter. You go ahead, sir. Get your room and I'll be along with your trunk shortly."

William headed off in the direction the porter indicated, turning over in his mind how much "a quarter" might represent and what it was a quarter of. He soon passed the Fancy Nancy (with its sign depicting a young woman with an exceptionally low neckline skimming over alarmingly large breasts) and arrived at the Wild Turkey.

The brightly painted sign was obviously the work of an amateur, he thought, since the strange looking bird could just as easily have been a goose or a chicken.

Inside, there was a fire burning to ward off the dampness and a trestle table with benches on both sides running the length of the room. He paid two dollars for a room for the night and a dollar for his supper—roast chicken and potatoes with a thick slice of buttered bread and a large tankard of ale.

He took his supper at a spot near the fireplace. As he ate he watched men arrive for their own meals. Some were travellers like himself; others could be single men boarding at the tavern. It was certainly a workingman's drinking spot. As the dining room filled up, William found himself surrounded by a group of patrons who laughed and joked with each other like old friends. He caught the names of some of them: Tom and Joseph and something like 'Blink'.

Suddenly, the man who seemed to be called Tom turned to William and asked, "Who might you be? Your clothes seem a little too fancy for this fine establishment." He swept his hand in the direction of the other diners.

Taken aback, William paused for a moment. Then he stood up and bowed, "My name is William Forsyth, just arrived from Scotland. Pleased to meet you all."

He sat down and took another drink of his ale, but Tom wasn't through with him yet. "And what is your business in our country, might I ask?"

"I'm heading to the frontier to find employment. I hear ministers are in great demand in Vermont."

"A minister, did you say! Well, fellows," Tom said as he turned to his companions, "I guess he hasn't heard what we did to the Church of England ministers during the Revolution!"

The men all laughed uproariously.

Tom continued, "We put them and their wives and children out of their homes, took their property and ransacked their churches… even shot a few."

"Why ever would you do such a thing? It isn't Christian or even gentlemanly to treat people so."

"Why, we do what we want now that we are free from the tyranny of that English King."

The rest of his entourage nodded in agreement.

"Free to harass and kill helpless people? I say that is abuse of freedom. It is the actions of brigands and murderers!" William said emphatically.

"Already beginning to preach to us and you've only been in our country one day!"

"I hope to find a more Christian attitude in Vermont."

"Well, preacher, we shall see how long you last on the frontier," Tom said as he and his companions made ready to leave. "What do you think, boys, will he last a year?"

William listened to them laugh and watched as they clapped Tom on the back and left the tavern.

After that disconcerting first experience, William decided to retire to his room, which he found to be very small. The porter finally arrived, dragged his trunk up to the room and pushed it into a corner. After paying the man, William got ready for bed.

Just before saying his prayers and pulling the covers up to his shoulders, he thought several times, "I'm in America. I'm finally in America."

~

It seemed now that only moments ago he had been standing on the quay in Greenock, Scotland, his trunk at his side, waiting to board the ship that would sail him into the future—the future he dreamed about every day. His father and mother had come up to Glasgow from Ecclefechan to see their son off on his great adventure. It seemed harder to think about leaving when he looked at his parents—they might never see each other again.

On the way to Greenock, the departure point for trips to North America, every tree, bush and stream seemed to be dearer and more beautiful. He looked at the ring his parents had given him with the family crest, incorporating the griffin, symbol of vigilance and strength. It seemed to speak of his roots that spread deep into the land of his birth, roots he hoped would soon spread as successfully in the land of his future.

On the dock, his father hugged him and said, "Write soon and let us know how you are doing." His mother held him tight and then turned away for a moment. Their private good-byes had been tearful, so he hugged each of them again briefly and turned away.

After paying the porter to take his trunk on board, he went up the gangway quickly. He did not linger on the deck to exchange painful farewells over and over with his parents.

Once the ship was underway, William walked briskly toward the bow and stayed there for hours as the ship passed into the Firth of Clyde and made for the passage between the Isle of Bute and Great Cumbrae. The route ahead lay past the Isle of Arran on his right, across the Irish Sea, to pass north of Ireland and Rathlin Island and out into the great, heaving, North Atlantic Ocean. He wondered what waited for him in the New World as he watched the seagulls soar and scream around the ship before finally going below deck to check out his second-class accommodations.

After getting his sea legs and overcoming some initial sea sickness, William slept well each night and awoke each morning with excitement. After breakfast and when the weather permitted, he often walked along the promenade, watching the clouds and the sun sparkling on the waves.

While watching some dolphins, he bumped into a rather large gentleman in a fine-looking suit and smoking a cigar.

"Watch where you're going, laddie."

"Sorry, sir. Are you all right?" The cigar smoke made William cough.

"Most certainly. I take it you don't smoke cigars. What do you do?"

"My name is William Forsyth and I've just graduated and become a licentiate of the Church of Scotland."

"Have you now? Why don't you join me for supper in the first class dining room and I'll test your knowledge."

"Gladly, but I'm not sure that second class passengers are allowed in first class dining rooms."

"Well, you will be if I invite you. You don't know who I am, do you?"

"Nay, sir, I'm afraid I don't."

"Well, we'll leave it that way for now. Come to the main dining room at seven o'clock. We'll see what kind of minister you'll make."

William didn't know how he felt about the gentleman with the cigar or his invitation, nor did he relish being thrown out of first-class. But this seemed like a bit of adventure and he was all for adventure.

At seven o'clock he arrived at the first-class dining room and looked past the maître d' to see where his host might be seated.

The maître d' moved to block his view. "I'm sorry, sir. You seem to have lost your way."

"Nay, I have been invited."

"And by whom?"

William kicked himself for not having learned the man's name. But then he saw his cigar smoking host blustering across the room.

"All correct, all correct," his host said. He wrapped one large arm around William's shoulders and whisked him off to his table. William resisted the urge to look back to see the maître d's reaction.

William didn't get much to eat as his host cross-examined him first in Latin, then in Greek. Once satisfied with William's linguistic ability, he moved on to rhetoric and philosophy.

The inquisition came to a close with the last bite of pudding. "Well, that's enough for one night, laddie. We'll leave scripture studies, history and mathematics for another day. I appreciate that you speak in such a clear and logical manner. You have been well-taught. I hope you enjoyed your supper?"

"I did, indeed. But I have two questions for you. Where did you get your education?"

"Private tutors. My parents were comfortably well-off and believed in education. I have little need of Latin and Greek in my business, alas, so it is a treat to be able to exercise them with you. And the other question?"

William blushed slightly. "Uh, your name…?"

"Did I never say? My name is James Fraser and I am a partner of William Forsyth, businessman and merchant of Glasgow and Halifax. I own one of the largest lumber businesses in Nova Scotia and New Brunswick. I'm on my way to meet some shareholders in Boston."

"Very pleased to meet you, Mr. Fraser. I hope one day to be as successful in my calling as you are in your business."

From time to time during the voyage, Mr. Fraser invited William to dine with him, often adding other first-class passengers to the table. The talk often turned to business and politics and, occasionally, religion.

"I hear that the people in Europe are much engaged with their Enlightenment philosophers and their encouragement of skepticism, deism, or even atheism," Mr. Fraser said on one occasion to one of the dinner companions.

"Aye, aye. I hear that as well. Thankfully, most of the Enlightenment proponents in Scotland are ministers in the Church of Scotland. That has kept our society from becoming radicalized, although I believe the Church has now become divided into Evangelicals and Moderates. The Moderates—although in the minority—have become the dominant power elite in the Church of Scotland."

"And which are you, Mr. Forsyth?" Mr. Fraser asked.

"I am most firmly not a Moderate, sir. I am part of the majority of ministers who profess the tenets of the Presbyterian faith and are bitterly opposed to what the Moderates are proposing. I fear for the Church if this new philosophy takes hold in Scotland. It seems like a fidfad that might lead the less-informed astray. I find it deeply distressing for ministers to hold court in taverns, discussing philosophy and getting drunk."

"But surely you enjoy a good debate?"

"Indeed I do. I think it sharpens the mind and often adds to our understanding of the subject debated, but not if the question is poorly stated and only one side has had the opportunity to prepare their presentation."

The men nodded in appreciation of William's reasoning.

During the day, William explored the ship, asking the seamen about their work and marvelling as they, cat-like, climbed up and down the ship's rigging—raising and lowering the sails as the direction and strength of the wind demanded.

He regularly visited the sick and others on the lower decks, distressed at how many people were crammed into such close quarters. On his way back from one such outing he met a boy on the stairs down to third class. "Excuse me, lad, are you travelling with your family?"

"Nay, Mister. Well, not with my parents, but with my aunt and uncle. My family died of smallpox two years ago."

"I'm very sorry to hear that. You must miss them very much."

"Indeed, sir. But we lived in the workhouse and I do not miss that. We were fed poorly and worked almost to death. They took us away from our parents, so the parents would work harder to get out of the workhouse and get us back. I hope there are no work-houses in America."

"I think, lad, that there are more opportunities for the poor in America. I am sure you are a good worker and will do well. How are your aunt and uncle?"

"They have nine children...well, eight now. They were a little better off than my parents and decided to find a new life in Amer-ica."

"Where are you heading?"

"I think Boston, the next stop after Newburyport."

"Well, God bless you and your aunt and uncle. I hope you find great success and happiness in the New World. By the way, what is your name?"

"James Stewart from Dumfries-shire, sir. Pleased to meet you."

Since there were people trying to ascend and descend the stairs, William squeezed his way back up to second class.

When not exploring the ship, he had plenty of time to write several sermons and composed some hymns. The voyage passed pleasantly with only one storm. The sailors said the high seas and waves washing over the deck were not unusual on this sea route. Passengers like William, who had not been on an Atlantic voyage before, were a bit shaken.

But even the most pleasant voyage can wear on one's spirit. After seven long weeks, the sea-weary passengers heard the shout from the crow's nest, "Land ho!" He had arrived in America!

~

Upon awakening at the Wild Turkey Inn on his second day in the

New World, William said his morning prayers, then pulled back his long brown hair into a queue and tied a black grosgrain ribbon around the hair band. He dressed, put on his buckled shoes and his jacket, placed his tricorn hat on his head and went downstairs to have a breakfast of porridge, bread and ale.

After breakfast he asked his host when he might travel to Vermont, specifically the area around Ryegate.

"Well, you're lucky," the man said. "The wagon only goes once a week and you can catch it tomorrow morning right here at the Inn. But why would a lad like yourself want to go out to the frontier? Nothing but log cabins and farmland barely cleared out of the forest."

"Have you been there?"

"Nay. Just what I've heard. Why don't you stay here in Newburyport or go down to Boston. Now there's a busy place with lots happening."

"Well, Ryegate is settled by Church of Scotland people from around the Glasgow area so I think I would adjust better to the New World among my own people. Besides, I heard ministers and school teachers are in short supply."

"Well, my advice—if you asked for my advice—would be to stay on the coast where it's been settled longer and there are many more opportunities. But the young don't usually take advice from us oldsters, so I wish you well in your travels."

William thanked the Inn owner for his information and advice and decided to take a stroll around town. On the high street, he saw beautiful homes and well-dressed people riding in horse-drawn carriages. The poorer areas of town were closer to the waterfront—their shabbiness a sad contrast to the high street. There was a market square where fresh produce from the countryside was sold each week—with some rotting produce scattered here and there. It smelled unpleasant.

Walking even more quickly, he turned onto a street that he hoped led back to his lodgings, and ran right into the tavern crowd.

"Well, well, Mr. Minister from Scotland I do believe," Tom said.

His friends quickly filled in behind him blocking the path.

"Tom from the Tavern, good day," William smiled. By their clothing, he imagined they were sailors, perhaps on furlough.

"Still in Newburyport. Maybe cold feet about going to the frontier?"

"I'll be leaving tomorrow. Now excuse me as I'm on my way back to my lodgings."

William shouldered his way through the little crowd and continued on down the street. The last thing he heard was, "He won't last a year. Mark my words."

The next day, excited to see this new country, William climbed into the wagon, drawn by four horses, which would take him to Ryegate. As he glanced around his transport, he noticed there was a rounded canvas cover which could be raised if it rained and a bench along each side of the wagon. There was a place to stow trunks, parcels, and the mail close to the back. The driver and his spare sat in front on a bench with a backrest.

As they drove through the cobblestone streets of Newburyport, William saw that most of the houses of the ordinary people were made of unpainted boards weathered a soft grey. He saw boys on their way to school and servants busy buying food for their employers or engaged in other tasks. Shopkeepers were just beginning to open their doors for the day. Their servants were sweeping the sidewalks and washing the store windows. The wagon driver avoided the lovely mansions of the rich that lined the high street and instead took a route through the poorer part of the town.

They were soon in the countryside. As people on horseback or in wagons passed, they tipped their hats; the driver and his second nodded in acknowledgement. The jolting drive over the ruts and the dust of the road kept William from fully enjoying the trip, but he did get a chance to look at the countryside with its neat farms and herds of cattle, horses, sheep, as well as fields of barley, oats, wheat, and flax.

At one point, William slid towards the front of the wagon and yelled over the noise, "Why do they raise so many pigs?"

"Not sure," the spare replied, turning to look at William. "Pigs just seem to grow well in this climate as best I can tell."

At the first stop to water the horses, there was a small inn. William bought his lunch and two men with no luggage climbed on board with their lunches.

"Good-morning, lads," William said cheerfully.

"And you would be?" one said.

William introduced himself and noted he was on his way to Ryegate.

"Never been there. Abner, have you ever been there?"

"Nay, Samson. Why would anyone want to go there?"

"I've heard that they are short of ministers and school teachers on the frontier," William said.

"That may be so. And which are you?" Abner asked

"I'm a licentiate of the Church of Scotland just arrived in America."

"Never had the need to go to church. Have you, Samson?"

"Nah. Prefer to go to the horse races. Or do a little gambling."

"Are either of you married?"

"My old woman nags me to stay home with her and the children —eight so far—but I tell her I work hard and that a man needs some fun," Abner said.

"What about you, Samson? You go to the horse races, too?"

"Nah, mostly I go hunting and fishing with my friends. As soon as I can afford to buy some land, I think I'll marry and have a passel of children like Samson here."

"And what about you, Minister? What do you like to do for pleasure—if ministers are allowed to have pleasure!" Abner looked at his friend gleefully, smiling like someone who enjoys his own jokes.

"Well, I've been studying hard for many years. I've almost forgotten what I used to enjoy. Let me think a minute. I enjoy swimming and flying kites, in the summer, of course. In the winter I like to read and go on sleigh rides."

"Children's pastimes," Abner said, wrinkling his nose. "Real men gamble, and go to taverns, and maybe wrestle or box. I guess it has been a long time since you've done anything for pleasure."

"I did take boxing lessons for a time when I was younger. Perhaps once I'm settled in a parish, I'll take that up again—if my parishioners don't object."

They finished eating their lunch and drank some bottled ale to clear away the grit in their mouths from all the dust of the road. Then the men settled themselves as best they could and had a nap.

William began to consider his opinion so far regarding the people he had met. They were less disciplined and less well-mannered than he had expected and he wondered if this would be conducive to the success of their new republic. The ones he met so far certainly were not church-goers or people who had any appreciation of his hard-won education. He decided to withhold his final assessment until he had met more Americans.

As it grew dark, the wagon pulled into a clearing. William saw a log building with a horse shed and storage shed. He and his travelling companions climbed out and went to the inn to get a hot meal and some more ale.

There was roast pork or mutton, bread and butter, roasted potatoes and Indian corn. Full of good food and, therefore, guaranteed to have a good night's sleep, William went up to a small room with a large bed. His trunk was kept in the shed to await the wagon that would take them the next step of the journey.

Before he undressed, Samson and Abner came into the room. That was when William discovered the uncomfortable fact that all the male guests of the inn slept in their clothes in the same bed, only removing their hats, coats, and shoes.

As the men threw their coats and hats over the rail of the bed and kicked off their shoes, William hesitated, but saw no option but to follow suit. He carefully folded his coat and put it on a small stool in the corner of the room, putting his hat on top and, taking off his shoes, put them beside the stool.

Hoping there were no fleas in the bed, he lay down with his back to one of the men and, despite thinking he would have a long wakeful night, soon fell asleep.

As the sun came up, William awoke with a start. He could hear birds singing outside the window and the beginnings of the hustle and bustle of the day. He was thankful the other two men were already gone as he tried to smooth the wrinkles out of his clothes and pick the lint off his stockings.

Smoothing his hair back, he put on his coat, hat and shoes and headed downstairs to the dining room. There, for the first time, William experienced maple syrup. The pancakes and sausages were delicious but the syrup poured in abundance over the pancakes was…he searched for the word that would do justice to the experience.

"What is this syrup? It's, it's …divine!"

The guests seated at his table laughed. "We call it maple syrup— it's the boiled down sap of the sugar maple tree," a pretty young lady, one of the waiting staff, said.

"I think it was worth my whole trip so far, just to taste maple syrup."

His table companions smiled.

The morning was bright and sunny. The great North American forest surrounding the inn heated in the sunlight, filling the air with the scent of pine and spruce and enhancing William's feeling of aliveness. It was soon time to climb up on the new wagon and continue the journey.

He reminded himself once more, "I'm in America," before the wagon jerked forward. It would be two more days of travel to reach Ryegate.

The further they progressed, the fewer the farms and the deeper and darker the forest.

The inn he stayed at on his second night had the same arrangement—the men all sleeping in one bed. He learned all the women slept in one bed in another room.

As he and his travelling companions finished their late supper, William decided to ask about the sleeping arrangements. "This expedient of the men all together in one bed. Being from Scotland, I'm not familiar with this arrangement."

"Well, you're not in Scotland anymore," a large and rather dishevelled man said.

"We Americans get tired of strangers acting like they're better than us. They're just snobs as far as I'm concerned," an older man added.

"Gentlemen," William said, "I only meant I was unfamiliar with the practice and meant no offence. Every country does things a little differently, I think."

"True, true,' the dishevelled man agreed. "No offence taken."

William didn't add that it wasn't a practice he found particularly pleasing, but what could he do?

~

The closer they got to Ryegate, the more vivid the dream became—the dream of his future. This dream had sent him across the Atlantic to a new land, and it ran like a bubbling brook through his mind.

He could see himself as the minister of a large and flourishing congregation—preaching, visiting his parishioners and catechizing the young and old. Men would tip their hats to him and young women would curtsy. Here was a place where he wouldn't be hemmed in by the hierarchies and traditions of the Old World. He felt like the whole New World was opening before him with the promise of adventures and opportunities.

But for now, he was bumping along a dusty wagon road with his trunk jouncing behind him as the long day stretched before him. People without luggage got on and then off a few wagon-stops later.

As the wagon jolted and rocked along the rough road, one of the passengers next to him, an older man, said to another, perhaps his son, "This young man is quite the dreamer—hardly a word to say."

"Wonder what he's dreaming about," the younger man said with a chuckle.

William said, "I am dreaming about my future in America, gentlemen."

The older man snorted, "America, land of hopes and dreams! You can see by our gorgeous attire that we have achieved our dreams!" They both laughed uproariously.

William didn't mind that they got off at the next stop.

A woman and little girl boarded. They both smiled warmly and

William tipped his hat to them. Shortly after the wagon began to move, the little girl fell asleep. Amid the jouncing of the wagon, the thud of the horses' hooves, the squeaking of the horses' harnesses, and the dust from the road, William said, "I'm William Forsyth and I'm on my way to Ryegate. Pleased to meet you."

"Pleased to meet you as well, Mr. Forsyth. I'm Mrs. Norris. We have a hundred acres nearby, and I'll be getting off at the next watering place where my husband will be meeting me and my little one, Annie Martha."

"And how old is Annie Martha?"

"Just turned five a few days ago. I like your accent, Mr. Forsyth, is it Scottish?"

"Aye, Mrs. Norris. I arrived a few days ago."

The conversation was cut short when the wagon came to a halt at the watering place for the horses. William jumped down from the wagon and Mrs. Norris passed the sleeping Annie Martha to him so she could jump down herself.

"Good luck in your travels, Mr. Forsyth."

"Good-day to you, Mrs. Norris," William said as he climbed back onto the wagon. The horses having drunk their fill, the wagon was shortly on its way again.

William returned to dreaming. He saw himself running a grammar school for young people so they could be educated and find important roles in this new nation. He saw powerful and well-placed people seeking his opinions on their plans. William often felt that it was important to consider policies from the eyes of the poor or disenfranchised. This was a missing element in the wild scramble for those with some power and wealth to gain even more. He could at least bring attention to the fact that there was more to life than grasping and controlling all the resources of a country. Taking a break from his dream, William watched the sides of the road. As the farms grew fewer and the forest grew larger, he saw birds he did not recognize, including one that was a beautiful sky blue."Driver," he said, "what is the name of the blue bird with the harsh call?"

"Ah, sir, that's a blue jay, or some call it a jaybird. Remarkably noisy. Not as noisy as the woodpeckers, though. They can drive you crazy with their pecking at the trees."

There were many squirrels, only a bit different from the ones they had at home. Towards evening he saw a bear—he was sure it was a bear as he had seen pictures of those creatures. The bear and her cub seemed out for an evening stroll.

Late on the third day of the journey, the driver announced they were about to reach Ryegate. William sat up and paid close attention as he began to see small, one-story farm houses and large, three-story barns the closer they got to their destination. Then there was a spacious clearing with a hitching post and a watering trough ahead.

The driver pulled the team up to the watering trough. William climbed down, and a local man appeared and helped him to lower his trunk to the ground.

"I'm John McDonald. Welcome to Ryegate."

"Thank you, Mr. McDonald. Would you know of a place to stay?" William noticed Mr. McDonald's overalls looked a bit tattered and splashed with mud. His gray hair seemed unkempt under his broad-brimmed hat.

"Indeed I would. You see that house over there?" McDonald pointed to a house made of grey clapboards on the edge of the clearing.

William nodded.

"My wife and I keep a boarding house. Would you like me to take your trunk over there?"

"Aye, Mr. McDonald."

"You see that other building across the clearing?"

"The one that looks under construction?" William asked.

"The same. That building—which you can see, is just a shell at the moment—is our new Meeting House. Its construction seems to be stalled. We will soon have a Township meeting to find out why."

They were soon at the boarding house. Mrs. McDonald greeted him warmly in a loud, friendly voice. She wore a blue gingham dress covered with a white apron, with her sleeves rolled up to her elbows and her hands covered with flour. Her grey hair was braided, with the braids coiled around her head and a few stray hairs falling toward her blue eyes. It looked like she had flour on her forehead as well. Her face was pale but her cheeks were ruddy.

"Come into the kitchen, laddie. I'm just getting supper ready for the table."

She poured him a glass of ale. William had arrived.

Back in Scotland, William had learned from the Presbytery that the townships of Ryegate and Barnet had written and asked them to send a minister. William wanted to waste no time in locating the committee members and presenting himself as a candidate.

At supper, he asked, "Mr. McDonald, how would I meet with the committee to hire ministers?"

"Lucky for you the Township will meet in two days to find out about the delay in construction of the Meeting House. I'll ask the committee to meet with you at that time."

Before the meeting, William did his best to prepare himself—he even had a bath and washed his hair. He opened his trunk and found the new suit his parents had purchased for him. It was made of fine black wool and had a cream-coloured linen shirt and fine wool stockings, as well as new buckled shoes and a new tricorn hat.

Feeling well-dressed, he consulted the small mirror in the room and saw the excitement in his blue eyes. If he had had a larger mirror, he might have noticed how wrinkled his suit and shirt were after seven weeks at sea and the jostling ride from Newburyport to Ryegate.

However, Mrs. McDonald did notice and soon he was on his way back upstairs to remove his suit so she could iron it. "Laddie, couldn't you see those wrinkles, for Heaven's sake!" she scolded.

"I confess I was too excited to notice, Mrs. McDonald. Thank you for ironing it. I'm sure I'll make a better impression now."

Secretly, William felt he was being 'mothered' and it was comforting to feel 'at home'.

Now dressed in his freshly ironed clothes, he returned to his trunk and took time to neaten its contents. Under the new clothes in his trunk were his winter coat and boots, and below that were his Greek and Latin texts, Biblical commentaries, history books and writing material.

As he touched his new clothes and looked at his books, he thought of all the sacrifices his parents had made to get him an education and give him a start in the world. In the excitement of coming to America, he had forgotten what this meant to them. He promised himself that he would write them when he had the good news he hoped would soon be forthcoming.

And so on May 30, 1798, William walked the short distance from the boarding house to the Meeting House. The place was so far from completion that it was like entering a notion rather than a building. There were benches scattered about and a few chairs, but no pews and no pulpit.

The meeting was a little tense. William understood from the debate that the members had expected the building to be completed over a month ago. The contractors could offer no satisfactory reason for the delay. The meeting voted on a new completion date, with dire warnings of what might take place should the contractors fail that date as well.

The hiring committee members stayed behind after the township meeting dispersed. William removed his hat and walked toward them with confidence.

"Good evening, gentlemen. Thank you for meeting with me."

"Ah, Mr., Mr. Forsyth. Is that right?" a man replied.

"William Forsyth, at your service."

"Well, Mr. Forsyth, we'll have you sit across the room. We're not quite ready for you yet. See that chair on the far side? Sit there."

As he sat on a wobbly little chair, William gathered his first impression of the committee. Their slight lack of manners and preparedness left a disconcerted feeling in his stomach. However, he knew that what he lacked in experience he more than made up for in education, confidence, and a quick wit.

"Mr. For..., yes, that's right. Mr. Forsyth. We're ready for you now. Quickly, please."

William walked over at his own pace and said boldly, "Where I come from, gentlemen, people greet their guests with more hospitality. However, I shall try to overlook this in our conversation."

The men stared at him for a moment, seemingly in consternation, then introduced themselves as the committee to appoint preaching and settle with the minister agreeable to the Acts of the State. John Gray introduced himself as an Elder, and Andrew Brock as a Deacon. William Neilson, James Henderson and Hugh Gardner were managers of the Scotch-American Company of Farmers on the American side of the Company.

Mr. Gray, acting as chairman, said, "And do you have credentials, Mr. Forsyth?"

"Licentiate of the Church of Scotland."

"And your experience?"

He looked to William like a farmer, as he was dressed in homespun clothing with his shorter pants, above his bare feet, spattered with mud.

"During my studies, I had preaching duties at the local churches, on a rotating basis, along with the other students."

The committee members looked at each other.

"So you're a new graduate with no experience?" one said.

Once again, William felt the uneasy feeling in his stomach. "I am highly trained in ministry by the Church of Scotland."

"Well," Mr. Gray said, "we will give you a chance to demonstrate your ability by hiring you for the summer. You will preach in the mornings at Ryegate and in the evenings at Barnet."

The Committee voted "that the money due for pine timber from the Glebe lot be paid for preaching done after this date, Mr. Goodwillie to have one-third and Mr. Forsyth two-thirds."

They also voted that "the money to pay Mr. Forsyth for preaching through the summer be paid by subscription when the timber money is done."

Mr. Gray asked, "Can you ride?"

"Most certainly," William nodded.

"Then we will provide you with a horse."

William walked out of the meeting house in a mild tumult of elation and unease, with a resolve to prepare for Sunday coming. There was a lot he needed to figure out about this meeting and he hoped his landlady could give him the information necessary to understand what just happened.

"Did you get the position?" Mrs. McDonald asked when he entered the kitchen.

"For the next month or so."

"Those folks have been looking for a permanent minister for years. You know what it is—they hope to find a way to hire you cheap. See if I'm not right."

William was surprised at her indignation on his behalf. One of her braids, already loose, fell down over her shoulder and her ruddy face became more flushed.

"Mrs. McDonald, I need to understand what happened in the meeting. Who is Mr. Goodwillie and what is subscription?"

"Mr. Goodwillie is a Presbyterian minister who comes by after his crops have been planted and preaches for the summer. He goes home in time for harvest. He lives quite a distance away from Ryegate. As for subscription, this is often the way ministers are paid on the frontier. Each household promises to pay what they can towards the salary of any ministers and schoolteachers."

"And are people satisfied with the services Mr. Goodwillie is able to provide?"

"Nay, many people want their own full-time minister. A committee was set up, maybe ten years ago, to search for a full-time Church of Scotland minister, but so far no one has applied."

He nodded. That would explain the cool reception and the way the committee dismissed his credentials. The elders of the church were probably happy just to go along as usual. Their leadership in church affairs may be very satisfying to them, and hiring a permanent minister would take away either their power or their pleasure or both.

Sunday came bright and sunny. William walked to the Meeting House in his new suit, sermon and Bible in hand. The house was packed—everyone in the community eyeing the newcomer. By then everyone knew he was a new graduate, new to America, and, of course, new to Ryegate. There was even a group of people from Barnet in the congregation hoping to be the first to carry their impressions back to their township before the evening service.

William sat with the congregation as the elders led the service. When the time came for his sermon, he strode to the pulpit. With the confidence of one who knows his gift and how to use it, he preached a sermon that clearly demonstrated his ability.

With a clear and powerful voice, he began, "You who are sinking under the burden of suffering and oppression, be comforted; the day of your deliverance draweth nigh; the morning of your salvation which you are so ardently soliciting. All your afflictions and fiery trials which are but for a moment, will work out for you an high degree of felicity through all the ages of eternity."

The elders and the congregation were silent. Some had their mouths open in amazement.

At the end of the sermon, the Barnet people quietly slid out of their seats and headed for the door. After the service, the congregation of Ryegate took turns to shake his hand and tell him how much they hoped he would stay and be their minister. The Committee members were not among the well-wishers.

Once the congregation was gone, John Gray came up to him as he gathered up his hat and papers."Well, there, Mr. Forsyth, the committee considers your sermon adequate. You can continue on with us for the next little while. Don't forget you're supposed to be in Barnet by seven this evening."

He turned on his heel and strode away.

~

It being the beginning of June, William decided to wait until the end of the month to see how things would turn out. He told his landlady how his first Sunday seemed to him. "The committee doesn't seem too welcoming, Mrs. McDonald. I have a bit of a sinking feeling about their interest in a full time minister. I could be wrong, of course."

She said, "You wouldn't leave us now, would you? The congregation is really impressed with your preaching."

"We shall see," William said, not sure himself what he would do.

Just then, Mr. McDonald and one of the other boarders, who assisted Mr. McDonald with the farm work, came in for their lunch, after stamping their feet loudly on the back porch.

Mr. McDonald sat down with a sigh, "It's a good thing I've got Sam here to help with the hoeing. I'm getting a little old for such back-breaking work."

Sam smiled, evidently pleased with the acknowledgement of his usefulness. "And how are you, Mr. Forsyth? You seem a little distracted."

"Sam, I am a bit worried about something, but I'm sure in time it will all get sorted out. You're looking very sunburned, Sam."

"Aye," Mr. McDonald said, "he won't wear the straw hat I bought him. Sam, I insist you wear your hat. Mr. Forsyth is right. You look like your face is on fire! The girls won't be interested in you if you look like you're scalded."

Sam laughed. "You're right, Mr. McDonald. I'll wear my hat. Don't want to scare away the girls."

The cheerful banter around the kitchen table lifted William's spirits and the split pea soup with ham, and the homemade bread and butter, were delicious. *It will all work out*, he told himself.

In the following days, he set himself the goal of visiting as many of the families of Ryegate as he could, setting off each morning with his lunch in his saddlebags and arriving back at the boarding house each evening with stories for his landlady, mostly about getting lost or falling off his horse when it stumbled on the rutted and muddy roads.

The homes in Ryegate were a mixture of log cabins, more recently-constructed plank houses, and even more-modern frame houses. Almost every house had a three-story barn with room for animals to overwinter, a hayloft, and a loft to store grain and the necessary seeds for planting in the spring.

The farmers and other tradesmen—blacksmiths, cordwainers, carpenters, and others—were friendly and helpful, glad to meet their minister and, if time permitted, to have a chat over a glass of rum, or—even better from William's viewpoint—a cold glass of buttermilk. All were from the Glasgow area or descendants of those first pioneers, so William felt right at home with them and they with him. Most of the conversations started with, "do you know the ___ family from ____?"

Mrs. MacDonald was one of the first settlers at Ryegate. She remembered all the recipes from around Glasgow and would make them for William. As he ate, she talked about her experience of crossing the Atlantic, taking the wagon trek from Newburyport to Ryegate, and living off their supplies as they cut logs, built cabins, and began to clear the land for planting. "We were all experienced farmers who knew each other from the Old Country, so we were well able to work together, but nothing could have prepared us for the winters—howling blizzards and six feet of snow and ice. We were never warm unless we were in front of the fire."

She told William about each of the families and about how the township was run. "Now, a township is not a town. It is a farming community that has bought or been granted a certain number of acres of land that are divided into farm lots, each farmer owning his own lot. The lot owners make the necessary decisions about the township. each having a vote, or by a special committee, like the committee to find and settle a minister."

One of William's early visits was to the home of General James Whitelaw, Surveyor-General for the state of Vermont, and perhaps the most important man in the township. On a warm June day, William rode up to General Whitelaw's home which was several miles away from the meeting house.

The General was sitting on his front veranda in a rocking chair. Recognizing William, he rose to greet him. "Welcome to my home, Mr. Forsyth. Very pleased you've come to visit. Just a second until I pull over a comfortable seat—my wife's chair is a little too small for you."

William took a seat in the comfortable-looking rocking chair with a high back and a cane seat, just as General Whitelaw's wife opened the front door and came over to meet the newcomer.

"Mr. Forsyth, this is my wife, Suzanna. Suzanna, you recognize our new minister, Mr. Forsyth."

"You're most welcome at our home, Mr. Forsyth. Would you like some rum or cider?"

"Pleased to meet you, Mrs. Whitelaw. And I'll have some cider, please."

By the time she returned, William and General Whitelaw were already well into talk about family and family history.

General Whitelaw described how the Scotch American Company of Farmers sent him and David Allen to look for land for the township. "Mr. Allen was a farmer of good judgment and I was trained as a surveyor. There were about one hundred and ninety-three families in this joint-stock company. Each farmer had contributed the same amount to the company. With the money we bought 23,000 acres! Unfortunately, shortly after the American Revolution broke out. The Royal Navy blockaded the coast, so that not all of the families that signed up were able to arrive until after the war ended in 1783. I think that everyone that intends to come has now arrived."

"And how did you become Surveyor-General for the State of Vermont?"

"More and more people moved into Vermont and the State needed the land surveyed. I had some experience and they hired me. So for the last twenty-five years I have been surveying Vermont. There were few roads and it was hard work tramping through forests and swamps all the way up to the Canadian border, sleeping in the woods summer and winter. Now that I'm about to turn fifty, I've decided to take it easy and enjoy my family and my farm."

General Whitelaw gave William a tour of his farm. As they walked, he told William that his eldest son, Robert, now twenty, had managed the farm for the last five years while he was away surveying. His second son, William, seventeen, also helped out.

There were fields of wheat, oats, and barley sprouting in the spring sunshine. The herd of dairy cattle—black and white—stood out against the fresh green grass of the pasture.

"Well, here are our dairy cows. We are now at the stage where we produce an excess of butter and cheese that we can sell to the markets on the coast, mostly to Newburyport or Boston."

"Do you use the barter system or use cash?"

"Cash. It's just easier. But we buy lots of things from the coast that we can't manufacture here like fashionable shoes, gloves, quality clothing, buttons, new plows—the ones we brought with us are mostly worn out by now—hay forks and the like. It's easier to buy these things than to manufacture them yourself."

"Now, we're just getting back towards the house. It's rather a point of pride that I have the first frame house in the Township. Our first house—a log house—is now being used as a shed to store winter rugs and curtains during the summer."

"Its a very nice house, General Whitelaw, and I especially like that front porch with the rocking chairs."

"Everyone likes our front porch," he smiled.

They sat for a while longer while the General talked about his family.

"I've already mentioned my sons and would be remiss if I didn't mention Abigail, just fifteen and named after her mother, my first wife, and Marion, eleven, named after my mother. All my children are by my first wife, Abigail Johnston of Newbury which is our nearest 'English' town. She died in 1788 when she was only thirty. It wasn't until 1791 that I remarried Susanna Rogers of Bradford."

"Sorry to hear about your first wife. It must have been very difficult on you and the children to lose someone so dear to you."

"Aye. But it is still too difficult to talk about so we will leave it at that, if you don't mind."

"Of course, of course."

As it was getting close to suppertime, William said good-bye to General Whitelaw. He rode back to the McDonalds', thinking how comfortable he felt sitting on the porch, drinking cider with the General.

Having a few month's worth of work with the promise of continuing employment, William sent a letter to the Grafton Presbytery, the governing body for Presbyterian and Congregational churches in central New Hampshire and Vermont, to ask them to ordain him. It was located at Dartmouth College, in Hanover, New Hampshire, about twenty miles down the Connecticut River from

Ryegate.

~

In mid-June, General Whitelaw and several members of the Committee attended William's ordination ceremony. There were fourteen ministers and numerous lay presbyters present as William walked to the front of the classroom where the lay elders stood. After a hymn and prayer, the elders asked William the essential questions about his faith and his call to ministry.

Then, with William kneeling before the assembly, two lay presbyters laid their hands on his head and prayed, "In the name of Christ and in obedience to His most blessed will we do now ordain William Forsyth and appoint him to be a minister in Thy Church, charging him with the administration of Thy Holy Word and Sacraments. We beseech Thee that he may be faithful and wise servant in all that is committed to him and may so fulfill his promises and vows that he may hold fast to his profession without wavering. So guide and govern his ministry by Thy Holy Spirit that it may be to the praise of Thy Name, the comfort of the Church, and the inbringing of many from their wanderings unto the true fold, and finally to the assurance of his own conscience in the day of the Lord. Enrich him with all knowledge and utterance, and fill him with the wisdom and gentleness of Christ. Amen."

All the members of the Presbytery came forward to shake William's hand and welcome him. The ordination ended with a hymn and the apostolic benediction.

William was ecstatic. After all his studies and training, he had the recognition needed to fulfill his hopes and dreams.

"A very moving event for you, Mr. Forsyth," General Whitelaw said, smiling at the happiness shining from William's face.

"Aye, General," William said. "And since my parents are not well off, it was a great sacrifice for them to support my education. I was never sure if I could finish my studies and reach my heart's desire. So this is an amazing day for me—and for them."

As they rode back to Ryegate, the elders told William about the other ministers and lay people in the Presbytery. William tried to pay attention, but his head was a bit in the clouds.

When he got home, Mrs. McDonald was waiting, eager to hear the whole story from the beginning to the end. She was very happy for him. Then, as it was very late, William wished her good night and headed off to his room.

Still filled with enthusiasm, he opened his trunk to find a piece of writing paper, then sat at the small table. "Dear Mother and Father," he wrote. "Good news. I have this day been ordained by the Presbytery of the Connecticut River. I scarcely can believe I have achieved this goal after so many years of study. Without your encouragement and financial support this would never have happened. I am filled with boundless thankfulness to you both."

William's energy began to wane and he decided to finish the letter in the morning.

Upon arising, he completed the letter with descriptions of the ordination and some more details about Ryegate, General Whitelaw, and his parishioners and signed it "your most devoted son, William."

Shortly after his ordination, at the end of a long day of visiting his parishioners, William and General Whitelaw sat on the general's porch drinking cold buttermilk against the heat of the summer. As they chatted, a man on horseback rode up, let himself down from his horse and walked up the path to the house.

General Whitelaw rose, and William followed suit

"Mr. Forsyth, this is our good doctor, Dr. Samuel White, of Newbury. He has a large number of patients in Ryegate. Dr. White was a surgeon during the Revolutionary War."

"I am honoured to meet a friend of General Whitelaw," William said as the men shook hands.

More buttermilk made the rounds, and the chat carried into early evening.

"I heard you just got ordained," Dr. White said.

"Indeed I did, Doctor! Did you know that the President of Dartmouth College is one of the members of the Presbytery? He told us that he was educated in Edinburgh and he knows the south of

Scotland very well.

Doctor White and General Whitelaw looked at one another with a smile.

"And," William continued, "they were pleased to grant me the ordination of an Evangelist with ample power to execute all the offices of the ministry wherever I went—even to establish churches. This was without any request of mine."

After Doctor White's departure, William decided to bring up his latest plan. "General Whitelaw, I know there are a goodly number of students in the Township who have attended grammar school. I thought I might start a normal school to educate them to be teachers. What do you think?"

"What an opportunity for the young men of Ryegate, Reverend Forsyth."

General Whitelaw had been calling William 'Reverend' all day. William smiled happily each time.

"You can get started whenever you want, Mr. Forsyth. I'll make sure the townsfolk know about this opportunity and I'm sure you'll readily get fifteen or twenty students. We'll figure out a way to pay you, and the students can pay for their own supplies."

Within a month, General Whitelaw had offered his home as a place to teach. Twenty-one students showed up the first day to enrol. One of the first was John Page, whom everyone called 'Lame John' behind his back. He got around on homemade crutches and was never going to be able to farm or do any of the jobs on the frontier that required physical labour.

"Mr. Forsyth," Page said, "this is a matter of great excitement for me. I plan to be your best student."

All the others were equally enthusiastic. And so the first normal school in Vermont was begun.

General Whitelaw was a local leader of the Masonic Order. During one of William's weekly visits, he suggested that he would offer William's name to the Masons of Harmony Lodge, who were looking for a sermon for the celebration of the Festival of St. John the Baptist, June 25. This service was to be held at Danville, a nearby town.

William jumped at the opportunity and was soon working on both a sermon and a hymn for the occasion. The work had to be done soon enough to have it printed before the event.

"I believe," General Whitelaw said, "this sermon will be the first printed communication in Ryegate Township. Fancy that!"

William searched the commentaries for a theme suitable for the occasion and decided that he would preach on one of the Beatitudes—'Blessed are the merciful, for they shall obtain mercy'. He got to work crafting his sermon with the Masons in mind.

After many hours of pondering and writing, he needed a break and a second opinion. With his notes in hand, William entered the kitchen and found Mrs. McDonald intent on her cooking, surrounded by the usual cloud of flour, the result of baking their daily bread. "Mrs. McDonald, would you have time to listen to my sermon for the Masons?"

"Aye, Laddie. Just give me a moment to put the meat into the pot and I'll have a short time before I need to start peeling the potatoes."

Mrs. McDonald was careful to refer to William as 'the Reverend' or 'Mr. Forsyth' in public but in private she usually called him 'Will' or 'laddie'—usually laddie, which made William homesick as this is what his parents called him.

Mrs. McDonald dropped the cubes of meat into a large iron pot suspended by a crane over the fire, wiped her hands on her apron and put the lid on the pot. Pulling out a kitchen chair, she sat down and looked at William. William stood behind a chair and, notes in hand, began to deliver his sermon.

> 'Blessed are the merciful for they shall obtain mercy.' The Gospel according to St. Matthew, Chapter 5, Verse 7.
>
> The truly merciful man flies with feeling heart, and open hands, to the assistance of every known distress; and exerts his whole powers, as far as the law of God and nature directs, in labours of love and acts of benevolence. It is true indeed that he is sensible that the powers and capacities of particular men are limited; and since no individual can as-

sure the care or procure the happiness of all, he is first attentive to those relations of friendship, kindred, or society, in which the universal father has more immediately placed him. But his kind wishes and his benevolent intentions are not confined to these. No, his boundless and inextinguishable desire, like the God who framed his capacious soul, embrace the whole universe of which he is a member; and if his influence extends beyond the welfare of those whom nature and Providence has more immediately committed to his care and protection, he hears the voice of God and humanity within calling him to exert his powers to their full extent.

The sermon continued for some time in the same vein, even though William eschewed the dramatic pauses he felt would be appropriate when he actually delivered it before a congregation.

When at last he was done, and looked up from his text, Mrs. McDonald rose from her chair and said with great seriousness, "I can tell that you really feel all this in your heart, laddie. We cannot be reminded of the importance of loving our neighbour too much. You are truly suited to preach the Gospel and I hope the hiring committee realizes how much you have to give Ryegate and Barnet. I know the people of our Townships feel this way."

"Thank you, Mrs. McDonald. I truly appreciate all your support," William said, wishing that the hiring committee were more like her.

The sermon was a great success. William's name and ability were spreading throughout Vermont.

"Mr. Forsyth," General Whitelaw said one evening toward the end of the summer, "I'm hearing excellent reviews from your normal school students. Strict but fair is what they are saying. The students feel confident that they will be able to follow your methods and educate our children. We are very fortunate to have someone of your ability come to Ryegate."

William glowed with pride. "Thank you for your kind words, General Whitelaw. I have always wanted to teach and I take great joy in the success of my students."

On September 17th there was another town meeting. The town voted: 'To pay Mr. Forsyth $6 per week for the time he had preached to date out of the pine money. To hire Mr. Forsyth and settle him as minister of the town as soon as he produces proper credentials. 40 yeas/ 6 nays.'

The Township also voted 'to pay Mr. Forsyth $200 for the year ensuing and increase his salary as the grant list increases, 'til it amounts to $250.'

The minutes read: 'Mr. Forsyth declined the offer.'

Compared to the salary and benefits he would have received in Scotland, the offer seemed not just inadequate but perhaps offensive. Maybe the Township didn't really want to hire a full-time permanent minister? And, besides, there was no manse offered. He hoped to marry and have children. Where would they live?

William continued to preach and teach, but he began to search for another job.

General Whitelaw tried to temper William's expectations. "The frontier of America is not the same as the parishes on the estates of the large landowners of Scotland, Mr. Forsyth. People do pay what they can, but it all depends on the success of their crops."

William had great respect for General Whitelaw and his advice but, still, had his parents sacrificed their own well-being to see their son perhaps worse off than they were? Were his years of study to result in a threadbare life in a boarding house? Had he made a great mistake leaving Scotland for...for a pittance?

To an observer, the town might seem to run on as usual; but behind the scenes there was a battle going on between the townspeople, who wanted to negotiate with Mr. Forsyth in order to keep him in Ryegate, and the committee members, who wanted to save money and let Mr. Forsyth know who was in charge.

William knew what was going on, of course, because Mrs. McDonald was keeping up on the progress of the debate and filled him in with what she knew.

For a while everyone's energy had to go entirely into getting the crops harvested and into barns and cold cellars for the winter ahead. As soon as the last potato was dug up and buried in straw in the cold cellar, however, the debate resumed, with the majority of towns folk wanting to keep William.

On November 13th at another Township meeting, it was voted: 'To pay Mr. Forsyth $200 for the first year and let the salary advance with the list til it amounts to 80 pounds per annum.'

The minutes read: 'The offer was declined.'

General Whitelaw had already explained to William that all the members of the joint-stock company who were going to come to Ryegate from Scotland were already here. The list was not going to increase and so neither was his salary.

William shook his head. "I cannot accept this offer. It seems disingenuous."

"Let's call it what it is, Mr. Forsyth: devious and deceitful. No gentleman could accept such an offer," the General said, shaking his head.

~

It was winter in Vermont and when the sky was covered with flat, grey clouds that threatened snow, they usually delivered on that threat. Even though Mrs. McDonald had mentioned how unused the newcomers from Glasgow were with the snow, William had yet to experience what this meant. The first snow of the season brought his visiting and teaching to a complete stop as his horse couldn't make it through the drifts.

Some things, though, cannot wait for a reprieve from the weather, as William learned when he got the message that Mrs. Henderson and her infant had died in childbirth at the height of the storm.

"How do I reach them, Mr. McDonald? What happens now?"

"Some of the men will come for you and help you over the worst of the drifts on the way to the cemetery. Others are digging a grave and some are bringing Mrs. Henderson and the baby's coffin to the graveyard. The Hendersons and everyone who can make it there will attend." He glanced out the window. "None will hold it amiss if it is a *brief* service, laddie, as they all must fight their way home again after."

Almost as soon as William was dressed in his warmest clothing, his cloak, and riding boots, there was a knock at the door and the stamping of feet on the porch. Mr. McDonald let the men in. Their long, sad faces said it all.

"Pray, come with us, Mr. Forsyth," one of the men said.

William nodded and followed them out into the dark, overcast day, with the wind blowing snow off the tops of the drifts, almost blinding the men as they struggled through the deep snow.

William watched as a couple of men pushed their way up a drift and then lay on the snow, waiting for him to be pushed toward them. Grasping his arms they pulled him up the drift and then all three rolled down the other side. It was exhausting, but they finally made it to what must have been the graveyard, where a small group huddled, backs turned against the wind. William saw there were even some children, so wrapped up it was impossible to tell whether they were boys or girls.

The coffin was already in the grave, dug no doubt with great difficulty.

William said the graveside service from memory, as any service book would have been ripped from his hands by the gusty wind, and on the heels of his last "amen" the men began to fill in the grave. The Hendersons watched on, scarves wrapped around their faces and hats pulled down over their ears.

William remembered his pleasant visits with the Hendersons just in the early fall. Then Mrs. Henderson was a pregnant, cheerful woman with six or seven children, all in good health. Now she was lying in the cold earth, her baby in her arms, while her family bid her farewell.

William felt like crying, but struggled to keep calm as he shook hands with the mourners before they all departed.

Once the men returned him to the McDonald's, he sat for a long time before the fire, warming up and, when no one was looking, crying tears of sadness for the Hendersons, especially the little children returning home with no mother.

Mrs. McDonald was busy cooking meat for the stew she was making for the Hendersons. Some of the young, strong men would be by soon with a large sled to collect all the food the women of the Township were cooking. She didn't say anything to William and he was glad he didn't have to chat with anyone.

He continued to teach and preach until spring, still casting about for another job, having concluded that he would never be accepted by some members of the committee and that his salary would never progress. He also knew—if he cared to admit it to himself— that he was a gifted preacher and teacher and that the salary offered seemed to show no real appreciation for his abilities. He hoped it wasn't pride that caused him to refuse the final offer of the Township.

At a regular meeting of the Presbytery at Dartmouth College in May, 1799, the agenda included the approval of building churches in new communities, raising money for the care of the poor, and the education of ministers to fill the usual shortage on the frontier. Then the secretary read the correspondence received since the last meeting.

"I also have a letter," he said, "from, let me see, Cornwallis Township in Nova Scotia. They say they will be looking for a minister. Their minister of fourteen years will be leaving this year."

That would be tight shoes to step into," someone said.

"I wonder they even raise the question," another said. "Any who went there would place himself back under that mad King George."

As soon as he returned to his lodgings, William wrote to the Elders of Cornwallis Township, knowing that a reply would take several weeks. He walked the letter down to the wagon stop where the wagon driver took his money and placed the letter in a leather pouch with the rest of the outgoing mail to be sent down to Newburyport. His letter would go from there to Halifax, Nova Scotia, and from there to wherever Cornwallis Township might be. William also sent a letter to his parents to let them know what was happening. Then the waiting began.

William's routine of teaching, preaching and visiting continued in Ryegate and Barnet. He often sat in the evenings with his friend,

General Whitelaw, who knew of William's decision and regretted, as he said to his friends and family, that the town was 'so short-sighted to lose such a valuable man.' He recommended William to His Excellency, the Governor of Vermont, as worthy to preach the election sermon, to be preached to the Governor, the Lieutenant Governor and Council and House of Representatives of the State of Vermont at Windsor on October 10, 1799.

It was quite unusual for a minister who had only been in America for two years to be invited to preach to the Government of a State—any state. But William's friends and supporters knew he was someone they wanted to keep in Ryegate and in Vermont. In the first week of July of 1799, Mrs. McDonald went down to the wagon stop to pick up the mail. A letter was waiting for William when he returned in the evening.

With his landlady, he sat on the porch drinking ale as she waited for him to open the letter. William was of two minds about opening it and finding out what his fate would be. If the Cornwallis people said, 'No', then he might have to accept the Committee's offer, inadequate as it seemed to him. If the Cornwallis people invited him for an interview, that would be a positive sign. If he was offered the job, he would have to leave his friends and parishioners as well as his normal-school students. He was no longer sure what he wished for.

As he drank his ale and struggled with what he wanted for himself, his landlady, no longer able to stand the tension, said, "Well, Mr. Forsyth, are you ready to open the letter?"

William's reverie was broken, "Oh, I am sorry. I was lost in a maze of anticipations."

He reached for the letter and tore it open. He scanned the several sheets, then went back to the start to read slowly.

"Are you committing it to memory?" his landlady said.

A slow smile spread over his face. "I might just. They wish to interview me for the position."

Her face wrinkled in consternation."So, will you go for the interview? Across the sea and all?" She was clearly upset about the thought of losing the man the Ryegate people now called the 'Ryegate minister.'

"I need to sleep on it," William said slowly.

"Aye, do that," she said. "But know I will not be sleeping at all."

Once away from his landlady, he had to admit he felt quite excited that he had been invited for an interview.

At breakfast the next morning, Mrs. McDonald put William's porridge down in front of him with a thump and said, "Well?"

Mr. McDonald looked up from his plate of eggs and bacon.

"I've decided to go, Mrs. McDonald. I have to see what they will offer before I can finally make up my mind."

Mrs. McDonald just stood there looking at him.

Finally, her husband put down his fork. "Now, my dear, you've got to let the lad figure out what he wants for himself. As sad as you'll be if he decides to go, he can't stay where he's not satisfied. All young men have to do a bit of exploring before they settle down. That's hard for you, I know, since our sons were killed in the Revolution, but it's just life."

That was a shock to William. Neither of the McDonalds had mentioned their sons before. That explained the way she 'mothered' him. *It seems that no matter what you do*, William thought, *you have an effect on those close to you*. He remembered how hard it had been on his mother when he left for America.

~

A week before the date of his interview, William rode to Newburyport and booked passage on one of the small commercial sailing ships that plied their trade between Windsor, Nova Scotia and ports along the New England coastline, or the 'Boston States'.

After four days of sailing, they reached the southern end of Nova Scotia and entered the Bay of Fundy. William spent most of his time watching the Nova Scotia coastline. Just a short sail up the Bay of Fundy, the sailors pointed out the entrance to the Annapolis Basin, called Digby Gut. On the shores of the Basin, they told him, were the towns of Annapolis Royal—the old capital of Nova Scotia from 1710 to 1749 until it moved to the newly-built town of Halifax—and Digby.

The rest of the coastline was rather monotonous, as a line of high hills covered with forest blocked any view of the interior, so he turned his attention to the whales that often spouted nearby. Squinting into the bright sunshine, he tried to spy the coast of New Brunswick with its seaport of Saint John. No matter how clear and bright the day, it seemed there was always a fog bank in the Bay of Fundy obscuring the western horizon.

The weather being clear and fine, the ship arrived in Windsor after six days at sea. The Reverend Hugh Graham, the Church of Scotland minister who was leaving Cornwallis Township for the congregation in Stewiacke, met William at the dock.

As they were to ride to the township, Mr Graham led William to a stable where he could hire a horse. Mr. Graham was warm and friendly. They chatted about family and church matters in Scotland and Nova Scotia before Mr. Graham took William on a brief tour of the township.

Cornwallis Township looked so beautiful to William—lush green marshland, crops ripening in the sunshine, herds of cattle, sheep and pigs, and small but comfortable homes and big barns. It seemed like a heavenly place.

"People call it the garden of Nova Scotia," Mr. Graham said, "so excellent are the soil and the climate."

"A very Eden," William said. But then a thought struck him. "But are there...serpents?"

Mr. Graham made a rueful face. "Were people not always battling the devil, we would have no work at all. But I should tell you that I have had a bit of a falling-out with the Church folk."

"But you've been here for fourteen years, Mr. Graham. Surely your relationships with your congregation were very solid and well-established."

"That's what I thought," Mr. Graham said, "so I decided to bring up the possibility of moving to the new Church of Scotland hymnbook. That's when I found out how attached the congregation were to *Watt's Hymns*."

William knew it well: a solid, if stolid, New England Congregational hymnbook. "What happened, then?"

"They were so vehement about keeping their old book, I fear I got a little defensive and said things I wish I hadn't."

"Such as?"

"Well, I called the hymns 'Watt's brats' and said they were not spiritual like those in the Scottish hymnbook."

"And?"

"The rancour was so great that when an opening for a second minister among the Scotch-Irish Presbyterians of the Musquodoboit Valley was advertised, I applied and was offered the job."

Knowing that they were soon going to lose their minister, the Elders were pleased at William's interest, although they would have preferred a Congregational minister. This was out of the question since after the American Revolution all Congregational ministers were trained in the newly minted United States of America and did not choose to move to the English colonies.

After all had offered William welcome and were seated, Deacon Newcomb spoke. "Our friends and relatives in Vermont speak highly of your abilities, Mr. Forsyth, and that encouraged us to invite you for an interview."

"It is certainly kind of your relatives and acquaintances to speak well of me. I appreciate that."

"Well, now, first we want to hear why you are not satisfied in Ryegate and are looking for a new congregation."

William knew that this valid question had a trap-door within it. They would be looking to hear whether he would speak ill of his current employers. "Mr. Newcomb, gentlemen, the people of Ryegate seem not to have the means to hire a full-time minister and, since I wish to marry and have children, I must be able to earn enough to support a wife and family."

"Quite a reasonable decision," Mr. Newcomb said, looking around at Mr. Morton, Mr. Cogswell, and Mr. Beckwith.

Mr. Morton spoke up. "Tell us what you know about the Congregational Church, Mr. Forsyth."

"Mr. Morton, as you may know, Grafton Presbytery serves both

Presbyterian and Congregational Churches. I get to meet Congregational ministers and hear their concerns at each meeting of the Presbytery. My impression is that the Congregationalists have a sincere desire to serve the Lord with all their heart and soul."

"Well said, Mr. Forsyth. I might also add that we are very loyal to our customs and traditions that we brought from England starting in 1620."

William could see the Elders sitting back in their chairs and relaxing as their conversation continued. There seemed to be no vexing concerns.

So, with the caveat that William would accept the preference of the Congregational Church for *Watt's Hymns*, the Elders offered him the position. He was to arrive as soon as possible and certainly before the end of 1799. The salary and benefits offered were far better than what had been offered in Ryegate and they had a manse for the minister as well.

William promised to consider their offer and reply promptly. He knew he would first have to give proper notice to the Ryegate and Barnet people.

On the trip back, William debated the offer from the Cornwallis people. Besides the salary and benefits, there was the fact that the Americans were still anti-English, the American Revolution having only ended fifteen years before. William and his family were loyal to the King and the Royal Family, but William thought that the United States had freed itself from the old traditions that resulted in strict class hierarchies. There seemed more freedom to move in the United States. William had been struggling with the thought of abandoning his loyalty to the Crown and becoming an American. He would not have that struggle of conscience in Nova Scotia.

Mrs. McDonald was in her kitchen cooking supper when he arrived. She turned and looked hard at William, then gave a little nod. "You're going to leave, aren't you?"

"It was a very good interview and they offered me the job. I'm still considering the pros and cons."

She turned back to her cooking and soon Sam and Mr. McDonald came in from the barn, hanging their heavy coats just inside the door to allow them to dry off. Mr. McDonald looked at his wife and then at William, and decided not to ask any questions.

They ate their supper with a little forced conversation about hay prices and the cost of a new plough. Sam, not noticing the tension in the air, continued to ask questions and make observations.

"Well, Mr. Forsyth, if it's Nova Scotia for you, I hope you'll remember your friends here in Ryegate. Maybe I could come up for a visit. How far would it be, I wonder? Does it cost much to go there? It would be by ship, I suppose."

William answered each question briefly, hoping that his tone of voice sounded calm and neutral.

With the pros and cons still swirling around in his head on his first night back in Ryegate, after many hours he finally fell asleep.

~

By morning, the answer was clear and the only question was how to let the people of Ryegate know.

At the end of the Sunday service, just before the benediction, William spoke of his sincere appreciation to the town for the opportunity to be their minister and to the State of Vermont for inviting him to offer the election sermon. He told them how much he enjoyed teaching at the normal school.

Then he said, "Dear friends in Christ, as you know, I have been to Cornwallis Township for an interview. They have offered me this soon-to-be vacant position. After serious consideration, I have decided to accept. I hasten to assure you that this was not an easy decision, but the Cornwallis people have offered me salary and benefits commensurate with my desire to marry and have children. You have all been most kind to a new minister trying to find his way in the New World and I will always remember all I have learned from you. I hope you will wish me well and I'm sure you will soon have a new minister who will be much to your liking."

He said the benediction and walked out the door of the church, leaving behind a shocked congregation. As he stood on the path outside, blinking in the sunlight, he could hear surges of conversation like the waves in a troubled sea.

After a time, the congregation left the meeting house. Most walked over to William, shook his hand, and said how sorry they were things had not worked out. Others left without acknowledging him.

As soon as William returned for supper after having preached in the evening at Barnet, Mrs. McDonald greeted him with a glass of ale and an offer to be seated in the kitchen.

"Laddie, I must apologize to you for being so upset at the thought of you leaving. My husband is right. You have to find your own way in life. Finding happiness is truly what I would wish for you. You seemed so like my own sons that died that I became too attached to you. Please forgive me."

"Mrs. McDonald, there is nothing to forgive. I readily let you 'mother' me as I was missing my own dear mother. Perhaps I gave you good reason to get attached to me. We were both missing loved ones and that explains it all. Please don't feel badly, only wish me well and pray that I have made the right decision for my life."

"I will, laddie. I will."

On October 7, 1799, William and General James Whitelaw set off for Windsor, Vermont, where William would preach the election sermon to the Governor, the Lieutenant-Governor, the Council, the House of Representatives and the House of Assembly. The title of his sermon was 'Palida mors, aequo pulsat pede, pauperum tabernas, regumque turres' ('Pale death, with impartial step, knocks at the cottages of the poor and the palaces of kings,' from the poet Horace). The Scriptural text was from the Book of Job: 'There the wicked cease from troubling, there the weary are at rest, there the prisoners rest together, they hear not the voice of the oppressor, the small and the great are there, and the servant is free from his master.'

In his sermon, William spoke about the common destiny of all rivers and how some become great and mighty while others are just small streams, but in the end all flow into the ocean and disappear. Applying this metaphor to humans, he said, "next to the influence of our passions, the most of the calamities which man inflicts on man arise from the unequal though necessary distribution of property and power. Dazzled with riches and distinctions, we are apt to consider ourselves when we obtain possession, not as men appointed to collect and preside over the common stores of providence, but as undoubted heirs of exclusive advantages and superior in the very nature of things to the common mass of mankind. Than this there cannot be an error more fatal either in theory or in life."

Calling on the leaders of Vermont to consider the nature of life and death, William concluded, "Would you, my brethren, trace all these streams of vice to their sources and sincerely repent of your sins; would you adopt the resolution of Zaccheus, the publican, 'Shew mercy to the poor, and if you have taken anything from any man by false accusation, restore it to him four fold,' you would be the happiest people on earth. As I am a stranger and without political view or interest at stake, I hope you will listen to me with an unprejudiced ear!"

The applause was strong but subdued as each of the newly elected officers considered the words of the minister and the application going forward for the people of Vermont, who had elected them to do what was best for the people.

"Well said," General Whitelaw exclaimed as they returned to their accommodations. He had already begun to feel the loss of his friend, and realized William could have done much good, not just in Ryegate or Caledonia County, but throughout the state. They had some sherry in the tavern nearby before turning-in early to be rested for their return to Ryegate in the morning.

The following week, the General showed William the note in *Spooner's Vermont Journal,* an influential newspaper:

> On Thursday last the General Assembly of this state convened in the town at 2 o'clock P.M., the Governor and Council, a number of the members of the House, and a large concourse of people assembled at the new Meeting House, where a well-adapted discourse was delivered by Reverend William Forsyth.

The minutes of the Vermont General Assembly read:

> On motion resolved, that Mr. Hay be requested to wait on the Reverend William Forsyth, to return him thanks of this House for the election sermon, delivered on Thursday last before his excellency, the Governor and both branches of the Legislature; and to request a copy thereof for the Press.

"I had a chance to talk to Governor Tichenor and the Lieutenant-Governor," General Whitelaw told William during one of their weekly meetings. "They were very pleased with your sermon, as it went right to the heart of what governing is all about. Well done, Mr. Forsyth."

As he laid his head on the pillow one night in mid-October, William realized that in his mind he had already moved from Ryegate to Cornwallis. Having already notified the Ryegate people, the Cornwallis people and his parents, he was concentrating on his plans to travel by wagon to Newburyport and then, by ship, to Halifax, Nova Scotia.

The morning of his departure was bright and sunny. In a glorious send-off, the leaves of the hardwood trees—maple, birch, beech, oak—covered the hills and valleys of Vermont with brilliant reds, yellows, oranges, and rusty browns.

Mrs. McDonald and William said their good-byes at the boarding house. "God bless you, Laddie. I'm sure you will do very well for the people of Cornwallis Township, off in the wild north. I will miss you."

"You've been like a second mother to me, Mrs. McDonald, and helped me to adjust to America and to Ryegate. I hope I find such a kind and caring friend in Cornwallis."

There was a tear in her eye and one rolling down William's face as well. He turned quickly and left the boarding house.

William's friends, students, and congregants waited with him at the wagon stop, their subdued dispositions a contrast to nature's display of enthusiasm. As the wagon drew close and stopped, the men shook hands with William and the women hugged him. General Whitelaw and Mr. McDonald lugged the trunk from the boarding house and loaded it onto the wagon. William climbed onboard.

As the wagon picked up speed, he continued to wave until they were out of sight.

2: Cornwallis Township

The wagon ride back to Newburyport gave William time to consider his experience at Ryegate. Had he made the right decision? He had arrived with such high hopes and then found that he was not going to be fully accepted or appreciated by some of the leadership. Why was that? What could he have done to change the response of the hiring committee?

He didn't know. That shook his confidence a bit. One thing he did know for sure now: ministry is more than preaching and teaching. It is also about politics.

Sadder but somewhat wiser, he hoped, he tried to turn his thoughts to Cornwallis Township.

At Newburyport he paid for his passage and arranged for his trunk to be stowed on the passenger ship heading for Halifax in His Majesty's Province of Nova Scotia. On board, he still couldn't stop thinking about his Ryegate experience. It gnawed at him.

Perhaps Ryegate was the exception to the rule, he thought. Surely Cornwallis Township would be the land of his hopes and dreams. But when he thought about the salary and benefits he was offered at Ryegate, he still got angry and he didn't like that feeling. Every time he tried to work on forgiving the hiring committee, he remembered that they had not even paid him what he was owed before he left. He had to remind himself, again and again, that there's no sense in mulling over the past. Look toward your bright future.

And, at that point, he would get up and take a walk around the deck, along with many of the other passengers. They all braved the winds of winter on the open ocean, but William didn't mind the wind, as he knew it was blowing him towards a new and fresh beginning.

It took a week to sail from Newburyport to Halifax. What William could see of the Atlantic shore of Nova Scotia didn't look too hospitable. The land was covered with stunted birch and spruce and was very rocky. As the ship sailed up the coast, the passengers could see deep indents of harbours, rivers, coves and bays, with the occasional twinkling of a settlement.

"Where are you heading, young fellow?"

William turned to see a man dressed much like himself, with a bit of grey in his hair. "Cornwallis Township. Do you know Nova Scotia?"

"Well, Halifax. I work as a clerk for James Fraser. He's in the shipping business."

"You don't say! I met Mr. Fraser on my voyage from Scotland to Newburyport."

"Small world. Mr. Fraser spends most of his time in New Brunswick as his lumber business is there, but he is a business partner with William Forsyth, a Scottish businessman who, at the moment, is residing in Halifax."

"Why, that's my name as well. I'm the new minister for Cornwallis Township in Kings County."

"Pretty country, but I've heard that the Puritans who settled there are even more persnickety than the Presbyterians from Scotland."

"Persnickety?"

"You know, too precise...picky...I'm looking for the right word—priggish."

"I, sir, am a Presbyterian of the Church of Scotland variety. I would contend that your evaluation of Presbyterians is quite imprecise...I'm looking for the right word...sloppy—and rude as well!"

"Well, well, you do have blood in your veins. A bit of a temper, maybe," he teased.

"Perhaps so," William said as he began to cool down. "But I see that you, sir, are a provocateur, and I have been the object of your enjoyment. What is your name, if you dare to tell me at this point?"

"Iain Fraser, nephew of James, at your service, my dear Mr. Forsyth." He made a sweeping bow, with his hat in his hand coming very close to William's nose. "Very pleased to make your acquaintance."

William wasn't sure if he was pleased to meet Iain Fraser, but thought it best to finally cool down before he said something he might regret.

"Pleased to make your acquaintance as well, Mr. Fraser. However, I believe I'll return to my bunk."

William could hear Iain chuckling to himself as he headed to the nearest door to the inside of the ship.

Lying on his bunk fuming, William suddenly laughed out loud. It really was funny. Iain had poked him and he had over-reacted. Once started, he couldn't stop laughing. It was a great relief to let go of all his emotions about leaving Ryegate.

Jumping up from his bunk, he went back up on deck. Iain was still there, engaged with some men who looked a little hot under the collar, leaning toward Iain and yelling something he could not hear for the wind.

Striding over, William said, "Mr. Fraser, would you have time for a drink before dinner?"

"An excellent idea, Mr. Forsyth. Please excuse me, gentlemen. This is an offer too good to refuse."

He left his acquaintances still fuming and went with William to the dining room.

"Really, Mr. Fraser, one of these days you're going to get a punch in the nose when you poke the wrong person."

"I believe you're right, my dear Forsyth, but until then I'll take my fun where I can get it."

They agreed to let bygones be bygones and chatted about Nova Scotia. Their conversation continued after their drinks were done and dinner lay before them.

As the voyage continued, William often leaned on the railing and watched the coastline. Nova Scotians, who were always happy to answer questions, explained to William that from Yarmouth Township at the south end of Nova Scotia along the Atlantic seacoast towards Halifax were townships founded in 1760 by New Englanders, such as Shelburne, Barrington, Liverpool and Chester. Lunenburg Township was the exception. 'Foreign Protestants', mostly German and Swiss, settled it in 1752, not long after the founding of Halifax in 1749.

The closer they got to Halifax Harbour the more ships they saw. Some were passenger ships, some freighters, some fishing boats. There were also a few of His Majesty's war ships—imposing vessels with three tall masts and pierced for many guns. When under full sail, they were quite an impressive sight.

On a clear day, William enjoyed looking at the horizon. You could see that the horizon was not flat but slightly curved. That curve gave the sense of the roundness of the earth and the sense of his smallness in relation to the vast sea and sky. William felt the same way when he gazed at the stars at night. The sea, the sky, and the stars put his life in perspective. It felt better not to be so wrapped up in his thoughts and concerns.

But being so wrapped up in his own thoughts about not being wrapped up in his thoughts, he almost jumped with surprise when one of his fellow passengers spoke to him. The man wanted to point out Chebucto Head, at the entrance to Halifax Harbour. As they looked at the rocky headland, the ship turned west and headed into the mouth of the Harbour.

The man, a Mr. Lydiard who owned a brewery in Halifax, took great delight in describing the scene to William. "There's Sambro Island with its lighthouse, and over there is McNab's Island. Now we can begin to see the town of Halifax which is close to the Narrows—the passage between the end of the Harbour and the entrance to Bedford Basin. This is one of the finest harbours in North America—a thousand vessels could fit in it and it's free of ice year round. That's Halifax on the west side of the Harbour and just across from it is the village of Dartmouth. The little island between them is George's Island."

At that point several other Haligonians joined them. Mr. Fairbanks, a merchant, and Mr. Watson, a druggist, were only too eager to describe their town to the newcomer. "You see," Mr. Fairbanks said, "Halifax has been the capital of Nova Scotia since Governor Cornwallis brought about two thousand English people here in 1749. We were in the midst of the French and Indian War and it was from Halifax that His Majesty's navy would go to fight the French at Louisbourg, and Quebec. Since then, we have been quite secure and Halifax has flourished, as you will soon see."

"See the hill there behind the town?" Mr. Watson said, "That's Citadel Hill, and Fort George at the top. The town is located between the Hill and the Harbour."

"It's a spiteful little place compared to your London or Paris," Fairbanks said, "but it has room to grow when more people come. We're fewer than five thousand souls the now."

Mr. Lydiard pushed a little closer to William in order to be heard. "Now here's something you'll need to know about Halifax and Nova Scotia. There is still a military presence in Halifax despite the American Revolution being over, and all the government, upper class, and military leaders are Church of England. Besides that, the place is run by the merchants. You'll see ships from England, the American colonies and the West Indies here in the port."

"Where does that leave the others in the province—the Presbyterians, the Congregationalists, the Baptists, and Methodists?"

"The dissenters? For the most part, if they want to get a top job in this province, they have to become Church of England."

"I see," William said, wondering to himself how exactly that was going to affect his life in this colony.

He thanked the men and thought to himself that few places he had seen were as pleasing as Halifax viewed from the Harbour. The streets were regularly laid out and the plentiful trees and church spires scattered throughout made it very picturesque.

Iain caught up to William just before the ship docked. "Best of luck in your new job. Perhaps you'll look me up if you're in Halifax and we'll enjoy another rum, or sherry, or whatever you prefer to drink. Just ask anyone where Forsyth and Sons is located. We're on the waterfront."

"Thank you, Mr. Fraser. Are you going home to your wife and children?'

"Aye. Four youngsters, two boys and two girls. They miss their home in Scotland, but for now we have to be in Halifax in the cold and snow."

The men shook hands and each went to look for his luggage.

Once the ship arrived, the crew threw heavy ropes overboard and men on the wharf tied them to bollards to secure the ship. The gangplank was lowered and the passengers carefully stepped down the slippery passage to the wharf, gentlemen assisting the lady passengers.

William noticed that there was a little bit of snow on the roofs of the warehouses and patches of snow on the dock. He wrapped his cape more snugly around him. Looking forward to hot food and a warm bed, he asked the porter, "Is there an inn you might recommend?"

"Many travellers choose the Split Crow, which is the closest inn to the wharf."

After his trunk was unloaded on the wharf, the porter wrestled it onto his little horse-drawn cart and headed to the inn. William followed behind.

The buildings near the waterfront were large stone warehouses for storing materials destined to be shipped, the porter said—lumber for England, and grain, hay, potatoes, apples, and salt fish to other ports. Also stored were the materials received from far-away places—rum, molasses, some tropical fruits from the West Indies. From England, luxury clothing, fine furniture, fine china, wine, and many other materials for living an upper class life were stored.

Past the warehouses were stone and some brick buildings of the local businesses. At the corner of Salter and Water Streets, William could see the light from a large stone building with a sign above the door swinging in the wind. The picture of the split crow reminded William of German ensigns he had seen of the double eagle. *Was the split crow a parody of the double eagle?*

The room was small and clean. The supper was good but plain, but William began to be concerned once the entertainment began for the evening. It was a little too raunchy for his taste, and when a few fights broke out, he took a brisk walk around the block.

It was late evening and the streets were empty. Everything was grey and bleak now that the sun had set; the light from oil lamps cast long shadows across the sidewalk.

He was glad to see the sign of the inn as he turned the last corner. He strode even more quickly, wanting to be warm again. Before the walk, he had thought about spending a few more days in Halifax to explore the town. The cold and damp dissuaded him.

The next day the innkeeper arranged for him to take public transport to Windsor. "Now, remember, Mr. Forsyth, there are only two real roads in the Province, one to Windsor and the other to Truro Township. You travel out Windsor Street, around the Bedford Basin and at the head of the Basin the road splits in two. If you have to switch carts, be sure to have them put your trunk in the cart taking the left fork, which goes to Windsor."

"What happens when I get to Windsor? How does one get to Cornwallis Township?"

"You'll have to hire a horse and cart to take you the rest of the way."

The four-horse drawn wagon had a covering over it but was open at both ends. The driver and the spare had overhead protection and windbreaks to shield them from the weather. Their legs and feet were shrouded in sheepskins. William had on most of his clothing and his winter cloak. Two men loaded his trunk into the baggage section and he climbed on board. There were sheepskin blankets in the wagon for the passengers.

Two men who had been loading kegs and barrels into the back of the cart climbed on board. "Afternoon, Mister. Cold enough for you?"

"Indeed. My name is William Forsyth. Pleased to make your acquaintance, gentlemen."

"My name is Fultz and this is Mr. Anthony. We both live in Sackville. We work for an inn along the Halifax-Windsor road."

"Now, what's your occupation, if you don't mind me asking?" Mr. Anthony said.

"I'm the new minister for Cornwallis Township. That's where I'm heading."

"Pleased to meet you as well, Mr. Forsyth. I hear the Congregationalists in Cornwallis Township just lost hold of their previous minister."

"Aye, he is moving to Stewiacke. I've met him. A good man from what I can tell."

"Aye, that's what we've heard as well."

With that Mr. Fultz and Mr. Anthony turned their attention to assuring the kegs were tightly secured.

As they travelled along Windsor Street, the wagon lurched and shook so that William had to hold on to the handle on his side. He hoped his trunk would not slide out the back of the wagon. He worried the kegs of rum would roll out as well. That would only delay his time in the frosty weather.

Mr. Anthony and Mr. Fultz had a running discussion about the cost of commodities for operating their inn and then a long speculation about buying up land for logging, so it was quite a while before they turned their attention to William.

"A cold day for travelling to Windsor, Mr. Forsyth."

"Aye, aye. I'm about to perish."

"Well, you've got to wrap those sheepskins more tightly and sit on one as well. And there's another secret to keeping warm." He pulled out a flask and shoved it towards William. "Have a drink of this."

"What is it?"

"The best of rum. It'll warm you right up."

William hated rum. His dislike for the taste was in part because rum came from sugar cane grown in the Caribbean and processed by black slaves. Slavery was now illegal in Scotland, but was still an institution in England and America. With every drink of rum, he knew he was supporting the slave trade.

"Nay, Mr. Anthony. Thank you for your generosity, but I cannot stand the taste."

"Very well. I suppose I shouldn't take offence as there's only more rum for me."

"Indeed, sir. A perfect way to look at it. Now, can you tell me how much longer the trip will be once we reach your destination?"

Mr. Anthony cocked his head. "I have never tried it myself. It is such a long road, even a young man such as yourself might be quite mature before ever you arrived."

Mr. Fultz smothered a laugh. "Here, take another sheepskin. You're going to need it."

He's right about that, William thought.

William noticed there were many inns along the road that ran beside Bedford Basin, most only a few miles apart. When necessary, the wagon-driver pulled into an inn to rest and water the horses, depending on the horses themselves, and also on the terrain. After hauling the wagon up a hill, the horses had to rest for a while before the journey could continue. William and the other passengers usually got out to stretch their legs and get a sense of where they were.

When the team of horses had to be exchanged for a fresh team, William and the other passengers went into the inn and got a tankard of ale and a hot meal. The passengers told him that if the weather was bad, it might be necessary to stay overnight at an inn. In this case, the horses would be put in a shed to protect them from the weather and the baggage would be stored in a baggage shed. He found it was forty-four miles from Halifax to Windsor—a full day's wagon ride in good weather.

William peered out the front of the wagon as they drove along the Bedford Basin. Although the water looked blue, there were whitecaps. He saw many ships at anchor in the Basin with their sails furled.

Part way around the Basin, there appeared a round building with Greek-style columns.

"Pray, what might that round building be, Mr. Anthony?"

"That is Prince's Lodge. Built by the Duke of Kent for his, well, his lady friend."

Mr. Fultz snorted. "'Lady friend'."

"Madame de St. Laurent is quite the thing. You know it as well as I."

"I have not heard of this lady," William said.

"It's a very touching story, though it may singe your ears a little."

Mr. Anthony cleared his throat as if about to address an assembly. "Yon duke had his friends search for a French, um, mistress for him while he was stationed in Gibraltar, and this lady suited him well. She came with him to Quebec City when he was stationed there. After that they came to Halifax and they've had the most salubrious effect on our town."

"How so?"

"The elegant dances, parties, and all the business produced by his building projects and having his Regiment in town, has enlivened the whole population."

"Am I to understand that they are not married?" William said.

"As to that," said Mr. Fultz, "they royals do things a little different. Your King Solomon, now, had a shoal of wives, I do believe."

William had to acknowledge that point. "How do the people feel about his French, his French mistress?"

"Only the proper ladies do not accept her as their equal," Mr. Anthony said, "and I don't think she cares that they do not. I have seen her on several occasions and she is a lovely, graceful, and cordial woman. Any person of merit would be pleased to have her company, I am sure."

"Do they have any children?"

"Nay. Not that I know of."

"I suppose he will have to leave her and marry someone acceptable to his family."

"That could well be. But it would be very sad, as he seems completely devoted to her. He had a heart-shaped pond built and the winding pathway to it spells out the word 'Julie.'"

"How very touching, Mr. Fultz. It must be wonderful to have found true love."

They left it at that.

Eventually they came to the head of the Basin and the area known as Sackville. There was a small fort in the area—Fort Sackville. It was just across the bridge over the Sackville River and to the right, close to Bedford Basin.

"There are always about thirty officers and men of the Royal Nova Scotia Regiment stationed there," Mr. Fultz said.

"When was the fort built?" William asked.

"Oh, way back when the English were fighting the French, the Acadians and the Mi'kmaq for supremacy over Nova Scotia. There were battles throughout the Province, so there are little forts in many places. They came in handy during the American Revolution, too, when pirates, privateers and American militias were raiding Nova Scotia. Not much use for them now."

"Well, that's good."

"You might like to know that just near the Fort is a lovely house owned by Mr. Joseph Scott, a Halifax merchant, now in the lumber business. It is a very fine building."

"Then, I may have had a glimpse of it just before we arrived at the inn. I could see it just where the Sackville River runs into Bedford Basin."

"Yes, that's it. It's harder to see in the summer as it's surrounded by many trees."

At the head of Bedford Basin the road split as foretold, the left fork going to Windsor and the right fork to Truro Township. The cart stopped at an inn there, and William's travelling companions unloaded the rum and supplies they had bought into a two-horse wagon that a man had standing ready for them.

"We wish you well on the rest of your journey and your time with the Puritans," Mr. Anthony said. "Some say they're not easy to get along with, but you never heard me say that."

"Thank you for your well-wishes, Mr. Anthony. A pleasure to meet you, Mr. Fultz."

No one joined him—because of the cold, he suspected. As the wagon continued towards Windsor, William just watched the passing scene. There were a few small farms but, other than the inns, most of the land was forest. William guessed that was because of the rocky nature of the soil.

"You've been rather quiet up to now, Mr. Andrews," William shouted at the driver.

"Aye, well, you had Mr. Fultz and Mr. Anthony to answer your questions. Will you want me to point out a few landmarks?"

"Aye, that would be appreciated, but can you turn towards me when you speak so the wind doesn't carry your voice away?"

The driver turned to William and said, "There's a lot of logging going on in this area. Most of the forest is owned by Mr. Joseph Scott—you saw his house there at the head of Bedford Basin. We're about to go through a very wooded area for quite a few miles, but I'll tell you about the Attorney-General's estate when we reach it. At that point we'll be about halfway to Windsor."

William pulled all the sheepskins in the wagon around him to make a barrier against the cold and spent the time daydreaming about his new congregation until Mr. Andrews turned again.

"There, on your right, is the almost five thousand acres of land—some granted, some purchased—belonging to Richard John Uniacke, the Attorney-General for Nova Scotia, an Irishman by birth. He's going to build a summer home here, although why not in Windsor, I do not know. Now, there isn't going to be much to see until we reach Windsor, so imagine how welcome that town will be with its inns, hot food and a warm bed."

"Thanks, Mr. Andrews, I am already anticipating that with all my heart!"

After what seemed an interminable journey, the driver turned again.

"There's Windsor just up ahead, Mr. Forsyth."

William moved forward to look out the front of the wagon, dragging his sheepskins with him.

"What are the two rivers?"

"The Avon and the St. Croix. They run into the Minas Basin. Windsor used to be a township owned by landlords in Halifax and rented to Presbyterians from the North of Ireland, but now it boasts the summer homes of many wealthy Haligonians. It is also an important shipping centre for traffic to the New England States and to the Caribbean."

In Windsor, William stayed overnight at an inn and the next day hired a Mr. Smith to transport him and his trunk by wagon to Cornwallis Township. The weather remained clear and cold, but Mr. Smith had a diverting line of conversation about the local sights to keep William's mind off the chill.

"Now, there's Fort Edward, built in 1750. This is where the English soldiers went out from to round up and deport the Acadians in 1755."

"Where did they all go?"

"I care not, so long as they was gone. Flora MacDonald of 'Bonnie Prince Charlie' fame spent the winter of 1779 in that fort with her husband, a captain in the Royal Highland Emigrants Regiment. They had been driven out of the Carolinas in the Rebellion. From here they made their way home to the Isle of Skye."

William said, "She was a truly brave woman. She guided Bonnie Prince Charlie as he tried to escape the English. I greatly admire her."

"Aye. Everyone who hears her story is inspired by her bravery."

A few minutes later, Mr. Smith said, "Now here's King's College, founded by the Provincial Assembly in 1789 at the instigation of the Loyalists."

"I'm impressed that Nova Scotia has its own college."

"No need for you to be impressed. It's only for the wealthy sons of the Church of England—Anglicans they call themselves. No dissenters study there."

They took the ferry over the Avon River and continued along the wagon trail that led around the Minas Basin, through Falmouth and Horton Townships, to Cornwallis Township. The ruts in the trail were frozen in place like wrinkles in a poorly ironed garment. As they lurched along the trunk bounced and slid in the wagon.

Each time the horses pulled the wagon to the top of a hill, William was greeted by a most beautiful view out over the Minas Basin sparkling in the winter sunshine. He could just make out the outlines of farms in the near distance silent under a light blanket of snow. It was a scene of peace and tranquility, William thought.

The sky threatened snow, but by the time they reached Mud Creek, a sixteen mile journey, the wind had blown away the dark clouds and some blue sky was again visible.

Mr. Smith said, "Judge Elisha DeWolf is the most important man in Mud Creek. He had thirteen children, do you see, and they married into most of the other smart families in the village."

William had to laugh. "A plan like that requires a lot of fore-thought and patience."

"When that Duke of Kent travelled down the Annapolis Valley a few years ago, he stayed overnight at Judge DeWolf's, at his old house. Just this year, the Judge built a larger, more attractive home where he and his wife entertain."

"Mud Creek isn't a very attractive name for a village," William said.

"No, indeed. There are many in the place who would like to see it renamed."

They drove another ten miles or so along the Cornwallis River, passing farmhouses and barns until they reached Horton Corner and the river that divided Horton and Cornwallis townships.

"You know," Mr. Smith said, "the people in Horton Township called it the Horton River and the people in Cornwallis Township called it the Cornwallis River."

"Are they rivals of some sort?"

"Nay, nay. They all arrived at the same time in 1760 on twenty or so ships. Each of the settlers decided whether they wanted land in Horton or Cornwallis. Then some thought some others had gotten a better deal, and so a bit of contention arose. I think that's pretty well over by now. What's done is done, I say."

At Horton Corner, there was a ford. Some split pine trees formed a bridge of sorts across the two-named river.

As they waited their turn to cross, William counted fourteen houses, as well as a general store and a blacksmith. "Henry McGee owns the store and the mill," Mr. Smith said. "Being a Loyalist, he found it a little too hot to stay in those United States."

After crossing the River, they were in Cornwallis Township. The rolling hills and beautiful meadows, the woods filled with mostly hardwood trees, now denuded of their leaves in anticipation of the coming winter, and the large and well-organized farms impressed William. The Minas Basin, a part of the Bay of Fundy, came in view from the tops of the hills. Grey clapboard houses, smoke rising from the chimneys, had large barns and outbuildings surrounded by apple orchards—small, leafless trees with twisted branches, dark against the blue sky. Sometimes he caught a glimpse of neat kitchen gardens in their lazy beds which had been harvested and made ready for winter. William thought it was a most beautiful place and his heart leapt with excitement.

"Now, Mr. Forsyth," Mr. Smith said, "I suppose you'll want to know a bit about Cornwallis Township."

"Please."

"The rivers are what attracted first the Acadians and then the New England Planters: the Cornwallis is the largest, and then there's the Canard, the Habitant and the Pereaux. They all empty into the Minas Basin. On either side of the rivers are marshlands—intervale—which are protected from the tidal surges by dykes—the Acadians built them, but we keep them up. Some Acadians escaped deportation and the English made them teach the New England settlers how to repair and maintain the dykes.

"I thought all the Acadians were deported."

"Many hid in the forests and were routed out by the English from time to time. Thousands of acres of marshland depend on these dykes. It is pasturage for the cattle and sheep and gives the hay supply to keep the animals over the winter. Yes, it's the intervale that makes Cornwallis Township an ideal area of the province."

"I thank you for the lesson, although I may lose the names of the rivers."

"Anyone can tell them to you, if you need. Now, sir, where exactly am I to take you?"

"Before anything else, I would like to see the church."

"That yon great thing? You can see it from here," Mr. Smith said with a smile. "But I will drive you and your luggage there."

As William looked intently at the church, a man in his late sixties dressed in farmer's clothes—pantaloons made of wool cut very full with cartridge pleats, heavy wool socks in his wooden shoes, a heavy wool jacket over his linen shirt and a broad-brimmed hat—stepped out of the church door. Seeing the horse and cart with two men in it, he strode over. "Good-afternoon, gentlemen. My name is Elkanah Morton and I am an elder of this church."

"Then I am your new minister, William Forsyth!"

The older man's eyes crinkled in delight. "I didn't recognize you, Mr. Forsyth, in all your winter clothes. How can I help you? Would you like to see the church now? Or perhaps you could come to my farm just up the road where my wife can give you a cup of tea and a bite to eat?"

"The cup of tea sounds very welcome. I imagine you can also provide for Mr. Smith, my driver. He has family not far away but he has my trunk in his wagon and will need to leave it wherever I will stay tonight."

"We are always pleased to offer our hospitality to travellers," Elkanah said.

So they drove the mile to his farm house, where Mary, Elkanah's second wife, was just taking fresh bread out of the oven. She was soon feeding her guests with bread, cheese, preserves and strong, hot tea.

As they ate, Elkanah introduced his son, Samuel, and his daughter, Rebecca. "These are my two youngest children. As my wife and I are getting a bit older, we need and appreciate their help with the house and farm."

Samuel welcomed William to their Township and Rebecca curtsied. William smiled in appreciation.

Samuel was dressed like his father. Rebecca and Mrs. Morton were dressed alike—blue homespun skirts and flowered overblouses covered with work aprons front and back with ties in the front. They had woollen shawls crossed in the front and tied. Their hats were made of linen and completely covered their hair. They wore no rings or jewellery. They had heavy woollen socks in their wooden shoes.

As William finished the last bit on his plate, Mary said, "We have a little something to finish the meal, if you would like."

"That would be lovely," William said, thinking there might be an apple left from the last harvest.

"Most kind," Mr. Smith said.

What appeared were dishes of cherry preserves with fresh cream. "Ma'am," William said, the Duke of Kent could not expect a more perfect pudding." He was quite aware that Elkanah and Mary were assessing him all this time—it was to be expected, really.

Just then there was a knock at the door, and a man invited himself into the house. He was dressed like Elkanah.

"Just saw the horse and cart in the driveway and wondered who it could be."

"Mr. Beckwith, it's my pleasure to introduce you to our new minister, the Reverend William Forsyth. Mr. Forsyth, this is my near neighbour, Mr. Asa Beckwith—a member of our church."

William stood. "A pleasure to meet you, Mr. Beckwith."

"And you as well. Welcome to Cornwallis Township."

"Sit down, Mr. Beckwith," Mary Morton said. "Will you have some tea and a dish of preserves?"

"I surely can't resist that offer. How are you, Mr. Morton? Have you got all your salt hay stored away?"

"I have, aye. I am thankful I have Samuel to help me, or else it might still be out on the intervale."

Mr. Beckwith cast an eye over Mr. Smith, who was steadfastly eating, then turned his full attention on William. "Well, now, Mr. Forsyth. Did you have a smooth journey from Vermont?"

"I did, sir; thank you for asking. But I am glad to have finally arrived and to such a warm welcome."

"Mr. Forsyth," Mary said, "we would be pleased if you would stay with us until we can secure you proper accommodations."

"Mrs. Morton, I gratefully accept your kind offer."

"If you're through your tea, Mr. Smith, I'll help you bring the trunk inside and put it in the guestroom," Mr. Beckwith said.

That accomplished, the driver departed patting his stomach in satisfaction. Mrs. Morton showed William to his room so he could rest before supper. Asa Beckwith left to begin to spread the news that the new minister had arrived and was staying at the Morton farm.

~

Right after breakfast the next morning, members of the congregation began to arrive to greet the minister and, of course, observe him. William, now a bit wiser after his days in Ryegate, kept his own observations to himself. He greeted his new congregation with words of warmth and cheer, displaying just enough of his true self to satisfy those who were trying to assess him. Soon Mary Morton's kitchen was almost filled with well-wishers.

When Asa Beckwith returned, a young woman was with him. "Mr. Forsyth, I would like you to meet my daughter, Mary Morton Beckwith. Mary, this is our new minister, the Reverend William Forsyth, late from Vermont. He is from Scotland."

William stood, cup of tea in hand, and inclined his head.

"I am very pleased to make your acquaintance, Mr. Forsyth." She curtsied. "I do hope you find everything to your satisfaction so far."

"Thank you for your kind greeting, Miss Beckwith. It is a pleasure to meet you."

With a small smile, Mary Beckwith went to sit with Mrs. Morton.

As she turned, William's heart skipped a beat. With every lull in a conversation, he glanced over at the pretty, brown-haired girl in the rose dress with lace collar and cuffs. Her ringlets fell over her shoulders and bounced as she chatted with others around her.

Asa noticed William's glances and smiled to himself.

After the many, many guests had departed, Elkanah took a chair facing William. "Now, then," he said, "what do you think they think of you?"

"They seemed happy to meet me," William said, "but what they truly thought..."

"They thought this," Elkanah said, and paused.

"Don't torture the poor man," Mary said.

"The general consensus, then," Elkanah said,"is that...you...will do." He folded his hands across his stomach in satisfaction.

The people of this Township aren't given to hyperbole, William thought.

Mary said, "The women are all hoping that you might find a wife among their daughters. Surely that is a sign of approval!"

Two days later, William borrowed Elkanah's horse, determined to return to the church before Sunday just to get his bearings. The road to the church was muddy and a light covering of snow blanketed the fields. William was thankful he had bundled up with his woollen riding cape over several layers of clothes.

There was no need for directions as the land was rather flat and the largest object on the horizon was the church. It couldn't be missed! The frame, Elkanah had said, had been brought up by ship from Machias, Maine, and put together by the men of the community. According to him, the church could hold about one thousand people.

Upon arrival, William observed the outside of the large, square building with slanting roof and side steeple, two stories in height, and covered with grey, weathered clapboard. There were long, slim windows on the long walls and on either side of the double front door. William tethered his horse at the rail at the front door rather than in the long low horse sheds behind the church, then walked up the two wide stone steps and opened the door with ease.

Inside, it was cold and dark. William was used to that. He walked up one of the two isles to the dais, and was soon at the foot of the small, winding set of stairs that led up to the high pulpit. He ascended the steps slowly, running his hands over the polished wood railing, until he reached the roomy pulpit. Grasping the edges of the lectern on either side of the very large Bible, he stood silently for a while, looking out over the pews on the ground floor and high in the balcony.

The box pews had high backs to keep off the drafts and little doors on the side. He knew a whole family would squeeze into their pew each Sunday, cuddling together to keep warm. Blankets and foot warmers helped as well. The rent for each family's pew helped pay for the upkeep of the building.

All this William was familiar with from Scotland. Ryegate had had a much smaller and only partially-finished Meeting House, so this church felt more like home.

He looked up to inspect the sounding board that would help project his voice to all corners of the building. Then he practised projecting his voice until he felt comfortable he had the pitch just right for the space.

Aye, he thought, *I have arrived at a goodly place.*

If he had any complaint about this Church, it was the plainness. There was not one decoration of any kind; not a stained glass window or a carved pulpit; it was the very definition of plain and simple.

Even so, he looked forward to his first Sunday.

~

Although William had total confidence in his preaching ability, he had some concerns about meeting the expectations of the elders and the congregation. It was crucial that he convince them that he was the right minister for them—that they all get off on the right foot.

He decided to take as his text Jesus' admonition to his disciples in Matthew, "You are the light of the world…Let your light so shine before men that they may see your good works and give glory to your Father who is in heaven." It was critical the whole congregation regard themselves as shining bright for all to see. Bitterness, rancour, fighting, gossip would be a clear sign that their light had gone out—that they were a church in name only.

He did not know at this moment that bitterness, rancour, fighting, and gossip were exactly what had been going on in the congregation for many years, and that the congregation had split in two. The 'reformed' Congregationalists called those who stayed with the original congregation 'old lights' and themselves 'new lights.' This was a very touchy subject for the congregation.

Before nine o'clock Sunday morning people started arriving by horse and wagon or on foot, all dressed in their Sunday best. The men wore knee breeches with stockings and buckled shoes. Over their fine linen shirts, they wore colourful vests under long, wool jackets. They had pulled their hair back into queues and wore tricorn hats. Over these clothes they wore ankle-length woollen cloaks. The women, under their ankle-length woollen cloaks, were gaily dressed in flowered dresses over a multitude of petticoats. They had their hair pulled up in elaborate styles over which they wore warm woollen bonnets. William almost didn't recognize these as the same people he had been meeting all week dressed in homespun clothes, most commonly dyed blue.

The church had been carefully cleaned and looked fresh and neat. Elkanah, being one of the elders, led the service. It began with opening prayers for which, to William's surprise, the people all stood and then turned their backs to the person praying.

The service continued with hymns. There being no musical instruments, a presenter lined out each hymn, singing two lines at a time, or sometimes offering a kind of rapid chant of the words.

One hymn in particular stood out for William. He scribbled down the words as the presenter lined them out:

> Who would true valour see, Let him come hither;
> One here will constant be, Come wind, come weather.
> There's no discouragement Shall make him once relent
> His first avowed intent
> To be a pilgrim.
>
> Whoso beset him round With dismal stories
> Do but themselves confound His strength the more is.
> No lion can him fright, He'll with a giant fight.
> But he will have a right
> To be a pilgrim.
>
> Hobgoblin nor foul fiend Can daunt his spirit,
> He knows he at the end Shall life inherit.
> Then fancies fly away, He'll fear not what men say,
> He'll labour night and day
> To be a pilgrim.

When the time came for the sermon, Elkanah introduced William to the congregation. William rose, strode to the dais, and ascended to the pulpit. He paused and looked out over the people who seemed to be waiting with bated breath to see what kind of minister they had hired. Hundreds of eyes looked back at him, their bodies upright with anticipation.

William said a prayer for illumination and began his sermon. As he progressed, he could see the looks of consternation on the people's faces. It was the last thing that William expected to see. What was happening? William was at a loss to explain the murmuring and discomfort his words seemed to elicit.

Half way through the sermon, a man stood up and began to wrap his scarf around his neck. "I am sure I don't need to listen to this, this hogwash! Come on, Ann. Hurry on, children, we're going home. Enough of this."

Ann looked up pleadingly, reaching and hoping to pull her husband down by his scarf, but he pushed out of the pew and headed for the door. None of the elders or congregants intervened. Ann and the six children hurried out behind him.

William returned to his sermon. What else could he do? But he felt totally in shock and hoped the shakiness in his voice was not obvious to the congregation.

As the people filed out of the church to have their lunch, William could feel his words had touched a nerve, and not the nerve he had wanted to touch. The people were polite but reserved towards him.

After lunch, which each congregant had brought in his or her pockets, the service continued in the afternoon. This time the sermon was on Colossians 4:12, "Put on then, as God's chosen ones, holy and beloved, compassion, kindness, lowliness, meekness, and patience, forbearing one another and, if one has a complaint against another, forgiving each other, as the Lord has forgiven you."

This time William experienced the congregation nodding in response to his sermon. He felt that whatever happened in the morning had been, at least partly, overcome in the afternoon. What had happened? He needed to know.

As she left the church that morning, Mary Beckwith shook William's hand and smiled sweetly. William thought she looked very attractive in her lavender dress and bonnet with deep rose and green ribbons. Never at a loss for words, William couldn't seem to find an appropriate greeting.

As he stammered a bit, he noticed Mary's brothers and sisters smiling and winking at one another—seemingly at his discomfort. All he knew for sure was that he hoped Mary Beckwith might be as interested in him as he was in her.

Back at the Mortons' farm, William brushed and fed his horse, trying to imagine what had befallen him. He was going to have to ask Elkanah.

As Elkanah, Mary, Rebeccah and Samuel began their supper of ham with potatoes, turnip and carrots. William cleared his throat and said, "Mr. Morton, what was the name of the man who left church this morning in the middle of the sermon?"

"Oh, that's one of the Smith family—Hezekiah. He has a big farm not too far from us. A touchy fellow."

"Who was he upset with?"

"Why, you, Mr. Forsyth."

William sat back in his chair, feeling rather appalled. "Upset with me? Why would that be?"

"You said that bitterness, rancour and fighting were a sure sign that our light had gone out."

"Aye."

"Well, he's still bitter that one of his brothers has joined the 'New Lights' and told Hezekiah that he and Ann aren't even really Christians."

"My goodness! I had no idea at all about New Lights."

"I guess maybe the hiring committee didn't want to get into that at your interview."

"They should have explained that to me. Wouldn't that be something a new minister ought to know?"

"Well, well, I suppose so. But according to your preaching, you're going to have to forgive us, I guess."

The family all smiled down at their plates, but William was not willing to drop the subject. "What else haven't you told me? Let's hear it all so I can forgive you for everything all at once. At least we can be efficient about forgiveness."

"Now, now, Mr. Forsyth, let's calm down before you have your own need for forgiveness. I'll answer all your questions and fill you in on the history of the congregation, but let Sunday be a day of rest."

"Very well. I think I'll try to enjoy the rest of the Sabbath."

On Monday, before William could get out and start visiting his parishioners, a great snowstorm started—actually two. The first began as the flat gray clouds covered the sky and it was so dark that one needed a candle or two to do any task such as sewing or reading. Then the great white snowflakes began to fall, slowly at first, and then with amazing speed. The wind picked up and soon all to be seen outside the window was a swirling mass of white. It lasted all day and lessened towards suppertime.

Elkanah and Samuel rushed out to feed and water their horses, cows and sheep and to clean out their stalls. Rebecca milked the cows. The milk had to be brought inside the house immediately or it would have frozen solid. The men, including William, split firewood just inside the back door to keep it as dry as possible. Mary and Rebecca kept the fires going and cooked the meals. But sometime after midnight when all were asleep under a pile of quilts and assisted by warming pans, the storm started up again with equal ferocity.

By noon on Tuesday it was beginning to let up. Elkanah, Samuel and Rebecca began shovelling out a path to the barn so they could milk the cows and feed the animals. William continued to chop wood at the door.

When they finally finished the work, William peered outside. The landscape looked magical with snow swirled into fantastic shapes. The whole of Cornwallis Township was buried under several feet of snow. William was used to snow from his experience in Vermont, so this was no surprise to him, but it was certainly going to prevent him from getting out to do his visiting.

Finally, late in the week, William was able to borrow Elkanah's horse and start following the footpaths to some of the neighbouring farms, but it was slow going. In the evenings, after evening prayers led by Elkanah, William would ask questions about the Church or the Township or about Elkanah and his family and other families. One evening, Elkanah told him about all the religious turmoil in Cornwallis and Horton Townships during the previous twenty-five years.

"As you know, Mr. Forsyth, the official religion here is the Church of England or, as some call it, the Anglican Church. When Governor Lawrence advertised in the Boston newspapers in 1759 for farmers to come up and settle in Nova Scotia following the expulsion of the Acadians, those interested wrote to the Governor asking to be assured that we could practice our religion without interference. We also wanted to continue to run our townships as we had done in New England. We were promised these liberties. But now we find that the Anglicans want to have all the say about religion in this Colony and our clergy are not even allowed to perform marriages, which have to be performed by the Anglican Church ministers as set out in their Book of Common Prayer. So, as you can imagine, we are not too happy with this. In addition, we do not have full say within our townships, as most of the laws are made in Halifax by the Legislative Assembly. The members of the Assembly are mostly rich merchants and the King's representatives, Anglicans all."

"What else can you tell me about the history of your Township and congregation?"

"Well," Elkanah continued, "it may have been remiss of us not to tell you about the 'New Lights' in Cornwallis Township. About the time of the American Revolution, a young man over in Falmouth Township had a religious experience and began preaching against the Congregational Church. He actually preached in our church here at one point. His name was Henry Aline. Mr. Aline convinced about half of our congregation to leave our church around 1778. Those that left called us 'old lights' and themselves 'new lights'. The 'new lights' consider themselves superior in every way to the 'old lights.' This caused a schism in our congregation and even in families. We reached a very low point as a congregation."

"I can only imagine how you must have felt."

"Aye, we were desperate enough to ask the Congregational church in Yarmouth Township to loan us their minister, a Mr. Scott, for a season, and that buoyed us up for a time. We asked for him to return to us but the Yarmouth folk felt we were imposing on them

—and so we were. We heartily apologized to them for our lapse in good Christian concern for their congregation."

"What else could you do? The Revolution must have prevented you from getting another Congregational minister."

"You are right. We were no longer on speaking terms with our relatives in New England. At that point, we decided to write to Scotland, to the Glasgow Associate Synod of the Secession Church of Scotland, and ask for them to send us a Presbyterian minister. Our doctrine is very similar to theirs. Well, they sent us the Reverend Hugh Graham. He was a good minister but preferred his Scottish psalter to the extent of making fun of our Congregationalist hymnbook. I think he will be happier among the Scotch-Irish in Musquodoboit."

"What is the current situation regarding the New Lights," William said.

"Since 1795, their minister has been the Reverend Edward Manning at Jaw Bone Corner. Father Manning, as his congregants call him, is a big man with a wonderful speaking voice, but with not much scholastic training. He is a man of strong convictions and ready to express them. The New Lights, I hear, are now transforming themselves into Baptists."

"No doubt I will meet him soon enough in my travels. Are the relations between the Old Lights and the New Lights any better now?"

"Somewhat. Most of the bitterness over the schism and the claims by the New Lights that we are not even Christians has lessened. But you will soon find it under the surface, especially in those families that were divided."

On another winter evening, William and Elkanah enjoyed some cider together after supper, and William asked, "Would you tell me about your New England background, and how your family came to Nova Scotia?"

"We all like to talk about our families," Elkanah said, "so this could take a while."

William looked out the window at the high snow banks and laughed. "Mr. Morton, I think I have all evening. If your good wife will let us sit in front of the fire and sip our cider, I am ready to listen."

Mary nodded. "Mr. Forsyth, I've finished my chores and will sit and listen while I knit some socks. I'm sure Samuel and Rebecca will join us when they finish their chores."

Elkanah began, "Our family, as well as nearly all the people in these Townships, are the descendants of the Pilgrims and Puritans who came to New England—Plymouth Colony and Massachusetts Bay Colony—starting in 1620 with the arrival of the Mayflower. Pilgrims and Puritans rejected the Church of England. They wanted to try to recreate the Early Church—the Church as it existed shortly after the death of Jesus. In their minds, hierarchy, robes and vestments, incense, processions, feast days to celebrate various saints, even Christmas, were unnecessary and 'popish'. What was needed was for each church to be self-regulating and able to hire its own minister. Everything should be very simple and plain. Each congregation should covenant with each other and agree to how the church would be organized and run. These folks dissented against the Church of England and they were persecuted for this. They left England to practice their beliefs in the wilderness of North America."

"I understand that the dissenters themselves could be quite aggressive against those who did not agree with them. I recall a story about dissenters breaking into an Anglican church and breaking their altar and candles and windows."

"Those were troublesome times indeed. Everyone thought that their way was the only right way. They were quite willing to attack others for their beliefs. Except for the Quakers—the Society of Friends, as they call themselves. They are dedicated pacifists."

"I believe it was the Puritans who rebelled against King Charles, leading to a war. The Puritans won and had the King executed. They tried to set up a republic. As I recall, the severity of Puritan rule eventually led the people to restore the monarchy and the Church of England. "

"Your memory serves you well, Mr. Forsyth. All this is true."

"Being a Presbyterian, I think I can understand the Puritans' desire to live in a way that would be pleasing to God. Perhaps God is not as concerned with strictness as he is with love."

"Well said, Mr. Forsyth."

"Please continue with the story of your family, Mr. Morton."

"My family is descended from George Morton and his wife, Juliana Carpenter, who arrived at Plymouth Colony in 1623 on the ship *Ann*. George died six months after he arrived and his five children were taken in by the governor of the Colony, William Bradford, who had married Juliana's sister, Alice. We are descended from Ephraim, the youngest child, who was born at sea. Ephraim had a son, George; George had a son, Ephraim; Ephraim had a son, Elkanah—my father—who was born in 1702. I was born in 1730."

"So you are six generations in North America? That's quite a family history, Mr. Morton. Do you have it written down or did you memorize it?"

"We have a family Bible, Mr. Forsyth. Each time we have to replace an older one we transcribe the details into the new Bible and then continue to add each birth, marriage and death. We also have a Township book, like the one we had in New England. The Township tries to keep track of all births, marriages, and deaths as well."

"That is an important service to the community."

"Father and I decided to come to Nova Scotia, and so we did in 1760. My mother, Elizabeth Holmes, died very shortly after we arrived and father died in 1779. My first wife, Rebecca, died in 1778 when Samuel was about eleven and Rebecca about thirteen. I married my second wife, Mary, the next year."

"So soon after your wife died?" William realized as he spoke that the question sounded like a judgment, but he could not call his words back.

"You will find, Mr. Forsyth, that no man can manage both a farm and a household, especially if there are young children to be cared for. And that applies for women who lose their husbands. No woman can care for a house, children, and a farm. So everyone marries just as quickly as possible if they lose a spouse. We certainly frown on staying unmarried unnecessarily. Men and women should marry. That is our belief."

"I hope to marry as soon as I meet a good woman, Mr. Morton."

"I wouldn't worry about that, Mr. Forsyth," Elkanah said with a sly smile. "There are many comely young women in these townships. You will surely find just the right one to be a minister's wife."

"Thank you for the encouragement. I can see that the descendants of the Pilgrims and the Puritans are very independent people with firm ideas about how their church and community should be run. This helps me understand the people of Cornwallis Township."

"We are by nature Congregationalists. The congregations in the Massachusetts Bay Colony developed the Cambridge Platform, which spelled out who could become a member and how we would choose our minister. In New England each of our churches was totally independent and we chose our own ministers. But during and after the American Revolution we could not get Congregationalist ministers to come to Nova Scotia."

"The Americans wouldn't send Congregational ministers to Nova Scotia?"

"Hard feelings from the war fed over into church affairs, I fear. Since Congregationalists and Presbyterians agree with the doctrines propounded by John Calvin, we decided to write to Scotland to find our previous minister, Mr. Graham. But by 1799 we had better relationships with our American relatives, and we wrote to the Grafton Presbytery of the Connecticut River Valley to see if they could help us find a minister. We were used to Presbyterians by then, and were willing to accept another Presbyterian minister, although we still want to retain much of our Congregational traditions."

"I can understand that, Mr. Morton. You have a fine heritage of which to be proud."

"It was your willingness to appreciate our traditions that allowed us to agree to call you as our minister. If you continue in this opinion, then it will make our lives and your life easier."

Elkanah always called a spade a spade and William appreciated always knowing where he stood with this Elder and the rest of the congregation.

"I wrote down the words to the hymn, 'He Who Would True

Valour See'—a very stirring hymn."

"Aye, John Bunyan, a Puritan in England, wrote it. He was imprisoned on and off for twelve years for not following the regulations of the Church of England. He wrote his great story, 'The Pilgrim's Progress', while he was in prison. This hymn is in that book. It does express much of what it takes to be a Pilgrim or a Puritan."

"Then we will have to sing it often," William said.

Elkanah nodded with a smile.

"Now, Mr. Morton, you must tell me why it is that when a person leads prayer, the people stand and turn their back on him."

"I'm not sure where or when this tradition started. I've only heard that it may have begun as a protest against reverence for the minister as priest, but more than that I do not know. It has always been a custom in my lifetime."

"It gave me quite a start," William said with a smile.

~

As Christmas approached, William kept learning all he could about Cornwallis Township and the Annapolis Valley. As was his practice, he visited the homes, farms, and businesses of his parishioners, and that was how he ended up at the home of Asa and Mary Beckwith's farm close to supper time one day.

At his knock on their front door, Mrs. Beckwith answered and greeted him with pleasure. "Mr. Forsyth, do come in. Let me take your hat and coat. Come this way to the parlour."

As she guided him towards a comfortable seat, she called out, "Children, tidy yourselves and gather round: our minister has come for a visit. James, take care of Mr. Forsyth's horse."

She hung his hat and coat on a hook in the hallway, then led William into the parlour—kept pristine for visits by the minister and the laying out of the bodies of loved ones prior to their funeral.

William soon had a glass of hard cider and some homemade biscuits with butter and strawberry preserves. The younger children crept in and sat quietly as the adults began to chat about the Beckwith family.

"Are the Beckwiths all New England Planters?" William asked.

"Well, all of Asa's brothers and sisters were born in Connecticut and came here with their parents. Asa's family all worked together to build up this farm and the children consider themselves Planters. I suppose they are not, technically, because they did not receive an original land grant. Asa's father received one and one-half share, about one thousand acres. He also had five sons and so was able to purchase some additional land as time went by, so our own family now has five hundred acres.

Just then there arrived in the parlour doorway what William could only describe as a vision of loveliness. Mary wore a simple dress in an apple-blossom pink floral; her long, shiny brown hair was in ringlets held back by a fresh green grosgrain ribbon

"Oh, mother," she said with 'surprise', "has Mr. Forsyth come to call? How lovely. Dear Mr. Forsyth, may I bring you some more cider?"

Before he could reply, she had whisked his glass off the side table and disappeared through the doorway in a swirl of pink. The children giggled behind their hands and made knowing glances toward each other until their mother shooed them out of the room.

"Now, Mr. Forsyth, you must agree to stay for supper. We only have simple fare but we would be honoured to share it with you. Please say yes."

Of course, William had been hoping to be invited. "Dear Mrs. Beckwith, you honour me with your invitation. I am very used to dining simply and I much prefer it to elaborate and costly fare."

"Then I will go and search my cupboards for what we might provide," Mrs. Beckwith said.

As if on cue, as Mrs. Beckwith left, Mary arrived with William's cider and placed it daintily on his side table. "Oh my, Mr. Forsyth, it seems my family have deserted us. I do hope you will tell me about your life in Scotland or your travels in America. I myself have never been outside Cornwallis Township and I do love to hear tales of adventure."

William took a sip of his cider—it was stronger, he thought, than the previous glass—and began to tell the story of his travels in

America. He described the port of Newburyport and the wagon road to Ryegate. He also told her about Ryegate and the Church of Scotland there. He told an amusing story about his landlady as well.

"But why did you leave Ryegate? The people loved you and you surely could have found a good wife there among people who were from your area of Scotland."

William mused a bit. The effect of the cider allowed him to speak more freely than he had planned to do. "I think it disappointed me that the Committee would offer me little money and made their offer dependent on whether the community grew. I hoped to find a situation that would make my parents proud and justify the money they spent on my education. Perhaps my reasoning was a reaction to that, as I do admit to having some pangs as I was leaving. But now, I am here—wiser, I hope, and ready to commit to the Cornwallis Township folk."

William could hear Asa arriving at the back door, and just then Mary's mother called that dinner was ready. Soon, and with great enthusiasm, their children arrived and took their seats at the table. Elizabeth, age twenty-two, was the eldest, with her seven siblings descending to one-year-old Nehemiah, who sat on his mother's lap.

The table was laden with all things delicious, as the smell of roasted chicken and potatoes with gravy wafted through the room. Asa said grace and everyone said, "Amen."

William ate with great gusto and asked for seconds, to the delight of Mary's mother. There were two options for dessert—apple brown betty or cherry cobbler—and William had both. The family looked amazed that such a slim man could have such an appetite.

After dinner, William complimented Mrs. Beckwith many times for the splendid meal. Asa and Mary, his wife, seemed cheerful and happy. The children seemed to be excited that William was visiting them. William was happy to see what an interest this beautiful young woman took in him.

The family said good-bye to William at the door. Only Mary went out to the porch to wave as William rode off.

~

It was mid-afternoon on December 25th, 1799, Christmas Day. Only a few days and everyone would see in a new century. William was busy writing his sermon in a corner of the kitchen. Looking up from his second paragraph, he realized there was more bustling around than usual. Then he noticed Samuel smiling at him from beside the fireplace.

"We're going to celebrate Christmas with a special supper, Mr. Forsyth. Mrs. Morton has prepared a goose to roast over the fire. I'm going to tend to that chore while Mrs. Morton and Rebecca are making a Christmas cake. There'll be roasted potatoes, turnip, carrots, and cranberry sauce."

"I thought Congregationalists didn't believe in celebrating Christmas."

"Oh, well, we don't. Too much like popery and Church of England holy days. But it can't hurt to have a good meal, you'll agree."

"I'll certainly agree. Only one question—may I help?"

"Thank you for your kind offer, Mr. Forsyth. I'll get you to wash off the potatoes before we roast them. Here's a bucket of water and a pile of potatoes. Put the washed potatoes in this pan with the long handle. They roast well in that."

As he washed potatoes, William thought about his childhood in Scotland. Ever since the Protestant Reformation, Christmas—or Yule, as it was called—was outlawed. It was just another ordinary working day. The Roman Catholics in Scotland had to celebrate Christmas—that is, Christ's mass—in secret. There were severe penalties if they were caught. To replace Yule, which had some pagan Viking elements, the Protestants celebrated New Year's Eve, or Hogmanay. This also included pagan Viking practices but did not carry a tinge of Roman Catholic or Church of England holy days.

Hogmanay included lots of food and whisky and music and dance. Groups of enthusiasts carried torches through the streets. It was a wild celebration. William was pretty sure the Congregationalists would not approve.

William and the Mortons drank lots of cider and thoroughly enjoyed their special supper. William just hoped the Church of Scotland would not frown on a special Christmas meal. But who was around to tell them? Certainly not him.

Soon it was back to the normal routine of winter in the household.

~

Months went by and William was still staying with the Mortons. However, everyone knew the Mortons wanted to keep him as long as they could as a sort of status symbol. He didn't object, as the alternative was to stay with each of the families in his congregation on a rotating basis—much better to be fed and cared for by Mary Morton. Besides, he could learn a lot from Elkanah and Mary about the Township and the other families.

On Monday evening, after evening prayers led by Elkanah, William asked Elkanah some more about his family.

"Well," Elkanah said, "in 1761 I brought the family house up from Massachusetts and re-assembled it here on my farm lot. Phoebe, my sister, and her new husband, Seth Winslow, Jr. came with Mother and Father. My first wife, Rebecca Tupper, and my first four children were all born in Massachusetts. My other children all came along here."

Elkanah continued, "Lemuel, our first born, is a Major in the Militia and Member of the Legislative Assembly. He married Martha, daughter of John Newcomb, Jr. Martha was the first child born in Cornwallis Township, just after we all arrived in 1761. Lemuel and Martha got married in 1780. They just had their ninth child this past year. Her name is Mary Alice—a really sweet child."

"Then all your children are married now?"

"All except Samuel and Rebecca. Sarah married Pern Terry, son of Captain John Terry, owner of Terry's Creek—a port for shipping on the Cornwallis River. Roland, our second son, is a farmer. He married Martha's sister Alice, who died, and he has re-married Hannah Gore. Mary married Asa Beckwith, of course. Elkanah III had a terrible accident and lost his leg, but that hasn't slowed him down much. He is married and living in Digby. George Augustus got his own land grant in Penobsquis, New Brunswick, and is married and a very successful farmer."

"Tell Mr. Forsyth what happened to Elkanah's leg," Rebecca pleaded. She loved to hear family stories—except the one about Elkanah's sister Phoebe, whom the neighbours accused of living in sin with a man other than her husband, and who petitioned the court to address the issue.

"As you may know," Elkanah said, "all the men in the Townships have to have some militia training just in case we have to defend ourselves, although, thank God, we have not had to do so recently. When my son was sixteen, he joined the local militia and began his training. The time came for their first parade and the Lieutenant-Governor came all the way from Halifax to review the troops on the parade ground next to the church. No one knows exactly what happened, but as the Lieutenant-Governor approached Elkanah, his holster pistol discharged accidentally and shot Elkanah in the leg. In the end, his leg had to be amputated. He gets around on crutches now. For a while he was up on the Saint John River in charge of building the ship *Lord Sheffield*, the first one of its kind built in New Brunswick. Elkanah was a Justice of the Peace over there before he moved to Digby."

"I'm afraid I'm going to have a hard time keeping all the names and relationships straight," William said.

Elkanah laughed. "If you try going back into New England and all the family inter-relationships you'll certainly find it quite a tangle. For a long time, in New England and later here, there were only so many families, so most families are related to some degree. This is a good thing to remember when you go visiting!"

~

As William began to visit the people in Cornwallis Township, he learned that most were farmers who raised cattle, sheep and pigs. They grew potatoes, wheat and barley, corn and pumpkins and they cultivated apple orchards. Everyone grew apples that were dried for use in the winter and made into hard cider. They kept the cider in kegs and drank it on a regular basis, and especially if a family had visitors. It would be the height of rudeness not to offer a guest a drink of an alcoholic beverage. Water was not usually drunk as it was considered unsafe. *And probably they are right*, William thought.

The Planters, William discovered, were hard-working, industrious, religious and no-nonsense people. Their society was not very stratified and so each grant owner had a say in the affairs of the Township and within the Church. There were a few men who had jobs of special privilege, such as judges, members of the legislative assembly—elected by the people to represent them in the decision-making that took place in Halifax. Halifax itself was mostly run by the merchant class for its own self-interest.

Elkanah told William the story of two of the men who had been a big part of the life of the Township and who had died just before William arrived. The first was Handley Chipman. "Handley lived at Chipman's Corner, where the Congregational-Presbyterian Church is. He was born in 1717 in Sandwich, Massachusetts and was raised in Rhode Island, where he became active in civic affairs. Handley and his first wife, Jean Allen, accepted a land grant of one thousand acres in the Township and arrived here in 1761. He became Justice of the Peace, chief officer in the Township, and was elected first Judge of Probate of Kings County."

"It would take a special character to fill all those roles well."

"He was a good and just man," Elkanah said, "but hot-tempered. When Captain Samuel Beckwith, Hezekiah Cogswell, John Newcomb, Deacon Caleb Huntington, and I wrote a letter to New England for some financial help for the Church, Handley was very angry. He called me a 'snake in the grass' because he thought we had gone behind his back. We just thought we were trying to solve the problem that together we had paid the minister three hundred pounds of our own money and had no more to give."

"Did you and Mr. Chipman reconcile your differences after that?"

"I'm not sure that he ever forgave us, as he spent more time at the Anglican Church than he did with us after that. However, he did leave some money to this church in his will."

"Then he seems to have reconciled himself to your church and to the other congregations in the Township."

"Perhaps," Elkanah said thoughtfully.

After a pause for thought, he continued, "The other man was Major Samuel Starr, who came to the Township in 1761. Starr's Point, where our ships landed, is named after him. It was Colonel Starr who donated the land for our Church, the cemetery, the Parade Ground and a school. The story is that he was one of a committee in Norwich, Connecticut in 1759 to make arrangements with the Nova Scotia Government for the settlement of Connecticut people in the province. He and Handley Chipman were leading lights in the Township. When they took a dislike to our first minister, Benaniah Phelphs, they started going to St. John's, the Anglican church. The colonel's son, Joseph, is a prominent man hereabouts."

The winter had been long and hard: lots of snow, sleet, freezing rain and high winds. Visiting was difficult, but William had been snug and warm as he was still with the Mortons. As April began, so did hopes of spring. Each day the warmer weather reduced the snow and the rivers and streams began to be dangerous as they roared and tumbled toward Minas Basin. There were days when the ferry from Terry's Creek across the Cornwallis River to Mud Creek was not running and mud presented a challenge to getting around on any road.

On the first mild, dry day, Asa Beckwith rode over to the Morton farm and called on William. "Let me take you on a tour of some of the Township you haven't seen yet, Mr. Forsyth," he suggested.

"What a good idea!" William said.

So off they went. They visited Starr's Point, and William saw the place where the Cornwallis Township folk had first stepped ashore.

Asa said, "There were twenty-two ships full of passengers, so it took quite a while to get all the people and all their belongings ashore."

"How did it feel," William said, "to finally arrive at the place of all your hopes and dreams—your new home?"

"Well," Asa said, "it was rather a disconcerting experience.

There, just as we set foot on this new land, were sixty ox carts and sixty yokes, just as the Acadians had left them as they, with their few belongings, were forced into ships. They were taken all down the eastern seaboard of New England and as far south as Louisiana. This had happened just five years before. The bones of their cattle were piled along the edges of the meadows where they had fallen from lack of food through the winter. It made us all very aware that this land had been owned by others."

"Did it bother you that this had been Acadian land?"

"At that time, we considered the French, including the Acadians, and the Indians our enemies. We had just fought a long war with them in New England and beyond. The English won this war with the French. When the Acadians wouldn't agree to swear allegiance to the English king and, indeed, seemed to be giving aid to the French at Fortress Louisbourg, the English deported them. So at the time of our arrival, we didn't have much sympathy for the Acadians. Since then, those who escaped deportation helped us repair our dykes and our attitude has certainly softened. I think a great many of them have returned to Nova Scotia and taken the oath of allegiance to the king. Some live south of Digby and some on Cape Breton Island."

He gave himself a little shake. "Well, enough of that! Look, over there is one of our parade grounds and the little fort to be used in case of an attack by the French or Mi'kmaq—which never came. We were raided a lot, though, during the American Revolution by American privateer ships. That certainly caused a rift between us and our New England relatives. If we had ever thought of becoming American, all the raids of our Township put an end to that. But all that's over now, as well."

Asa looked over to find William deep in thought. "Why, I don't believe you heard a word I said!"

William looked up from his reverie. "My apologies, Mr. Beckwith. I find I have been very absent-minded just of late—having something of great import on my mind."

William paused and Asa waited expectantly. "I have something to ask you. I would like your permission to court your daughter,

Mary."

William studied Asa's face and thought he saw no surprise, but rather amusement and pleasure in Asa's response. "I will consider your request most seriously and reply to you very soon, Mr. Forsyth."

3: Mary Beckwith

Every night William went to sleep thinking first about Mary Beckwith and second about his new congregation. Occasionally he tried to think about his new congregation first. One thing he was not thinking about was his salary. He was still staying with the Mortons and he was very comfortable.

Every morning William woke up thinking about Mary Beckwith. He was so energized by the very thought of her he practically leapt out of bed to prepare for the day. Each day he wondered if this was the day her father would give him permission to court Mary or, alternately, if he should go and see her father and ask when he would have a decision. It seemed impossible to wait to see how this would turn out.

Over a week after Asa and William had taken the ride out to Starr's Point, Asa came by the Morton farm. They went into the parlour and sat on chairs facing each other. William's emotions were all over the place. Would Asa bring happiness and joy or disappointment and despair?

"I won't keep you waiting, Mr. Forsyth. My wife and I have talked about this and we gladly give our permission for you to court our daughter...with a few caveats. Mr. Forsyth, you have only been in our Township for a few months and we know you left Ryegate because you were not satisfied. So you may court Mary, but not exclusively. If another man were to wish to court her, we would not prevent it. We would like you to be here at least a year before you ask Mary for her hand in marriage. Do you agree?"

William was concerned and relieved all in the same moment. But he saw no alternative. He could understand Asa's concern. "I gladly accept these conditions," he said.

Then another thought struck him. "Mr. Beckwith, does Mary know about your decision?"

"Now that I have your word, I will tell Mary and ask if she wishes to be courted. Why don't you come by our house after church on Sunday and have supper with the family?"

"Thank you, Mr. Beckwith. I'll be there."

It seemed like Sunday would never come but, of course, it did. William found himself seated next to Mary at the table, and as she smiled sweetly at him William's heart soared.

Asa and Mary's younger children rolled their eyes and giggled behind their hands. Asa and his wife smiled at each other. William was almost oblivious—William was in love.

In the coming weeks, William struggled to keep his focus on his congregation. As a minister, he saw one of his roles as learning to love his parishioners, and this meant getting to know them on their farms or in their businesses. So he set off on his horse each morning to visit.

The roads were a great challenge—narrow and muddy during most seasons of the year—and when he got home each day it would take him quite a while to brush his horse and get all the dried mud off. His horse, Blackie, was a patient and peaceful an- imal and she and William were very compatible.

Not that William was always peaceful and patient. He had a great deal of energy and not much patience with those who did not put their whole focus on what was necessary for a good result. "Blackie," he said, "I'm grateful you are so patient and such a good listener."

It became their habit that, as William brushed Blackie and Blackie munched her oats, William poured out his heart to her about all the issues of the day. Blackie seemed to quite enjoy the routine and William often felt that Blackie was a great blessing to him. He knew he could not share his feelings with anyone in his congregation, as everyone in the Township—and probably in Hor- ton Township as well—was related to everyone else in some way.

On a fresh spring morning, William saddled Blackie and headed out from the Morton farm to Upper Dyke Village on the Canard River. His plan was to visit the Cogswell family.

Spring was in the air and the dyked lands were starting to show little signs of awakening from their winter slumber. If you pushed aside the dead grass of the year before, underneath were bright green shoots of this year's grass. The flat grey clouds of winter had changed to fluffy white clouds against the bright blue sky of spring. Farmers were out ploughing their fields and getting ready to plant wheat and oats and corn as soon as the risk of frost was over. The whole Township bustled with energy and eagerness for the summer and William was bursting with energy and eagerness, too.

As he rode along, he looked for the dykes. There were two types, he had learned: long dykes that ran parallel to the rivers to prevent salt water from the high tides reaching the farmland and cross dykes that prevented the high tides from flooding the marshes with salt water. Beyond the cross dyke closest to the Minas Basin were the unprotected salt marshes which flooded with sea water that flowed in with every high tide.

The Acadian settlers had built the cross dykes—Upper Dyke, Middle Dyke and Grand Dyke, the one closest to the incoming tide. William learned that the English army forced the Acadians who had escaped deportation to show the New England Planters how to repair and maintain the dykes. Dyke land was precious as it provided grazing for the cattle and sheep, as well as hay to keep the animals over the winter. Hay from the salt marshes provided salt and other minerals that the cattle could not get from their regular feed.

Maintaining the dykes was a community responsibility, and a formal elected officer called the commissioner of sewers and dykes was responsible for organizing the regular repair and maintenance of all dykes and drainage ditches in the Township.

On his regular travels in the Township, William had noted a curiosity out in the salt marshes—scattered here and there were groups of poles, twenty or so in a group, sticking up out the marsh and surrounded by water at high tide. No one had mentioned the phenomenon and William had forgotten to ask about it.

Seeing a boy of seven or eight years on the road ahead, he reined Blackie in. "Lad, are you from nearby?"

The boy had a straw hat over his tousled hair and wore short pants and bare feet. He lifted up his freckled face so he could see William better. "My name is John, sir. I'm one of the sons of John Newcomb. Father has been wondering when you'll visit our farm. He is an Elder, you know."

"I'll make a point of visiting in the very near future, if you would be so good to let your father know. In the meantime, could you satisfy my curiosity and tell me why there are groups of poles here and there in the salt marshes?"

"They're called 'hay straddles', Mr. Forsyth. You'll see how they're used in August when we harvest the salt marsh hay for cattle fodder."

"Thank you," William said. "Give my regards to your father and tell him I will visit soon."

At Upper Dyke Village, William found the home of Captain Mason Cogswell and his wife, Lydia Huntington. A man made sure Blackie was well taken care of in the horse shelter with a few oats to enjoy.

Inside, Mrs. Cogswell offered him some hard cider which he drank rather too quickly to help warm himself, there still being somewhat of a north wind despite the blue sky.

The Cogswells, once they were seated in the parlour, were only too happy to tell about their family history. Mason said, "This is the farm I inherited from mother and father, Hezekiah and Susanna, whom you will meet shortly. Mother is ninety this year and father is ninety-four. We came to Cornwallis Township when I was ten years old." He smiled. "There is a family story about that."

"I would like to hear it."

"When we visited my grandparents to say good-bye, grandmother didn't want me to go. I was the youngest child at that time and her favourite. So she hid me and told me to be quiet. My parents searched for me when it was time to leave. At some point, my father got frustrated and said very firmly, 'Mason!' and without thinking, I said, 'Aye, sir,' and was found—to my grandmother's distress."

"A difficult day for the family you left behind."

"Just so, Mr. Forsyth. And for us leaving, both a sad and exciting day."

"I hear you have been blessed with many children."

"We have seven children, and three who died in infancy."

"And you have grandchildren as well?"

Our son William married Eunice Beckwith and they have five children. Our Eunice married Charles Chipman and they have eight. Henry Hezekiah, isn't married yet but is courting a young woman from Windsor. So we are grandparents many times over."

Just then Hezekiah walked into the parlour. William rose to greet him. "You are the pioneer. I'm very glad to meet you."

"Sit down, Mr. Forsyth. I am very pleased to meet you as well." Mason hurried to provide his father with a chair and made sure he was comfortable.

"Yes, I am a pioneer. Would you like to hear how the Cogswells arrived in America?

"Indeed," William said. He really enjoyed pioneer stories. He thought of himself as his family's pioneer to North America.

"Well, the year was 1635 when my ancestor John Cogswell and his wife, Elizabeth, and eight of their nine children departed Bristol, England, on the *Angel Gabriel*, bound for Massachusetts. John was a wealthy man. He brought with him several farm and household servants, and farming and housekeeping implements."

"A man who would be very well situated in his new homeland."

"But this is where fate comes in. They arrived at Pemaquid, Maine, and were at anchor when a huge storm struck them with high wind and even higher tides—in places more than twenty feet, followed by a tidal wave. The *Angel Gabriel* was blown apart and all aboard cast into the sea. It seems miraculous that only three or four seamen and one passenger lost their lives. So my Cogswell ancestors spent their first night in America on a beach in Maine, as penniless as Adam."

"It is incredible to me that your ancestors were able to survive all that they did—and as a result we are here in your parlour today, enjoying this beautiful spring day."

Hezekiah nodded. "I was fifty-four when we arrived at Starr's Point. I brought my house up from Lebanon, Connecticut, and put it together and here it stands to this day—with some additions for my growing family. Susanna and I had eleven children. Not all came up to Cornwallis Township. We only managed to get Mason here with great difficulty," he chuckled.

"I just heard the story," William said. "I also heard you were an Elder of the Church."

"Yes, until I got too old to get to church regularly. My legs don't take me as far as I would like anymore."

Mason said, "I was just telling Mr. Forsyth that Lydia and I were married by the first minister of Cornwallis Township, Mr. Phelps, Father."

William noticed the glance that Hezekiah gave to Mason at the name of Mr. Phelps—or at least that seemed to be the reason.

Lydia appeared to announce that lunch was served, and they all followed her to the dining room. The table was set with their best pewter cutlery and earthenware dishes with homemade bread and butter already on the table. As they were seated, Susanna Bailey, Hezekiah's wife, who was quite frail, was helped to the table. She greeted William with warmth and asked him to sit next to her.

"With great pleasure." William said.

Lunch was very satisfying—ham with cabbage and potatoes, with strawberry preserves and cream for dessert.

"Did you know, Mr. Forsyth," Susanna said, "that Hezekiah and I have been married seventy years this year?"

"Amazing," William said. "Being a pioneer must have been good for you both!"

"It was such hard work," Susanna said, "but I'm glad we made this decision. It was best for most of the children, especially the boys."

"What about you, Mrs. Cogswell,"William asked Mason's wife, Lydia Huntington, "do you have any pioneer stories to tell?"

"I have a good pioneer story for you, Mr. Forsyth, about the very first Huntingtons to arrive in America. My ancestors were from

Norwich, England and in 1633 Simon Huntington and his wife Margaret left England with their five children, the youngest, and our ancestor, Simon, junior, being just four years old. They were part of what is now called the Puritan Great Migration from England to Massachusetts. But before they reached these shores, Simon, senior, became sick with smallpox, died, and was buried at sea. This left Margaret on her own in a new country with five small children. Simon and his brother, Christopher, were among the founders of Norwich, Connecticut. He was the first deacon of the church there, and he married Sarah Clark.``

"But what happened to Margaret Barrett?" William asked. He was trying to imagine what it would be like to be a widow with children in those circumstances.

"We know she married Thomas Stoughton in Dorchester, Massachusetts, and they moved to Windham, Connecticut the following year. As far as we know, they had no children of their own. Thomas raised Simon, senior's children as his own and he willed his estate to Thomas Huntington."

"So, all these many years later, you also became pioneers to a new land—Nova Scotia,"William said.

"I don't think it was as difficult a move as from England to North American," Hezekiah remarked.

Then the conversation shifted to Mason and Lydia's second son, Henry Hezekiah—named after his grandfather.

"You may have heard, Mr. Forsyth, that our second son was chosen to go into the professions. Heaven knows he was not suited for farming. We sent him to Kings College over in Windsor in 1789 while it was still open to Dissenters, and since then he has gone to Halifax for legal training and clerked in the law practice of Richard John Uniacke, the Solicitor-General. He was admitted to the bar in 1798 and is now building up a law practice in Halifax. There is currently a lot of legal business concerning prizes of war. We're very proud of him. The Cogswells have always been good at business and Mason has developed our farm until it ranks among the top Township holdings. So we're proud of all our children and how they have contributed to the family's success."

After lunch and a long chat, William left to visit a couple more farms before returning to the Morton farm at suppertime. "Blackie," he said, "this was a good day for you and me."

William didn't hear Elkanah enter the barn. "Hello, Mr. Forsyth, I thought I heard voices."

"Hello, Mr. Morton. I guess I was just talking to myself."

William's face flushed red with embarrassment. He knew farmers took very good care of their animals but saw them only in the light of their value to the well-being of the family. Animals were food or horsepower or a source of products like wool or butter or leather. William didn't feel he could say that he was very attached to Blackie and talked to her like a friend.

That evening, after supper, the Church Elders arrived for a meeting with William. After Mrs. Morton poured a glass of rum for each of the visitors, Mr. Newcomb began by saying, "Mr. Forsyth, you seem to be settling into our Township."

"I'm certainly well cared for by Mrs. Morton and going further and further afield visiting all my parishioners, but I think it will be some time yet before I visit everyone."

"We, the Elders, are pleased with your sincere proclamation of the Gospel each Sunday and with your visiting during the week. We hope you can fit in a catechism class for our young people."

Mr. Webster and the others nodded in agreement.

"Mr. Newcomb, that would be a wonderful opportunity to get to know the young people. But where could we meet?"

"I believe Mr. and Mrs. Morton will let you gather in their parlour during the winter. Isn't that right, Mr. Morton?"

"It is indeed, Mr. Newcomb. It may be a tight fit, but they're more than welcome to use the parlour."

The other Elders nodded, seemingly pleased to have finalized their agenda, and spent some time talking about crops and the weather. William hoped there would be some mention of his salary, but in the end decided it was not the time for him to bring this up.

The meeting ended with a prayer, and then the men bundled up and headed out into the cold night air.

~

Cornwallis Township, William was discovering, was a farming community. Each farm was almost completely self-sufficient, making or growing all the family needed to sustain itself.

One evening Elkanah and William were sitting near the fireplace as Elkanah smoked his white clay pipe. As the smoke rose, forming a little cloud over Elkanah's head, he continued to explain how things worked in Nova Scotia. "There is hardly any money in circulation here, as you may have noted."

"If you need something you can't make or barter for, how do you purchase it?" William asked.

"Well, you have to have a surplus of some kind—hay, animals, grain—and then you need a market that pays cash, like Halifax, Boston, or the West Indies. Then, of course, you need a way to transport your surplus to the market."

"If you transported hay to Halifax, you could get cash for it?"

"Aye, especially so if the garrison is filled with soldiers. All their horses need fodder and they have to pay to get it. For the most part, we use barter in the Township, keeping accounts of all our transactions and the cash value. Some years, due to poor crops, no one has a surplus of anything to sell or barter."

William found this information interesting but as yet did not see the implications for himself. He was living with the Mortons and being well taken care of. He had things on his mind other than salary at the moment.

Shortly after William's visit with the Cogswells, Mason arrived at the Morton farm. William was up in his room, working on his sermon, when he heard Mason's voice calling him.

As he reached the bottom of the stairs, Mason stated flatly, "Mother has died. Will you come back with me?"

William grabbed his jacket and went to the barn to saddle Blackie. Soon they were galloping towards Upper Dyke Village.

The family were gathered in the parlour., sitting quietly as neighbours and friends came and went bringing food and offering to look after the animals until after the funeral. Susanna's body had been washed, wrapped in a shroud, and placed in a wooden coffin.

When William entered, the family stood up and William began the prayers for the dead. "Blessed be the God and Father of our Lord Jesus Christ, which according to His abundant mercy hath begotten us again unto a lively hope by the resurrection of Jesus Christ from the dead, to an inheritance incorruptible, and undefiled, and that fadeth not away, reserved in heaven for you. Precious in the sight of the Lord is the death of His saints."

The old, familiar ritual brought a sense of peace and comfort to the family and friends.

The burial took place the next day. The coffin was placed in an ox cart and led to the Church at Chipman's Corner. Family and friends gathered and almost filled the church. After the service the coffin was taken across the road to the cemetery, with William leading the procession of family, friends and neighbours. Since everyone in the Township knew each other, the whole community felt every death and the support of neighbours and friends was a great comfort to the grieving family.

After the prayer service at the grave site, William shook hands with all in attendance, starting with the immediate family. He said to Hezekiah and Mason, "I am so glad I met Susanna, a true pioneer woman and Christian lady."

Mason and Hezekiah nodded quietly but had no words.

The pioneers and their children were so used to losing loved ones on a regular basis through illness, childbirth, and accidents, that they seldom expressed their sorrow openly. Indeed, William had learned that many pioneers brought coffins and their own tombstones with them when they came, knowing that in the early years these necessities would not be available.

Faith and community were their mainstays, and sentimentalism and emotionalism were not pioneer traits, William was discovering. Widows and widowers with young children married again quickly after the death of a spouse. Men married, usually to a much younger woman, and often had second and even third families of children.

Sunday services, baptisms, weekly visiting, and funerals were to be major parts of William's routine. However, dissenters from the Church of England were not permitted to perform marriages—the ministers of the Church of England officiated at weddings.

At the end of a beautiful spring day, William rode over to the Beckwith farm, hoping to visit with Mary. As he jumped down from his horse, he saw one of Asa's children, James, and asked if his sister was inside the house.

"Aye", was the reply, "she has a visitor."

"One of her cousins?"

"Nay. She has another beau come to court her, Mr. Forsyth."

What happened next was completely out of the realm of William's experience. He felt shaky and confused, and then his heart seemed to stop as his stomach dropped down into his riding boots. As he tried to compose a question in his mind, nothing came out of his mouth and he couldn't seem to move. All his daydreams of proposing to Mary and thoughts about their wedding day exploded into a thousand little pieces.

Finally, after what seemed like hours, William stammered goodbye to James and rode back to the Morton farm.

He had a sleepless night, but in the morning it seemed clear what he had to do. He rode over to see Asa.

Finding him in the barn, William blurted out what he had come to say. "Mr. Beckwith, I came to visit Mary yesterday and James told me she was entertaining a suitor. I have to admit I wasn't prepared for this, even though you had mentioned it. I would like your permission to visit Mary twice a week—Sunday evenings and Wednesday evenings. I need to know how Mary feels about me and so I need to see her on a regular basis. My desire is to stay in Cornwallis Township and I cannot do that without a wife and the opportunity to have my own family. My heart is set on Mary, so if you cannot agree that I can court her regularly, then I do not know where my disappointment will take me."

"Mr. Forsyth," Asa said, "you are right that Mary has to get to know you and that sooner than later. You will want to move into the manse and you cannot do that without the help of a woman. I feel I have been unfair to you in the interest of protecting my daughter, whom I love dearly, so I will agree to your suggestions. Furthermore, I will suggest to Mary that, if she is interested in you, she should encourage your regular visits."

The men shook hands and William left, feeling like a huge burden had been lifted from his heart. He had gotten too far ahead of the courting process and, before he planned proposals and weddings, he needed to see if Mary felt the same way.

With William's regular visits and his sweetheart's encouragement, the Township was buzzing about the Minister and Mary Beckwith. Mrs. Morton always shared the local gossip with William. It was positive—the general opinion was that they would make a good match. Everyone was watching and waiting to hear any tidbit of news that they could pass on to everyone else.

Excitement was in the air, but the Township would have to wait. William was going to honour both Asa and Mary by slowing down and enjoying every minute he spent with Mary.

In May, William had a wonderful new experience. The apple orchards that were everywhere throughout the Township had been desolate rows of small trees with twisted branches since his arrival the previous November. Suddenly they were filled with blossoms. The pink and white flowers turned the trees into clouds of loveliness and the scent of everything fresh and green and beautiful filled the air. On a fine day with blue sky and big fluffy clouds and the green grass and the apple blossoms, there was nowhere short of heaven that was like Cornwallis Township. That was what William told Blackie as they headed over to the Beckwith farm.

Mary was waiting on the front porch for William to arrive, and they walked together over to the orchard and down one of the rows of blossoms. They had been courting for a while and there was an ease between them that warmed William's heart and let him believe that Mary was fond of him and enjoyed his company.

They stopped by a tree with branches close to their height and Mary held a branch still so William could smell the blossoms. "Be careful, Mr. Forsyth," she teased, "there could be a bee in the flower and you don't want to get stung."

William laughed, but double-checked just to be sure. As he smelled the flower, he closed his eyes to experience the moment, and the blossom rewarded him with the scent of the divine.

When he opened his eyes, he saw Mary's smiling face next to his and without thinking, he put out his hand toward her. With a smile she put her hand in his and they strolled together hand in hand through the pink and white heaven.

~

The next experience William had was far from heavenly. In fact, it left him feeling quite disconcerted. Elkanah invited him to a barn-raising. He was excited to go—a good chance to meet some more of the men and perhaps work with them.

When he got to the farm, the other men were just arriving. He walked over to the foundation of the barn and saw that the frame for the walls was lying on the ground with ropes attached. But before they began to pull the walls into place with the help of oxen, the host began to pass out mugs of what turned out to be hard cider. Before any work began the men had had several brimming mugs. William had one, which was more than enough.

Then the process began of pulling on the ropes to raise the walls and secure them to the stone foundation. After that was accomplished, it was time to raise the frame for the roof into place. More cider seemed to be required before the work began.

Several of the men were staggering around by this time and others were lying on the ground, passed out. It surprised William that the other men were able to get the roof into place and secure it.

That being done, the men drank some more, until it seemed like no one was capable of doing any work. William was appalled. This was so out of character for the usually very sober and pious and hardworking men of the Township.

Without bidding farewell to anyone, William untied Blackie and rode home. None of the men ever mentioned this event to William and he never spoke of it, but it troubled his heart.

One morning as William was working on a sermon, Major

Lemuel Morton, one of Elkanah's sons, arrived for a visit. William had, of course, met him at church. He had come with his parents to Cornwallis Township in 1760 when he was six years old and later married Martha, daughter of John, Jr. and Mercy Newcomb, who was the first child born in the Township after they arrived.

As usual the talk turned to family. "How many children do you and Martha have?" William inquired.

"Nine: John, William, James, George Elkanah, Holmes, Charles, Guy, Rebecca and, of course, Mary Alice, just about the time that you arrived, Mr. Forsyth."

William felt a sense of despair rising up inside him. Everyone had so many children and grandchildren and, to make it more diffi-cult, you had to know whether a person was the child of the first, second or third wife.

Lemuel read William's face and smiled. "Don't worry, Mr. For-syth, if you stay with us it will eventually sort itself out. It takes time and goodness knows how much patience."

Lemuel suggested that he and William go over to Terry's Creek that afternoon so William could see how it was growing as a port. William thought 'creek' and 'port' didn't seem to go together, but he was all for a break from his sermon writing. So, after lunch, they set off for Terry's Creek, on the north bank of the Cornwallis River.

Along the way, they passed the farm of Benjamin Belcher.

"Mr. Belcher is married to Sarah, the daughter of Stephen and Elizabeth Post," Lemuel said. We're going to see some of his ships over at 'the Creek'."

It turned out that 'the Creek' was a bit more impressive than William had thought. There were several medium-sized sailing ships at the docks, among them one of Mr. Belcher's.

"What do they ship from here?" William asked.

"Mostly cargoes of horses, potatoes, oats, fish, beef, pork, and lumber to the West Indies. They bring back molasses, sugar, rum, and some West Indian fruits.

"A more impressive trading operation than I was expecting. Is Mr. Belcher a Planter?"

"Nay, he's from England but he has a land grant in this Township."

"But what happens to his ships when the tide goes out?" William asked as he noticed the ships barely afloat.

"They just sit on the mud of the riverbed until the tide lifts them again."

On the way from Terry's Creek to Town Plot, they rode past the farm of Colonel John Burbidge, until recently a Member of the Provincial Parliament. Lemuel told William a bit about the Colonel.

"He's one of the most important people in our county. I think he's about eighty-four or eighty-five. He came with the first English settlers to Halifax in 1749. Then he came up to Cornwallis Township around the time we all arrived, in 1760. He's the Registrar of Deeds, a justice in the Court of Common Pleas, a magistrate for the Province and a Colonel of the Militia. He and his friend William Best paid for the building of St. John's Anglican Church."

"Should we drop in and see if he's home?" William said.

They rode up to the house, but the Colonel was not there—in Halifax on business. William was surprised that the man who opened the door was black.

"The Colonel has some black slaves," Lemuel said as they rode away. "He's not the only one: Mr. Benjamin Belcher has them as well, but most of the Township folk with slaves call them 'servants'. Usually people with slaves are either directly from England or Loyalists. For the most part, we're not very comfortable with this, and from what I hear in the Legislature, there is a move afoot to end this practice. I'm not sure what the black folk would do if they were freed, as they don't have any land or any way to support their families."

"Slavery became illegal in Scotland in 1778," William said. "Surely this practice cannot continue here."

They were both silent for a while.

William was starting to get a feel for the layout of Cornwallis Township and 'who's who' in the running of the affairs.

As William and Lemuel rode back to the farm, they dropped in to see Dr. Isaac Webster, who had been the doctor in the Township since about 1788. William knew he was a staunch Presbyterian who never missed a Sunday at Church unless a patient had need of him.

Dr. Webster was home so William decided to stay for a visit. Lemuel left them after they had a glass of cider together.

William immediately liked Dr. Webster, who was close to him in age and had young children.

'Our Cynthia was born in 1795, William Bennett in 1798. So we're just getting started. I heard you mentioned to the hiring committee that you might start a grammar school. When you get it up and running, we will have to send you Cynthia and William."

"It would give me great pleasure to teach your children, Dr. Webster," William said with a happy smile.

The men chatted about Scotland, as Dr. Isaac had attended Edinburgh University. They had a lot in common and the time passed swiftly.

"You should visit my uncle Abraham. He and his wife, Margaret, are from Lebanon, Connecticut, while my parents were from Mansfield, not far away. I didn't know him that well until he moved to Cornwallis Township. He is an Elder of the Church and a great supporter of yours. I am enjoying getting to know him now that we're both here."

William nodded in agreement at the suggestion and made a mental note to have that visit as soon as possible.

Back at the Morton farm, William shared his day, first with Blackie, who had been with him the whole time, of course, and then with Elkanah and his wife.

"Lemuel sure toured you around the place," Elkanah laughed.

"And how's Miss Beckwith, Mr. Forsyth?" Mary asked. "I hear you two are an 'item'. Is that right?"

"Mrs. Morton, I believe Miss Beckwith may be as fond of me as I am of her. In any case, that is my hope."

"Perhaps there will soon be a wedding in your future? You must be anxious to move into the manse and start your own family."

"I am trying to take one step at a time and just enjoy courtship, which is a new experience for me. But I hope the time will be right very soon."

It was almost time for supper and William was hungry. He wondered what was on the menu that evening and it turned out to be his favourite—roast chicken with mashed potatoes made with butter and cream, and new green beans and little carrots right out of the garden.

That evening he strolled through the kitchen garden with its raised beds of sprouting vegetables—onions, carrots, cucumbers, beans, peas, squash. William checked to be sure there were no tomato plants. Everyone had heard of the plant common to the Americas called the tomato. It often grew in the flower beds. Mrs. Morton told William that everyone knew those were not good for you—poisonous, no doubt. The red fruit they produced was certainly beautiful to look at, but they were to be avoided at all cost.

One thing the Planters had found and made good use of was rose hips. Once the rose blossoms had fallen off the wild rose bushes, they produced round red fruit. You could boil the pulp with sugar and make rose hip jelly. It had a delightful flavor and went well with biscuits or bread for afternoon tea.

Further from the house, William could see fields of corn, which was good for boiling and eating right on the cob or grinding into cornmeal for making cornbread. Just the thought of hot cornbread with fresh butter and some rose hip jelly made William hungry, even though he had just eaten.

~

On Sunday as he greeted all the people at the door after the service, William felt that he was making some headway in getting to know everyone, but he certainly had a long way to go. There were still many faces to which he could not easily connect a name, or even a family. But his thoughts soon turned to his regular visit with Mary on Sunday evening—the highlight of his week.

As usual, Mary met him at the door and they sat together at supper. Then they went for a walk, accompanied, to avert gossip, by a couple of Mary's younger siblings. It seemed to William that the world was such a wonderful place with Mary in it that he just couldn't keep from smiling as they chatted about day-to-day happenings in the Township. They looked happily into each other's eyes, ignoring the giggles of their young chaperones, and knew they were growing closer each day.

Many of their longer rambles took them past the Manse on Middle Dyke Road. If Mary found this more than coincidental, she did not say. William wondered if she dreamed as much as he did about them marrying and moving into the manse as husband and wife, but he tried to keep the talk casual and enjoy the children as they tried to catch frogs or sneak up on dragonflies settled on the marsh grass as it swayed in the wind. Occasionally, a sword fight broke out when the children managed to break off cattails and use them to tickle each other. William and Mary laughed a lot at the children's games and antics, glancing at each other to see if the other was enjoying themselves.

He hoped he would know when the time was right to ask Mary to marry him.

On Monday, William decided to take his first foray into Horton Township, just across the Cornwallis River. He wanted to meet the Presbyterian Minister, the Reverend Mr. George Gillmore. After crossing the river at Horton Corner at low tide, William rode along until he came to Mr. Gillmore's manse, where he found the minister at home.

"Welcome, welcome, Mr. Forsyth,' Mr. Gillmore said heartily. 'I have been looking forward to meeting you."

He led William into the parlour. and they sat on two rocking chairs near a little tea table. "How are you doing so far?"

"I'm doing well, so far as I can tell. I hear you've been here since after the Revolution."

"Right you are. I'm from Ireland and decided to come to America after my graduation from Theology Hall. So we, my wife and three children under ten, sailed to Boston, and I was ordained by the Presbytery of Boston later that year. But I was forced to stop preaching by the Rebels and taught school for a while. Finally, I was forced to escape through the woods to Quebec in 1782. It took a couple of years to get permission for my wife and children to join me and then we all sailed to Halifax."

"What terrible difficulties the Rebels caused for you and your family. I am shocked at their behaviour towards harmless people. During my stay in Vermont, I found many of the loudest partisans of their new country were poorly educated, seldom went to church, and were involved in all sorts of questionable behaviour—gambling, horse racing, and seeming to ignore their family's well being."

"After all my family suffered, I cannot speak well of them. But to continue, I came to Windsor around 1786 and then to Horton in 1791—been here ever since. I was sixty-six when I came to Nova Scotia and I'm going to be eighty this year. But here is a bit of excitement: we are in the midst of planning a new church and, God willing, I hope to preach the first sermon once it is built!"

William was amazed at Mr. Gillmore's energy and enthusiasm. He was pleased to meet another minister and learn what he could from one so experienced. After they had tea, Mr. Gillmore asked him if he had heard the story about the Reverend Benaiah Phelphs, the first minister in Cornwallis Township. William had not, although he remembered Mason Cogswell's mention of Mr. Phelphs.

"Mind you, this is all second hand—just as background information. When the Cornwallis Township folk arrived here in 1760 they did not have a minister, and it took them nearly five years to arrange for one. Eventually Mr. Benaiah Phelps, a Yale graduate, was ordained for this ministry. He arrived at Halifax in 1765. The Governor of Nova Scotia, gave him a grant of land in his own name, and I think Mr. Phelps borrowed money to pay for a house and barn."

"From whom did he borrow the money?"

"I suspect from Handley Chipman and Colonel Starr. In any case, it seems that Handley and the Colonel took a dislike to him. Some say he didn't seem too attached to his calling, but in any case those two were not people you want to be at odds with. In fact, Handley started to attend the Anglican Church part-time and Colonel Starr and his brother became full members of that church. This would have been a big blow to the Church at Chipman's Corner."

"I can imagine that the congregation was pretty distressed, losing two of the senior leaders of the Township."

"Aye. Then the rumours of the American Revolution began to circulate and it was said that Mr. Phelps was in favour of this. In the end, probably because he had not received all or most of his salary, he sold his property and went back to New England, around 1776. His wife was from Horton Township and they had young children, so that must have been a difficult decision. The Cornwallis folk were angry about that and, despite the fact that the land was in Mr. Phelps' name, they thought it was terrible that he sold it. They believed the land was for future ministers as part of the Township. Then the Revolution broke out, so they couldn't look south any more and they turned to Scotland to seek a minister. Eventually they got Hugh Graham in 1785."

"And he is no longer here. Why did he leave?"

"I am not at liberty to say everything I know, save to say he hated their hymnbook and wanted to replace it with the Scottish psalter."

The story seemed to match what the Reverend Graham had told him, so William moved on to another topic. "I understand that you were part of the formation of Truro Presbytery, the first Presbytery in Nova Scotia."

"That's true. It was formed in 1786, the same year I arrived here. The minister at Truro Township, the Reverend Daniel Cock and the Reverend David Smith of Londonderry Township met with Hugh Graham to plan for the first meeting. It took place in August and included the Reverend James McGregor of Pictou District and myself as well as two elders from Londonderry."

"What are the current concerns of the Presbytery?"

Mr. Gillmore sat forward. "This is an important issue, Mr. Forsyth, and I want you to bear it in mind. We spent a good part of the October 1792 meeting discussing 'the poverty of their ministers and the destitute situation of many comers to this province.'"

William could feel his heart sink. Why had no one in Cornwallis ever mentioned his salary? Surely, it was just because he was living so comfortably with the Mortons. Surely, Asa would not let his daughter marry an impoverished minister. Surely, Asa would know the facts about his salary.

"When is the next Presbytery meeting?" William asked

"Oh, not until October. Will you stay for supper, Mr. Forsyth?"

"Thank you, nay," William said. "I have to get back to my Township before dark or else you will have to put me up overnight, and that was not my plan. But I hope we will meet again soon. You certainly have given me lots to think about, Mr. Gillmore. Your personal story has been instructive about the rift that existed between the Cornwallis people and their relatives in New England. I also appreciate all the information about the Presbytery. Thank you very much for tea."

"God speed, Mr. Forsyth. Come again soon."

~

William thought about everything Mr. Gillmore had said, but especially the discussion of the poverty of the ministers. Surely he had not left one place offering a pitiful salary only to arrive in a worse situation. He would have to bring his concerns to the attention of the Elders.

As he rode along, another question arose: why had previous ministers of his congregation left under adverse circumstances? Did the problem lie with the ministers or with the congregation?

As concerned as he was about salary, he couldn't help returning to his daydreams about Mary Beckwith and their future together. It was starting to get dark, so he urged Blackie to a trot after they had forded the river again.

Later, in the barn, as he brushed Blackie and she ate her supper, he told her of his concerns. In the end, he was still certain he had to bring those concerns to the Elders. With that decision made, he patted Blackie and wished her a good-night.

In the morning he went out to saddle Blackie and she wasn't there. Instead, there was a rather larger male horse.

William ran to look for Elkanah and found him coming out onto the porch. "Mr. Morton, Blackie's gone!"

"Who?"

"Blackie, my horse—or rather, your horse that I ride!"

"Oh, I've managed to get you a younger and more energetic horse. Had to trade two of my older mares for him."

"But, I'm sorry, Mr. Morton, I don't want any horse but Blackie. I'm used to her."

"You'll soon get used to the new horse and you can call him anything you want," Elkanah said cheerfully. "Are you not pleased with my gift?"

"Where is Blackie?" William insisted.

"Why, she's on her way over to Terry's Creek to be shipped wherever they are going to take them. I'm not sure—didn't ask."

William saddled and bridled the new horse and set off at a gallop towards Terry's Creek. He found the herders before they reached the docks.

"Who's in charge here? I need to speak to whomever is in charge!"

One of the herders pointed to an older man up ahead riding a bay stallion. William pushed his horse to catch up, yelling, "Hey, mister, slow down. I need to speak to you."

The man ignored him and William had to push his horse even harder until he was beside the man. "You've been given my horse by mistake!" He looked over the backs to several horses to see Blackie, now looking at him with what he thought was dismay.

"That black mare right behind the brown gelding, that's my horse. I want her back right now!"

William could feel his anger beginning to boil over as the man looked at him and then shrugged his shoulders. With a supreme effort, he rode his horse in front of the man, bringing his horse to a halt. "My name is William Forsyth and that black mare is mine."

"We bought these horses from Mr. Morton. If you have a problem you should take it up with him."

"There's no time for that. I will arrange to pay you for the horse."

"We only deal with Mr. Morton."

"I live with Mr. Morton and am the minister of his church. He sold you my horse by accident."

For the first time, the man seemed to be considering William's demand. The whole time the rest of the herd had been moving towards Terry's Creek and the ship that would transport the animals to the West Indies.

Suddenly, the man kicked his horse, and sped ahead to catch up and William was right on his heels. He heard the man yelling at the other riders, "Samson, cut that black mare out of the herd and bring her over here!"

Then the man turned to William. "Seeing as you're a minister and we have a good relationship with Mr. Morton, we will give you ten days to pay us in full."

"Agreed," William said quickly, before the man could change his mind. He grabbed Blackie by her bridle and led her back to the Morton farm.

When Elkanah saw him riding up the lane with Blackie in tow, he rose from his chair on the porch, a picture of confusion.

"I have to pay the herders in ten days, Mr. Morton, so I need to meet with Elders about my salary," William said without ceremony.

"Mr. Forsyth, don't worry. I will give them another horse to replace the one you call Blackie. We want you to be comfortable and get off to a good start in the Township. There will be time enough to talk about salary when you settle into the manse. Until then, I hope you think we are taking good care of you."

William swallowed several things he had been about to say, and composed his features into a pleasant mien."Thank you, Mr. Morton, for paying for Blackie. And, yes, you and Mary are taking very good care of me. I want for nothing."

William noticed Elkanah breathe what seemed a sigh of relief.

As soon as William had Blackie back in the barn, he gave her a double ration of oats and brushed her until she shone. When he crossed the barnyard towards the house after making his horse comfortable, William, too, breathed a sigh of relief. Blackie was back in the barn and all was right with the world.

~

As promised, William rode over to the Newcomb farm on a pleasant summer day. It was not a long ride and he took his time, enjoying the beauty of the Township.

John Newcomb was pleased to welcome his visitor, and they sat on the front porch with glasses of cider and chatted about the crops and the weather. Almost every Nova Scotian seemed obsessed with the weather—not just farmers, you could understand that—but doctors, lawyers, housewives, everyone. The *Farmer's Almanac* had begun in 1792 and contained health advice, weather predictions, jokes, recipes, charts detailing sunrise and sunset, phases of the moon, tides, and more 'new, useful and entertaining' information than one might think possible. So William could always launch a conversation by inquiring how accurate the *Farmer's Almanac* had been this year at predicting the weather. The second most common topic of discussion was family origins and family achievements. So, eventually, John Newcomb began to talk about how his family came to first New England and then to Nova Scotia.

"I'm the third generation on this farm, Mr. Forsyth, and it will pass on to my son, John, whom you met on the road. I have older sons, but for some reason our family has decided to honour the first of our family to come to Nova Scotia in this way. Deacon John Newcomb, the pioneer, was a New England Planter. He and his brothers came here from Connecticut when he was seventy-two years old. Deacon John died in 1765, aged seventy-seven years. Four of his eight children arrived as well, including my father, John, Jr. Father died in 1778, and the farm came to me."

"How long had your family been in New England?" William inquired.

"Let me see....It seems the first of our family to come to North America was Captain Andrew Newcombe. We had an 'e' on the end of our name at that time. He was a sea captain and travelled up and down the coast from Boston to Maine. His son, Lieutenant Andrew, was engaged in the fisheries near Portsmouth, New Hampshire. Later he moved to Martha's Vineyard. He was engaged in merchandising and seems to have been very prominent in his community. His son, Simon, was born in 1666 in Kittery, Maine. In 1713 the family removed to Lebanon, Connecticut."

"Mr. Newcomb, excuse me for breaking in on your story, but I just have to say that I am amazed how often the New England families moved. Hardly anyone stayed where they first settled."

"Aye, when you have a whole continent to choose from, it always seems the grass might be greener somewhere else. Of course, if you have five or six sons, you need to provide for them, as well."

"Oh, aye, I can understand that."

"Where was I? Oh, Simon had a farm of one hundred and sixty acres and held many town offices in Lebanon. He married Deborah Buell and they lived together for fifty-eight years. They are the parents of Deacon John Newcomb who was their eldest son. The Deacon, his wife, and his son, John, Jr., my father, came to this very farm in 1761."

William said, "I thought I was on a great adventure, coming to America by myself, but now I can see that the first families in New England were even braver. Not only were they coming to a completely unknown place with unknown dangers, but they had to create the society in which they wanted to live. I am always amazed how they were able to survive and thrive."

William thanked Mr. Newcomb for his hospitality and set off to see who else he might visit.

He was still pondering the marriage of Deacon John Newcomb's daughter, Catherine, to Abraham Webster's father, Noah, when he rode up to Abraham Webster's farm on Upper Dyke Road.

They made themselves comfortable on the front porch with glasses of rum. William pretended to sip at his. They jumped right past the weather, and Abraham set into how he, his first wife, had had their first child just before they came to Cornwallis Township in 1760.

"As you know, my son, Abraham, Junior, is looking after the farm. He and his wife have ten children. My daughter, Margaret, married David Bentley and they have three. Olive and her husband have moved to Stewiacke. Isaac and his wife, Abigail, live nearby and have four children. Our twins, Cyrus and Darius, are also nearby. Cyrus is married to Elizabeth English and they have seven children.

Darius is married to Elizabeth Kennedy."

"So you have six children, then?"

"Well, nay, we had eight. Daniel was born right after we arrived in the Township and died in 1765 and David was born in 1767 and died the next year. Children bring great joy and sometimes great sorrow."

William mused on that until Abraham changed the subject to the Church.

"Not everyone will tell you this, Mr. Forsyth, but the people are very pleased with your ministry. Myself, I have the highest regard for you as our minister."

William smiled warmly. "My dear Mr. Webster, it fills me with great pleasure to be so well regarded by you, a respected Elder of our Church."

On the way back to the Morton farm, William felt warm all over at the kind words of Mr. Webster, and he reflected on all that he had learned recently about the people of his congregation. He was starting to see a pattern in the stories of the New England Planters in Nova Scotia. They had moved from England to New England in the 1600s and settled near the coast until they ran out of land to give to their sons. Then they moved to where land was available, such as Connecticut. And when they began to run out of land *there*, they came to Nova Scotia. The Governor had promised them land on very good terms and that they could keep their township form of self-government and practice their religion. From their stories, William deduced that they were among the most successful people in their townships.

~

It was a delight to watch the summer pass in the beautiful world around him. The crops ripened in the warm days and the soft rains and, as fall approached, the pace of the farm work began to increase in readiness for the most important event in the life of the Township—the harvest. On the harvest depended their very lives, so every person had to turn out to gather the apples, potatoes, corn, wheat, barley, hay, and flax.

They preserved the root vegetables in cold cellars. The apples had to be sliced and dried; the corn dried, shucked, and ground into flour; the wheat and barley threshed, winnowed and finally also turned into flour. The hay had to be cut with scythes, stacked in the fields to dry and then gathered into the barns to feed the animals over the winter. Harvesting flax was just the beginning of the incredibly long process of turning it into linen.

All farm work is hard, physical labour, and that is especially true at harvest. There was no time for visiting and chatting until the last potato was tucked away in the straw in the cold cellar.

In late August William watched as men with scythes cut the salt marsh hay, then raked and hauled it to the straddles on a drag. The straddles were constructed of poles approximately twenty feet in length driven into the mud, leaving about five feet above the ground and placed about a foot apart. They carefully pitch forked the hay onto the straddles to form a rounded stack, then threw wires with boards attached to each end over the stacks to secure them from the wind. In the winter when the marsh was harder with frost, the farmers would bring the hay on sleds from the marshes to the farm for winter feed.

Late fall was a time of resting and recovering from the harvest. William and Mary had become even closer over the year and William planned to ask her to marry him at Christmas. He puzzled over just how he was going to do this—the right time; the right place.

He finally settled on Christmas Day. He would have been in Cornwallis Township a little over a year by then, and should leave his generous host and hostess and begin his life as a married man in the manse.

It was a snowy Christmas Eve, 1800, when William opened his trunk and began to rummage around inside. After a few minutes of feeling around for a small box covered with dark blue velvet and not finding it, he got quite excited and started throwing items out of the trunk until he remembered he had put the box in the pocket of his best suit coat, the one he kept for special occasions.

Sure enough, there it was. He opened it to assure himself that the contents were secure, then put it in a safer place. Later in the day, he would be visiting Mary, and he was determined to obtain Asa's permission to ask Mary to marry him.

The ride was not a long one and, once there, with Blackie comfortable in a stall in Asa's barn, William walked to the house and knocked quickly on the back door before letting himself into the kitchen. Evening prayers were about to begin.

Asa lifted down the family Bible from its shelf. He lit another candle near at hand, and said to his family, "Let us worship God."

Then, turning to the Gospel of Luke, he read the story of how Jesus, taking human nature, was born in a manger and an angel visited the shepherds who were watching their flocks by night. The shepherds were alarmed, but the angel spoke to them in kindly words about their saviour. The family then knelt and closed their devotions with thanksgiving to God.

After the final prayer, it was time to prepare the fireplace for cooking the roast of beef on Christmas Day. Asa used tongs to pull out the andirons. James caught the largest log with the hook on the back of the poker and pulled it out onto the hearth. Mary, Asa's wife, swept the partially burnt kindling and ashes forward into her dustpan and took them out to the ash heap far from the back door. Then Asa and James wrestled and rolled the new back log into place at the rear of the fireplace. It had to be big enough to burn all day.

They then built up brands and kindling in front of the log and restored the andirons to their places. By then everyone was coughing from the smoke and dust which had begun to settle.

Meanwhile others had twisted a long cord from the coarse fibres of home-grown flax, for suspending the Christmas roast before the fire on Christmas Day. Now it was time for bed.

There was so much commotion on Christmas Eve, it wasn't until quite late, after most of the family had retired for the night, that William was able to ask Asa the question burning in his chest. Asa's smile was all he needed, and he left in high spirits. Tomorrow, Christmas Day, he would propose to Mary Beckwith and fulfill one of the big parts of his hopes and dreams—securing a wife and, God willing, a future with a family of sons and daughters.

Christmas Day was crisp and cold. At the Beckwith's the Christmas roast was suspended in front of the fire. One of the family had to keep the roast ever on the whirl to bring all parts in turn directly to the heat. Under the roast was a pan to catch the drippings used to make gravy.

All the other preparations for dinner were underway: potatoes peeled, turnips and carrots chopped. The women of the house had baked cakes and puddings and made cranberry sauce earlier in the week. The younger children set the big kitchen table with plates and cutlery, napkins and the salt dish, serving dishes and spoons.

William arrived to cheery shouts of *Merry Christmas! Merry Christmas!* and immersed himself in the pleasures of the day. After the meal was done and all were sitting back in their chairs, enjoying the satisfaction of such a feast, he said to Mary, "I have a Christmas gift for you, Miss Beckwith."

While the whole family watched, William reached into his jacket pocket and took out the blue velvet box. He held it out to Mary.

She received it with a smile and said, "What is this? May I open it now?"

"Aye," William said with enthusiasm, his face flushed with excitement.

Mary opened the box and there, on the dark blue velvet lining, was a silver brooch—two overlapping hearts surmounted with a crown.

"It is beautiful, Mr. Forsyth, but what does it mean?"

"In Scotland, it is given as an engagement present. It is called a Luckenbooth brooch. The body shows two hearts joined together and the crown represents loyalty. I brought it from Scotland to give to my bride-to-be. Mary, will you marry me?"

The whole family was silent for the split second it took for Mary to laugh and say, "Yes, Mr. Forsyth, I will marry you."

William quickly picked up the brooch and pinned it to Mary's dress. Everyone clapped.

Asa said, "We must have a toast to the engagement of my dear daughter and her husband-to-be."

And so more cider was poured into the empty cups and everyone clinked their cups together. "To the happy couple!" they cheered

4: Salem Cottage

William and Mary set their wedding date for September 9, 1801.

Between now and then, Mary knew there was much work to be done—a wedding dress to be made and a trousseau to be prepared. She and her mother spun flax into thread to weave into sheets, pillow cases, towels and nightgowns, and their busy fingers sewed hems and embroidered the initials of the bride and groom on the pillowcases. Mary's father took several ox carts full of hay to the general store at Horton Corner to exchange for material for Mary's wedding dress, a deep blue silk taffeta and some white lace for the collar and cuffs.

On one of William's regular visits, Mary told him about it. "Oh, Mr. Forsyth, it is the most luxurious fabric I have ever seen. I have imagined my dress so many times, and I can't wait for Mother and me to finish it."

"When will I be able to see it, Miss Beckwith? I'm sure you will be a vision of loveliness and the envy of all other brides," he said with a fond smile.

"Oh, everyone knows it would be bad luck for the groom to see the bride in her wedding dress before the wedding. So you will have to be as patient as can be, Mr. Forsyth." Then she giggled. "But it will be worth the wait, I assure you."

The new couple would need many things to set up Salem Cottage. Most of these items would be wedding presents from relatives, friends and members of the congregation: pots and pans, bowls, a spinning wheel, a loom, a quilt frame, laundry tubs, and irons. As well, the congregation would make sure the cottage was cleaned right down to the fireplace, the andirons and the fireplace implements—the crane, shovel, hearth brush, broom, tongs and poker.

While Mary's family was busy with the wedding plans, William continued his exploration of Cornwallis Township. On a beautiful spring-like day in late April, Lemuel rode over to his father's farm and invited William to go to Apple Tree Landing and nearby Indian Point. These were in the northeast part of the Township, closer to the North Mountain. "If time permits," Lemuel said, "we'll try to go up to the Look-off and get a view of the whole Township. Then, if all goes well, we'll try going over the North Mountain to Hall's Harbour."

William thought this was a fine plan and he looked forward to the day.

Despite the blue sky and fluffy clouds, there was a chill in the air intensified by the brisk April wind which made it hard to converse. So from time to time, Lemuel would stop and let William catch up before pointing out landmarks and points of interest.

They rode along Grand Dyke Road and crossed the Canard River to meet up with Canard Street. The flat marshland was grey and dull, its winter-worn look awaiting the arrival of the lively green of spring in Nova Scotia. A few more miles and they crossed the Habitant River and took Washington Street heading east. They soon reached Apple Tree Landing.

The ancient stump of an apple tree, said to have been planted in Acadian times, was still visible near the landing spot for ships on the river. Lemuel led William toward the wharf which was obviously under construction. There was a substantial pile of boards that would finish the framed-in deck.

Lemuel introduced William to the three men hammering the boards to the frame, John Wells, John Sheffield and William Woodworth. The men nodded to William.

"The old wharf is not enough no more," Mr. Wells said. "So bigger she must be."

"Ship building is going to be the up and coming industry in the Township," William Woodworth said.

"Pleased to meet you gentlemen," William said. "I hope to see you in church soon."

"My father always said they should never have built the church at Chipman's Corner. It's too far for us on this side of the Township to travel," Mr. Sheffield said.

"Shush, John," Mr. Wells said. "We'll try to make it as often as we can, Mr. Forsyth. Thank you for coming over to visit us. We'll let the other families know you were here."

The men went back to work and William followed Lemuel down the road towards Indian Point, on the Minas Basin. There, Lemuel introduced William to Ebenezer Bigelow at his boat shed and workshop.

It was a busy place, but Ebenezer broke away from the frame of a boat he was putting together. He was a young man, with broad shoulders and a face roughened by wind and weather.

"Mr. Morton, good to see you. How are you getting along in the Legislative Assembly?"

"Very well, Mr. Bigelow, as far as I can tell. I'd like you to meet our new minister, the Reverend William Forsyth."

"Good-day to you, sir. I hear you're getting married to Miss Beck-with."

"A pleasure to meet you, Mr. Bigelow. Yes, September 9th is the big day. How about you, are you married?"

Ebenezer flushed even redder. "Not yet. My business is growing and just yesterday I hired two new men to help me. As soon as the business is making a profit, I'll be looking for a wife."

"I hear ship building is the up and coming industry in the town-ship."

"Why, that's right, Mr. Forsyth. Now, you haven't seen me at church yet—no doubt that's why Mr. Morton brought you over for a visit." Mr. Bigelow and William looked toward Lemuel.

"The thought did cross my mind. I was hoping to see you in the near future."

"Well, it's a long way from here to Chipman's Corner, and with the business booming and all..."

"I'm sure when the time comes for you to marry and have chil-dren, you'll want them baptized and brought up in the church?"

William said.

"Ah, well, aye, we will."

"And will you not want to set a good example for your children?"

"Aye."

"Then it would be a good thing to begin now and get into the habit, would it not?"

"True. I'll think about what you're saying, Mr. Forsyth. It bears some consideration."

"And your parents, would they not expect you to follow in their footsteps? By the way, do you live with your parents?"

"Now, my father died in 1799. He was a ship builder and I apprenticed as a ship's carpenter. I live with my mother. But come now, have a seat and let's have a drink of rum before I have to get back to work."

There was only a board balanced on two tree stumps to sit on, so William and Lemuel sat and Ebenezer stood chatting about ship building for a comfortable interval. But William could see his mind was partly on his work, so they wished him well and headed back towards Apple Tree Landing in order to pick up the trail to the North Mountain.

The path up the mountain was a tangle of roots and the small rocks which seemed to break loose with each hoof step and made the path seem treacherous. But Lemuel was urging on his horse, so William encouraged Blackie to keep up. The forest on either side and arching above their heads reminded William of a tunnel.

After what seemed a long time, they arrived at a level area where the trees on the east side of the mountain had been cleared away. William dismounted and tied Blackie to a little bush, and then looked out to see the whole eastern side of Cornwallis Township laid out before him.

To his left was the sparkling blue water of Minas Basin. Closer to the shore, the water was reddish due to the tidal mud. The rivers that ran into Minas Basin were red and the fields were green and brown patches, making the Township look like a quilt. William was amused at how small the houses and barns looked from their vantage point. Over the whole scene was the blue sky with the clouds scudding by, chased by the April wind.

"What a glorious sight, Mr. Morton!" William hollered over the wind.

Lemuel smiled, "Worth the climb, then?"

William smiled back. "I'm a little concerned about the ride down the mountain, though."

Going down was tricky but William was learning how sure-footed Blackie was.

At the foot of the Mountain, and after some consideration, they decided to eat their lunch as they rode along. Lemuel wasn't quite sure how long it would take them to get to Hall's Harbour as it was several miles to the west along the path at the foot of the North Mountain.

It was slow going along the path, but they finally reached the gap in the Mountain that led to the Harbour. They, and the horses, took a break before heading up and over the gap. This gave Lemuel an opportunity to tell William how Hall's Harbour got its name.

"Have you heard this story before?"

William shook his head, no.

"Well, during the American Revolution, a fellow from here who had given up on farming and returned to New England joined a band of privateers and directed them to one of our fishing sta-tions. This was one Samuel Hall. They planned to rob Mr. Sher-man's house and store at Town Plot. They had already been raiding cattle and stealing from houses in other parts of the Annapolis Val-ley. The Militia under Abraham Newcomb got wind of this and went to the Harbour and found just three men left to guard their vessels. The Militia fired on these men and shot two of them— wounding them. The third, Samuel Hall, got away.

"They found out from the prisoners where the privateers were going and chased off to Town Plot, it was too late. The privateers had robbed the store and house, and had disappeared. The militia heard later that Samuel Hall was seen in Annapolis Royal at the other end of the Valley. We presume that he found a way back to New England."

"So Hall's Harbour is named after an American privateer!" William exclaimed.

Lemuel nodded with a smile.

"I can well see why there was such a rift between the Planters and their American cousins due to the raids along this coastline. How unfortunate it was for the families on both sides of the American Revolution to be divided by that War."

Then William had a thought. "I suppose some of the Planters might have been torn between loyalty to the Crown or to the Rebels."

"Oh, it certainly was a concern of the Governor, so all the men had to take an oath of loyalty to the Crown. For quite a while there was tension within families and within the Township until it was finally clear that Nova Scotia was going to be neutral during the American Revolution. Besides, we had other causes to divert our attention."

"Such as?"

"There was a great religious upheaval that was splitting church and families," Lemuel said, shaking his head. "Of course, there was only one church building in these parts, the church that we brought with us from New England. Congregationalists were all Dissenters from the Church of England and had come to North America in order to practice their beliefs freely."

"Oh, yes," William said. "Your father told me about that."

"Then there were the Scotch-Irish at at the head of Cobequid Bay."

"There is a road from Halifax to Truro Township. Is that the location you're talking about?"

"That's right. Some of the Scotch-Irish were directly from Northern Ireland while others came up from New Hampshire. The ones from New Hampshire supported the Rebels, even hid Rebels who had been captured by the English and then escaped. All of Cobequid were so united in this regard, that several Rebels were able to build themselves a boat in broad daylight just across the Salmon River from the Deputy Provost-Marshall's house. There was a great to-do when this was discovered. The English arrived by ship to force the men to take the oath of loyalty to the King. It took them quite a while to accomplish this. You know, in those days if you took an oath that was your word and your bond. No one wanted to take an oath to something they didn't agree with. But they finally did and I'm not sure what would have happened if they did not. Anyway, they were a nest of Rebel sympathizers, for sure."

They started up the steep incline that led to the top of the pass on the way to Hall's Harbour. William had hoped to see quite a distance over the Bay of Fundy from the top of the pass but all he could see was fog.

They soon arrived at the fishing station and could see fishermen's huts and fish flakes from the previous year, but it was too early for the fishermen to have arrived and begun their work. The tide was out and the red mud flats extended out from the shore until they disappeared into the fog.

"The difference between low tide and high tide is about thirty feet of water," Lemuel explained.

"That's amazing," William laughed, "I hope I get to see that!"

Lemuel smiled at William's enthusiasm.

The horses had been enjoying some early spring grass when Lemuel suggested that they return home before supper. William was ready. It had been a long day.

The horses picked their way along the narrow path back to Washington Street and then to a bend in the road.

"We call this Jaw Bone Corner," Lemuel hollered over the wind. Looking around, William saw that the house on the corner had as a gate the two sides of a whale's jaw bone.

"The whale got stuck on some mud flats nearby. Once he was just a skeleton, one of the farmers brought back his jawbone to make this gate."

William nodded vigorously rather than try to yell over the wind.

Back at the Morton farm, William thanked Lemuel for the day exploring the Township.

"It is a lovely part of God's earth," Lemuel said as he took up his reins and urged his horse toward his farm. "I am glad to have shown you some of it."

It took William quite a while to get all the burrs and tangles out of Blackie's tail. He didn't say much. They were both tired.

After supper, as they sat near the fireplace enjoying the crackling of the logs and the dancing of the flames, William told Elkanah and Mary about his adventure and also about his visit to the Beckwiths.

"Ah, now," Mary said. "How are the Beckwiths coming with the plans for the wedding?"

"As far as I can tell, Mrs. Morton, they are doing very well. Everyone seems happy and excited. Oh, and Miss Beckwith has selected the material for her wedding dress, but I am not allowed to see it until the wedding day."

"Nay, of course not, bad luck for sure."

Elkanah decided to call a meeting of the Elders and discuss what they might do in addition to cleaning and refurbishing the manse. William went to the meeting.

"Mr. Forsyth will have to buy a new suit and shoes and maybe a wedding ring for his bride," Elkanah suggested. "We could give him some cash or we could barter with Henry McGee at Horton Corner for these items and give them to Mr. Forsyth as a gift."

In the end, it was decided that John Newcomb would take some cider and some ham to the store and order the clothes and shoes from Halifax.

"Take Mr. Forsyth with you," Elkanah said, "so he can be measured. And be sure to tell Mr. McGee that we need the items back from Halifax by August 1st."

Someone else said, "Let's pool some cash and so Mr. Beckwith can go up to Halifax with Asa to buy the wedding ring."

They agreed.

~

William hadn't been back to Halifax since he had arrived in Nova Scotia. Winter was a beautiful time, but now he would see the city in the spring.

It was late spring, so the roads had dried up and the leaves on the trees were about to open into their fresh green fullness. Asa said that the leaves in the Township were about two weeks ahead of the trees they would see on their way to Halifax.

They set off in a spring shower, but very soon the sun came out and a rainbow seemed to promise a beautiful day ahead. The farms along the way were hubs of activity as farmers planted crops, and their cattle, horses and pigs were all out to pasture enjoying fresh spring grass. Once they reached Windsor, they found an inn to water the horses and then continued along the Windsor-Halifax road, stopping whenever the horses reached the top of a hill to let them rest and to take in the view.

The last hill gave them a view of Halifax. Although the leaves of the trees along the road had been just in bud and gave the forest a pale green gauzy effect, the trees in Halifax were in full leaf, giving the town a fresh green appearance. The white church steeples, reaching towards the blue sky, made the scene very picturesque.

They continued along the Windsor Road until it met Barrington Street, just two or three streets up from the waterfront, and there they found a store that specialized in jewellery. William bought Mary a small gold wedding band and the clerk carefully placed it in a little red velvet box.

Then they walked around the streets and docks, amazed at the apple and cake stalls old women kept in front of the established stores, and the boiled lobsters and gull eggs available on the wharves. There were stalls to buy clothes, horses, hot gingerbread and potatoes, even places to get your knives sharpened, all surrounded by countless street musicians, the deafening noise of horse and carriages, the stench of horse manure, the sight of fallen and dead horses, and poor children gathering up manure to sell for a few pennies. It was overwhelming.

While Asa went to see a family friend, William decided to visit his acquaintance, Iain Fraser at Forsyth and Company. As he climbed the stairs inside the old stone building that also served as a warehouse, he wondered if Iain would remember him from their sail from Newburyport to Halifax in 1799.

Iain spotted him just as he reached the top of the stairs, "My dear sir, there you are! Wonderful of you to pay me a visit." He grasped William's hand so tightly it made William wince.

"Chaps," Iain said to the others in the office, "Mr. Forsyth and I will be going out for a drink." He recalled himself and turned back to William. "You do have time for a drink?"

"Aye, Mr. Fraser. But only one," William said with a smile.

As they walked to the tavern, Iain said, "Now you must let me pay for your drink as it will be the last we have together, at least in this god-forsaken colony."

"How so, Mr. Fraser?"

"I've been called back to the Scottish side of the company and we are leaving within days. My wife and children are rejoicing to see our families and friends again, and so am I."

"That is quite a sea-change, if I may put it like that."

"Very droll. But, come now, what is your news?"

William felt a smile stretching his face. "I am here in Halifax to buy a wedding ring for my bride-to-be. Her name is Mary Beckwith and we'll be wed in September."

"So, you're going to stick it out in the colony...with the Puritans."

He paused. William waited for the expected saucy comment.

"Well," Iain finally said, "how can one not be overjoyed that a fellow countryman has found happiness? Congratulations, my dear Forsyth. May your wedded life be as blissfully happy as mine is. Or will be once we are home again. May God bless you."

The two shared details of their separate plans until it was time for William to rejoin Asa. Iain did not share what dissatisfaction or sorrow had led him to take his family home to Scotland, and William did not press the point. *Had I not found my Mary*, he thought, *perhaps I would now be contemplating a similar journey.*

William and Asa had supper and stayed overnight at the Split Crow tavern and hostel, and were early back on the road to Windsor. The two chatted happily about the upcoming wedding and about Salem Cottage. The time passed quickly and soon they were back at Asa's farm.

William took some time to talk with Mary about the trip to Halifax and his impressions of the Province and the Town. Then he shyly took the velvet box out of his inside jacket pocket and opened it to show her.

"Oh, Mr. Forsyth, how lovely!" Mary reached over and, with more spontaneity than anyone could have imagined from a Puritan, hugged William and kissed him on the cheek. Just as suddenly, she sat back down and spent some time blushing and smoothing out her skirt.

William waited tensely for the Beckwiths' response.

Asa looked at his wife and she at him, trying to hide their smiles and be stern about this display of emotion, but to no avail, and they burst out laughing. As soon as William and Mary were sure of this response, they laughed, too. *We should laugh more*, William thought. *It feels good.*

The last step in William's preparation for the wedding was to ride over to the Reverend William Twinning's house and ask him if he would perform the ceremony, as only Church of England ministers could do this according to English law. It was a source of great irritation to the Planters that the governor had not fully kept his promise that the New Englanders could practice their own religion.

St. John's Anglican Church, at Fox Hill, was very small. There were plans being considered for a larger church building. Although only about ten percent of the population of Cornwallis Township were Church of England, they were some of the most influential people.

The Reverend Twinning agreed to perform the ceremony at the Beckwith farm on September 9, 1801. He would read the banns from the pulpit on the previous three Sundays to let everyone know about the upcoming wedding and to allow anyone with objections to the marriage to notify the minister. The Crown had two main issues—were either the bride or groom already married and, if not, were they within the illegal degrees of consanguinity, such as uncle and niece, or first or second cousins.

Having finalized this detail, William felt he could breathe a sigh of relief. He hoped his new suit would be ready on time and he wondered how Mary was coming with sewing her wedding dress. It was all so exciting.

In early August William learned that his suit and shoes were ready. He tried on his suit in the storeroom of Henry McGee's store and, as looked at himself in the mirror propped up against some barrels, he felt pleased. The suit was made of the finest black wool. The jacket lapels were edged with black velvet, and it fitted smoothly over a waistcoat made of blue silk. His shoes had silver buckles and the higher heels made him look a little taller, he thought. He still had a new shirt and stockings in his trunk and the Mortons bought him a new tricorn hat as a wedding present.

Standing there in front of the mirror, looking at himself in the finest of clothing, he imagined that Mary would be impressed with her groom. He put his new suit and shoes back in the cloth bags they had come in and left the storeroom.

"Congratulations, Mr. Forsyth, on your upcoming wedding," Henry McGee called from the top of his ladder, where he was organizing bolts of cloth.

"I thank you kindly," William said with a broad smile. "You have contributed greatly to it.".

William told Blackie all about the wedding plans while he brushed her mane. Blackie seemed to know William was excited, but William was sure she didn't know she would soon have a new home.

The big day arrived.

"Don't forget the ring!" Elkanah called to William as he dressed in his room.

"Don't worry, I have it!" William shouted back.

Blackie was already saddled and bridled and had been curried and brushed to within an inch of her life. She looked very special indeed.

"I'll see you at the Beckwiths'!" William called, after he had brought Blackie around to the front of the house. Then he rode toward his future.

Farmers tipped their hats and women smiled as he rode by. He felt both shy at all the attention and, somehow, strengthened by it.

When he arrived, Samuel Beckwith took Blackie to the horse shed. William walked in the front door and met Asa and two of the younger children.

"Mary's upstairs with her mother, getting ready," Asa said. "Her mother says she is dressed and seems amazingly calm—just looking forward to the wedding and her life with you in Salem Cottage. Wait until you see her. She has made a beautiful job of her wedding dress.'

William so wished he could go straight up, but knew he wasn't to see Mary until the wedding, so he went back outside and paced. It seemed the only thing he could do to calm the butterflies.

Asa, dressed in his Sunday best, came and paced with him. They greeted the guests as they arrived and directed them to the parlour.

"The manse is all ready," Asa said. "I've taken all the wedding gifts over and put them in the kitchen until you and Mary can sort them out. The women have stocked the larder with food—everything you will need for a while. My wife says the manse looks very cosy."

Shortly, the Anglican minister arrived. Mr. Twinning had a good laugh at William and Asa pacing in the front yard. Then the three of them went into the house together, William to stand in the parlour with Mr. Twinning and his groomsman, Lemuel Morton, dressed in the fine clothing he wore as Member of the Legislative Assembly in Halifax. There they waited, along with the guests, for Asa to return with the bride.

Very soon, Asa appeared with his daughter, who had her arm through his. William couldn't believe how beautiful she looked in her deep-blue taffeta dress with the high, white lace collar and matching cuffs. Her hair was pulled up and ringlets fell to her shoulders, and she wore a blue taffeta bonnet with a white taffeta ribbon tied in a bow under her chin.

Asa led Mary up the 'aisle' between the chairs that had been placed in the parlour for the guests. Her bridesmaid was her sister, Elizabeth, who followed behind her wearing a new yellow taffeta dress with a sprinkling of flowers, and a pale green bonnet. Family and guests smiled at the bride.

When they arrived where William stood, Asa kissed his daughter on the cheek and went to sit with his wife. Mary put out her hand and William held it gently as they turned to face Mr. Twinning.

They held right hands as they took their vows and William gave Mary her ring. Then Mr. Twinning pronounced them man and wife.

For the first time, William was able to kiss Mary. He felt the heat from her lips might cause him to ignite. They smiled at each other and the family and guests clapped enthusiastically.

After a final prayer and the blessing, Asa invited the guests to enjoy the food and drink prepared for them. William and Mary, hand-in-hand, strolled among their guests and received their congratulations.

When all the guests were gone, William mounted Blackie and Asa helped Mary up onto the pillion behind William. As the family waved, William and Mary set off on their life together.

Blackie started to automatically turn right towards the Morton farm, but William directed her toward Middle Dyke Road and Salem Cottage.

The cottage looked lovely to William as Blackie turned up the lane lined on both sides with acacia trees. "Mary, I feel like the most blessed man in the world. I've long dreamed of marrying a wonderful woman. And you are that woman. What more could a man ask for."

"Remember our first meeting in Grandfather's kitchen? In just that brief encounter, I felt that we were going to marry."

"I do remember that meeting. I kept looking at you and wondering if you already had a beau. I never had eyes for anyone but you, Mary. I just knew you were the one for me."

"And now, here we are, married and about to move into Salem Cottage. I feel like I'm in the happiest of all dreams."

There were still many people at the manse to welcome them. William dismounted and helped Mary down from the pillion. Someone took Blackie to her new stall.

William and Mary entered through the front door, into the hallway. The parlour was on one side and the dining room on the other. They found their way to the kitchen, at the back of the house.

"Sit down, sit down," said one of the women, "and refresh yourselves. You must be exhausted from your ordeal."

The other women laughed, and Mary and William could not help joining in. Above all things they wanted to be on their own, but they could not very well shoo all these kind people out of the manse. So they sat and ate, and declared the food to be just what they had needed.

When William could stand it no longer, he said, "Come, Mary. We should see how Blackie is installed."

"You must say 'Mrs. Forsyth' now, you know," a woman said to further laughter.

They finally escaped to the barn, where Blackie was in a very comfortable box stall. The brief respite let them catch their breaths and gaze lovingly on each other before returning to the crowded cottage.

As evening came, the well-wishers left and William and Mary climbed the stairs to their room. It was freshly whitewashed, and white linen curtains moved in the evening breeze. The bed was made with white linen sheets and pillow cases and a fine, cream-coloured wool blanket, and folded at the foot was a beautiful quilt with a wild rose pattern in pink and green. There were rag rugs on either side of the bed and, on the dresser beside the wash bowl and pitcher, was a vase of purple asters and white Queen Ann's lace.

William and Mary smiled shyly at each other and closed the door.

The next morning they were both up at sunrise. Mary had cleared two places at the kitchen table and laid out bread and butter. She had raked out some hot coals onto the hearth and was frying eggs and ham in their new long-handled frying pan. They smiled at each other and both ate a big breakfast.

~

As William reviewed all the events of the day before, he felt he had not just married Mary but in some way had married the Township.

He felt more part of his congregation now—not just a stranger from Scotland. William felt on top of the world.

True, he had not been paid his salary yet, but he had been so well taken care of by Elkanah and Mary Morton and now he was living in a lovely cottage with his beautiful bride. The congregation and her relatives had furbished the cottage with everything they would need, right down to the tea he was drinking.

William wrote a letter to his parents in Scotland and another to General Whitelaw in Vermont, to let them know the good news and to inquire into their well-being. The memories of some of his difficulties in Ryegate were beginning to fade as the people in Cornwallis Township had been so welcoming.

Another good thing about the Cornwallis Township people, in William's view, was their character. They were honest to a fault. You didn't have to worry about people working against you behind your back; no, if anyone had anything to say to you, they said it to your face. It was true as well that sometimes some things didn't need saying but William realized he was much like his parishioners. He said what he thought and, if necessary, he stood his ground. You could correct him but you had better know what you were talking about and be prepared to defend it. *So, in a way*, he thought, *we are much alike and that is why we get along so well.*

After lunch, William decided to check on Blackie and take another look at the barn. Blackie was gone. The stall door was open. He looked out into the paddock. No Blackie. He looked over the field behind the barn. No Blackie. He ran into the cottage.

"Mary, Blackie is gone!"

She looked puzzled. "Where could she have gone?"

"I know not. Perhaps Elkanah could help me find her. I will walk over and see."

As William reached the end of the lane, he could see Elkanah walking up the road leading Blackie.

"Mr. Morton, how did you find her? Where was she?"

"I imagine she got lonely, for she came back to the farm to see the other horses. Horses are social—they like being with other horses."

William had never thought about how this move might affect Blackie. "What can I do to keep her from running away again?"

"Get her a goat."

"Get her a *what*?"

"A goat, for a companion. The Barnabys have a few goats. Ride over there and ask for a goat."

"What will it cost?"

"Oh, Barnaby will give it to you. He's a member of the congregation. Tell him I sent you."

Soon William was riding back to the cottage, leading a goat and thinking of the curious way in which his household was growing. He put Blackie in her stall and untied the goat. Blackie was curious. She sniffed the goat and the goat sniffed her. Then they settled in together. William was amazed.

"Do you have a name for the goat?" Mary inquired with a smile on her face.

"I'm going to name him Peter."

"Peter it is," Mary laughed.

William and Mary and Blackie and Peter soon had a pleasing routine. William conducted Sunday services, wrote sermons and visited his parishioners. He attended meetings with the Elders and conducted baptisms and funerals as well as holding catechism classes for the young people. He also took care of Blackie and Peter, hauled water from the well for the cottage and the barn, chopped wood outside the back door and stacked it by the fireplace.

Mary took care of the house, making meals, doing dishes and keeping the kitchen garden. Every day she had to bake bread in the little bake on the side of the fireplace, sweep floors, make beds, and each week do the laundry and hang it out to dry, then using iron blocks with handles, heated in the hot coals, iron clothing, sheets and pillow cases. Another regular task was making candles and soap, and in the fall, she prepared food for storage over the winter and pickled vegetables.

As a minister's wife, Mary also visited the women of the congregation who had just given birth and hosted quilting bees and other social events. It was a very busy life.

~

William often thought about what his life would be like if he had been a farmer. Spring involved spreading manure over the fields, plowing, and planting the crops of wheat, barley, corn, potatoes, and flax. As well, in the spring, the farmers washed and sheared sheep. Summer involved hoeing crops, repairing dykes and roads, taking turns watching over the animals turned out to pasture, and maintaining farming implements and buildings. In August the harvest of hay, including the hay on the salt marshes, began. Fall was harvest and the threshing and winnowing of grain, which the farmer then took to the mill to be ground into flour. The apples had to be picked and prepared to hang to dry.

Winter included looking after the animals in the barns, as well as slaughtering and butchering them to be put into salt brine for storage. In February, those with sugar maple trees tapped them to get the sap, which they then boiled to make maple syrup, the favoured sweetener for much of the baking the women did. The winter was also the best time to log trees and drag them back to the farm to be cut and stacked.

Every day included chopping logs into firewood, stacking it by the fireplace, and hauling water for the house and the animals.

All in all it was a very busy life for the men and the women, but there were social events such as quilting bees for the women and barn raisings for the men, as well as Sunday church services.

William got to see most of his parishioners every Sunday, and visited them regularly during the week. He had learned that the best way to do this was to meet with them wherever he found them.

As he rode through the Township one fine day, he saw someone walking down the road leading an ox. It looked like Benjamin Burgess, a faithful member of the congregation. He, his wife, Abigail, and their children were usually at Church on Sunday.

As William drew closer, he called out, "Is that you, Mr. Burgess?"

"Indeed, it is, Mr. Forsyth. How are you this fine day?"

"Very well. May I walk along with you for a way?"

The farmer nodded. "I've sold this ox to the farm next door and so I'm walking it over there."

William dismounted and led Blackie by her bridle. "How are your wife and children? You have six now, I think."

"Indeed. Our youngest was born in January 1800 and I haven't had him baptized yet. Would you perform the sacrament for us?"

"Aye, just remind me before the service this Sunday and I will baptize—sorry, I don't remember his name."

"John Newcomb Burgess, and fine lad he is."

"Your wife's maiden name is Hovey, Abigail Hovey? That doesn't sound like a Cornwallis Township name."

"My wife's parents were Loyalists from Massachusetts. After the Revolution they settled in New Brunswick. I was up there visiting some relatives when I was introduced to her."

At this point they reached the lane to the neighbour's farm and parted ways.

That evening Lemuel came over to Salem Cottage to tell William that there was going to be a Town Meeting the following week to plan the auctioning of the poor.

"Plan the auctioning of what?" William thought he had not heard Lemuel rightly.

"Auctioning the poor, Mr. Forsyth. We do this as a Township on a regular basis. It is our duty as to care for the poor. We have to raise money for the care of the poor and then auction them off to the lowest bidders."

"Start from the beginning," William said, "and explain this to me."

"Well, at the Town Meeting we will decide how much money we need to raise to care for the poor this year. All the rate-payers will then be assessed for their portion of the money needed and then we will appoint some among us to go out and collect this money. We then bring the poor together, and certain rate-payers bid-off one or more of the men, women and children for sums they will be paid weekly by the Town. If possible, the poor are made useful in their homes in exchange for room, board, and clothes. There are actually some men in the Township who make their living totally or partially by boarding the poor. Oh, and, included in the money we raise is a sum set aside for care by a doctor."

"Thank you, Mr. Morton. I did not know how you took care of the poor in this Township. In Scotland, we have Poor Houses supported by taxes on all the property owners in a shire. I will be glad to go with you to see just how this system works."

William and Lemuel continued to chat over a glass of cider—William was finally getting a bit of a 'taste' for cider—about how the Township was run.

"In all the Townships in Nova Scotia settled by New England Planters, the Town Meeting is the local form of self-government. We meet in conjunction with the Court of Sessions, which is the magistrates or justices of the peace, the chairman of which is the *Custos Rotulorum* and the secretary, the Clerk of the Peace. This court appoints constables, assessors, surveyors of highways, school commissioners, pound keepers, fence viewers, and trustees of school lands. In the Town Meeting, the rate-payers meet to discuss freely all local affairs, including the relief and support of the poor and the appointment of overseers and a clerk of overseers for carrying out the provisions for the needy."

Having answered all of William's questions, Lemuel said goodbye to Mary and William, as it was almost dark.

William's plan for the next day was to visit the Reverend George Gillmore in Horton Township. The red sky predicted a fine day and he looked forward to their visits every month or two. He wanted to see how the new church building was coming along and have a chance to talk about ministerial issues. He smiled as Mary snuggled beside him and they were soon fast asleep, having had a busy day.

~

No matter how good his intentions, Mary was always up before him and cooking their breakfast. She often made oatmeal porridge once she realized how much William enjoyed it. They ate it with a little butter and cream. Delicious!

When William arrived at the manse in Horton he realized that something must be wrong. Usually George would be out on the front porch to offer him a hearty welcome, but not this time.

After he knocked, a man of about thirty came to the door and invited him in. He introduced himself as Deacon Elihu Woodworth, of the Horton Congregational-Presbyterian Church. "Mr. Gillmore has had a bad spell—not himself at all, I'm afraid. But he will recognize you. Come, he is in bed."

William followed the Deacon to the room where George was lying quietly with his eyes shut.

"Mr. Gilmore," Elihu said quietly, "it's your friend from Cornwallis Township, Mr. Forsyth."

Immediately, George opened his eyes and smiled weakly. "Sorry I wasn't there to greet you, Mr. Forsyth. I am very happy to see you. Can you sit with me for a while?"

William nodded and sat down in the chair by the bed. The Deacon left the room and the two ministers were left alone.

"I had a weak spell a few days ago. To be expected, I guess, since I am eighty-two years old. But now I'm feeling better. Thought I would stay in bed a few more days just in case it's rest I need. I'm glad you've come to call. Tell me all about the wedding and how you and your bride are doing in the manse."

William chatted for a short while, until he saw that George's eyes were getting heavy. He left his friend to get more rest and went out to chat with the Deacon.

"How does he seem to you, Mr. Forsyth?"

"Needing more rest, as far as I can tell. He surely likes to be out and about, so maybe he is just worn down and needs to take things more slowly."

"That's my opinion as well. I'm going to have to give him more help whether he wants it or not," Elihu said with a smile.

William instantly liked Elihu, and decided that when he visited George in the future he would take time to visit the Deacon as well.

"I think we may be about the same age," Elihu said.

"Indeed. I think you are right. I've just married and have begun living in Salem Cottage."

"I've been married to my wife, Sabra, since 1793. Our eldest son's name is Joseph, after my father, Joseph Woodworth, the Planter, who died in 1794. Mother and Father came here from Lebanon, Connecticut. We live at Island here in Horton Township and my mother lives with us. We would be very glad if you had time to visit us at Island, Mr. Forsyth."

"I'll make plans to do that. I will take my leave now, but will be back when Mr. Gilmore is feeling better. I think you have some relatives in Cornwallis Township. Perhaps you could send me word through them."

Elihu escorted William to the door.

"Tell Mr. Gilmore that I wish him a speedy recovery."

"I will, Mr. Forsyth."

At suppertime, William told Mary about his day and she told him about hers. It was a helpful routine.

One evening Mary decided to tell William what he should know about the children of Handley Chipman. "I think you already know that Handley Chipman was a very influential member of the Township and that he died in 1799."

"Aye, I think it was your father who told me about him. He and Handley didn't have the best of relationships."

"You are right about that. However, Handley had fifteen children by his two wives, and they are very prominent in the Township. I'll just mention a few. John is in the provincial parliament, is a Justice of the Peace and Judge of the Inferior Court in Kings County. He married Eunice Dickson and they have fifteen children. William Allen Chipman is a merchant, a Member of the Legislative Assembly for Cornwallis Township and a Judge of the Inferior Court. He and Ann have four children, I think. Holmes and his wife, Elizabeth, have eleven children. And, of course, the Reverend Thomas Handley Chipman is a pastor of a Baptist Church in Annapolis Royal."

"Mary, I think that's all I can hope to remember for right now. I can see that Handley's children, and soon his grandchildren, will continue his legacy for the foreseeable future."

Mary nodded. William wondered to himself how many children he and Mary would have. What would it be like to have fifteen or twenty children? *Five or six would be enough,* he thought.

~

In late January 1802, as William and Mary snuggled down in their bed, Mary kissed William on the cheek and said, "William, you are going to be a father!"

It took a moment to sink in, and then William smiled and asked, "When?"

"Probably in late June or July. Are you pleased?"

"More than pleased, Mary. I've been hoping for children. All children are a blessing, but I hope to someday have a son who will return to Scotland to be educated at Glasgow or Edinburgh University. If we have a son, let's name him William after my father. And if we have a daughter, let's call her Mary after your mother.

Mary laughed and agreed. They fell asleep dreaming of the baby and its future.

As Mary became larger, the women in her family came over regularly to help her keep up with the housework.

One evening in early July, 1802, William came home to find a group of women in the room prepared for the birth, with a midwife in charge of the process. William could hear Mary crying out in pain and it really distressed him, but the women kept him away from her.

"Please tell her I am here, at least," he pleaded, and one of the women crept off to carry the message.

William didn't know what to do with himself. Sitting down was out of the question, so he paced...and paced...and paced for what seemed to be forever.

Many hours went by, and William was at the point of desperation as each cry or groan seemed to cause him to feel pain, so much so that he thought he might be having a baby himself. No one ever told him about sympathetic pain.

His pain was relieved only when he heard the unmistakable cry of a baby. He ran towards the birth room and pushed past the women to see Mary looking pale, wan, and exhausted. But she still managed a small smile.

"It's a girl, William, our daughter, Mary."

William smiled back.

The midwife brought Mary a little bundle and she reached out to receive her daughter, Mary Forsyth.

William's main feeling was relief—relief Mary and the baby were going to be well and healthy. Just under the relief was another feeling. It kept bubbling up until William realized it was joy.

He sat beside Mary on the bed and they gazed at little Mary. She was beautiful, he thought, and she reminded him of his mother, for some reason unknown to him—maybe it was the bright blue of her eyes. Yes, that was probably it. He wished his parents were closer so they could see their granddaughter.

Another of his dreams had come true. He was now both a husband and father.

He wrote to his parents about the wonderful news.

5: The missionary

Drip, drip, drip. The rain ran off William's hat and dripped down onto his oil slicker. Despite the rain, he was in high spirits.

"Blackie," William leaned forward to pat the side of her neck, "are you as excited as I am to begin this journey?" For once, Blackie didn't seem to hear him. *Probably focused on the trail ahead,* he thought.

If Blackie had been listening, William would have explained that, despite his excitement, he had mixed feelings about his missionary journey 'down the Valley'. He greatly desired to exercise the authority conferred on him at his ordination, but Mary was pregnant with their second child and he couldn't help being concerned about her. Her first pregnancy had gone smoothly, but he knew of many examples of pregnancies that had resulted in the death of mother or child, or both. However, he should be back at least two weeks before she was due to give birth. "I'll be just fine," Mary said. "You need to attend to those poor folks who have only silent Sabbaths for lack of a minister. You need not worry about me. My family and the women of the community will support me. Go."

So William decided to go on his first missionary trip down the Annapolis Valley. Mary's parents, Asa and Mary, stood beside Mary, who was holding his daughter, as he left Salem Cottage to saddle Blackie.

He recalled the last meeting of the Presbytery. A letter was read from a Mr. Turnbull from Digby Township, asking for a visit by a minister. After a short discussion, it was decided that William was the logical minister to make the journey as the next closest Presbyterian minister was in his eighties. The Presbytery carefully outlined the duties of a missionary on this first trip—first, find some Presbyterians; then organize them into a society and instruct them on their responsibilities.

"Here's what we expect, Mr. Forsyth," Mr. Smith, minister of Londonderry Township, had said. "The men must hold it as their highest duty to hold Sunday prayer services, catechize the young, and make sure that everyone can read their Bibles. That means that all the children must be taught to read."

"Do we expect that all the adults can read and write?"

"Most who came here from England or New England can read and write as they had schools in those places, but I'm afraid their children have often gone without schooling. This must change in Nova Scotia, and most especially among Presbyterians, as it is our belief that everyone must be able to read their Bibles."

"Certainly an excellent objective," William remembered replying.

The Presbytery wanted him to hold a worship and communion service and baptize all who requested it on his first visit. It was also important for the society to organize such a service each summer thereafter when William could attend.

"That seems like a great deal to accomplish on one trip," William said. "I doubt that my congregation will give me permission to be away for any more than two weeks."

"If you do not tarry in any one spot, Mr. Forsyth, you may be able to do it in two weeks," Mr. Smith said with the assurance of someone who was not going to have to do it. "Let your Elders know that we are counting on you to meet this need."

When William presented the Presbytery's decision to the Elders of his Church, they had been none too pleased.

"Well, Mr. Forsyth," Mr. Newcomb said, "as Congregationalists we pride ourselves on being independent of any higher earthly authority, so it displeases us that your Presbytery would take you away from your duties here."

William hadn't heard that tone of voice before and it rather surprised him. "Don't think of it as interference in your independence, sir, but rather as a Christian duty to your fellow Christians who are not as fortunate as you."

All William got for his attempt to reframe what the Presbytery had tasked him to do was a big "Humpft!" All the men in the meeting had their arms crossed and were sitting back in their chairs.

In the end, they gave William permission to travel during the end of August and beginning of September. Just two weeks, they had said with finality. If he was going to visit down the Valley in 1805, this was the time.

Now that he was at the beginning of the trail that would lead down the Valley and ultimately to Digby and Bayview, he decided to focus on the advice that Elkanah and other Elders had given him. His son, Elkanah, Jr., was a customs officer at Digby. He was also a school teacher appointed by the Church of England organization, the Society for the Propagation of the Gospel—usually referred to as "the Society". "Now," Elkanah had said as they sat on his porch sipping cider on a warm summer evening just before William was due to leave, "when it comes to your journey, just follow the Post Road—it's really just a blazed trail. You have to be very careful, for if you were to slip and break your leg, no one would know you were missing for days or weeks. You could die."

"Oh, dear!"

"And if your horse were to break her leg, you would have to leave her to the mercies of the wild animals, and carry your saddle, bridle, bags and blanket as you searched for a horse you could borrow."

Elkanah seemed to be enjoying laying out the rigours of the journey. "Oh, and find a place to stay before dark. You don't want to wander off the trail and get lost. Most people will welcome a stranger. Because the roads are so bad, there are not many inns until you get to Annapolis Royal."

"That is more of a settled town, I collect."

"Indeed, with a fort and garrison."

"People make this journey and survive, I suppose."

Elkanah seemed to be stifling a laugh. "Oh, aye. As long as they watch out for bears. Mothers with cubs are very dangerous, so keep your eyes peeled. Your horse will probably alert you before you see anything, but don't get lost in a day dream and overtake a bear by accident. There are other animals out there but it's the bears that I'd worry about."

"*Other* dangerous animals?"

"Well, wildcats. But they don't usually attack people and it would be highly unusual for you to see one as they are silent creatures that blend into their surroundings.

Perhaps I should bring the Elders along as bodyguards, William thought.

"Oh, and another thing," Elkanah said. "The towns you will travel through are usually either Congregationalists like the Planters or Church of England—mostly Church of England."

"Are there many Presbyterians in the Valley?"

"Scattered here and there but you will have to hunt hard to find them. And both Annapolis Royal and Digby are strongholds of the Church of England." Elkanah had nodded sagely. "Aye, your Presbytery is sending you as Daniel into the Anglican lions' den."

When William at last took his leave, he privately determined to share none of Elkanah's more grisly warnings with Mary.

~

For his journey William packed an extra suit of clothes, towels, soap, a razor, a mug, utensils and a bowl, fruit, tea, some dried meat—and a smoked ham that a well-wisher handed to him at the last minute. All that was to sustain his body. For his mission he added his Bible, a baptismal cup in a red velvet bag with a gold drawstring, and a special cup and plate for the sacrament of communion in a similar velvet bag. He had a supply of catechisms, copies of the Westminster Confession and a few Bibles.

Just before he left, the Church of England minister, Mr. Twinning, paid him a visit. "We have heard of your upcoming trip down the Valley, Mr. Forsyth. There are many of my congregation who still remember the Reverend Mr. Bailey, who was their minister. They asked me to request that you take their fond greetings to Mr. Bailey."

"Of course, Mr. Twinning. of course. I'd be honoured to visit him and to bring your greetings."

So now William was on his way despite the rain.

Blackie was pretty much in charge of finding the best path forward as William trusted her implicitly with his safety. Her sure-footedness had saved them from many a mishap where the spring rains made the paths throughout the Township slippery and treacherous.

Eventually, they picked up the Post Road down the Valley. *What a mess of ruts, holes, tree roots, and fallen branches it is*, he thought, *but at least it's going to take us in the right direction*.

He didn't have to worry about a map: there was only one road down the Valley.

They rode through a heavily forested area for about eleven miles without seeing a soul. William entertained himself with his daily prayers and thinking about Mary and their unborn child. He loved his darling little daughter with all his heart, but also hoped he would someday have a son.

The rain continued to fall as they picked their way along the Post Road, but William was lost in a daydream about preparing his future son to study at one of Scotland's great universities to become a minister, a doctor, or a lawyer—he didn't care, just as long as his son had every advantage in life to become an educated man.

Just then, William thought he heard a sound, like a baby crying —or rather, screaming. He drew on the reins to bring Blackie to a stop.

There it was again, off to the right.

He turned Blackie off the trail and tied her reins to a tree branch. As he struggled through the underbrush, he kept pausing to hear the sound. There it was.

Eventually, he came out into a tiny open space only to see, yes, a rabbit in a snare.

Upon seeing William, the rabbit tried desperately to get away, hysterically twisting and turning, all to no avail.

She thinks I'm going to club her to death, William imagined. He grabbed the wire and loosened the loop, and as soon as the rabbit was free it flung itself into the brush and was gone.

That's when William felt the first strike, a blow that knocked his hat off his head. A second stone hit him on the chest. Then two voices yelled at him, "You stole our rabbit! You stole our rabbit!"

William dodged a flung stick. "Come out, you cowards, and show yourselves like men!"

He almost laughed when two boys of about ten or eleven stood up from behind a bush. They seemed equally prepared to flee, or to pelt him with more missiles.

"So you are the attackers of strangers. I will have to report you to the magistrates."

"No, no!," the taller boy cried. "You stole our rabbit. You are a thief."

"Snaring little creatures is very cruel. Have you no mercy?"

"No." They looked at each other as they shook their heads. The taller boy said, "No, we are getting food for our family. Father hurt his foot and has been laid up for over a week. We just wanted to help our family."

"Well, that put a different complexion on this. How is your father doing? Is he on the mend?"

"We think so," the smaller boys said. "He could walk today for the first time since the cow stepped on his foot. Don't you think so, Sam?"

The taller boy nodded.

"Well, you brothers are to be praised for wanting to help provide for your family. Perhaps I can make up for your loss. Come with me."

They pushed their way back out of the underbrush to where Blackie was waiting patiently.

"Is this your horse?"Tom asked.

"Indeed. I am the Reverend William Forsyth on a missionary journey down the Valley."

The boys looked at each other with concern. Then Sam said, "We're sorry we attacked you, Mr. Forsyth. If our parents knew we had attacked a minister we would be in big trouble."

Tom nodded vigorously. They both looked down and rubbed their bare toes in the dust.

"Well, boys, I'm not going to tell your parents or a magistrate, but I am going to give you this piece of smoked ham to take home to your parents. Just tell them that we met up on the road and that, when I heard of your troubles, I wanted to help out. And I want you to remember, the animals you snare feel as much fear and pain as you would in their circumstances."

The boys nodded. Holding the ham, they disappeared back into the woods.

William mounted again and continued on his way. After several miles, he said, "Blackie, I have to shake off my day-dreaming, pay attention to the road, and heed Elkanah's warning about black bears."

Blackie was still not listening, but carefully raising her hooves as she stepped over the obstacles and skirted the ruts and puddles.

William began to focus more on his missionary trip. First, he decided, he needed to find whatever Presbyterians were in a township and try to form them into little 'societies'. Then he could guide them as to how to conduct prayer meetings on Sundays and provide religious instruction on a regular basis. Although the postal service was almost non-existent, he would find a way to be in contact with the societies during the year until he could again visit them.

After that, he would baptize all the babies and children, conduct Sunday services and help the societies to organize an annual communion service—a several-day affair they could hold in an open field or in a barn each summer so that relatives and friends from far and near could attend. It was a big event for Presbyterians each year.

By working closely with each society, he would get to know the people and their joys and sorrows. He hoped that, each year, he would get to know everyone better.

This trip was just a beginning, as William saw it—a chance to get people organized so they could get more of their needs met. It was going to be the best he could do, as the Elders had made it clear that they would only approve him making one trip per year.

After about six hours, there was an opening in the forest ahead and William saw a small group of buildings. There was a plank house surrounded by several log buildings large and small.

He rode up to the front door of the house and, despite the fact he was a stranger riding alone in the rain, the owner was quick to open the door.

"Welcome stranger, come in. Alexander, go see to the man's horse."

William took off his wet hat, oil slicker, and boots at the door and the man led him to a welcoming fire in the huge stone fireplace.

As they sat down, William introduced himself. "I am the Reverend William Forsyth of Cornwallis Township, on a missionary journey down the Annapolis Valley. I thank you, sir, for your warm welcome and this fire. I hope you will let me dry out for a bit."

"So you shall, and have a bite of lunch and some tea—unless you would rather have rum?"

"No, indeed. Strong, hot tea would be my preference!"

Soon, Jabez Benedict, his host, introduced William to Mary, his wife, and to their children. While William sat by the fire, Sarah, the eldest, helped her mother prepare the lunch. The small children played with dolls made of stuffed cloth with button eyes.

Lunch was ham, cheese, and bread with butter and cherry preserves with fresh cream. Between the tea and the meal, William felt revived.

Eventually Alexander, the oldest boy, came in out of the rain. "Mr. Forsyth, your horse is drying off and I've given her some hay."

"Thank you, lad."

It was of the utmost importance to travellers to have their horses well taken care of. Besides, he knew how reproachfully Blackie would look at him if she was wet and hungry and he was dry and well fed!

As they sat by the fire, William said, "You mentioned this is Aylesford Township. How is it developing?"

"As best it can," Mr. Benedict said. "Our grant of land is not much —one hundred acres. We're doing well, but like many others we're thinking about moving to Wilmot Township. More land is available there. John Fowler and I applied together for five hundred acres. But now that we have that grant for Wilmot, Mary doesn't want to move."

Mary, a little flustered, said, "It's just that we're fairly settled here. To move again so soon..."

"We came in 1784," her husband said with a wry look.

"So you're a Loyalist?" William said.

"I suppose so. We didn't come in any big group of settlers. Just heard there was land available. I am from Connecticut but met Mary in Smithtown, New York."

There was a pause in the conversation, and William realized he might be holding his hosts back from the work they had planned for the day. He set his teacup down and stood.

"Well, Mr. and Mrs. Benedict, I thank you kindly for your hospitality. I would ask if there is anything I could do for you or your community but I've guessed you are Anglican and have your own missionary."

"Right you are, Mr. Forsyth. My children are all baptized."

"Well, good." He looked around for his hat, "I wonder if it is still raining."

"It's stopped, sir," Alexander said. "I can see some blue sky."

"Time for me to be on my way then, dry and well fed." He headed over to pick up his hat and rain gear.

Alexander brought Blackie around to the front porch. She felt dry. "Many thanks for your hospitality."

As the family waved, William picked up the trail again.

~

It was hard to enjoy the beautiful countryside when the mud and ruts demanded all his attention, but he remembered Elkanah's warning about what would happen if he or Blackie slipped and broke a leg, so the fear kept him focused.

As it got toward evening, William knew they had to find a place to stay for the night. There was no travelling at night, as one could easily wander off the road and become hopelessly lost.

Just as it seemed apparent they would have to spend the night in the woods, William saw a small glimmer in the distance. "Blackie, move as fast as you can, so we can find out what that light is—and let's hope for both our sakes it's a house."

It was a house, and quite a fine one, from what William could make out in the glow of a lantern. William called out many times, fearful the lantern-holder would go into the house and he would no longer have the light to guide him.

"What's all this noise, stranger?" The man said with a smile as William dismounted.

William introduced himself and explained his purpose for being in the area. John Magee—for that was the name of his host—called to a man to take William's horse to a barn to feed her and rub her down.

Once inside, William said, "You wouldn't be the son of Henry Magee of Horton Corner, would you?"

"Indeed I am. Everyone knows my father, for sure."

"True," William said. "I often go to your father's store to get my catechisms and New Testaments, which he orders in for me. I enjoy looking at all the supplies he offers—nails, ropes, shingles, butter churns, plows, wheat, rum, snuff, those fish called gaspereaux. It's a great place to meet with folks from all the Townships."

"Aye, it is a great meeting place."

"Did you come here with your father and mother after the American Revolution?"

"Before I answer that, would you take some rum or cider?"

"Cider, please."

As the strong apple cider trickled down William's throat, John Magee told William the story of his family. "When I was six years old, father, mother, and I left Northern Ireland. We are what you call Scotch-Irish, our ancestors having come from Scotland to Ireland in the early 1600s. But the constant wars and the lack of land for farming—we were flax farmers and weavers—caused father to decide to move on. We travelled to Pennsylvania in 1773 and had just got settled and built a mill when the Revolution broke out. Henry was born during this time. Father was loyal to the King so they threw him into jail with Loyalist officers."

"My goodness, Mr. Magee, that left your mother all alone with two little children."

"Aye, and some of the rebel militias and even neighbours broke in and stole our animals and food, leaving us nearly destitute."

"How did your father get free?"

"I am not quite sure how, but he and the officers escaped and fled into the mountains where many more Loyalists joined them. They started attacking the rebel militias until one of their number betrayed them. Then everyone split up. Father went to New York. The King's officers gave him £7 New York currency for his troubles. He came to Nova Scotia late in 1778 and that's where we were re-united. So that is our story!"

"Your father is a brave and loyal man," William said. "I correspond with an American in Vermont. They seem to be making a good job of organizing their new country."

"Aye," John said. "Many Loyalists have returned to the United States since the war ended."

Just then, John's wife, Ann, called them to supper. William and the family, which included five children, gathered around a large table next to the fireplace in the kitchen. William noticed how clean and neat the children were. They seemed in very good health and respectful of their parents.

John asked William to say grace, and William was glad to see that this family thought it important to give thanks to God for all their blessings.

"Thou who art the giver of every good and perfect gift, bless this food unto us and us to thy service, for Christ's sake. Amen"

Toward the end of the supper of potatoes, chicken, fresh peas, and corn, William asked if the family were Presbyterians or Congregationalists.

"Back in Ireland, we were Presbyterians," John said. "But one day father was sent to break up a crowd of people listening to a Methodist preacher. Instead of breaking up the crowd, he became Methodist."

"I guess he must have been pretty dissatisfied with the Presbyterians. Or, perhaps, the Methodists were much more persuasive and converted him on the spot."

"I think the former," John said.

"Do you have a Methodist Church or preacher here at Auburn?"

"We do not. The Anglicans built a pretty little church here in 1797 at the instigation of their Bishop Inglis, who owns a large property here. I believe he prefers to live in Auburn as much as possible rather than in Halifax."

John then cleared his throat and shifted in his seat. "Speaking of churches, I was wondering if you could baptize my children, since we don't know the next time a Methodist preacher will come by."

"By all means," William said. "I will get my baptismal cup from my saddlebags and I will need some water. Have your children learned the Lord's Prayer and some catechism?"

"The three oldest know the Lord's Prayer and the first bit of catechism."

As Ann poured the tea, she mentioned that the baby had torn up the little catechism they had, so they had to rely on their memory.

"And do you have a Bible?" William asked.

"Yes, and we have devotions each evening with the children, reading from the Bible and leading in prayers."

"Very good. I see you take your duty for the spiritual life of your children seriously and I have no hesitation in baptizing them."

So it was on that lovely August evening that William stood in the parlour, surrounded by John and Ann and their children. He had filled the silver baptismal cup and carefully placed it on a little table Ann had covered with a white cloth. The wide, shallow cup was engraved with the letters, IHS—the first three letters of the Greek word (IHSOUS) for Jesus—and the silver gleamed in the sunlight and the water sparkled when the faint breeze blew the curtains open.

Her parents chose Margaret, the eldest at eight years, to be baptized first.

After a prayer, William asked John and Ann, "Do you present this child for Christian baptism, and do you solemnly promise that this child shall be brought up as a Christian child in the nurture and admonition of the Lord?"

"We do," they answered.

Margaret, who had been staring at her parents and the stranger with increasing anxiety, asked in a low voice, "What is the Reverend going to do?"

"Children," William said, "we are just going to say a prayer and put some water on your foreheads. It is called baptism. We ask God to bless you and be with you all your lives."

Margaret exchanged a quick look with her brother John, then gave a little nod. "Yes, please, then."

William offered a prayer over the water and held out his hand to Margaret. She took his hand and he led her the few steps to where the cup was sitting on the table.

"Margaret, I baptize you in the name of the Father, and of the Son, and of the Holy Spirit."

As William named the three persons of the Trinity, he wet his fingers and dropped some water on Margaret's forehead, wetting her hair and allowing a few drops to run down her forehead.

"That tickles," she murmured, to the delight of the other children.

William repeated the sacrament with each child and then said a prayer of blessing,

"The Lord bless thee, and keep thee; the Lord make His face shine upon thee, and be gracious unto thee; the Lord lift up His countenance upon thee, and give thee peace. Amen."

He then announced, "We receive this child into the congregation of Christ's flock, in the faith that hereafter this child shall not be ashamed to confess Christ, but shall walk in His footsteps, rejoicing to do His will unto life's end. Amen."

Everyone said the Lord's Prayer together. William gave Ann a new catechism and told the family he would be back next year. "The children know the Lord's Prayer so I suggest you teach them the 23rd Psalm next."

The parents looked pleased and proud, and the children smiled up at their parents, feeling something important had happened that included them.

~

The next morning, after a breakfast of porridge and tea, William saddled Blackie, who seemed to have spent a good night. He put the baptismal cup, now back in its red velvet drawstring bag, into a saddle bag. After he had mounted, Ann gave him some food wrapped in a linen cloth, which he tucked away in a pocket.

He waved good-bye and headed further down the Valley, following now the north bank of the Annapolis River. As William and Blackie moved along, William said his morning prayers and enjoyed the beauty along the fast-moving river. The trail was a little better along the river—at least there were no tree roots to worry about. The sun sparkled on the water, birds chirped and warbled.

Despite the fact it was still August, William could feel the season had turned. The slant of the sun's rays made longer shadows and the freshness and verdure of spring had taken on a mature green. "Blackie," he said, "what a day!"

Blackie's ears turned back toward William's voice and she turned her head slightly to determine if anything William said had included the word oats. William often teased her, saying, "You must be Scottish like me, Blackie, you like your oats so much!"

Halfway through the morning, William dismounted to allow Blackie to drink from a little stream that ran into the river. As they stood together, he heard someone approaching on horseback. Blackie raised her head and turned her ears toward the sound.

Shortly a rider appeared on a brown horse and came to a halt beside them. As he slid off his horse, he introduced himself as Samuel Chesley.

"We have been here in Wilmot Township for quite a few years. Came up from Granville Township."

"That is down closer to Annapolis Royal, I collect."

"Right on its doorstep, I pride myself in the apple orchard I've planted. It is producing well."

"I was told that you are a leading magistrate in this area," William said.

"That is so. I came to Nova Scotia hoping to be part of the force to take the Fortress of Louisbourg up in Cape Breton from the French, but as fate would have it I arrived too late. I spent that winter and the start of 1759 in Halifax. In the spring, they sent me to Granville Township to survey the lots they were going to offer to the New Englanders. I decided to take up one of those lots myself, but later changed my mind as there was more land available here in Wilmot when it opened up for the Loyalists in 1783. So I moved here and was able to plant my orchard."

"Do you grow apples from seed?"

"You do if you are starting fresh, as my brother and I did. But once we had some trees that gave good fruit, we were quick to graft from them onto the root stock that was not doing so well."

"It must have been a long labour," William said.

"It has been, but a more profitable one than throwing oneself at the walls of a French fortress," Samuel said with a laugh. "My brother and I have twenty-two children between us, twenty-two!"

"A small village!"

"Indeed. And to provide for their futures, we need to have land to give to each of our sons and some to sell to provide for our daughters." He shook his head ruefully. "You know, Mr. Forsyth, the rebels took our land in New England and we had no option but to start over here, but those days are now long behind us and we are doing very well for ourselves."

Samuel invited William to come for lunch, so William mounted Blackie and rode with his new acquaintance. As they chatted, Samuel mentioned the names of some of the other settlers in Wilmot Township,

"There's John Baker, who tried several places in the Valley before finally settling in Wilmot. He married Persis Wheeler. Not sure how many children they have now. Then there's John Charlton from England. By 1765 he had cleared fifty acres and had twenty-five head of horned cattle. He built the first sawmill in 1786. If you go to Hicks Ferry you'll probably run into Jesse Oakes and Robert FitzRandolph, both Loyalists. Oakes has a blacksmith shop and FitzRandolph owns Bell Farm nearby."

Samuel cast an eye at William. "I am afraid that none of them are Presbyterians that I know of."

"I enjoy meeting and learning about all of God's children," William said.

"Then your journeys will never disappoint you."

After lunch, William was on his way again to Hicks Ferry, hoping to see the bridge that was under construction there. It would allow travellers to cross from the north side of the Annapolis River to the south side without using a barge or a boat.

Besides the bridge there was also a building called the 'Mud House'. It was a local landmark, having been built—so they said—by the Acadians. No one knew exactly its purpose.

He was barely underway when he noticed large, ominous, black thunderclouds on the horizon and it seemed prudent to dismount and pull his rain slicker out of a saddlebag. He had barely pulled the slicker over his head and adjusted the hood over his hat when a great crash of lightning struck a nearby tree, splitting it in two and leaving it a tangled mess of leaves and branches hissing and steaming from the heat of the strike.

As William tried to gather his wits, he realized he was lying on the ground—with no memory of falling—and that Blackie was gone. As he checked and found himself in one piece, the enormity of his situation dawned on him. He was alone with no horse, no food or drink, and still shaking from fright.

Then it began to rain like it had never rained before and he rushed to find shelter under the smallest tree—remembering that lightning strikes the tallest objects. All he could think was *where is Blackie?*

When the rain finally let up, still wearing his rain slicker, he returned to the spot where he had been standing and tried to find Blackie's hoof prints, but the rain had washed them all away.

If I were a horse, where would I go? he thought. The answer came after a bit: as far in the other direction as I could run.

So he set off in the direction in which they had come, following the blazed trail and hoping he found Blackie before it got dark. After about two miles, he thought he heard something, but the swaying of the trees in the wind made it hard to tell the direction.

Standing still and turning slowly, he thought he heard it again. Aye, there it was—a faint whinnying. *Where was she?*

"Blackie, where are you? Blackie, girl, whinny again. Where are you?"

Then he saw a faint movement. There she was, lying, legs folded under her, in a little gully.

He rushed over and started to examine her carefully. "Can you get up? Just go slowly. Don't rush."

When she was up on four feet, he examined her legs very carefully. "So far, so good, girl. Let's see if you can walk."

Once out on the trail, William led her slowly, checking to see if her legs were good. "What do you think, can I get on?" He noticed she had stopped shaking as much, so he took a handful of oats out of his saddlebags and she ate them gratefully.

Still unsure, he slowly ran his hands over her legs and hips, then he mounted and they started towards Hicks Ferry again.

Of all the things that could happen on the frontier, no one had mentioned thunderstorms, he thought, as he checked the sky for any sign of those black clouds but found only white fluffy clouds and blue sky. He was still a little shaken and he thought Blackie was, too, but there was nothing to do but continue to his next destination.

~

Arriving in Hicks' Ferry, William went to see the bridge and discovered it was open to travellers. There were four piles on either side to support it and low sides to the surface of the bridge.

The Mud House did not live up to its fame, being built of logs, stones, mud and clay, with walls four feet thick. It was possibly built for protection.

After viewing the Mud House, William found Jesse Oakes' blacksmith shop, close to the bridge. After dismounting, and hitching Blackie to the post outside the shop, he entered.

"Welcome, friend," a voice near the door said.

After his eyes adjusted to the lower light, William saw a man sitting on a tree stump. He wore soft brown clothing, with his broadbrimmed hat perched on his knee. "Art thou a traveller?"

William nodded.

"Welcome to the community. I present to you Mr. Jesse Oakes, who owns this shop. My name is Robert FitzRandolph. Thou canst probably tell by my speech and dress that I am a Quaker."

Mr. Oakes, who had been adjusting the fire with bellows in order to bend some iron into horseshoes, nodded over his shoulder. "Welcome, Mr...?"

"Forsyth—the Reverend William Forsyth of Cornwallis Township. Very pleased to meet you both. I am on a journey to provide my services to Presbyterians in the Valley. However, my horse had a great fright and ran until she collapsed. I imagine you are both good judges of horses and I would be grateful if you could examine her in case I'm missing something."

"You're able to ride her?" Mr. FitzRandolph asked.

"Aye."

"She's not tried to buck you off?" Mr. Oakes was drinking great gulps of water between each word.

"Nay."

The three went out of the shop into the bright sunshine. Mr. Oakes began to run his hands over Blackie's legs while William held her bridle and reassured her, and all the while Mr. FitzRandolph walked around, taking in her appearance from all angles.

Mr. Oakes spoke first. "She feels solid to me. What do you think, Robert?"

"Well now, methinks she looks like a horse standing on her own four legs with all her parts intact and able to be ridden. No reason to believe she'll keel over any time soon."

"Many thanks, gentlemen. Well then, I am also hoping you can tell me a little bit about Hicks Ferry and the Presbyterians in this area."

"We are always happy to narrate," Mr. FitzRandolph said. "Come back in out of the sun."

They re-entered the dark shop and sat on some tree stumps

provided for clients.

"Settlers started to come to this area in the 1760s. It is as far up the river as ships can come, and also the best place to cross it.

The story had to wait while Mr. Oakes pounded a horseshoe into shape for Mr. FitzRandolph's horse. That being accomplished, he plunged the red-hot shoe into a bucket of cold water and they all watched as the heat caused the water to hiss and turn into steam.

Once the horseshoe was complete, Mr. Oakes took a break. William noted that a large leather apron covered him from his neck to his ankles, almost eclipsing his heavy leather boots. His face was flushed from the heat.

"My first land grant was in Digby Township," Mr. Oakes said, "but this seemed to make it a good place to open a smithy. I do believe I was the first person to settle right at Hicks Ferry."

"Now that you have a bridge to replace the ferry, you'll have to consider a new name for this place," William said. "Maybe Bridgetown would be a good choice?"

The men smiled and nodded in agreement.

"What did you do in the American colonies, Mr. FitzRandolph?"

"I was a farmer, a distiller, and a merchant in New Jersey. I was also the Township clerk of records." He glanced around as if looking for unwanted listeners. "And in 1776 I refused to give the records to the rebels. They rightly suspected I was giving information to the English, so I had to escape to the English Army at Ruth Amboy. They made me superintendent of building a redoubt. Finally, the rebels confiscated my property and so my wife and I, along with our five children, came to Nova Scotia."

"Some of our children have married," Robert said. "Not so surprising as there were fewer choices here when they were younger."

"So you two are in-laws," William laughed.

"Yes, we have to get along for our children and grandchildren's sake."

William thought they seemed like old friends. "Mr. Oakes," he said, "what is your story? How did you come to live in this part of Nova Scotia?"

"Well, I was born on Long Island, New York, and when the War broke out it was obvious we were going to have to take sides, even though we didn't want to. Then the English asked us to take a loyalty oath and the rebels from Connecticut attacked those that did, and we had no way to defend ourselves. So my brother, Joshua, and I chartered a ship in 1783 and sailed here with our families. I settled first in the Digby area on two hundred and forty acres. I have one child by my first wife and five more by my second."

"It is good to see that your families are flourishing," William said. "I have a daughter, Mary, and my wife is expecting in three or four weeks. Now, gentlemen, can you tell me if there are any Presbyterians or old standing order Congregationalists in this area that we might meet for worship and sacraments?"

"There are, indeed, a few Presbyterians in and around Hick's Ferry," Mr. FitzRandolph said "I can get them together for you by tomorrow late afternoon. I'll try to find a place for you to meet, as well."

"Many thanks," William said. "Are you a Presbyterian, Mr. Oakes?"

"Nay, I've thrown in my lot with the Church of England. However, I would like to invite you to supper and to stay at my house. Mr. FitzRandolph, you're invited to supper, as well. Let us go together, Mr. Forsyth, so I can inform my wife."

~

The next evening, local Presbyterians gathered in the home of Mr. and Mrs. Daniel McEwan, anxious to hear Mr. Forsyth preach and to receive communion. Men and women arrived in their Sunday best. The men wore breeches with stockings instead of their shorter work pants, and buckled shoes. Their silk vests were brightly coloured and their long jackets matched the breeches. The women were transformed from their dull blue work dresses and aprons into ladies in fashionable taffeta dresses with lace trim and lovely bonnets with bright ribbons and bows. The smiles on their faces showed their appreciation of the occasion.

The McEwans had arranged the chairs in the parlour in rows facing the back of the room. The children sat on the floor in front of their parents.

At the front of the room by the fireplace there was a table with a white linen cloth on which stood the bread, on a paten, and the wine, in a chalice. After the prayers, hymns, baptism of the children, and a two-hour sermon, it was time for communion.

It began with a prayer of confession. "Almighty God, unto whom all hearts be open, all desires known, and from whom no secrets are hid: cleanse the thoughts of our hearts by the inspiration of Thy Holy Spirit, that we may perfectly love Thee, and worthily magnify Thy Holy Name: through Christ our Lord. Amen."

William continued, "Beloved in the Lord, As we celebrate the Holy Communion, we are gratefully to remember that our Lord instituted this Sacrament to be observed in His Church for the perpetual remembrance of the sacrifice of Himself in His death, to give a visible assurance and seal of all the benefits thereof unto true believers, to be a bond and pledge of their union with Him and with one another as members of His body which is the Church, and to engage them further in the fulfillment of all the duties they owe to him."

The people said the Lord's Prayer together.

William said the blessing over the bread and wine. Then he raised the loaf of bread, broke it, and said, "The body of Christ broken for you." Raising the chalice, said, "The blood of Christ poured out for you."

One of the men brought the plate with the bread on it to each adult, who broke off a portion and ate it. Then each adult drank from the cup.

After receiving the remaining bread and the cup, William pronounced the prayer after communion. "Now may the God of peace, Who brought again from the dead our Lord Jesus Christ, that great Shepherd of the sheep, through the blood of the everlasting covenant, make you perfect in every good work to do His will, working in you that which is well-pleasing in His sight, through Jesus Christ— to Whom be glory for ever and ever. Amen"

After communion, while the women chatted and cared for the

children, William took the time to gather the men together. He encouraged them to form a Presbyterian society. William was pleased they seemed willing to do so.

"As heads of households, you are required to provide spiritual leadership to your own families first and foremost, so have daily devotions and be sure your children learn to read so they can read their Bibles. Next, you must be leaders in your Presbyterian society. Hold meetings on Sundays and take turns reading Scriptures and leading in prayers and hymns. Visit all the Presbyterians in your area—and any old order Congregationalists as well—and encourage them to attend the society."

A younger man asked, "How often will you come to preach, Mr. Forsyth?"

"Once a year, I will try to attend your annual communion service. Encourage all families near and far to attend. It is a good time for families to reunite so that you can see your family members living at a distance and for the children to meet their uncles, aunts and cousins."

Another man said, "But what if we have concerns that we need to ask you about?"

"I will keep in touch with you as best I can through letters. If someone from Cornwallis Township is going down the Valley, I will send you a letter and you can respond and have the person bring your letter to me."

And from a third: "Do you think we will ever have our own church and our own minister?"

"If your society flourishes and others are encouraged to join you, who knows what may happen? You are only asked to be faithful to your baptismal vows, day by day."

It was a joyous occasion and one and all thanked the missionary for coming to their community and begged him to return soon.

The next morning, William was on his way again. He thanked Jesse Oaks and his wife for all their Christian kindness.

"You are doing the Lord's work. It was our pleasure to help you."

Mr. FitzRandolph and his wife came over from Bell Farm to say good-bye. William thanked them for organizing the gathering and finding a home where the service could be held.

"It was a pleasure to help thee. God go with thee on thy journey."

William had not met Quakers before and he smiled at the old couple—she in her brown dress with a white bonnet and a kerchief around her neck and he in his brown suit and broad-brimmed hat.

"God bless you both!"

"Where to now, Mr. Forsyth?" Mr. Oakes asked.

"To Annapolis Royal."

"Not many Presbyterians or 'Old Lights" there!"

"I hope to find any Presbyterians that are in Annapolis Royal and to see the Church of England minister, Mr. Bailey. He was minister in Cornwallis Township for three years—before my time—and I hope to have a chat with him."

"Well, God bless you, Mr. Forsyth, and come to us again soon."

~

William crossed the Annapolis River at the bridge and rode along the road toward Annapolis Royal, taking note that the roads began to seem better cared for and were less treacherous, and that the farms were more plentiful.

But as he rode past a tidy-looking farm, he could hear muffled shouts and screams and decided to investigate.

He rode up the path towards the house, looking for the cause of the sounds, which were only getting louder, until he saw a man beating a woman while a boy of around eleven was trying to pull the man away.

William encouraged Blackie to a gallop until he reached the trio, and, tying Blackie to a tree, he marched directly over to the scene of the scuffle. "What do you think you're doing, sir? I insist that you stop at once."

"And who are you to interfere in my affairs, mister? Take your horse and get out of here, or you'll get some of the same."

The man had loosened his grip on the woman, and she and the boy rushed over to William.

"What is this about, ma'am? Why is he beating you?"

"Sir, he bought my farm after my husband died. I and my son became his indentured servants so that we could live here and not become destitute, but he is interested in more than my work, and I have refused to comply. My son was only trying to defend me as best he could."

"I can find myself other servants," the man said, "and I have no more need of you! If you think you can do better elsewhere with this man, then go. Get out of here!"

He turned and stomped back to the house.

"Oh, no," the woman cried, "What shall we do?" She hugged her son as the tears ran down her face.

Suddenly, William realized his interference had left him responsible for these two lives. He was silent for a while, desperately trying to decide what to do, while the woman wept and her son tried to comfort her.

Finally he said, "Madam, I feel some responsibility for what has happened and, although a stranger in these parts, I will try my best to find you a better situation. Do you have a horse?"

"Mister," the boy said, "I'll take one of the horses that used to be ours if you will wait here."

William nodded and he sped away. "And, Madam, if you would try to stop crying, perhaps we can think of what would be best to do."

She wiped the tears from her eyes on the hem of her apron, smoothed back her hair and neatened her clothing. "My name is Annie Inglis and my son's name is Isaiah. Thank you for interceding and for your concern. I have often thought that it would be better for me and my son if I were to go to Annapolis Royal. Perhaps I could get a job as a housekeeper for a well-to-do family. I am a good and reliable person and would not fail to please any family who hired me." Another tear escaped and ran down her cheek, which she hastily wiped with her apron.

"What a fine idea. I think anyplace would be better than here. We will travel together and I will try to help you find a place to stay."

When Isaiah returned with a saddled horse, the woman mounted and pulled him up behind her.

But before they could take a step, the man came back out onto the porch. "You're stealing my horse! Don't take that horse or you'll be sorry! Give me back my horse!"

They urged the horses to a gallop and were soon back on the Post Road, but it was another few miles before they brought the horses to a walk.

"I haven't even asked your name, stranger," Annie said.

"William Forsyth, I am a minister from Cornwallis Township on a missionary trip down the Valley."

"Then, I think you were sent from God to save me and my son from my master. I am starting to feel that brighter days are ahead for me and my son."

"It would not take much for them to be better than what you had, Mrs. Inglis. What kind of a man would beat a woman. It is unconscionable, unchristian, an absolute abomination!" William could feel hot anger arising and cautioned himself about letting it take over his reason.

They rode for about fifteen miles until they saw ahead the spires of Annapolis Royal, the former capital of Nova Scotia, just where the Annapolis River runs into the Annapolis Basin—a beautiful setting with the green forest surrounding the town as it nestled near the sparkling blue Basin. He knew that in 1749 Halifax had become the new capital of Nova Scotia, but there was still a garrison at Annapolis Royal, and many fine homes.

Being hungry, and imagining that Annie and Isaiah might be as well, William paused to water Blackie at a stream. As she grazed on the fresh, green grass, William and his charges ate some of his bread and cheese and drank a little cider. Refreshed, they continued into the town where he hoped to find the Reverend Jacob Bailey, the Church of England minister.

Mr. Bailey's house was easy to find, it being on the main street of the town. William knocked on the door and a woman answered.

"Would the Reverend Bailey be at home?"

"Yes, sir. May I tell him who is calling?"

"The Reverend William Forsyth of Cornwallis Township."

Mr. Bailey arrived in the hallway and greeted him. "Come in, come in, Mr. Forsyth." He then saw Annie and Isaiah. "And are these your family?"

"Nay, Mr. Bailey. They have been released by their master and Mrs. Inglis wishes to find a position as a live-in housekeeper. Would you be able to help them find a place to stay until she can get a job?"

"I will speak to my housekeeper about this, in the meantime they are welcome to stay in the servants' quarters and we will send them some food and drink."

Mrs. Inglis stepped forward and curtsied. "May God bless you Mr. Bailey. We will never forget your kindness."

"Hilda, please get my stableman to take care of these horses, and find food and a bed for these good people."

"Could you arrange for your stableman to return the grey horse to Mrs. Inglis' former master? She can give him the directions," William said.

"Of course, Mr. Forsyth."

Soon William and Mr. Bailey were sitting in the parlour, drinking tea. Mr. Bailey looked like a man in his seventies but full of vigour and very elegantly dressed.

"If I recall Mr. Twinnings' story," William said, "you are a Loyalist from Pownalborough, Maine. He said that you and your family had to escape from the rebels who were threatening to kill you because you continued to pray for our King during Sunday worship."

"Yes, they killed my farm animals—shot them—and threatened my family. Several times I had to hide in the forest to escape from them. They broke into the church during worship and threatened me. Our friends arranged for a boat to take us to Halifax. We left at night and arrived with only the clothes on our backs. I was forty-eight at that time and the thought of starting over was daunting."

"You certainly have a place in the hearts of your former congregation. Mr. Twinning came to see me on behalf of his congregation to ask that I bring you their greetings and loving regards."

"My dear Mr. Forsyth, it does my heart good to know that they still remember me. The beauty of that area and the fertility of its soil certainly rival Annapolis Royal. And the people—not just my own parishioners—were good and kind to us, poor refugees. When we left for Annapolis Royal after three years, they all came to say good-bye. Some of them followed us almost all the way to here."

"And now, you have been rector of St. Luke's Parish for over twenty years. I have been minister at Cornwallis for only five years and wish to be a missionary for old order Congregationalists and Presbyterians from Cornwallis Township to Digby Township. I hope you can tell me about the Annapolis-Granville area."

"Gladly, but have you had your lunch, Mr. Forsyth? My servant is at the door with news that lunch is on the table."

"Servant?" William raised an eyebrow.

"I know only the wealthy in Cornwallis Township have servants, but here in the former capital, my employers—the Society for the Propagation of the Gospel—require me to look the part of a man of means. As a frontier minister, I am not much inclined to dress as a gentleman, but I have discovered that the parishioners expect it of me. I learned this one day when I arrived at a wedding wet and covered with mud because my horse could not make it up a slippery riverbank and I had to get off and lead him. The parishioners reported me to the Bishop for not looking like an appropriate representative of the Church of England."

"My sympathy is with you in that story, Mr. Bailey. It seems quite unreasonable for your parishioners to complain about unavoidable circumstances. A muddy minister, how unacceptable!"

"There have been many other instances of my unacceptable behaviour over the years, Mr. Forsyth. I am getting quite used to it, much to the consternation of my wife."

"I believe that you have six children?"

"Indeed, three boys and three girls—but only the unmarried children are still at home."

"Very shortly my wife and I are expecting our second child. Our daughter, Mary, is now almost three years old," William said.

"A delightful age. They help you see the world through fresh, new eyes."

"You have a lovely home, Mr. Bailey."

"And quite a bit of land as well. This means I can indulge my passion for flowers. I shall show you my garden after lunch. Come now: let us be fed."

Having had his bread and cheese, William planned to eat lightly at his host's table in order not to take advantage of his hospitality. The table was set with good pewter tableware and china dishes. There were flowers from the garden—late-blooming English roses, pink and white with greenery.

Mrs. Bailey appeared in a rose-coloured dress with lace collar and cuffs, her hair tastefully arranged in curls on the top of her head. "Mr. Forsyth," she said, "you are very welcome at our table."

After Mr. Bailey said grace, the servant brought in the dishes of roast beef, garden vegetables, and roast potatoes. The dessert was a blueberry and cranberry compôte in red wine with meringue. William's good intentions flew out the window and he did not restrain himself.

After dinner, the two men enjoyed a glass of sherry in the parlour. William was effusive in his praise of the hospitality.

"You must stay overnight, as well," Mr. Bailey said. "We pride ourselves on offering food and lodging to missionaries and, of course, to visiting dignitaries."

"That is beyond kind, sir. I had planned to ask the names of some local Presbyterians—"

"There are few Presbyterians in this place at present," Mr. Bailey said. "You would have to go to Digby to find any number. So that is not an option. Besides, we can chat longer, my dear Mr. Forsyth, if you stay here."

"I would be delighted."

After their sherry, Mr. Bailey conducted the promised tour of his flower gardens. As William was not a botanist, his attention strayed a bit as his host expatiated on the subtle differences and challenges of the many varieties of what all seemed to be the same plant. But he became alert again as the discussion moved on to missionary work.

"During and after the American Revolution," Mr. Bailey said, "there was much turmoil in religious matters. The people in Cornwallis Township were nearly all dissenters, and only about twenty of the two hundred families in the Township were Church of England. However, Annapolis Royal was an English town and the majority were Church of England, so the Society for the Propagation of the Gospel decided their money would be better spent supporting me here, where there was also a garrison needing a chaplain. But I always think fondly about my time in beautiful Cornwallis Township."

"The harvest calls for the labourers."

"Indeed. The religious turmoil has mostly died down now. Most of the former Congregationalists who settled in this area have become "New Lights". And many of them are now becoming Baptists. The Baptists are the fastest-growing denomination. That means there are very few Presbyterians and they are without ministers or churches. I am sure they will be very glad to see you...if you can find them."

"Are there any Presbyterian families in Annapolis Royal? Perhaps I could meet with them and ask them about others in the Township. I need at least one family to help me build a Presbyterian society in this area."

"We had two Ritchie families: Andrew Ritchie and his wife, and Andrew's nephew, John Ritchie and *his* wife. They were originally from Scotland and their families are probably Presbyterian."

"It is not unlikely."

"John was a merchant, and during the war he traded goods between here and Boston and supplied the Loyalist forces. His business was in financial difficulty when he died in 1790. His son, Thomas, was admitted to the bar in 1795. Their daughter, Ann, married Daniel James, who lives in the area. And there is their younger son, Andrew Sterling Ritchie.

"I look forward to meeting some of them."

"Now, Andrew Ritchie and his wife, Margaret, had eight children. They came to Nova Scotia in 1781, and most of his children have settled in this area."

Mr. Bailey looked around at his garden with a faint regret. "Well.

Well. Let us see if we can find Andrew Ritchie. He may be at his business.``

They walked down St. George Street toward the Annapolis River. William admired the old wooden houses with their sloping roofs, dormer windows and centre doors, each surrounded by a picket fence enclosing a flower garden. "The houses are so lovely and charming."

"Aye," Mr. Bailey said. He pointed out the houses of various well-known businessmen. "And here, just across from the ferry slip, is the Commercial House Hotel. Well placed for travellers, I'd say."

William nodded. "Is the slip for the ferry across to Granville?"

Mr. Bailey nodded. "And for the ferry down to Digby. You get your ticket on board. You can walk your horse on but you have to stay with it for the duration of the ride."

"Who owns the hotel?"

"Mr. John Hall set up that hotel. He came here in 1760. He carries on a large mercantile business and his ships are built and launched right across the street."

William had to admire his entrepreneurship. "It seems he knows how to make money."

"Oh, indeed. But here is the house of an entrepreneur of another sort, Colonel William Robertson. He represents us at the Legislative Assembly in Halifax."

Mr. Bailey paused to admire the building. "Is it not a fine house —square, two full stories, with four windows on the second story and four on the first, two on either side of the large front door? It surely stands out from the older, smaller homes."

He drew William to him and lowered his voice. "You know, I think the Robertsons are Scottish, as well. They may be Presbyterian. Many people when they enter politics become members of the Church of England, as the whole Halifax establishment is Church of England. It pays to go to an Anglican church if you are a merchant or a politician."

Begrudgingly, William nodded to Mr. Bailey's logic.

But when they arrived at the merchant's store and warehouse, Mr. Ritchie's clerk suggested he might be at home. He was not to be found there, either.

"Perhaps I will find him another day," William said.

"Missionaries must be persistent," Mr. Bailey said with a small smile. "If I cannot reel them in on your current visit, I will speak to the Ritchies and Robinsons about you, and will write to you what they have to say."

"That would be most kind."

"Well, if we can't find Mr. Ritchie, perhaps you would like to meet the Society school master. Have you ever thought of teaching, Mr. Forsyth?"

"Indeed I have, and I should like to meet your school master, Mr...?"

"Corbett, Ichabod Corbett. He has been a school teacher since he was fourteen years old. The children and their parents hold him in high esteem. He and his wife, Elizabeth, have ten children and live at the foot of St. Anthony's Street. They use one large room for the school room."

Mr. Corbett laid himself out to be a gracious host. He showed William the school room with its seats made of planks and rather crude desks to write on. On the desks were inkwells—filled with the ink Mr. Corbett made himself.

The children were required to gather goose quills and bring them so Mr. Corbett could make them into writing implements. They did their practice writing with chalk on slates that could be washed off and used over again until the writing was acceptable.

"We have your basic array of texts," Mr. Corbett said. "The New Testament, of course. The students must provide their own copies of Murray's Grammar and Dillworth's spelling book."

"Is that a burden on the children of poorer families?" William asked.

"The families with means pay enough that we can provide for the poorer children," Mr. Bailey said.

"Reading and writing being mastered," Mr. Corbitt continued, "the students move on to history, mathematics, geography, Latin, Greek and catechesis—the Reverend Mr. Bailey provides the latter."

"Education is a serious business here," Mr. Bailey said. "Children who misbehave find we will 'improve' them by the application of a willow switch."

"One more question, Mr. Corbitt. How are you paid for this work?"

"The Society pays my basic salary and each child's family pays a certain amount toward their child's education. From this, I maintain the school and support my family."

"But what would happen if the Society did not support you?"

"All the support would have to come from the parents. A school could only take the children of the well-to-do unless the richer families were willing to pay a certain amount towards the education of poorer children."

"Any other advice, Mr. Corbitt?"

"Nay, Mr. Forsyth."

William thanked Mr. Corbitt for his hospitality and advice and he and Mr. Bailey went back to his home.

"Mr. Bailey, you and your wife have been kind and generous to me. I will take your greetings back to Cornwallis Township and tell them of your lovely home and garden. And I hope to hear that Mrs. Inglis and Isaiah have found a good situation. They deserve some peace and happiness in their lives."

"God go with you, Mr. Forsyth."

~

William turned Blackie back on the road to the Annapolis-Granville ferry and, after crossing, he took the road to Granville Centre. Once again, William stopped to eat from what was in his saddlebags, mostly just bread and cheese and dried fruit, as Blackie grazed on the lush green grass.

As he sat on a fallen log, he thought he noticed a red leaf on one of the branches in the distance and stood up to look more closely. There were, indeed, a few red leaves on one branch of a large rock maple tree—a sure sign that fall was approaching.

As William rode along the west side of Granville Township, admiring the tidy farms along the Annapolis River, he occasionally saw a church, and he remembered what the Reverend Jacob Bailey had told him about the state of affairs in this township over the past twenty years. Reading from his diary, Mr. Bailey had said, 'It is impossible for a place to be more divided in religious sentiment than Granville. I suppose that there be about four hundred families now, near half of which reckon themselves to be members of the Church of England, though subdivided into Deists, Socinians, Methodists and Whitefieldites. The remainder are Lutherans, Calvinists, Presbyterians, Seceders, Congregationalists, Anabaptists, Quakers, Everythingarians, mystics and New Lights. A number of illiterate and drunken teachers are daily following each other in rapid succession like waves of the Atlantic, the last of which always eclipses the glory of his predecessor.'

William wondered what to expect—were there any Presbyterians or Congregationalists left or had they all been absorbed? Some of the names he heard mentioned gave him hope; for instance, McCormick had to be Scottish or Scotch-Irish. He decided to try to find Samuel McCormick at Granville Centre.

Just ahead he saw several boys moving idly along the road; pushing, shoving, and running about. "Let's go, Blackie. Let's get some directions."

The boys saw him cantering towards them and stopped to see if it was someone they knew. As he drew closer, they peered at him rather boldly.

"Lads, I'm looking for Mr. Samuel McCormick in Granville Centre."

"And who might you be?" one of the boys asked. He was tall, thin, and his pale skin was highlighted by a shock of red hair.

"I am the Reverend Forsyth of Cornwallis Township."

"Are you Baptist, then?" another asked. William noticed that he had brown hair and buck teeth.

"Nay, Presbyterian."

"We don't have any of them around here," piped up another.

William said, "I had hoped you could direct me to the McCormick farm."

The red-haired boy suddenly remembered his manners. "Mr.

Forsyth, Mr. Samuel McCormick lives just a mile down this road. You'll see his farmhouse after you round a bend and go down a little hill."

"Thank you for your help."

Samuel McCormick was at home, as well as his wife, Mary. To be polite, William accepted Samuel's offer of rum and they sat outside on the porch.

"Aye, we're from Northern Ireland, but we got married here in Granville at the All Saints Anglican Church in 1781. There were no Presbyterian churches and, as you know, only Anglican ministers were able to perform marriage. Mr. Bailey officiated and we liked him, so we just continued on at All Saints. There are other Scotch and Irish families hereabouts—the Litches are from Ireland; the Riley family, also. I think the Weatherspoons are Scottish. Some of them went with the Anglicans, some with the Baptists as we still have no Presbyterian Church or minister."

"Ah. I see."

"But it is a great pleasure to meet with a Church of Scotland minister like yourself."

William began to rise.

"We have room for one more for supper. Will you stay?"

"I fear I will miss the ferry back to Annapolis Royal if I tarry."

"You've already missed the ferry for today. It only runs until three o'clock. There's always room for one more at this house. I'll get one of my sons to take care of your horse and tell Mary to put another potato in the pot!"

Well, William thought, *this is an offer too good to refuse, both for myself and for Blackie.*

Samuel and William chatted about Granville Township until supper was ready.

"I must tell you the story of Mr. Weatherspoon, a Planter in Granville Township. In 1757 he was cutting firewood near Fort Anne—now Annapolis Royal—and was captured by Indians and taken to the Miramichi River in New Brunswick. From there, he was sold or traded to the French and taken to Quebec. He was there during the Battle of the Plains of Abraham. He kept a journal in his own blood of all his trials and tribulations. After the battle he was released and settled here. He and his wife, Elizabeth, had six children. He died here around 1791. But the reason I'm telling you this story is that, first, he was Scottish and, second, that most of their one hundred and fifty great grand-children live in this area."

Before William could comment, they were called to the table.

Mrs. McCormick set a platter of baked salmon in white sauce in the centre of the table. She'd taken the trouble to decorate it with slices of hard-boiled egg, and she'd prepared dishes of boiled new potatoes and fresh corn scraped off the cob. The vegetables glistened with melting butter. *Heavenly!*

She smiled as William ate with gusto. "It is gratifying to see someone enjoy my cooking so much, Mr. Forsyth. Will you have blueberry grunt for dessert?"

He would.

Over supper, William learned that the McCormicks had six children. "Jane is our oldest child and she is married to Robert Young. Samuel, Jr. and John are also married. Daniel is courting Suzanna Young and Thomas has his eye on Elizabeth Winchester," Mrs Mc-Cormick said. "Hannah is still at home with us."

After supper, William and Mr. McCormick went out to look at the crops and then down to the wharf where the fishermen brought in their catch. William went into the barn to check on Blackie and found her in a stall with fresh, clean straw, a pile of hay and a bucket of oats. She barely opened her eyes to look at William as she munched her oats.

The next morning, William washed, dressed and joined his hosts at breakfast.

"Will you have a glass of rum to clear away the cobwebs, Mr. Forsyth?"

"Thank you, nay, Mr. McCormick. But I do look forward to the bacon and eggs I see your good wife frying over the fire."

"Will you have toast as well, Mr. Forsyth? I have this new long-handled toaster that I can hold over the flames."

"Please don't bother yourself with that, Mrs. McCormick. Your fresh bread and some butter will be equally enjoyable."

After breakfast, William was on his way to the ferry back to Annapolis Royal. He crossed the river with no trouble, and was in time to board the ferry from Annapolis Royal to Digby. He tied Blackie in a stall and went up on deck to enjoy the blue sky, strong breeze, and sparkling water of Annapolis Basin.

~

When William arrived at Digby, he began to ask the people he met where Mr. Elkanah Morton lived and soon found his home. William didn't quite know what to expect, as Elkanah had been working on the St. John River helping supervise the building of the ship, the *Lord Sheffield*—the first of its kind built in New Brunswick. Later, he had gone to work in Sussex Vale as a school teacher. Around 1800 the Governor of Nova Scotia asked Elkanah to go to Digby and take on some administrative duties for the government. Beyond these facts, William did not know Elkanah at all.

A servant met William at the door and bade him wait while she 'saw if Mister were at home.' She let William step into the front hall, but did not invite him further.

William heard Elkanah before he saw him. There was a muffled thump, thump, thump, and then Elkanah came into view on crutches. Tall, slim, dressed in breeches, stockings and a buckled shoe, he wore a buttoned waistcoat over a shirt of fine linen. His brown hair was pulled back in a queue. He appeared to be in his mid-forties.

"Welcome, Mr. Forsyth! Come in, come in! Elsa, get Mr. Forsyth a glass of cider and arrange for Mr. Forsyth's horse. Come into the parlour and make yourself at home. Please be assured that my home is your home whenever you visit Digby. You will be staying here tonight, Mr. Forsyth, and for as long as you please."

William was overwhelmed by the warmth of Elkanah's welcome. *Just like his father*.

"Come into my parlour, Mr. Forsyth. Here, I find this a most comfortable chair. How are Father and his wife? How are my brothers and sisters? How is everyone in Cornwallis Township?"

"Everyone is fine and they send their greetings to you. Your father tells me that you have a son and daughter. I hope to meet them as well, since your father wants to hear of the family's health and well-being."

"So you shall. Probably at supper. But now let us have some lunch."

Lunch was baked scallops with potato puffs and little vegetables. There was white wine with the meal and sherry in the parlour after the meal.

"We have a big fishing and shipbuilding industry here in Digby. It is possible to have fresh fish every day."

"The scallops were uncommonly good," William said, patting his stomach.

"I received a letter from my father, informing me that you would be arriving and wanted to visit any Presbyterians and standing-order Congregationalists."

"Indeed," William nodded. "I am hoping you know of them and their whereabouts."

"There are a fair number just north of here at Bay View, Broad Cove, Culloden and Mount Pleasant. I have notified them and they are anxious to meet with you and enjoy worship and the sacraments. They have many unbaptized children, I would think. At Bay View, you want to speak to Robert, George or William Turnbull. They came over from Scotland maybe twenty years ago now and they are staunch Presbyterians."

"Well, then, I hope to stay in that community and travel to the other communities in that area that you mentioned. It sounds like I will need at least a week."

"Then stay for supper and start out first thing in the morning. And, aye, there are a few things you need to know. You can only reach Bay View by travelling the beach at low tide—and the tides in the Bay of Fundy are the highest in the world."

"Are they dangerous?"

Well, there is a difference of twenty-eight feet between low tide and high, so you do not want to get caught on the beach as the tide comes in. It is not as though you can just detour up from the beach at any point: Bay View is on the top of North Mountain and, as you travel west, the cliffs get higher and higher with only one path up off the beach."

"North Mountain. This is the same range that runs from Cornwallis Township down the coast of the Bay of Fundy?"

"The same. Not really a mountain, just a very high hill, but very steep to climb in places, and there are no roads. When these settlers arrived that was the only land that was available and cheap, so they didn't have much choice. I'm not sure anyone would settle there if they had a choice, that is, if they wanted to farm."

"But many people prefer to fish, I collect."

"Best to do both, if you mean to survive. There is actually a small ferry from the Granville side of Digby Gut to very close to Bay View. Your horse would have to swim. You might think about that in the future."

William accepted another glass of sherry as he sat back and relaxed. The conversation turned to family and friends and the state of Presbyterianism in Digby Township.

Then Elkanah said gingerly, "Mr. Forsyth, I have to tell you that I and my wife have joined the Trinity Anglican Church. All my employment is from the government and my teaching position is from the Church of England." He paused to sense William's response.

"I think your family was hinting at this before I left on my journey. I can see your ancestors turning over in their graves—they who left England for the wilds of North America to escape persecution by the Crown and the Church of England."

"True, true, Mr. Forsyth, but after the Lieutenant Governor shot me in the leg—"

"By accident, I trust."

"An accident, I assure you. But since then, the Government has tried to make up for it by offering me employment, and the Anglican Church made me a school teacher as well. I feel they have acted honourably and I hold them in high esteem. Would you like to meet the Rector of Trinity Parish, the Reverend Mr. Roger Viets?"

"Indeed, I would, as I have heard many good things about him during my meeting with the Reverend Mr. Bailey in Annapolis Royal."

With that they set off to find Mr. Viets. He was at home in the rectory next to Trinity Church—a very plain, square, story and one-half home, just up from the waterfront. They were invited in very cordially.

When they were seated in the parlour, William explained his purpose for being in Digby Township. "You are a Loyalist, I presume."

"Aye," Mr. Viets nodded, "driven out of Connecticut by the revolutionaries."

"I would greatly appreciate your estimation of the current state of Digby Township."

Their host sighed deeply. "Mr. Forsyth, the situation is not good. I am the only Anglican minister in the Township. Most of the Loyalist settlers are Anglican, but have relapsed into a state of heathenism. Being subject to no restraint, gambling, cock-fighting, horse racing and drinking prevail to an alarming extent. One of the worst situations was an atrocious conspiracy, planned by a man named Young with fifty desperadoes, to murder a Justice of the Peace on a night when the principal inhabitants were at the Assembly. They planned to plunder the town, place the goods on board a vessel and make their escape to Boston. The plot was discovered just in time."

"Did that make the wilder elements more cautious?"

"Not a whit. Vice is triumphant and virtue ridiculed. Drinking, idleness, profane swearing, tavern-haunting, slandering, back-biting, lying, defrauding and stealing call loudly for the exertions of the magistrates to raise the sword of law and justice for suppression and punishment of these vices."

William tried to conceal his shock at Mr. Viets' blunt assessment. "I wonder, Mr. Viets, what this means for my missionary purposes. Is my personal safety at risk? I travel alone through the wilderness and to date my concern has been for bears and wildcats. Shall I now add to the list the citizens of Digby Township?"

"I am afraid so. You will be most safe in Bay View, Broad Cove,

Culloden and Mount Pleasant as these people are mostly direct from Scotland, with a love for law and order as well as for Presbyterianism. They will welcome you with open arms and much hospitality and respect. You must report any villainy you encounter to Mr. Morton, who will direct it to the magistrates to deal with. I wish you every blessing on your journey and on your purposes."

~

Elkanah showed William the little one-room schoolhouse used to educate the boys of the Digby and the surrounding area. "The Society pays my basic salary and the well-to-do of the town pay handsomely so that the poorer children can get an education. Teaching school and doing the work that the government has assigned me allows me to live at the level of a gentleman. It is what my employers expect."

As they returned to Elkanah's home, he began to talk about the Presbyterians in the town of Digby as well as the role of a school teacher. "There are quite a few Presbyterians in the Digby itself, as well as those Mr. Viets spoke. I'll introduce you to Mr. William Hewett Letteney, a Loyalist from New York. He and his first wife came here in 1783. They had six children. When his first wife died, he married Hannah Gould. She was eighteen and he was sixty-two. They also have six children. Many of his first family are married now. I expect this family alone could fill a church!"

William laughed at the thought of a church full of Letteneys.

"Mr. Letteney's son, John, is now courting one of the Baxter girls, Eleanor, I think, from Bay View. I hear a marriage is in the works."

"I heard from your father that the Presbyterians had someone with some training in ministry?"

"They have a student catechist, Mr. Samuel Thompson, who often leads prayer meetings for them. He lives in Mount Pleasant. This helps the Presbyterians to live in hope of having their own church one day. But at present there are not enough of them to support a building and a minister. Many have joined other denominations so that they will have a place to worship and receive the sacraments. And, to be perfectly honest, the choice of denomination is often determined by politics and personal benefits to themselves and their families."

William sighed. So much work to be done if Presbyterians were to remain viable in Digby Township. He knew he could only get away from Cornwallis Township once a year without causing quite a fuss from the Elders and the Congregation—and he needed their support for his efforts.

At supper, Elkanah introduced William to the family. "Mr. Forsyth is my father's minister, sent here by the Presbytery as a missionary to the Presbyterian societies in the Valley."

After a warm welcome, Elkanah introduced his family, "This is my wife, Lucy, and her father Obediah Wheelock of Annapolis Royal." William smiled and nodded.

Elkanah continued, "This sturdy lad is my son, John, just turned twelve. His late mother was from New Brunswick." John smiled and William nodded. "And this sweet little girl is my baby daughter, Lucy Ann."

"A fine family, Mr. Morton. Very pleased to meet you all, I'm sure. Thank you for your hospitality."

William turned to Mr. Wheelock while the soup was being served—pea soup with ham—and asked about his family. "Sir, could you tell me about your family? When I was in Annapolis Royal, I stayed with the Reverend Jacob Bailey, as there were few Presbyterians there."

"I am not a Loyalist, rather a Planter," Mr. Wheelock said. "My wife and I married at Uxbridge, Massachusetts in 1765. Then we came here with my parents, Obediah and Martha. Father died in 1765 and my mother a few years later. Rachel and I have seven children, including my daughter, Lucy, here."

"Well, Mr. Wheelock, you are indeed blessed. I hope someday to have as many or more," William said.

The main course was scallops, bread-crumbed and fried, along with mashed potatoes enriched with cream and butter, and fresh peas. The conversation was friendly and pleasant and then the dessert course arrived.

William took one taste and said, "How delicious! What is this dessert, Mrs. Morton?"

"It is one of our specialties, Almond Pudding. It begins with ten sweet and five bitter almonds, which you pound very fine with a mortar and pestle. Then you take a pitcher of rich milk and place it in a saucepan of hot water, and when it boils you add the almonds. We use ground rice from the Carolinas to thicken, then you boil it for half an hour, stirring often."

"Quite a process."

She laughed like a maiden. "I am far from done! *Then* you add the yolks of three eggs beaten with half a cup of fine sugar, and in about a minute you take it off the heat, mix in another half cup of sugar and pour it into a pudding bowl to cool. Just before you serve it you beat the three egg whites to a stiff froth and add a large spoonful of *fine* sugar. You drop this on the cooled pudding and set it in a hot oven until it is browned well on top. It is very good!"

"It is delicious! If you would write down the recipe, I will take it back to my wife. She is an excellent cook and I am an excellent consumer of all that she cooks."

"For a man who loves to eat, Mr. Forsyth, you are very trim, I must say," Mrs. Morton said, to the laughter of the others.

After supper Elkanah and William headed off to find William Letteney.

"William and his wife are Loyalists," Elkanah said. "Their eldest son, William, Jr. married Elizabeth Oliver and settled at Granville Ferry, just across from Annapolis Royal. Their daughter Anne is at Sawmill Creek. Daughter Margaret married one of the Pickles' boys from Boston and Hannah Letteney Pickles is in Annapolis Royal. Thomas and John are here in Digby. Mr. Letteney's second family of six are too young to be married at this time."

Mr. Letteney, a spry man of seventy-two, was sitting on his front porch with his second wife, Hannah. William was glad Elkanah had told him of the age difference between them, as he might have assumed she was Mr. Letteney's daughter. They seemed very compatible, sharing smiles with each other during the conversation.

"Mr. Forsyth, I consider myself a staunch Presbyterian. Nothing would give me more pleasure than to help organize a Presbyterian society here in Digby. My two sons can be counted on to provide leadership and I don't think it will be very difficult to find a place to hold our services." He looked at Elkanah. "Mr. Morton might even intervene for us with Mr. Viets. Perhaps we could use Trinity Church after their Sunday services."

"I will ask Mr. Viets to consider this. The Church is empty Sunday evenings, as far as I know. If not, I will ask about a place for you to worship," Elkanah said.

"For now, Mr. Forsyth, I will gather us all in my barn tomorrow evening so we can worship God together. You can baptize all the children requiring baptism."

The next day, the men and women in their best clothing with numerous children—of all ages and sizes—gathered in Mr. Letteney's barn. There William met Mr. Letteney's two sons that lived in Digby, Thomas, sixteen and a mechanic, and John, fifteen, a shipbuilder. He thought that John was much like his father—very strongly Presbyterian and willing to help with forming a society, although Thomas also seemed a willing worker.

After baptizing the children, William gathered the people together to have their first worship service with communion since the Loyalists had first arrived and settled at Digby in 1783. Many people wept out of happiness. They told William that his presence gave them hope that someday they would have their own building and their own minister.

~

The following day, Elkanah, who was very familiar with the tides, let William know it was the right time to ride up the beach to the turn-off to Bay View.

Blackie had had a few days rest and seemed to be ready to go. As William saddled and bridled Blackie he noticed that Elkanah's stable hand had cleaned and polished the tack and washed and even dried the saddle blanket.

"Many thanks, Mr. Smith, for the excellent care of my horse."

"My pleasure, Pastor."

Blackie was not sure about the day's plan, as she had not walked on wet sand before and wanted to be convinced it would hold her weight. William had always learned to trust Blackie's instincts, so he dismounted and walked along with her until she decided they would be safe. Soon she was walking confidently, with her normal stride. Then, finally, they were on their way.

The view along the beach was very beautiful. The water of the Annapolis Basin sparkled in the fall sunshine and a broad expanse of beach was covered with seaweed and sea shells, with some small rocks scattered here and there. Across the basin were tall cliffs of reddish rock, the tops of which were covered with forest. The smell of the salt air was bracing and the breeze brought him the scent of pine and spruce. Many of the hardwood trees were showing more and more coloured leaves. It was a great day to be alive.

He thought once again, *It seems Nova Scotia is going to be my land of hopes and dreams. I have a good pastorate and a wonderful wife and child and I'll soon be a father for the second time...and now a missionary as well.*

Then the thought, unbidden, jumped into his mind: *what if our next child is a boy and I have no money to send him to university?*

There'll be time to think of that if I have a son, he told himself, and put the thought out of his mind once again.

William was enjoying the experience of riding down the beach and not saying much. Usually, he told Blackie all his thoughts, and he noticed her turning her head to look at him and whinnying just to get his attention.

"All right, all right, my friend, it's time for a chat, isn't it?" So William started talking and Blackie seemed satisfied to hear all his confidences. The black mare and the man dressed in black cantered down the beach toward his meeting with the people of Bay View.

After about a mile, William heard voices calling out. *Are they calling me?*

He slowed Blackie and looked around. Several men were walking toward him and as he slowed down even more the men began to run. Then he felt Blackie's body tense and saw her ears go back. The closer the men got, the more agitated Blackie became, almost dancing in place.

"Hey, mister! Slow down. We just want to talk to you. Nice horse you have there!"

Suddenly, all of Mr. Viets warnings about the men in Digby Township flooded into his mind. As the closest man reached to grab Blackie's bridle, William kicked Blackie's sides and she reared. Then, with unexpected power, Blackie galloped down the beach for almost a mile before William stopped urging her on. Looking behind he could see the men, still standing where he had left them.

William then noticed how fast his heart was beating. Once he had calmed down, he patted Blackie on the neck several times. "You saved the day, Blackie!"

He felt he had learned a lesson—in dangerous places, day-dreaming and good manners will only get you into trouble.

After about six miles, they reached what he assumed was the turn-off. He could see the ferry wharf up ahead and started to look for a road. Like most paths this one was narrow and rutted and filled with tree roots. In addition, it was steep, very steep.

"Careful, Blackie, let's take our time!"

Blackie ignored the caution and picked her way forward, lifting her hooves high to avoid getting them entangled and putting each foot down strategically.

When they reached level ground, they could see a pathway through the forest. They followed it for a mile or so until William could see smoke rising. Shortly a log cabin came into view. There was a woman outside washing clothes and hanging them out on a clothesline that ran from the back door to a nearby tree.

"Good afternoon, Mrs....?"

"Mrs. Turnbull," she responded. "Who might you be, mister?"

"The Reverend William Forsyth, Presbyterian missionary from Cornwallis Township. I am pleased to meet you. Might your hus-band be home?"

"He is just in our woodlot, chopping some firewood. He will be back shortly. Will you come in, Mr. Forsyth, and have some rum or cider?"

"Cider, please. And some water for my horse." He had hitched Blackie to a tree where there was shade and some fresh grass.

"Beautiful horse."

"Her name is Blackie. She is my trusted travel companion. Very sure-footed."

As William and Mrs. Turnbull chatted about the excellent growing season it had been, William heard a great crash and thumping just outside the door. The door opened and the man who appeared smiled and said, "Excuse the commotion. I just brought back an armload of firewood and had to stomp the pine needles and leaves off my feet."

William rose, introduced himself and said he was from Ecclefechan, Scotland.

"Finally, a Presbyterian minister! We've been here eighteen years and you're the first we've seen. Welcome!"

The two instantly fell into reminiscing about Scotland until Robert's wife, Anne, asked about William's intentions.

"I came to Digby to find the Scottish Presbyterians I was told were in the area. I came to preach, offer the sacraments and catechize."

"Perfect." Robert said. "You can stay with my family. My wife and I have three children: Jane, Elizabeth, and wee William. My mother also lives with us, as well as my aunt Helen Brown. Father died in 1796. This was his land grant, and this is the first house we built after we arrived in 1786."

William looked around at the small log cabin. "It is a wonder you can all fit in."

Mr. Turnbull shrugged, "Family, d'you see. We make do. But my mother and her sister can go and stay with my brother, George, at his home nearby, so there is room for one more."

William laughed, "I see you can read minds, Mr. Turnbull!"

All evening they talked about Scotland. Finally, William asked how many people besides Robert's family lived at Bay View and nearby.

"Besides my family there are the Condons, Cornelius Hinxman, the Bells, Robert and James Adams, Joshua Burnham, Carrs, Rosses, Urquharts, MacIntoshes, Sinclairs, oh, and others."

"I will have a job to learn all the names."

"You can make a start tomorrow at supper, with my brother George and his family," Robert said. "They all will come over for supper tomorrow and we will talk about Scotland again, I'm sure."

Anne Turnbull sighed, but Robert's mother and aunt were 'all ears'.

"I was only fourteen when we came over on the ship *Lily*," Robert continued. "The Reverend James McGregor was aboard. Do you know him?"

"I do, indeed, and as you know, he was for many years the only minister in Pictou County. I hear several others have joined him now."

"Did you know my father is a captain?" young Jane piped up.

Robert laughed. "Indeed, I am a captain of Artillery Company Number 14 Battalion. In a way, I am also a sea captain. Since 1789 I've been in command of the ship *Mary Ann*, a packet that I sail weekly between Annapolis, Digby and St. John, New Brunswick."

"Father sailed all the way across the ocean and back, didn't you?" Jane said.

"I fear my daughter has heard me tell my story too many times. Yes, I sailed the *Mary Ann* home and brought back some crofters we knew in Scotland. We had only been in Nova Scotia a few years. I think most of these crofters are still in this area. They work hard and have prospered."

William was amazed. "You couldn't have been very old when you sailed back to Scotland."

"No, I was just seventeen. But I had been crew on the ship that brought us to Nova Scotia when I was just fourteen."

"You have an amazing and brave spirit, Mr. Turnbull. I am impressed."

Supper was boiled mutton with barley, potatoes and turnip. Dessert was fresh-made applesauce and cream. William enjoyed the typical Scottish fare and the warmth and closeness he felt with Scottish people. He hadn't realized how much he missed his own people and customs and food.

In a pause in the conversation, eight year old Jane said, "Mr. Forsyth, will you baptize me?"

"Most certainly, Jane, and your sister and brother, too. Have you learned the Lord's Prayer?"

"Aye, Mr. Forsyth. Shall I say it for you?"

"If you please."

And so she did, in a smooth flow only interrupted by pauses for breath, sometimes in the middle of a word.

William baptized children and prepared for Sunday worship, including communion. The Letteneys had sent along several bottles of communion wine and Ann Turnbull baked loaves of bread so that all those close enough or spry enough to travel through the forest trails from Broad Cove, Culloden and Mount Pleasant could be part of the first Presbyterian worship service conducted by a Presbyterian minister since they had arrived. There were Carrs and Urquharts, McKays, Rosses and McLeans, and some others whose names William did not retain.

Over the next few days he visited the other communities in the area to conduct worship and baptize children. Each community would gather after supper in a barn or in a field, bringing blankets on which to sit. William would begin with a Call to Worship followed by an Opening Prayer and a Hymn from the Scottish Psalter. One of the favourites was the twenty-third psalm—The Lord's My Shepherd sung to the tune Crimond.

> The Lord's my Shepherd, I'll not want,
> He makes me down to lie
> In pastures green, he leadeth me,
> The quiet waters by.

After the hymn, the minister and the people bowed down and said the prayer of confession.

"Have mercy upon us, O God, according to Thy loving kindness;

according to the multitude of Thy tender mercies blot out our transgressions. Wash us thoroughly from our iniquities and cleanse us from our sin. For we acknowledge our transgressions, and our sin is ever before us. Create in us a clean heart, O God, and renew a right spirit within us. Cast us not away from Thy presence and take not Thy Holy Spirit from us. Restore unto us the joy of Thy salvation and uphold us with Thy free Spirit. Amen."

After reading I Corinthians II, verses 23-26, William said a blessing over the bread and wine. He broke the bread and poured the wine. The men selected to do so distributed the bread and the cup. William was impressed by how well they remembered the patterns of worship, even after so many years had passed since they had last taken part in a service.

After all who chose to had eaten and drunk, William said the prayer after communion. and all sang the Gloria in Excelsis. After another hymn there was the final blessing:,

"The grace of our Lord Jesus Christ, the love of God and the communion of the Holy Spirit be with you and abide with you, now and forever. Go in peace to love and serve the Lord in all that you do and say. Amen."

William provided catechisms and Bibles to the heads of families who had none. He catechized all who wished to learn about the Christian faith. Everyone was happy to have William there. Many cried during the singing of the Psalms from the Scottish Psalter as they remembered their life in Scotland.

After each communion service, there was a community picnic. At Culloden, the women were just putting out the food and drink, planning to feed the little children first and then the adults, when a group of young men emerged from the forest on the other side of the field. Everyone could hear their loud voices and glanced to see which way they were heading. It was then that the young men noticed the picnic and headed towards the Culloden people.

William watched as the women began gathering their children to them and the men slowly stood up, two of them taking up guns they had brought in case of a bear sighting.

The young men crossed the field and boldly walked up to the

families. One said, "What have we here? Good food and drink, I wager."

William said, "Good evening, good sirs. I am the Reverend Forsyth, a Presbyterian minister visiting this community. Would you care to take a seat? We will gladly share our meal with you." He looked at the other men, who reluctantly nodded.

Their leader said, "Ah, we thought you might be that troublesome cleric, Mr. Viets. Always trying to spoil our fun and get us into his church."

"I have met Mr. Viets. A fine gentleman and very concerned about the behaviour of some of the inhabitants of Digby Township. He certainly has the best interests of the people at heart."

William could feel the tension between the young men and the families. They never took their eyes off the young men and the children were perfectly silent, taking their cues from their parents.

"Well, we think we know what is best for ourselves without his meddling. I think we'll just take some of the food with us. What do you think, boys?"

Several of the young men had spied the guns and were looking a little unsure about just taking the food.

William responded, "I think you should not behave in such an unneighbourly way. You have been offered a chance to sit and eat with us, but if you prefer not to do so, we will give you a portion to take with you as you go on your way. Ladies, will you make some sandwiches for these men? While you wait, please enjoy some cider. We'll serve you over there by the little apple tree."

"Come on, Samuel," the youngest and smallest of the young men said to his leader, "Let's sit by the apple tree. I'm hungry and thirsty. Please, let's sit down."

The others started to head off to the tree, but Samuel stooped to grab a pie.

William grabbed his wrist and the family men raised their guns. "You have no need to behave like a thief," William said quietly, "and you are frightening the women and children. Go over and sit down."

Seeing no alternative, Samuel twisted his wrist away and took himself over to the tree. There, two of his companions grabbed his sleeve and pulled him down.

Once the sandwiches were made, William brought them over to the young men and said, "We offer you this food in Christian charity. Although you were rude and threatening to innocent people, we hope you will consider amending your ways and becoming a positive influence in your own communities. God bless you."

The young men guzzled down the cider and ate ravenously. Before they had finished their last bites, they were up and on their way. Finally, the families could relax and enjoy their picnic.

"You took charge and handled that well, Mr. Forsyth," one of the men said. "Thank you for preventing what could have been a very unfortunate incident."

"There were lots of men spoiling for a fight back when I was growing up in Scotland, so we all had to learn to defend ourselves. However, I think it was the guns that saved the day," William said, thankful that a communion service had not turned into a brawl or worse.

William Turnbull and his brothers, Robert and George, agreed to provide leadership for a new Presbyterian society for the area, and to plan the annual Communion service for the whole area. William was deeply impressed by the dedication of these Scottish settlers to their faith. It was good to see.

Toward the end of the visit, Elizabeth, the wife of William Turnbull, Sr., brought out a small, worn letter from the Session of their Church in Scotland. The letter said that they were a family in good standing and commended them to their congregation in Nova Scotia.

"I've been waiting for eighteen years to give this letter to a Presbyterian minister here. Now, finally, I can give it to you, Mr. Forsyth."

William saw the tears in her eyes and realized how bereft these faithful people had been since they came to the New World and tried to build a life for themselves without the care and comfort of their church—no worship, no sacraments, no catechesis. And all he could do to fill their longing was to visit them once a year.

There and then he decided that he would do just that faithfully. They would have that annual visit, at least, to rely upon. He also intended to write to the Church of Scotland and ask for a minister to be sent to them.

As William packed his saddle bags and prepared to leave, people came out to see him and bid him good-bye.

"There is a little ferry between Bay View and Granville Township," Robert reminded him. "It could take quite a few miles off your journey home, but your horse would have to swim Digby Gut."

"Is it far?"

"About one third of a mile, and you have to choose your time. If the tide is running out, the current might take you off into the bay."

William pondered for no more than a moment. "Perhaps in the future. Today I plan to stop in Digby before I return to Cornwallis Township. Thank you all for your faithfulness and your hospitality. I will be back this time next year. In the meantime, read your Bibles each evening, teach your children their catechism and be sure they know the Lord's Prayer and the 23rd Psalm. I know you will organize your society and plan for the summer communion service. Until we meet again, God bless you all."

William stayed at Elkanah's home in Digby that night and took the ferry to Annapolis Royal the next morning. There he mounted Blackie and set out at a comfortable pace for home.

~

Five or six miles outside Annapolis Royal, William saw a bridge up ahead. There appeared to be two men standing on the bridge, in deep conversation. When he got close enough he hailed them with a friendly, "Good-morning, gentlemen."

They wished him a good morning and William decided to dismount and have a bit of a rest. The men introduced themselves as Benjamin Fairn and Jasper Williams.

"Mr. Fairn here supervised the building of this bridge," Jasper, the younger man, said. "We make a point of coming over to stamp on it from time to time, to make sure it is still sound."

"A noble bridge, indeed," William said. "But do you have to travel far to do your stamping?"

"Nay, nay," Benjamin said. "It be no more than a mile."

"Is bridge-building your trade?"

"We have turned our hands to many things since we settled here. I came from near to Boston right after the American Revolution. I was given land and started farming, but I didn't have any sons old enough to help me. That's where Jasper comes in."

"That's right," Jasper said, "I came over from Wales and Mr. Fairn hired me. However, our relationship changed when in 1798 I married his daughter, Sarah. We have five children, all girls. I guess we just keep trying until we get a son," he laughed.

"How many children do you have, Mr. Fairn?"

"Six, Mr. Forsyth. Our daughter Elizabeth is married to the school master, Ichabod Corbitt."

"I have met Mr. Corbitt," William said with a laugh. "He's a very successful teacher."

Benjamin Fairn smiled. "So I hear. I never had much learning, so have no basis for comparison."

"Have either of you heard about a battle called Bloody Creek?"

"Oh, yes. It's not far from here; just this side of Hick's Ferry. There's a bit of a bridge over the creek, so you can't miss it."

"Do you know the story of the fight?"

Benjamin thought a while. "I can give you a general idea, Mr. Forsyth. I only heard about it once or twice when I first came here."

"You start off, father-in-law," Jasper said, "and I will patch in what I can."

Between the two of them, they were able to lay out a tale that William could follow.

In 1711, a year after the English captured Fort Anne from the French, they asked the Acadians in the area to cut some logs and float them down the Annapolis River for repairs to the fort. When that didn't happen, a party of soldiers went up the river to find out why. The French and their allies, the Abenaki Indians from Maine and Maliseet Indians from New Brunswick, attacked the troops. All the English in the first of three boats were killed, wounded or taken prisoner.

"That was the first attack at Bloody Creek," Benjamin said. "There were little battles after that, off and on and here and there up the Valley, right up until when the government rounded up the Acadians and sent them somewheres else."

"1755," Jasper said. "But many Acadians fled into the woods, and the Indians helped them survive."

"And just two years after that," Benjamin said, "there was a second fight at Bloody Creek. A whole British detachment got cut up bad, right there.""

"A sad history," William said, "but an excellent recounting of it."

Upon departing the two men on the bridge, William considered his journey thus far and felt very satisfied with his first missionary trip. He missed Mary and their daughter and just wanted to be at home now.

He did stop at Bloody Creek, and walked down to the little bridge over the creek. The high banks on either side of the water would make escape from an attack very difficult. It was a perfect trap. In his mind, he could hear the musket shots, the war cries of the Indians and sense the satisfaction of the Acadians at seeing their enemy at their mercy.

William didn't feel any need to take sides. In conflict there is often enough blame to go around for all involved. But had he felt the need to take sides, he thought that in general he had more sympathy for the Acadians and the Indians. They had been caught in a trap set by the war between England and France for the control of the New World.

His mind was full of anticipation of hugging his wife and daughter. But first he would have to ride through the forests and fields of the Annapolis Valley. Reaching the tops of some of the hills, he could see out over a sea of vibrant colours—reds, oranges, yellows, russets—intermingled with the evergreen of pine, fir, and spruce trees. These trees were loaded with cones, like brown decorations.

Even when it rained, William enjoyed all the scents and sounds of the great forest. Occasionally, he caught sight of bears and deer. Cattle grazed in some of the cleared fields he passed and horses whinnied when they saw Blackie.

He had thought he could make it all the way home that day, but night overtook them and there was nothing to do but to find a place for Blackie and him to be safe until morning. A large oak tree on the side of the road seemed to offer the best shelter.

William tied Blackie to a low branch on one side of the tree, removed her saddle and saddle blanket and set up the saddle against the tree so he could be propped against it almost in a sitting position. He spread the blanket on the ground and sat down. He didn't plan to sleep. It seemed better to be aware of his surroundings in case a bear decided to check them out.

But weariness was stronger than will power and he was awakened by the morning sun filtering through the leaves.

He checked Blackie over carefully. She seemed very relaxed for a horse that had spent a night in the woods.

"Blackie, did you sleep or keep watch last night?" he asked as he threw the saddle blanket over her back. Blackie turned to look at him. He thought she had kept watch as he slept.

Once the saddle girth was fastened and William pulled himself up—stiff from lying on the ground—into the saddle, he paused to pat her on the side of the neck. "Blackie, you're the best travelling companion a man could want. Let's go home."

As they rode along, the mist and the dew disappeared in the sunshine. The sun warmed his stiff muscles and he said his morning prayers, especially including Mary and their unborn child.

He passed through wilderness and farmland, declined the temptations of the small settlements he passed, and refreshed himself with bits of food from his saddlebag rather than seek out an inn and a meal.

Finally, from the top of a hill, he saw the Cornwallis River glinting in the sunshine and the wonderful sight of the township's farms and fields.

Mary was baking when William walked quietly into the kitchen. She looked much less pregnant than when he had left. "Mrs. Forsyth," he said quietly.

"Mr. Forsyth!" Mary laughed as she ran to throw her arms

around him.

Then he heard a baby cry. He looked hard at Mary, puzzled.

She took his hand and led him to the crib in the corner of the kitchen, "I'd like you to meet your first son, William."

"When?" William asked.

"Just the week after you left."

They both gazed at little William, now sleeping soundly in his crib. They looked at each other and smiled happily.

"You can hold him as soon as he wakes up for his next feeding."

"You're feeling well, Mary?"

"Aye. Once again I was blessed with a fairly short labour and delivery."

Suddenly, William said, "Where's our daughter?"

"Over at her grandparents' house. They are caring for her very well."

As he stood watching his son sleep, he realized he was now the father of two. His dreams of having sons and daughters had come true.

It was good to be home.

6: The educator

The Sunday following his return, William reported on his journey to the congregation. The people were pleased that they could be good neighbours to others who could not find or afford their own minister, but they were glad to have their own minister back.

The harvest was over and the people could now spend more time at Sunday services and visiting each other on Sundays after church.

William had been aware before he left to go 'down the Valley' that there seemed to be a lot of interest among the congregation as to whether his second child would be a boy or a girl. Then, before he arrived home, the news went out: 'It's a boy!'

Mary told William that the news was spreading like wildfire around the township. "I think the Elders are going to have a meeting to discuss the needs of our family."

"That would be kindly of them," William said a little dryly. He had not received even half his salary since he left the Morton farm and moved to Salem Cottage. Now that he had a son, he needed to start saving for his education and he was certain that the Elders would rectify the problem.

But the meeting was not about his salary. The Elders wanted to know what he and Mary needed now that he had two children.

"We're pleased to hear that you have a healthy son, and we want to know what you might need in order to take care of your growing family. The congregation are asking what they might provide by way of gifts," Elkanah said.

"Well," William said, "I'm not so sure about what we might need. Mrs. Forsyth would know better than I."

"We thought we might give you a cow," Mr. Webster said. 'You'll need a cow now that you have a growing family."

"I suppose you're right, Mr. Webster. I don't know much about cows myself, but my wife is very knowledgeable about that, as well, I am sure. I can talk to her about a cow."

"Oh, we already have, Mr. Forsyth. Your wife suggested it to us when we went to congratulate her. You were away on your little trip, of course, or we would have first consulted you."

"Then, I guess we will be getting a cow."

Very shortly, a cow arrived in the barn. There being a second stall, the cow had a place of her own. Blackie seemed to show little interest. Peter, the goat, didn't care. Mary milked the cow morning and evening and made butter and cheese.

The cow was named 'Maisie'—a pleasant and cooperative creature—and she fit right in to William and Mary's usual routine.

There was only one problem, Blackie, Peter and Maisie needed a pasture and William had no dyke land.

One day when his father-in-law was over to visit, William mentioned to Asa in passing about the need for some pasture land.

"I have two acres of dyke land that I can sell you, Mr. Forsyth. If you are interested, let me know."

When William got home to broach the idea to Mary, he found it was she who had suggested the idea to her father. It made him feel a little dizzy, realizing how much must go on without his being aware of it.

"It would be ideal to have a good pasture for the animals, William."

"You are right, but your father said he would *sell* it to me. As you know, I have no money."

"I'm sure father would agree that you could pay him as soon as you get your salary."

"Well, if he brings it up again, I'll suggest that."

Of course, Asa soon mentioned it again on his next visit, first glancing over at Mary, "About the two acres of dyke land, have you had a chance to think about it?"

"Mr. Beckwith, as you know, I have no money to pay you. Mary suggested that you might wait for payment until I get my salary?"

"No problem at all, Mr. Forsyth. That arrangement suits me."

A few weeks later, Asa arrived at Salem Cottage with two men. "I've had the deed drawn up, Mr. Forsyth, and Mr. Abraham Webster and his son, David, have agreed to be the witnesses to the deed. Read it over. If you agree, then we'll sign it."

William read the deed carefully.

> Know all men that I Asa Beckwith of Cornwallis in Kings County, Nova Scotia, Yeoman, for and in consideration of the sum of thirty-one pounds eight shillings to me in hand paid by William Forsyth of the place aforesaid, Minister, have bargained and sold and do by these presents grant, alien, and confirm unto him the said William Forsyth his heirs and assigns a certain tract of diked marsh containing two acres and one hundred and nine square rods more or less bounded as follows: Beginning at the southwest corner of the Creek Dyke Bridge as called from hence westerly by the middle of the Creek twenty-two rods or until it crosses to the south-west corner of a tract of diked marshland belonging to William Robinson from thence south twenty-three degrees East twenty-six rods to the Highway then by way of easterly and northerly the several courses thereof unto the corner of the Bridge or place of beginning to have and to hold the above described tract of land unto him the said William Forsyth his heirs and assigns against all lawful claims whatever in witnesseth thereof I the said Asa Beckwith have hereunto set my hand and seal this eighteenth day of October in the Year of our Lord one thousand eight hundred and five and in the forty-fifth year of His Majesty's reign.
>
> Asa Beckwith
>
> Signed, sealed and delivered in the presence of
> Abraham Webster
> David Webster

"Mr. Beckwith, all seems to be in order," William said.

Asa and the witnesses signed the deed and William now owned two acres of dyke land—not exactly what he had been hoping for. He knew he would soon have to find out what was going on about his salary by the most direct route possible.

Wherever William went—the blacksmith, the general store, the church meetings—he often overheard men talking about what must have been something to do with him. He thought that because, as soon as they noticed him, they stopped talking and pretended to go about some other business. Soon, he could see a pattern and decided to ask Mary what she might know that would explain this phenomenon.

"Oh, I think I know what the men are talking about—your salary."

"You know I've always planned to teach my son myself and prepare him for university in Scotland, and that requires that I begin to save money. God knows we could have another son in the future and that would double my need to save."

Mary nodded, her forehead wrinkled, her mouth a grim line, and her hands deep into her apron pockets. "Husband, I understand your need and I support you. I also know the capacity of this congregation to pay you."

She took a deep breath, looked away, and then looked back at William. "William, it was wrong for them to promise you a salary they were unable to pay. I do believe they knew that at the time of the promise. There has been so much religious turmoil—people breaking away from to join the New Lights or Baptists or the Methodists or some other newly minted group, but that had settled down of late. The Elders must have thought that many would return to our congregation. But that has not happened."

"And without those families, and their contributions...?"

"They will never be able to pay even half of what they promised. But they want you to stay, William. They believe you are the best minister for them, although they would never tell you—it might go to your head."

She quickly looked down at her shoes, her hands still stuffed in her pockets.

It was what William had secretly feared. He felt his heart sink and his mind go blank as he stood silently, trying to absorb this news. He realized the move from Ryegate to Cornwallis Township had gained him nothing—nothing from a financial point-of-view. He was actually in a worse situation than he would have been in Ryegate, assuming the Ryegate people would have fulfilled their commitment to him. What would he say to his parents? Or to General Whitelaw? It dawned on him that fearing his suspicions were true was why he had not confronted the Elders a long time ago.

First Ryegate seemed his land of hopes and dreams, then Cornwallis. Now what should he do? What could he do?

Finally, it occurred to him that Mary was still standing there, one hand resting on the kitchen table while the fingers of her other hand rolled the hem of her apron back and forth. She looked at him with great concern in her eyes.

"Have you known this the whole time, Mary?"

"Not the whole time. When I asked father, he said that it was just a matter of time until they figured out a way to pay your salary. So I waited patiently, just like you. But while you were away, I put father on the spot and would not let him dodge. That was when the truth came out. He and the Elders have no idea how they could raise the money they promised you."

Seeing the tears in Mary's eyes, William took her hand and drew her closer so he could hug her. They stood thus for a while, shifting gently from foot to foot.

"I assume the Elders have all known this for quite a while."

"At first they hoped to find a way, but as time went on they saw that—short of a miracle—they could find no way to pay your full salary. They feel badly about it, William. They are rather ashamed and really don't know how to tell you the truth."

William felt rather ashamed as well. It was up to him to confront the Elders about his salary and, instead, his wife had had to force out the truth. It was embarrassing.

"Mary," he said, "I am proud of you for discovering this, and I honour you for it. But I must think a bit. Please, do not take it amiss. I just need to...organize my thoughts."

"Are you angry with me?"

"Never with you. But this is a strange situation. I will be back before long."

William took a long ride, crossing into Horton Township. Then he dismounted and walked, holding Backie's reins, along a path beside one of the dykes. He stared out over the beautiful marsh without seeing a thing.

After a while, it was clear to him. Pride—his pride in his education and abilities—had led him to leave Ryegate and then had prevented him from forthrightly finding out the truth about his situation in Cornwallis Township.

William knew he had to hear the situation from the Elders themselves. He needed to know exactly where he stood in relation to his salary. So he began to plan what he was going to say to them.

~

William—that is, little William, or Will, as they called him—was a most healthy and lively child. As his father watched him grow and thrive, he mused about Will's future and all the plans he had in store—all of which would require cash. The University of Glasgow would certainly not be interested in a side of beef or a dozen eggs as part-payment on a semester's tuition. Nay, he had to start assembling cash. There was no putting off the conversation with the Elders about his salary.

But before that could happen, life got in the way.

William had come to Cornwallis Township just as many of the 1760 Planters and 1783 Loyalists were coming to the end of their lives. A new generation was, of course, replacing them.

In many ways the Planters and William were alike: straight-forward, plain-speaking people—except when it came to salary. He had enjoyed getting to know and serve them.

Now he had to bury so many of them. There were many deaths —some quick and unexpected, others long and lingering—and many funerals. The new generation brought its marriages, births and baptisms. Those were the joyous occasions.

There were also the deaths of many young women and their infants in childbirth. If a mother died and her infant survived childbirth, the child would shortly become part of another family. Fathers remarried and began having children with their new wives. If the second wife died in childbirth, the children of the first and second wife could become part of a third family. Children or whole families could be wiped out by childhood and other diseases like typhoid or scarlet fever, diphtheria or smallpox. Death was a familiar and ever-present guest in most households.

Like all ministers, William had long ago discovered that Sunday comes every seven days no matter how many funerals happen during the week. He had to prepare the prayers and sermons for two services every Sunday and, of course, lead the services, teach weekly catechesis for the youth of the congregation, and conduct regular visits to the congregation members. He also attended monthly church meetings and semi-annual Truro Presbytery meetings.

Daily, he had to haul water for the house and the barn. Blackie, Peter, and Maisie had to be fed and he had to clean their stalls every day. Then firewood had to be chopped and brought into the wood box. He combed and brushed Blackie regularly and polished the riding tack, and, of course, took her on regular trips to the blacksmith to have her shoes changed. And so the days went.

William noticed that he and Blackie no longer had their long chats each day. He told her all about his feelings as he cleaned her stall and fed her each day, but it was rushed—not like the early days.

But soon enough William was bringing little Will out to the barn so he could sit on Blackie's back and pat her and pull on her mane. Blackie seemed pleased and proud. This made up a bit for the lack of long chats.

Blackie began to take Will on little walks around the barn and down the lane with William in close attendance. Occasionally, his sister Mary rode along with him while their mother watched her children with pride.

Usually, Mary kept her daughter busy with her in the kitchen learning to do little tasks and the rudiments of knitting and needlework. Mary thought of her household as her domain and as a factory where she took raw materials such as grain, or flax or wool and processed them into what her family needed to survive and thrive: meals, clothes, bedding, candles, and much more. It was a huge responsibility and girls needed to be carefully prepared to do all this even while they were pregnant and nursing babies, as well as caring for their other children from toddlers to teens.

If a husband had some money, he might hire a servant to help with all the tasks. Sometimes other family members, such as teenage girls and unmarried women, also helped. Everyone was up at dawn, putting wood on the fire, making breakfast, feeding the children and putting the dough in the warming oven to rise. As a minister's wife, Mary also visited women who had just had babies and taught Sunday School to the little children.

"Whoever said, a woman's work is never done, must have known me," Mary said often.

But there was another responsibility that mothers and fathers had toward their children—learning social skills. Mary would often take her daughter with her on visits to other families so the children could play together while the mothers talked. Fathers usually took their sons with them when they went to the store or the blacksmith shop or any place the men would congregate and talk about politics and crop raising. William, of course, in the future would talk to his sons about Scotland and becoming educated men working in the professions.

When they had a little time together, William began to share his plans with Mary. "I've told you about my meetings with the clergy and schoolteachers in Annapolis Royal and Digby. They all have experience in teaching, I believe I've learned a lot from them about what is needed to run a successful school."

Mary listened intently.

"Mary, I think I am going to propose that I begin teaching. Remember, I taught adults in Ryegate, so I do have some experience, and just recently I just received a letter from General Whitelaw informing me how well my Ryegate teachers are doing. Listen to this —General Whitelaw says all my students have become excellent teachers. He talks about John Page—you remember me telling you about 'Lame John?"

Mary nodded. "The man with the crutches."

"Well, he says John teaches around one hundred children and young people in a one-room schoolhouse with 'marked success'." William gave a small smile. "The General says John uses those crutches for the 'castigation of refractory students'."

Mary pondered what William was planning. What else could her husband do but teach school? But she feared how this plan would affect their family. "Will you board your students?"

"Well, not at first, but maybe eventually."

Mary sighed and so did William, but he also felt excited about the prospect of teaching—he loved teaching—and making money. He really needed money.

"The New England Planters and the Loyalists who came here often had very good educations themselves and had been very involved in government and politics in their former homes," he said. "However, they had to set aside their former lives until they could develop farms in this wilderness. Now that stage is over, they want their children and grandchildren to have the benefit of a good education."

"That is certainly true, but seems easier said than done," Mary said.

"Here's what I have learned about the state of education in Nova Scotia," William said. "Girls are educated in the home. They are expected to be able to read and write and complete a sampler of their needlework ability. If they are from a well-to-do family, they might be sent away to England, Scotland, or New England to learn manners, etiquette, poise and deportment. They will probably also learn singing, dancing, playing a musical instrument and perhaps French. This prepares them to marry well—that is, to marry into another well-to-do family."

Mary said, "There is reason in this, for all women are expected to marry. Women who don't marry look after younger siblings, their sibling's children, their aged parents or other relatives, or orphaned children. But nobody pays them or honours them for it."

"In Proverbs—" William began.

"Perhaps with words, dear husband. But they are fortunate to get their room and board with their parents or perhaps other siblings for this labour. A few unmarried women might teach in a school for young children or tutor children privately, but they earn much less than any male counterpart for the same amount of work."

William found this line of conversation obscurely troubling. "Now, consider the boys from poorer families. They usually learn to read and write in a haphazard fashion, if at all. Almost one quarter of the population cannot read. School teachers come and go from communities. They are paid poorly and usually have to receive room and board on a rotating basis in the homes of their students' parents. Poorer boys may learn their father's occupation or may be apprenticed to learn blacksmithing, carpentry, masonry or stone laying. They live with their master and his family until they have learned that skill, and then for some years after to pay for the room, board and education."

Mary said, "Upper class boys are expected to be doctors, lawyers, merchants, or members of the Legislative Assembly. They are the people who run the Province."

"You have become quite a Jacobin."

"It's true, William! The contacts they make with other well-to-do people during their university days, and the family they marry into, help the ruling class be in power and stay in power. They make all the rules that affect all of us. And they are the lads who go away to university in England or Scotland."

"It is a hard puzzle. Even our Kings College in Windsor is for Church of England people only. This means that there is no college for dissenters—which includes most of the people in Nova Scotia."

Mary nodded. "Don't forget that some boys enlist in the Royal Navy or Army as young as twelve or thirteen to learn to be sailors or soldiers. And during war years, men and boys can be pressed into His Majesty's service."

"Oh, aye," William said, "I remember someone told me that when I was in Annapolis Royal. However, all ruling class people are very aware of the example of the French Revolution. The last thing the people in power here want is to have a lower class of dissatisfied people clamouring for a change in the way society is organized."

"My Uncle Lemuel, who attends the Legislature, said that the state of education in Nova Scotia was a constant topic of conversation at the Legislative Assembly. He said he was sure action would be taken soon."

"As you said earlier, dear wife," William said, "addressing a need with words is easy. I will be glad to see some practical progress in the near future."

~

Just as it seemed that things had settled down in Cornwallis Township, another change took place. The Church of England minister who had married William and Mary, the Reverend William Twining, transferred to Cape Breton, and in his place in 1806 came the Reverend Robert Norris. Mr. Norris was married to Lydia, the sister of a wealthy Halifax merchant, Charles Ramage Prescott. They had two children.

"I'm going to visit the Norris family, Mary," William said at breakfast one morning.

"Then let me put together a basket before you go."

William wondered how she would be able to do that quickly, but soon there was a basket filled with fresh bread, butter, maple syrup and a dozen eggs all covered with a snowy linen tea towel.

"Now, Mrs. Norris will return the basket and tea towel to you before you leave, I am sure. If not, she will bring it back to me. Give her my best wishes and tell I hope to meet her soon."

And so William set off with the basket, walking down Middle Dyke Road to where he could turn left on Church Street that, unsurprisingly, headed toward St. John's Anglican Church. Upon reaching the rectory, he set the basket down, straightened his coat, and knocked on the door. After a little pause, it opened to reveal a smiling lady and a child of about five.

"You've come to see my husband, no doubt," the woman said.

"Aye. I am the Reverend William Forsyth, the minister of the Congregationalist-Presbyterian Church at Chipman's Corner."

Mr. Norris, appeared behind the woman. "Welcome, reverend sir!" he said. "You have already met my wife and Mary Ann."

"Hullo," Mary Ann said from behind her mother's skirts.

"Mrs. Norris, my wife has sent along this basket for your family, as a small welcome gift."

"How kind, Mr. Forsyth. Our family thanks your family. Tell Mrs. Forsyth I will get the basket back to her very shortly."

Mr. Norris led William into the front parlour and got him seated in a comfortable chair. He said,

"I've just come from a pastorate in New Brunswick. Previous to that I was in Chester, on the South Shore. The Bishop seems to think I would be a good fit in this Township, but I see that our church building is unfit for worship. I will need to set that straight as soon as possible."

William noticed that his host seemed very tense and anxious. "I understand that your family is in England and so, like me, you have no relatives in Nova Scotia."

"True, sir. But could I afford to return to England, I would have no family there either, for my relatives have disowned me and my father has disinherited me."

William was shocked. "Surely, whatever has happened in the past could be reconciled and you could be reunited with your family."

"I'm afraid not, Mr. Forsyth. My family are staunch Roman Catholics and I studied for the priesthood and was even ordained a priest. But I decided that this was not what I wanted for myself. I was in France at this time and, before I could act, the Revolution broke out. I was arrested, accused of being an Englishman and an aristocrat, and put in prison at hard, labour for fifteen months."

"This must have been terrible."

"I can barely describe it. Every day I, and my companions in the prison, thought we would be taken out and beheaded. Finally, though, I was released to return to England and to my family. It was a joyful reunion, with many tears shed."

"I should think so. But all did not continue well?"

"Alas, no. Upon hearing that I planned to become a minister in the Church of England, they disowned me. They will never relent."

They sat in reflective silence for a period. Then William said, "Sir, I am honoured that you chose to tell me your story and I suspect that what has happened to you still haunts you, as it would any man. I hope you will count me as a good neighbour and that we can support each other as ministers in Cornwallis Township."

The men agreed to meet regularly, and William wished his new neighbour best wishes for a happy and successful pastorate. He decided not to tell Mary about Mr. Norris' background unless it seemed necessary, as it was a very private story. However, he was sure that his daughter, Mary, would be thrilled to know that the Reverend Norris had a daughter just about her age. He hoped they could become playmates.

Late in 1806, William and Mary's second daughter, Jean, was born—a happy, healthy baby. William always said a prayer of thanks that Mary had come through another childbirth safely.

~

There was good news in 1808. Lemuel told William that the Legislative Assembly would offer bounties to Townships to set up and run grammar schools. There were no background requirements for teachers to be hired, so the quality of education provided would vary greatly.

"Teachers, like ministers," Lemuel said, "are very desirable people, but few communities have the cash to pay for either. Only the well-to-do have much in the way of actual money, and most of us make our way by barter."

"I am glad the Legislature has finally decided to provide for education for those who need it but cannot afford it," William said.

Lemuel smiled. "Yes, they will throw out their chests and praise themselves for this decision, but it was a long time coming."

After William discussed his plans to open a grammar school with Mary once more, and after much thought, he asked the Elders to meet with him the next week.

As the Elders arrived for the meeting, William could feel the tension in the room. When everyone was seated, he rose from his seat and walked to the front of the church. He paused, hands on hips, took a breath, then began.

"Brethren, you will recall that before I came to Cornwallis Township as your minister, you offered me a certain salary which I deemed satisfactory." He paused and looked at each of them intently with great seriousness. "But, brethren, I have not received even half my salary for the past six years. I could speak to you today as a minister of the Church of Scotland or as a missionary in this Province, but I plan to speak to you today as a father of three children, one a son."

The Elders were silent, attentive but wary.

"I plan to educate my son myself so that he can attend a Scottish university, and for that I need to save enough money, and I need to start now. God willing, I may have other children, some of them sons. I assume each of you, being honourable men, would pay me my full salary if this were possible?"

William paused again to look each man in the eye. Most of the men did not meet his gaze.

"Seeing that none disagree with me, I have a proposal for you. I will take on the role of school teacher for those of you who have sons you wish prepared to go to university, and will charge an appropriate fee. I remind you that I taught school in Vermont, to prepare young men to be teachers so I have a proven record of success."

The Elders looked around at each other in confusion.

Mr. Webster spoke first. "Mr. Forsyth, you know I have the highest regard for you, but you already have a full time—and more —job as our minister. I do not understand how this will work to everyone's satisfaction."

Mr. Newcomb chimed in, "That's my concern, as well." Others

nodded.

William, plain-spoken as always, asked, "What did you think would happen when you could not pay my salary? That my sons would become farmers? I have no land to bequeath them and no ability to teach them to farm. My dream has always been to send my sons to university in Scotland and that is what I will do. I want your blessing as I try to balance ministry and teaching. My only other choice is to find another position, possibly in Halifax or elsewhere in the Province, or to return to Scotland. I see no other options."

"Do you plan to do other things to make money besides teaching?"an Elder asked.

"I plan to continue my work for Horton Township and my missionary work by going down the Valley once a year." William looked directly at the Elders and waited for their response.

"Mr. Forsyth," Elkanah Morton said, "we understand your situation and I believe you understand ours. As I see it, none of us have a choice and you are taking the only path open to you if you wish to remain our minister. We want you to be our minister, and so we must support your decision."

The other Elders slowly nodded assent.

"We have to have a congregational meeting before we can ratify our decision," Elkanah said after looking around the room, "and we will do so within the next six weeks."

William had anticipated more opposition. Had the Elders disagreed, he have been in the very difficult position of having to look for another opportunity.

But in a few weeks the Elders reported to the congregation. The congregation, having heard all about the meeting in the interim, of course, reluctantly accepted the Elders' recommendation. William was free to begin teaching.

Given the lot that was now his, it was fortunate that William loved to teach. It gave him great joy to see his students succeed.

Mary, who knew the temper of the community before William did, was pleased for him and for their son, Will. He would get an excellent education and become a teacher, doctor, lawyer or minister—or maybe a politician, like some of her Morton relatives.

But there was a hint of sadness as well. How would William be able to take on all the extra work? How would this affect his health, and how would it interfere with their family life? The first disruption was that the dining room would have to become the school room. What would be next?

Word spread around the Township and beyond, and several of the more well-to-do came to visit William to arrange to have their sons educated. School was to begin right after the harvest, and long before then, William had as many students as the dining room would accommodate.

On the first appointed day, the boys arrived with slates and small cloths to wipe the slates clean with. They brought the recommended books, such as *The New Guide to the English Tongue* by Thomas Dilworth, Schoolmaster; goose quills and an inkwell; and a copy book with lined pages. They also carried their lunch. William's daughter, Mary, joined them.

"Boys," William began when they were all seated, "welcome to my home and to your schoolroom. I know your parents, who are all fine people, and so I expect you will be as well. I have received a copy of the School Orders for Cornwallis Township and we will be following these orders strictly."

He held the School Orders aloft. This did not seem to elicit the tone of awe and commitment he was looking for, so he began to explain the orders.

"First, there will be no unnecessary—and I will be the judge of what is necessary—talking and laughing in school or your parents must pay one-half pound of candles."

The boys looked around at each other, rather surprised at the penalty. "Why candles?" one of them whispered.

"Second, there will be no singing or humming, with the same fine as above."

The boys looked rather disconcerted.

"Third, each student must be present in his place when school begins and during each class. The fine is one pound of candles and two shillings. Fourth, there shall be no interruption while the scholars are singing but you shall wait to come in after the tune is sung. The penalty is half a pound of candles and one shilling. We are here to learn and all disruptions will be reported to your parents so that they may also deal with you as they see fit."

By then, the boys looked defeated. There seemed to be no way to have fun; only work, work and more work.

"Boys, if you wish to ask a question or answer a question, raise your hand and wait to be acknowledged."

He scanned the room sternly. In truth, he would have loved to embrace each boy and urge him to be of good spirit, for learning is a wondrous thing. But he did not dare leave an opening through which his authority might be undermined.

Finally he nodded. "Let us begin."

Reading and writing came first, and the boys started by copying the letters of the alphabet into their copy book. Later they would learn the numbers, and then they would be ready to read and do arithmetic.

Several days later, after the last scholar had taken himself off for the day, Mary came into the school room. "William, why do we have such a pile of candles in the supply room? I was about to make some, but it seems I don't need to."

"You may never have to make candles again," William laughed. "My students are rascals who can't sit still for long, and they have to pay their fines. I may have to start using a switch soon if they don't settle down to their studies."

"Are they making any progress?"

"Oh, indeed, and I am not too concerned about their hi-jinks. They seem to be quick learners."

By spring, the parents were bragging about their sons and complimenting William on his teaching skills. In the fall the same boys returned to continue their education and two girls of good family were added. Parson Forsyth's School, as they called it, was the place to send your sons and daughters.

In 1808 William received a letter from Captain Robert Turnbull in Bay View, Digby Township, asking him to make a special trip to visit them because of all the babies the families wanted baptized.

After consulting with the Elders, he wrote to Captain Turnbull with directions as to how the community should prepare.

> Cornwallis, 28 August 1808
> My dear Sir
> I have received your letter requesting me to come down this fall. When I received your letter I was just returned from Halifax after preaching a Sabbath to a congregation there. I presented your petition to the Session. They seemed unwilling as I had been a Sabbath at Halifax and as I preach every sixth Sabbath at Horton, but after deliberation they seemed willing that I should come one Sabbath. The Sabbath therefore which I appoint is this day three weeks. It is necessary that you give full warning to all the people that they may meet on the Thursday before for a day of humiliation and preparation for that holy ordinance. As it is a kind of favour for me to get away to your relief, I hope that you will consider it such and engage with all your heart in that undertaking. If you could assemble a part of the people the Sabbath before and pray, sing and read in your meeting, it would be very proper and be a means of effectually spreading the report and the design of my coming. I hope also that it may engage some in thinking of joining themselves to God in an everlasting covenant never to be broken. If men could see as well as I do the misery and superstition in which they are involved all between Annapolis and Digby would be there, for never were there a people on the face of the earth so blinded and bewitched as they are.

He was full of news and anecdotes upon his return from his Digby trip. Mary tried to follow closely, but there were so many names that she could attach to no faces, as she had never seen these people, that she had to content herself with general expressions of joy and admiration.

"They long so to have their own minister," William said, "and perhaps build a little church."

"If they build a church first, perhaps a minister will appear for it."

"I wish it worked as it does for birdhouses and birds," William responded. "However, Captain Turnbull showed me a plot of land that is going to be donated."

"Will it do?"

"Oh, I think so. And they are so confident of the donation that they are already using part of it for a cemetery."

Bay View was not the only place to celebrate babies. On September 8 William and Mary had their second son, John Elkanah. William now had two sons to support through university in Scotland.

There was another happy event that October. William heard that one of his most faithful parishioners had a new son as well, so he was not surprised when the next Sunday, after church, Benjamin Burgess approached him about having his new son baptized.

"Of course, Mr. Burgess. Of course. And how is your wife doing? This is your tenth child, I believe."

"She is as well as can be expected, Mr. Forsyth," Benjamin said in his gruff style—the style William always associated with Planters. Benjamin had a large farm for which he hired many labourers, and ran a general store. To sell shoes in his store he had hired a cobbler. He was a prosperous member of the community.

"Do you have a name for your new son, Mr. Burgess?"

"Yes I do, sir. With your permission, I plan to name him William Forsyth Burgess."

William smiled. "It would be an honour to have your new son named after me. I thank you sincerely, Mr. Burgess."

William told Mary about his conversation with Mr. Burgess.

"Well, there is proof of his great respect for you, William. What an honour."

In 1810, William and Mary's third daughter was born, Elizabeth Ann. They now had five healthy children.

By 1811 William's school was very successful and everything seemed to be going well when he heard terrible news, Major Lemuel Morton, Elkanah's oldest son, died on April 30.

William was shocked. Lemuel was only fifty-eight years old and had seemed to be in good health until his recent illness. It seemed like a form of the flu and, before anyone realized how serious it was, he was gone.

William led the funeral, and the church was filled to capacity—over a thousand people, including a detachment of the battalion of which he had been Major.

Rebecca, Elkanah's youngest daughter, also died that year, as did Lemuel's son, James. And it was only a short time after James' death, when Elkanah's second wife, Mary, also went to her rest. William didn't know how Elkanah could stand having to bury two wives.

Elkanah was now eighty-one years old and had survived the deaths of so many near and dear to him. William wondered if he could handle all this loss. *It is fortunate Planters are tough people,* he decided.

Despite William's hopes that he had seen the end of funerals for a time, he heard in September that the Reverend George Gillmore of Horton Township had died. William was very sad about Mr. Gillmore, who had been a good friend. He had been the only Church of Scotland minister close enough for William to visit regularly, and he would miss that very much.

Shortly after this, there was a bit of a bright spot when Elkanah loaned William one hundred acres of land near the Grand Dyke so he could raise some sheep. This would be a big help to William's family, whose need for woollen clothing and blankets would only increase as the children grew older.

Soon after Mr. Gillmore's death, William was invited to a meeting of the Horton Township Congregational-Presbyterian Church at Grand Pré. The Reverend Gillmore had been instrumental in having this church built, but as soon as it was ready for use he died, at ninety-one. This great age surprised William, as Mr. Gillmore had always seemed lively and energetic.

"Mr. Forsyth," Deacon Elihu Woodworth said, "we have called you to our meeting to ask if you would consider filling in part-time, on a regular basis, until we can find another minister. We will begin our search immediately and hope to find a new minister within a year. If you could consider our request and discuss it with your Elders, we would much appreciate it."

William agreed to bring the request to the attention of the Cornwallis Township Elders. That matter attended to, the groups took William to see the Reverend Gillmore's grave and gave him a tour of their new church.

"I very much enjoyed having Mr. Gillmore as a colleague," William told the elders at the end of the tour. "I will miss our meetings, and our lively talks."

The next week William met with the Elders.

"Most certainly not!" Elder Newcomb thundered. "How could the Horton people even think of asking our minister to take this responsibility? I hope you will all agree with me, brethren, that this is outrageous."

"In all Christian charity," Elkanah Morton said, "do we not have to meet with them and see if there is anything we could do to help? Many of our families are married into their families. We all came here together in 1760 and worked to build homes and farms and churches. What would we tell them is our reason for not meeting with them to consider what is possible?"

Many heads nodded at this assessment of the situation. Somewhat rebuked, Mr. Newcomb sat down.

Mr. Webster said quietly, "I will contact Deacon Woodworth and invite him and their Elders to a meeting."

The conclusion was that William could preach at Horton every sixth Sabbath "and no more." But, despite their agreement, the Cornwallis people were far from happy. First their minister had become a school teacher and now he was filling in for another congregation. It was not a good situation.

They did not blame William, they told him—he had sought their approval and they had given it. No, it was being backed into a corner with no good option that frustrated the Cornwallis Elders. William knew frustration often leads, unfortunately, to resentment and perhaps even jealousy.

Jealousy, of course, is one of the seven deadly sins. It can lead to disunity—squabbling, fighting, and rifts within the community.

And, in this case, jealousy was heightened because the Cornwallis Elders discovered that the Horton people could afford to pay their minister—in full and on time. The Horton people were also cheerful and supportive of William, and all he tried to do for them.

Soon the Cornwallis people began to let William know that, in their opinion, he was getting far too friendly with the Horton people. Perhaps he liked them better?

"What am I going to do, Mary?" William said with sadness. "The Horton folk need some support and I surely need the money. They make it very easy for me to offer to them what I can."

Mary was silent for a long time. She loved her husband and she loved her family and the Township. She felt caught in the middle.

Finally, she said, "William, I have thought long and hard about your—our—situation. I cannot see any clear way forward. If you terminate the arrangement with the Horton people, our people here might be less resentful, but we would all fail in Christian charity. So, my only advice is to not share your pleasure in the arrangement and the money you are receiving."

"Share my pleasure?"

"Yes, my love. People can read your face like a book, and they know how you feel without you saying a word."

"I did not realize..." William said. "And they take my happiness as...as a rebuke? As gloating?"

"They do. I do not say it is right, but it is the truth."

They sat in silence for a few minutes while William digested this news. Then Mary said quietly, "Do not speak of your good feelings with the Horton people either, lest it get back to Cornwallis."

"I am to express no feelings at all?"

Mary laughed. "Oh, my dear, you could never do that. Rejoice in the Lord, but not in a way that lifts Horton up and draws us here down."

"I see."

"You can do this. Just continue as agreed. I wish I could offer a better solution."

William took Mary's advice, but he could not unsay what he had already shared. So the resentment always simmered in the background as they all waited for Horton to attract a new minister.

~

By the end of 1811, with six young children to care for, Mary was quite concerned when William spoke to her about taking in students as boarders from different townships, especially Annapolis Royal.

"Heaven knows we need the money, William, but where will we get the space?"

"I think some of your Morton uncles might be willing to help me build an ell onto the house. That would allow us to make the area into a sleeping place for boarders. I think with the amount we would earn, we could hire a servant to cook and clean for the boarders and that would leave you free to look after the children and do the housework."

Mary nodded—a separate sleeping area and a servant would make it all possible. "Under those circumstances I would agree, William."

William and Mary were pleased that their eldest daughter, Mary, was growing into a serious student but also loved to socialize with other young ladies. Among them was Mary Ann Norris, daughter of the Rector of St. John's Anglican Church. Mary Ann was a year older than Mary but the two enjoyed each other's company.

The Norris family lived in a modest house with one chimney, but pleasant grounds. There and in the surrounding gardens the girls played happily, Mary often taking the role of teacher and Mary Ann and her younger sister, Catherine, playing students. Mary's sister, Jean, often joined them as well.

Occasionally the Norris family would invite Mary and Jean to go to Prescott House. This was the home of Charles Rammage Prescott, a wealthy Halifax businessman and Mary Ann and Catherine's uncle. His large house was surrounded by gardens and greenhouses where he fulfilled his interest in horticulture. His children often entertained their friends and guests with plays and other merriment. Besides the Norris girls, there were plenty of other children to play with. Right at Chipman's Corner, just kitty-corner to the Church, were the Gesner family. Although they were Anglicans, William often met Henry and Rebecca Gesner in his travels. They had twelve children and several were in the same age range as the Forsyth family.

Henry and his twin brother, Abraham, were Loyalists. They had fought with the English in the American Revolution and their unit, the Kings Orange Rangers, was disbanded in St. John, New Brunswick. They made their way to Cornwallis Township and worked as labourers to make enough money to buy some land at Chipman's Corner. Eventually, Abraham was able to get a land grant in Annapolis Township. Henry stayed in Cornwallis Township and married a Planter's granddaughter.

William had heard that one of their children, Abraham, who was a student in Reverend Norris's school, was doing very well. Indeed, he had rather a scientific outlook and planned to go to university and become a doctor. Everyone was pleased that the Township had so many promising young men.

In 1811, the Legislature passed a Grammar School Act that increased the amount paid to school masters and teachers. William applied and got some grant money.

Because of their interest in the education of the young, there was often much discussion on the subject among the people of the Township. At a regular meeting of the Elders, Elkanah Morton asked William if he had heard anything about 'common schools'.

"What I know is what I have read in some of the material that my friend in Vermont, General Whitelaw, sent me," William said. "The idea seems to have started in Massachusetts and is related to the social disorder in American cities since the Revolution. There is a fear that America will not be able to sustain its institutions or its workforce if something isn't done to improve the morals and education of the people."

"Do the papers say how this system would work?"

"As I recall, there would be a standard curriculum and professional teachers supported by tax dollars."

The Elders looked around at each other.

"And who would design the curriculum, then?" Mr. Webster asked.

"I think it would be the government of the province, through a department of education. And, oh yes, the Bible would be part of the curriculum but no particular doctrine would be taught."

"But, surely," another man said, "whatever people are part of this department of education or those training the teachers, it would be their interpretation of the Bible that would influence the whole system."

"I think you are right. I hear that many of those proposing the common school system are Unitarians. I am sure the Roman Catholics would not be in favour of this system."

"Nor will we, Mr. Forsyth, nor will we."

Looking around, William could see all the Elders nodding in agreement. It would be a while, he thought, before the Elders would be willing to consider the common school system. Still, the current system certainly led to class distinctions and the workforce of the future had to be considered. If Nova Scotia was going to keep up with the times, it would need a less haphazard system.

There was a happy event in 1811. William and Mary's sixth child and fourth daughter, Margaret Elliot, was born, a healthy baby and a safe delivery for her mother. William was so extremely grateful that Mary continued to have safe deliveries. Perhaps this will be our last child, he pondered. Six children: two boys and four girls. If that was to be the final size of his family, he would be satisfied.

So ended 1811. But what would happen in 1812? There were even rumours of a war.

7: Hopes and dreams

1812 began with a notice in the Nova Scotia *Gazette* of the opening of the Reverend William Forsyth's Grammar School. It said that

> his house was now ready for boarding gentlemen's children educating them in Greek and Latin languages and in other branches of literature and where their education would not be interrupted by Fasts, Feasts and Holy Days and where latitude will be given in all the efforts of genius and where unequal powers shall not be an interruption to one another.

The people of the townships laughed at the plain-spokenness of their minister in taking on the powers in Nova Scotia—His Majesty's Government and the Church of England. It was the Church of England that held Fasts, Feasts and Holy Days. Only the Church of England could perform marriages and the only college in the province was restricted to members of the Church of England. That left the 'dissenters' without an institution of higher learning. Additionally, members of the Church of England were preferred in public offices and had most of the say in running the province.

William, himself, was a member of an established church, the Church of Scotland, but he ministered to the 'dissenters', who had been promised religious freedom and representative government. There was a lot of resentment about the state of affairs that excluded eighty percent of the citizens of Nova Scotia.

At the next meeting of the Elders, there were lots of smiles. "Ah, Mr. Forsyth, you have set the cat among the pigeons with that ad of yours. Well done."

They all laughed. And the Elders didn't laugh much, so this was quite an occasion.

William soon had a 'full house' of gentlemen's children and had to hire a servant to handle the extra workload so that Mary could concentrate her efforts on their home and children.

In March, William heard from one of the Elders that another important person in the life of Cornwallis Township, Colonel John Burbidge, had died. The Colonel was ninety-six years old. The newspaper notice of his death spoke of him as a man 'revered and loved by all who knew him, for his piety, integrity and benevolence.'

William, of course, attended the funeral, and described the proceedings to Mary when he returned home.

"What will happen to his slaves?" she asked.

"I think he manumitted them in his will, but I'm not sure exactly when that will happen."

"What will they do when they are free—will they be given land? How will they support themselves?"

To all these inquiries, William could only reply, "I'm not sure."

Many other slave owners, mostly the English and the well-to-do Loyalists, were starting to feel the 'wind of change'. There was certainly no support for slavery in Nova Scotia, but it had not been officially legislated against. William hoped it would happen soon.

As he was pouring all his energy into the grammar school, William had less time to keep up with world events. He was surprised to read in the newspaper, in June of 1812, that the Americans had declared war against England.

The Americans invaded Upper Canada, a part of English North America. Many of the people in that area were Loyalists. Now they were being attacked by the same Americans who had expelled them after their revolution. They had firmly declared their preference as to how they wished to be governed. What were the Americans thinking?

The American newspapers reported that the former President, Thomas Jefferson, was quite optimistic about this invasion. "The acquisition of Canada this year as far as Quebec, will be a mere matter of marching and will give us experience for the attack on Nova Scotia the next, and the final expulsion of England from America. Canada wants to enter the Union."

As Halifax began to prepare to protect Nova Scotia from invasion, everyone in the province followed the events in the newspapers, which arrived in Cornwallis Township a day or two after publication in Halifax.

> July 1: 'His Majesty's ship, Belvedere, arrives at Halifax and reports she was chased of the 23rd ultime by an American squadron consisting of three large frigates, a sloop of war and brig and fired into by the leading ship. The captain and eighteen seamen were wounded and two killed.'
>
> July 3: 'The Governor of Nova Scotia issues a proclamation forbidding all persons from molesting the inhabitants of the frontiers of the United States bordering on New Brunswick.'
>
> July 9: 'The General Assembly convened at Halifax. The first class of militia from eighteen to fifty years of age ordered to hold themselves in readiness to march at a moment's warning.'

The militia in Cornwallis Township were called up to begin intense training. One of the parade grounds was right beside the Church at Chipman's Corner, and Township people came out to watch their men drill, and to cheer on their efforts at marching and musketry.

People talked of nothing but the prospect of war, and waited with bated breath for the next event that might clarify what the Americans might do and how the Government might respond.

> July 18: 'Orders received from England that in case of the absence or the death of the Governor or Lieutenant-Governor, the senior military Officer shall administer the Government instead of the senior Counsellor as heretofore.'
>
> July 21: 'Council advises Governor to issue letters of marque against the Americans and to prohibit the sailing of

all vessels without special license for one month.'

"Mr. Forsyth", one of the students asked before class began, "what are 'letters of marque'?"

The other children stopped whatever they were doing to listen.

"Beckwith, you know that the Americans have attacked Upper Canada and plan to attack here as well?"

"Aye, Mr. Forsyth."

"Well, one way that Nova Scotia has to defend herself is to attack, capture and plunder enemy merchant ships. A letter of marque is a license to arm your ship, hire a crew and go out to sea searching for American merchant ships. You and your crew would be called privateers. If you were to capture one, you would bring it back to Halifax and the ship and its contents would be sold off. You would get a cut of the profits and the rest would go to the Government. Of course, you would have to pay your crew out of your cut."

But what happens to the crew of the captured ship?"

"The crew are usually put in jail until they can be exchanged for our prisoners that the Americans have captured. You see, the Americans have privateers as well, out to capture our ships and take them back to American ports to be sold. What do you students think of that?"

Will spoke up first. "Father, I don't think the Americans should have attacked us. Both countries were living in peace. But if they do attack us, I think we have to fight back. But it upsets me that people on both sides are getting killed."

The others nodded.

But Beckwith said he would like to be a privateer. "It would be very exciting, Mr. Forsyth. It's like being a pirate, isn't it?"

"It is indeed, Beckwith. It is just like being a pirate, except pirates don't have letters of marque to protect them from arrest for their actions. Let's begin our studies now."

July 31: 'American privateer comes into Broad Cove near Digby and is driven off by the militia; the captain and prize master of the ship who were on the shore were taken prisoner.'

When William heard about this he was relieved for all his friends at Bay View and Broad Cove. He knew that Robert Turnbull was a captain in the militia and that Robert would bravely defend the settlers in those places. But this made the war seem very close to home.

In August the embargo on trade or other commercial activity on all vessels was continued to the 21st of September.

> August 16: 'General Hull and his army surrender to the English in Upper Canada.'

Once the news reached Nova Scotia there was widespread celebration in Halifax and the Townships.

"I guess we showed them!" Mary said to her father

"Best we not get too excited, my dear. The war is not over yet."

"Then when will it be over, Father?"

"That's the thing about wars. When you start a fight you can never be sure when it will be over or what it will cost in lives and treasure."

William didn't want to explain that, because of the War, the economy in Nova Scotia was booming. It was easy to sell all the meat, produce and hay that were available to the English Army and Navy. The privateers brought in lots of cash to buy goods as well. More and more of His Majesty's warships arrived regularly to add to the merchant ships and privateers in the Harbour and Bedford Basin.

It was good times for all because of the War and even William's salary was paid almost in full during these times. Nova Scotia was profiting from the War.

> Aug. 27: 'The English frigate, Guerriere, was taken by the American frigate Constitution.'

The people fretted over what that might mean to the war effort.

The English response came on December 31st, when the Prince Regent, the King being unwell, issued letters of marque for making reprisals on the Americans.

As the Napoleonic War was coming to an end, the English were increasingly sending their warships to Halifax. The Harbour and Bedford Basin were full of warships, privateers and merchant vessels.

A prison on Melville Island in Halifax's Northwest Arm held American prisoners of war until they could be exchanged. Because there were so many prisoners, there was overcrowding and disease spread quickly. Those who did not survive were buried on Deadman's Island, a tiny peninsula within sight of the prison.

By 1813 the Royal Navy had formed a blockade of the American coast so that the American shipping trade almost ground to a halt.

In June, Commodore Perry captured the English squadron on Lake Erie, causing great gloom in Halifax and the Townships. But the gloom soon lifted and there was wild excitement when, on June 9, 1813 His Majesty's Ship *Shannon* led her prize the American frigate *Chesapeake* into Halifax Harbour.

The newspapers told that people lined the waterfront to see those two great ships. Both the three-masted ships had their sails full with an easterly wind. The *Shannon* was slightly behind the *Chesapeake,* which was still flying the stars and stripes, but from the tallest mast flew the Union Jack that signalled that this was a prize of war. The news soon reached every corner of the province.

This was a turning point for the Royal Navy. The English were now overcoming their losses in the first year of the war, even though the American ships were newer, faster and more heavily gunned.

The newspaper account of the naval battle explained that on June 1st, the Halifax bound *Shannon* challenged the newly-refitted *Chesapeake* to a battle off Boston Harbour. Many people from Boston came out to watch the fight between these evenly-matched ships.

The onlookers didn't have to wait long for the outcome. The *Shannon* captured the *Chesapeake* in less than fifteen minutes in what would become known as one of history's deadliest single-ship actions.

As Nova Scotians heard the news, there was great celebration.

The tide of war on the Atlantic coast was turning in the Royal Navy's favour.

> Sept. 7: 'The Governor issues a proclamation requiring that all vessels arriving from Malta, where the plague is raging, to conform to Quarantine Laws.'

In the midst of all the news about the war, another event—which would be significant to education in Nova Scotia—took place in the town of Pictou. The Reverend James McGregor, the Reverend Thomas McCulloch, and others formed the Pictou Academy. Unlike the Church of England college at Windsor, the Academy was to be open to all denominations. That said, the founders were all dissenters from the Church of Scotland. Some called them 'the Anti-Burghers'.

1813 ended with a huge gale at Halifax. 'Upwards of seventy vessels were driven ashore, sunk, or materially injured and many lives lost.'

But the English blockade of the American coastline was holding.

~

1814 began with Lord Baltimore, the Governor General, ordering all American prisoners to be removed to Louisbourg on Cape Breton Island, as a 'place of safety.' A place of safety from whom or from what, people worried. What's going to happen next? Two days later a press warrant was granted to Admiral Griffiths.

William's older students followed the report of the war, of course, and peppered William for explanations of what was happening.

"What is a press warrant, Mr. Forsyth?"

"Well, Webster, if you were between the ages of sixteen and twenty and walking the streets of Halifax today, a 'press gang' from the Royal Navy could grab you and force you into service in His Majesty's Navy. And you would serve at the pleasure of His Majesty until your services were no longer needed—probably at the end of this war."

"Could you say 'good-bye' to your mother and father?" one of the smallest children asked.

"Nay, Miss Rebecca, not even that."

All the children looked horrified except Beckwith, who seemed to be considering the idea as an opportunity.

The people of Nova Scotia were pleased when they heard that the Legislature had granted £3,500 to aid the sufferers of the late war in Upper Canada as a testimony of its 'approbation of their loyalty.' The Elders in Cornwallis Township certainly agreed that Nova Scotia would not be in as safe a position if the Upper Canadians had not remained loyal to the Crown.

"After all they did to those who disagreed with their rebellion," one of the Elders said, "you wonder why they thought we would want to join their Republic.

"Well, they know now for sure how we feel. Let's hope this is the end of their designs on English North America."

"What do you think, Mr. Forsyth?" Mr. Newcomb asked.

"It's always been a puzzle to me why we and the Americans don't see things the same way. You are, after all, descendants of the first pioneers to North America, brothers in every way, and yet they drove out all who disagreed with their war and then, forty years later, they march north to try to include us in their Republic. Yes, I, too, hope this is the end of their wish to drive the English out of North America."

There were nods of agreement.

All this time, William had been thinking of his dear friend, General Whitelaw, in Vermont. They had no trouble agreeing. It was painful to know that he was probably suffering because of the English blockade of the coast of America.

But the war was not over yet. In July, a squadron under Sir Thomas Hardy captured Eastport, Maine and garrisoned it with the 102nd Regiment and a detachment of artillery.

~

One morning, Beckwith was reading a newspaper article to the other students just before class began. He was so excited and animated. "Mr. Forsyth, just listen to this. It's about an American privateer called the *Rattlesnake* that was just captured by the *Leander*."

"Read on," William said.

Beckwith scanned the article rapidly and then put it in his own words. "Well, the privateer *Rattlesnake* had just put back to sea from Wilmington, North Carolina in March after having captured eight or nine merchant vessels. Then she encountered an English frigate which she escaped by throwing all but two of her guns overboard. Then she captured two more vessels."

"With just two guns?" someone asked.

"That's what it says. But then the *Leander*, that has fifty guns, captured her near Cape Sable."

"I've been to Cape Sable," another boy said.

Beckwith said, "It says *Leander is* renowned for her speed, especially in heavy weather conditions. And it was stormy when she took the *Rattlesnake*."

Beckwith looked around the room to see if the other students were as thrilled as he was. The boys looked suitably impressed but the girls looked puzzled at his enthusiasm for privateers.

"A sad end to the *Rattlesnake*, but a great help to all the English merchant navy, I'm sure," William remarked.

> July 15: 'Lord Bathurst ordered the licensed trade with the Americans to be discontinued.'

The noose was tightening.

> July 23: 'The Prince Regent issued a proclamation announcing that English subjects, although adopted citizens, would be considered guilty of high treason if found in the land or sea service of the Americans.'

> Aug. 24: There was great rejoicing in Nova Scotia when the news reached Nova Scotia that the city of Washington, D.C., capital of the United States of America, was taken by the English. This victory was sweet and seen as fair recompense for the American attack on the city of York in Upper Canada in 1812.

"But why did they burn the city?" several children asked at once.

"Well, first we have to say that the Americans fled the city when they heard their defences did not hold," William said. "Major General Robert Ross tried to meet with the Americans and headed out with a white flag only to have his horse shot out from under him. Only then did General Ross order the burning of the public buildings—the White House, the Capitol, the Library of Congress, the Treasury Building and the Navy Yard."

"I'm glad it was not the whole city," one child said.

In September there was even more good news. An expedition sailed from Halifax and captured Castene, Maine, on the Penobscot River. The Americans, having blown up their fort, withdrew. The expedition then captured Machias, Maine, giving the English control of one hundred miles of seacoast with no waste of blood or treasure.

William read a newspaper article to his students about another action in September. "If the faintly disguised reaction to the burning of Washington, D.C. was jubilation, then outright gloom was the response to the news that the English had retreated from the Battle of Baltimore on September 15th."

"Why did they retreat, Mr. Forsyth?" Webster asked.

"Well, according to this account, the attack on Baltimore was just another diversion, like the attack on Washington, to dissuade the Americans from continuing to attack Upper and Lower Canada. When the fighting became too risky for the English, they simply withdrew."

"So, they could have won?" Mary asked.

"I think so, my dear. But as I read further, I see that General Ross was killed September 12th during the battle of North Point. His body is being returned to Halifax and he is to be buried in the Old Burying Ground."

"I wish I had been there!" Beckwith exclaimed, his eyes wide with excitement.

"But people were being killed, Beckwith!" Mary said.

"That's what happens in wars, Mary."

"It may be what happens, but they should never have started this war at all!"

"You are right about that, my dear," William said. "Some argue that war is necessary at times, but I think we can agree that nations should avoid it if they can."

One of the boys started to protest, but William pressed on.

"I have just spoken of the death of General Ross. Now, his family are in Northern Ireland and they may not have even heard the news as yet. Imagine how they will feel when they hear. You know that Major General Ross is a great war hero who had been injured in battle many times and received many medals for his bravery. "

The children were all silent, even Beckwith.

William continued, "He had a beloved wife and a child and family, and they will forever mourn and miss him. This is the story of all wars, children. Remember that. Now let us get on with our studies."

The children worked diligently but silently until lunch.

William heard later that Beckwith wanted his father to take him to the funeral of General Ross, but apparently Asa was not in flavor of a trip to Halifax.

> Sept. 30: Bad news. 'The English Squadron on Lake Champlain captured by Commodore McDonnough.'

"Are we winning or losing, Mr. Forsyth?" Beckwith asked. "My father says it's hard to tell."

"Your father is correct, it is hard to tell. But from what I understand, we're winning. I think the burning of Washington was the turning point and the complete blockade of their coast by the Royal Navy is certainly having an effect on their trade."

> Dec. 24, 1814: 'Treaty of Ghent signed between England and the United States of America.'

This would have been very good news, but there was no rejoicing in the streets as many people were dying of smallpox in Halifax. The outbreak continued with a high death rate through the winter.

None of the reasons the Americans gave for declaring the war were included in the treaty that ended it, and all captured territory returned to the original owners. The Americans learned that English North America did not wish to become part of their republic. The English were firmly in control of their colonies.

> Feb. 24, 1815: 'Peace ratified between England and America.'

Nova Scotia breathed a sigh of relief. There would be no further threats from the Americans. Nova Scotia would remain part of English North America.

"We're safe now, aren't we, Mr. Forsyth?"

"We are indeed," William said. "Now we Nova Scotians need to concentrate on being the best people that we can be."

"How are we going to do that, Mr. Forsyth?" Webster asked in a thoughtful and studious manner.

"You're already doing it, Webster. You're becoming educated and prepared for being a good and useful citizen. You are learning good moral values and your Christian duties by attending Church regularly. I am very hopeful about the future when I see how well you are all doing. I'm very proud of each of you, as are your parents, I'm sure."

The students fairly glowed with happiness. Mr. Forsyth did not offer praise without good reason and very sparingly, hence it meant something when he offered his praise.

Everyone soon found out that while a war can be good for the economy, the peace that follows may not be. The economy slumped into a depression as all the Royal Navy ships departed for England

and the militia were no longer on high alert. All the trade arrangements with the Americans would have to be re-negotiated. Everyone had to tighten their purse strings.

William hated to admit he had profited indirectly from the war, but it was true. He had gotten more of his salary during the three years of hostilities than he had ever gotten before, and now his salary was shrinking back to the pre-war levels. He ran his hand through his hair as he and Mary considered their budget.

"Well, William, at least you have your Grammar School and the salary from the Horton folk." Mary smiled, amused at William's rumpled appearance.

"Aye, we have to count our blessings, I know," he said a little sourly.

Now that William had a little money, he determined that he should pay his father-in-law, for the two acres of dyked marsh he had sold William in 1805.

"You know," Asa joked, "I never had a thought that your would ever be able to repay me, so this is a real windfall for me." Asa wrote carefully at the bottom of the deed:

> Cornwallis April 18th 1815: Received of William Forsyth the sum of £31 and 8 shillings in the above mentioned consideration money in full. Asa Beckwith

William considered himself lucky that Elkanah Morton had given him some land in the Grand Dyke for as long as he was minister in Cornwallis. This allowed him to raise some sheep. He now had a second cow, Elsie. Maisie and Elsie were great additions to the well-being of his family.

~

One of the people who had done well for himself during the war was Henry Hezekiah Cogswell, Mason and Lydia' son. His successful law practice in Halifax and membership in the Church of England put him in a position to be in touch with the Halifax oligarchy.

He advanced in 1814 from deputy provincial secretary to registrar of the Court of Chancery. It was rumoured that his salary was five hundred pounds per year. He played a leading role in the establishment of the Halifax Fire Insurance Company and the Halifax Steamboat Company. Henry Hezekiah was making Cornwallis Township proud.

Of course, William heard about Henry Hezekiah often as his sister, Anne, was married to Major Morton's eldest son, John, another up-and-coming young man from Cornwallis Township. All thought he was destined for greatness.

It wasn't until long after it took place, in August of 1815, that the people of Nova Scotia learned about the Battle of Waterloo. The Duke of Wellington's defeat of the armies of the Emperor Napoleon Bonaparte, near a little town in Belgium, ended Napoleon's attempt to regain power and brought a close to the war between England and France. Napoleon was exiled again, this time to St. Helena, a desolate island in the Atlantic Ocean.

William announced the news he had just received to his students and this was followed by much whooping and hollering. When the excitement had died down, William asked the students a few questions to evaluate their knowledge of this decisive battle.

"Beckwith, you are the one always interested in battles and wars. How did this war begin?"

Beckwith was on his feet instantly. "Mr. Forsyth, Napoleon had already been exiled to the island of Elba near Italy and replaced by King Louis XVIII. King Louis was a disappointment to his people so Napoleon saw an opportunity, escaped from Elba, gathered his armies, and marched to Paris. The English and our allies were in no mood to allow him to continue his passion for taking over Europe, so they took to the field to stop him."

"Very good, Beckwith. And what is the relationship between this battle that won the war in Europe and the war between us and the Americans?"

Mary and Webster both raised their hands.

"Mary?"

"Father, the English Army and Navy had been occupied in Europe."

Webster added, "the English hadn't been able to come to our aid at once."

"You are both right," William said. "Well done. They couldn't help us very much during the first year of our war. Now wars on both sides of our ocean are over and Napoleon is exiled again. We are at peace."

William turned the children to their lesson, but the jubilant mood continued.

~

Besides the slumping economy, 1815 held a tragedy much closer to home, the death of James Beckwith, Mary Forsyth's brother. James had been working up on the Miramichi River in New Brunswick as a customs officer when he became ill. Jennet, his wife, had just given birth in November to their daughter, Lydia. Lydia died on December 8, the same day as her father.

Jennet's surviving children, four boys and a girl, went to live with her parents, James and Elizabeth Kerr, at Fox River, near Parrsboro.

Two of the boys and the girl died while living at Fox River. Since Jennet had severe rheumatism, she could not look after her children. Her son James Kerr—called Kerr—went to live with the Forsyths. For all intents and purposes, William and Mary now had seven children.

They soon discovered that Kerr was a very bright young boy. He joined the Grammar School and his cousin Mary helped him learn his alphabet and numbers.

People referred to 1815 as the Year of the Mice due to the damage they caused to the crops, so everyone was looking forward to 1816 and a better harvest.

But spring 1816 was late and cold. That was not unusual in Nova Scotia; springs were never the best time of the year. So the people waited for the signs that it was time to plant their crops.

To add to the misery that spring, Mary's mother died in May.

There had been a lot of flu that year and, before they knew it, she was gone.

William held his wife's hand as she talked about her mother and all she had done for her family. "She was a great blessing to all of us, William. I can't believe she's gone so soon. Some of our children will not even get to know their grandmother."

William presided at the funeral. There was so much snow that May that nobody thought the gravediggers were going to be able to do their work, but with much effort they dug the grave and cleared a path to it from the church. As the snow fell and swirled around them, the Beckwiths and their friends and relatives stood in the cold and damp until the graveside service was finished. Later, Asa would erect a gravestone.

A major snowstorm struck the Maritime Provinces June 4th, and the weather stayed cold and the snow remained up to a foot deep in places. Then there was another snow storm on June 17th.

Now *this* was truly unusual. It was almost the annual planting time. There were some reports that people who were not close to home when the storm hit froze to death.

If June was cold then July and August were even colder. There were reports that ice on the lakes was a half inch thick.

With such unusual weather, people started to look about for a cause. William noticed that the numbers attending Sunday services had increased, after having decreased during the war when many people left the townships for Halifax and the cash to be had working in construction or for the Royal Navy.

Now that the war was over, people returned to their farms. But the Year of the Mice followed by the Year of the Frost had rattled them. Some said that the sun was cooling and others that the snow storms were punishment for the neglect of their farms during the war. Perhaps God was angry with them. In dire straits, people have always returned to the Church.

William, who was of a more scientific mind set, thought that the aberrations indicated a change in weather patterns that, although affecting the harvest, was not 'an act of God.' The people felt comforted and determined to support each other as best they could until 1817, when, please God, the weather would allow for an abundant crop.

And that is what happened. Careful preparation and diligent work during the winter and an early warm spring led to early planting and abundant crops.

~

It was almost six years since the Reverend George Gillmore of Horton Township had died and William had begun preaching for that congregation every sixth week. He had begun working with their Deacon, Elihu Woodworth whom William found a most agreeable and capable person.

William had received a great surprise regarding his salary—even though the war economy was over, the Horton Township people continued to pay in full and on time. William and Mary rejoiced over this, for now they could save more quickly for their sons' education.

So far, William seemed to be balancing ministry in the two townships and his grammar school for gentlemen's children quite well. The Cornwallis folk were, of course, not really happy with these arrangements so there was certainly grumbling among the Elders but no proposal of a remedy.

But beyond all that, William found that he was happy. "I think I found the land of my hopes and dreams, Blackie," he said as he cleaned Blackie's hoof with a hoof pick. He was standing with his back to Blackie's forequarters with one of her bent front legs held between his knees and poking around her shoe with the pick.

"Look, there's the stone that was making you limp. Better?"

Blackie tried it out and neighed her approval.

Just then, Will came running in. "Can I ride Blackie to the end of the lane and back, Father?" Blackie was still saddled and bridled after their trip to visit a sick parishioner.

"Aye, my son, I'll lead her out of the barn and lift you into the saddle."

Blackie seemed pleased. Will was now almost eleven years old and part of a father's duty was to make sure his sons could ride and also care for a horse, and Will was usually in the barn when William was caring for Blackie. William watched his son with pride as he trotted to the end of the lane. There was no better horse to learn on than Blackie, who treated the children like they were her own.

"Well done, Will!" William cheered as Blackie was almost back to where he stood.

In that instant, William felt completely happy. He was the minister of two parishes. He was running his own school. He had an excellent wife and six children, as well as his nephew, Kerr. His daughter Mary was fifteen and perhaps his best student. She helped the youngest students with their schoolwork and was just like her mother—calm, thoughtful and very capable. He could tell that Will would have no trouble learning and even at an early age was a very devoted Christian. A father could ask for no more. The other children all showed great promise.

After Will ran off to play with his friends, William removed Blackie's saddle and bridle while chatting with her, as was his custom. "Indeed, Blackie, I am a very blessed man."

Blackie looked William in the eye reproachfully.

William laughed out loud. "And I have the best horse in the world as well!"

William gave Blackie a big hug and some extra oats—which were gratefully received. He was still laughing as he opened the back door and went into the kitchen. He decided not to mention the source of his amusement. Those who did not understand his and Blackie's relationship would not understand and he had no desire to try to explain.

In 1816 Asa Beckwith gave William one hundred acres of land in payment for his son Elkanah's education.

~

William and Mary thought long and hard about what they should do with the land. Mary was of the mind that it should be rented and the money put into the university fund for their sons. William mulled over the idea that they should sell the land and put the money into the university fund. It seemed like a lot of bother to get into the business of renting. In the end, he was persuaded by Mary's sense that the land would appreciate in value—and even if it did not, they could will it to their children.

William put a notice in the Halifax newspaper and eventually the land was rented. The university fund grew each month. That was very satisfying.

The War of 1812 was becoming a distant memory. Now, other concerns rose to the forefront. But nothing new seemed to begin without some sad event preceding it.

December 12, 1816 Mason Cogswell died at sixty-six. His son, Henry Hezakiah, fast becoming one of the richest men in Nova Scotia, made sure his funeral gave due honour to his father. William was truly sad as he and Mason had been very friendly and he had often dropped by the farm to have a glass of cider and a chat. As he walked away from the cemetery, he wondered to himself how many funerals he had preached at. *Too many to remember*, he decided.

But it seemed that good news was on the horizon for Presbyterians in Nova Scotia.

In 1817 Truro and Pictou Presbyteries agreed to form a Synod of the Presbyterian Church in Nova Scotia, joining the Burgher and Anti-Burgher factions into one Presbyterian Church.

William travelled to Truro for this historic meeting and was seated among the nineteen Presbyterian ministers and six elders.

The gathering elected the Rev. James McGregor of East River, Pictou County as the first Moderator.

William was pleased with the choice. He knew a little of the history of Mr. McGregor and thought that he was worthy of the honour and most certainly capable of carrying out the office.

McGregor had been the first minister in Pictou County, his first placement after his graduation in Scotland. For years he had been the only minister in the county and had also travelled widely as a missionary to Prince Edward and Cape Breton islands and to various areas in New Brunswick. He was adamant about the need for schools and had been the chief supporter of the building of the Pictou Academy and the Seminary to train home-grown ministers.

William still remembered the story of McGregor's arriving on the brig *Lily* in Halifax Harbour in 1786—the same ship that his friends the Turnbulls in Digby Township had arrived in—and having to travel through the forest of Nova Scotia, first to Truro and then over Mount Thom to Pictou. He only went back to Halifax once, to get married. Like William, he had started as a new graduate with high ideals and principles learned in Glasgow University and Aloa, his theological school. Over time these sharp edges had been smoothed by experience and hard work. Yes, William liked and admired James McGregor.

Too bad he's an Anti-burgher. the thought popped into William's mind unbidden. *No*, he admonished himself, *we're all one Church now*. While William had been lost in thought, the Chair had the Clerk read out the plans for developing a Basis of Union that the Reverend Hugh Graham had prepared. Mr. Graham went over the main points himself:

1   Developing the Grounds of Union and stressing the Word of God and the Westminster Confession.
2   Affirming Presbyterian system of Church government and the use of the call process for settling ministers.
3   Upholding the place of Jesus, the love of God and spirituality of the Church.
4   Recognizing the authority of Presbytery and to be 'cordially attached' to civil powers.
5   Affirming Synod's role as mainly a liaison between Presbyteries and the Scottish Assembly.
6   Arbitrating problems between Presbyteries; between Presbytery and Congregation; and Congregations or Clergy and individuals.
7   Safeguarding the powers of both Sessions and Presbyteries.
8   Meeting at least once a year.

The meeting agreed to these points and added three others of minor consequence.

Upon returning home, William told Mary all about the first Synod. When he had held forth in perhaps more detail than a non-attender might have found fascinating, he said, "It's good to see all the dissensions carried over from Scotland put behind us. I think we can all now settle down to working for the greater good."

Mary, who was soaking some salt beef she planned to cook for supper, nodded in agreement.

"You look preoccupied. You usually have a thing or two to say about my church stories," William said. "Are you unwell?"

"No, William, not ill. Pregnant."

William was speechless for a moment. "Mary, are you pleased or...?"

"I am pleased, William. But pleased or not, we are going to have another baby."

"When?"

"Probably around Christmas. At first I thought I was 'going through the change' a little early because we had not had a baby for six years. But then all the usual signs appeared."

"We have four daughters and two sons, so I wouldn't mind another son."

"What would you name him?"

"I don't know. I'm going to think about it though."

William was still thinking about it when he met with the Elders the next week. "I suppose you know about our good news?" he asked.

"Oh, we have known for weeks," Mr. Webster said with a laugh.

William never figured out how they knew everything before he did, but fertility was the chief business of farmers—fertility of crops, of animals, and, it seemed, of people.

"Congratulations, Mr. Forsyth," Mr. Webster said. All the other Elders smiled and nodded.

"I thought I would give you a summary of the establishment of the first Synod in Nova Scotia and our new Presbyterian Church," William said, and launched into the account he had been rehearsing on his long ride home from Truro.

But after five or six minutes, Mr. Newcomb interrupted. "It is hard for us to be enthusiastic about the Presbyterians, Mr. Forsyth. We Congregationalists feel we are losing ground to these and other denominations. The Baptists are growing at a great rate and bringing in most of the 'New Lights' Congregationalists. The Methodists are very busy and active and, of course, the Church of England has the support of the King and government. So we are feeling more and more that our faith, that we crossed the ocean to practice and that gives us our identity, will soon be gone."

"I can see how you could feel that, brethren. I apologize for not seeing this more clearly as your minister. Enough with the Presbyterians and the Synod, then. What do we need to do for our Church here in Cornwallis Township?"

He didn't mention Horton Township, for that was another sore point for the Elders. The burning question was: when the Horton people would get their own minister. There had been no hopeful signs for years and the Elders all felt frustrated but unable to solve the problem.

If the new Presbyterian Church of Nova Scotia—the union of Burghers (the Kirk) and Anti-Burghers (Dissenters) of the Church of Scotland—thought that all would be smooth sailing into the future, they were about to be shocked. There was an invasion of Kirk ministers from Scotland to Nova Scotia and especially to Pictou County, the centre of the Anti-Burghers. The 'war' between Burghers and Anti-Burghers was still raging in Scotland, so the Kirk ministers were determined to bring all the Presbyterians of Pictou County over to the Kirk—'the Church of your fathers.' One of the aims of the Kirk ministers was to close down the Pictou Academy and the Seminary.

The first to come was the Reverend Donald A. Fraser, who immediately challenged the legitimacy of James McGregor, Moderator of the Synod. Although Fraser did not have enough troops on the ground yet to fully go to battle, he planted seeds of doubt in the minds of people.

~

William was glad at first that the Kirk was finally taking an interest in Nova Scotia, as he had often begged them to do. But soon he became concerned that their divisiveness would lead to...who knew what? His fear was that they loved 'war' more than they loved 'peace' and that he would have to choose between the Presbyterian Church of Nova Scotia and the Kirk of Scotland.

Early in 1818, Mary was delivered of a son. He was a happy, healthy baby and William was grateful and relieved.

"You've been keeping his name a secret, William," Mary said after she had rested for a while. "Are you going to name him after someone on your side of the family or mine?"

William swallowed hard and said, "Mary, I want to name him Barzillai Bezaleel."

Mary was silent.

"Let me tell you why," William said, a little too quickly. "Barzillai means 'iron-hearted' in Hebrew—a strong name. I thought that my parishioners would appreciate our son having a Biblical name. And Bezaleel means 'in the shadow of God', a good protective name. What do you think?"

There was a long pause, then Mary said, carefully, "I'm sure the folk will appreciate you thinking of Hebrew names for our son. I'm a little concerned that no one will be able to pronounce them. Why not something like Jacob or Isaac or something a little more common?"

"Well, I guess because they are common, Mary. I wanted something a little more outstanding for our boy."

"William, I'm fine with your decision. But be sure to teach everyone how to pronounce—will you call him Barzillai or Bezaleel?"

"I think Bezaleel."

Mary nodded, lips compressed.

After a long, not very companionable, pause, William drew breath. "Mary, I haven't looked at our University Fund for some time. Now that we have three sons and your nephew, I'll have to work even harder to make sure there is enough for all four. For now, I think we have enough for Will to go to Glasgow University. He's what?—only twelve, so we have a few more years before he will go. It's time to start saving for John Elkanah and then we'll worry about little Bezaleel."

~

After 1817 the 'troubles' in Pictou County got worse. Nothing changed concerning Williams arrangements with Cornwallis or with Horton or the Grammar School. Or so he thought.

In the early summer of 1818, William walked into the barn in the evening to make one last check on Blackie and to retrieve his jacket. He heard a 'psst', which startled him greatly.

"Who's there?!" he almost shouted.

"It's Elkanah Morton, Mr. Forsyth," the voice whispered.

"Mr. Morton! What are you doing here?"

"Speak softly, Mr. Forsyth. I don't want anyone to know I'm here."

William's adrenaline started to subside. "Come out of the shadows and tell me what's happening."

A shadowy figure drew close. Elkanah whispered, "Mr. Forsyth, the Elders got together and got themselves all worked up about you working for the Horton folk. They think you're spending too much time there and that you like them more than you like us. They're going to call a meeting and 'have it out', they say. I just didn't want you to be surprised."

"But why hide in my barn?"

"They made me promise I wouldn't tell you. But my conscience wouldn't let me treat my friend in such a way. Please don't let them know I told you."

"Thank you, Mr. Morton, for being such a friend. I will keep your secret."

William started to ponder this news, but then had a thought. "But how are you going to get home? Your eyesight isn't that good."

"Nay, but my old horse knows the way, and he'll get me home."

With that Elkanah was gone and William was left to wonder

how to handle this situation.

The next meeting time arrived, and William went prepared to address whatever concerns might arise. He found his mouth strangely dry, and that he had to keep swallowing.

The Clerk of Session read out the agenda. It included 'the Horton situation.'

"Well, Mr. Forsyth," Elkanah said when they arrived at that item, "what is the current situation in Horton Township? Have they found a new minister yet?"

"I'm sad to say they have not. They have written to Scotland to ask for a minister and have not had a reply. But it is my own opinion that they will not be successful. The Church of Scotland seems to be embroiled in its own problems."

"Then, Mr. Forsyth, we must discuss this situation. Our concern is that you cannot fully do your duty to us if you are also caring for them. We agreed that you could preach there once every six weeks. It seems that you are in touch with their Deacon on a regular basis and do other work for them. We believe that your job and your school take up all your time and that there is no time left over for other responsibilities."

William knew why Elkanah was taking the lead on this. He was trying to keep the meeting from getting too acrimonious.

"Brethren," William said as he rose from his seat, "it had been my perception up until now that I was balancing each of my responsibilities rather well, so I am surprised to hear that you would differ with me. I will lay out my concerns on this matter. It is true that it would be much better for the Horton people to have their own minister, and that is what I would pray for them. As I have already expressed, I do not believe that their efforts in that regard will meet with success. They are, however, trying their best, and I don't have to tell you that the Horton people are in every way your own friends and relatives who came up from New England at the same time as you. They are your Christian brothers and sisters. They are in this situation through no fault of their own. And, out of Christian charity, you agreed that I would preach to them every six weeks. That is what I have done and am doing. You will have to vote to see the will of the Session if you wish to change this. The only thing I can do is refuse any requests for baptisms or funerals or any other ministerial assistance except on my Sunday visit. Please let me know if this is the will of the Session."

He started to sit down, then straightened to deliver a final shot. "Speaking only for myself and my family, being paid in cash by our brethren in Horton has been a great help to our household economy. That is all I have to say."

He sat, with an outward expression of peace, while the debate raged about what should be done.

Finally, one of the Elders said, "We will leave the preaching arrangement as it is for now but we insist that you not provide any other assistance to them."

"Very well," William said.

The meeting adjourned and William walked back to Salem Cottage. Although he looked calm, it was only superficial.

Once he was sure the children were in bed and could not hear, he told Mary what had happened. She nodded, confirming to him that she had known something about the situation. They had not talked about it because if anyone questioned them they did not want to give away secrets or lie to cover their true feelings. Besides, Mary had enough on her hands with the new baby and the other children.

After much thought, William decided that he had to let Deacon Woodworth know. He paid the deacon a visit as soon as he could.

Once they were seated in the parlour and tea had been offered and declined, William spoke almost without preamble. "My dear friend, all the controversy in this Township has left me in a state of despair."

"Surely not."

"The claim that I prefer the Horton church to the Cornwallis church causes me pain, and perhaps, indeed, leads me to prefer the one over the other. Has my ministry here been of any value at all? And must I now abandon my friends in Horton Township, who have been so kind and caring, giving me much encouragement in my ministry?"

Deacon Woodworth open his mouth but, finding no words in it sufficient for the situation, shut it again.

"It seems my worst fears have been realized, as now the Elders have decided I can only provide a service every sixth Sabbath and provide no other assistance."

"But what, then, are we to do?" the deacon asked.

William felt the tug of apostolic obligation. Would Saint Paul have acted so churlishly in the face of evident need?

But you are not Saint Paul, a little voice in his head observed, and he stiffened his resolve. "Please convey to my other friends how deeply sorry I am about this decision, and let them know the next Sabbath service will be at first light two weeks hence."

~

In 1820 one of the steady and faithful families left William a small bequest. Alexander and Elizabeth Bols of West Cornwallis included a codicil in their will: "Rev. William Forsyth, the present minister of the Presbyterian Church in Cornwallis, £1 and 10 shillings annually."

They both died in January, and William preached at their funerals and led their committals at the Chipman's Corner Cemetery. He took the bequest as a good sign.

8: The bitter decision

Everything in William's life had been going well—maybe too well. True, the Elders and some of the congregation in Cornwallis Township were unhappy about his relationship with the Horton Township people, but they had not tried to prevent him from preaching there. The grammar school was making its contribution to the community, and to his purse, and his graduated students were having great success in their university studies. His university fund for Will's education had grown to the point that he would be able to send Will to the University of Glasgow.

But there was one thing that he turned over in his mind from time to time—the newly-arrived Church of Scotland minister in Pictou Presbytery, Donald Allan Fraser from the Isle of Mull. *One of those bloody Highlanders,* William thought, *hot-tempered and always up for a fight.*

For years, William had written to the Kirk Synod in Scotland asking them to send out more Kirk ministers. Horton and Digby certainly needed ministers of their own. Finally, in 1817 the Kirk in its wisdom sent a minister to—no, not Horton or Digby, but to Pictou County—a county with a good supply of ministers. True, these men were dissenters from the Church of Scotland but he knew them to be good and faithful ministers of the Gospel. They had even set up the Pictou Academy to provide education to young men of all denominations, and the Reverend Thomas McCulloch had added an informal seminary for men who wanted to become ministers. William knew the Reverend James Drummond McGregor, the first and only minister in Pictou County for many years —a man of great integrity.

Now the Kirk ministers newly arrived from Scotland seemed determined to undermine all that the Presbyterians in Nova Scotia had achieved. It seemed to William, and to many, that the chief reason the Kirk was sending ministers to Pictou County was to start a war against the Dissenters. He hoped he was wrong. *To transport all the divisions within the Church in Scotland into Nova Scotia, just after these divisions had been resolved in Nova Scotia, would not be a good and worthy cause,* he thought.

"William, what are you daydreaming about? What's on your mind?" Mary asked as she churned some cream into butter.

The sound of the paddle inside the churn kept William from hearing her the first time so Mary raised her voice, startling William out of his reverie.

"Sorry, my dear. I am hearing so many stories about the Kirk in Pictou County and the divisions among the people that the new arrivals of the Kirk are causing, that I am worried where all this will end. The latest news is that the new ministers plan to form their own Kirk Presbytery—dividing the Presbyterians in Nova Scotia once again."

"William, what will you do if they form a Kirk Presbytery? You're a member of The Presbyterian Church in Nova Scotia and their Synod. Would you break away and join the Kirk Presbytery?"

"I just hope it won't come to that. It would put me in a terrible spot. I honestly am not sure, but I will be praying for guidance."

William had more time to think about the situation in 1821 as he set off on his annual missionary trip down the Annapolis Valley. In addition to visiting the small societies of Presbyterians scattered as far as Digby, he also wanted to visit the families of his students in Wilmot and Annapolis Townships.

He was not taking Blackie. The Elders had convinced him she was too old. Elkanah offered him a new horse, named Star for the white star on her forehead. She was a lovely bay mare—*it's just that she's not Blackie*, William thought.

He kept Star at Elkanah's farm as he didn't want Blackie to know he was going without her.

Blackie seemed not to notice, though as Will and his younger brother John rode her every day. William hoped it was true that she was unaware.

The weather was good—crisp and fine. The leaves were beginning to turn red and yellow and russet, and the sky had thin, wispy clouds so unlike the big, fluffy clouds of summer. William wrapped his riding cape more tightly, as the wind was a bit cool.

Star seemed to be a good, reliable horse, so he let the horse pick its way and began to daydream. One of his favourite dreams was of Will—so smart and so caring—returning from Scotland with a degree. Will wanted to be a doctor, and William was fine with that.

William dropped in on Colonel James Delancey's widow, Martha, in Nictaux, near Annapolis Royal. She welcomed William with delight. The family were Universalists but greatly respected William for the excellent education of their son Peter, now nineteen.

William had always admired the Delancey estate at Round Hill, situated on hundreds of acres and fronting on the Annapolis River. The elegant, two-story house had a front veranda and the Georgian door surround was surmounted by a half-moon window with a fan design.

"Aye," Mrs. Delancey told William, "Peter is living at Round Hill and busy helping his brother William look after our estate. He's getting a good handle on farming and managing all aspects of our business."

"Remind me: the Colonel's father was a politician from New York before the American Revolution?"

"Aye, the family was very prominent in the colony of New York. Actually, James' grandfather was one of the wealthiest men in America."

She sighed, thinking back. "Well, the Americans confiscated our property, so we went to England to apply for compensation. With what we were granted James bought this land. There were twenty family members in all who settled here."

One thing William did not bring up with Colonel Delancey's wife was her late husband's attempt to make slavery legal in Nova Scotia. The servants the family had brought with them from New York were, of course, slaves. Richard John Uniacke, the Attorney-General of Nova Scotia, thwarted this attempt and everyone—except the slave owners—was glad about that.

As Martha Delancey waved good-bye to William, she said she would give his regards to their son, Peter.

~

After his visit with the Presbyterians in Annapolis Royal, William met with Mary Adelia Robertson, mother of two of his students.

"It's been about ten years since your husband died," William said gently, once they were seated in the parlour, teacups in hand. "How are you and the family doing?"

"We are well, Mr. Forsyth. And your family?"

"Very well. We now have seven children: three boys and four girls as well as my wife's nephew"

"How lovely. Our daughter Frances, who married Dr. Bayard in 1812, has a new son, William. And John, your former student, has become a Member of the Legislative Assembly. We are so proud of him."

"These cakes are delicious, Mrs. Robertson."

"Aye. I have an excellent cook now." She rang the little bell on the tea tray. "You may remember her, as she surely remembers you."

Annie Inglis appeared in a long grey dress, white apron and cap. "Mr. Forsyth! How wonderful to see you again. Blessings on you, dear sir."

William stood and smiled broadly. "Mrs. Inglis. I heard that you were doing well and I am glad to see you for myself. My goodness, you look well! And how is Isaiah?"

"All grown up and about to marry. He was able to apprentice as a blacksmith and now has his own shop."

"What excellent news. The day I met you being ill-treated by that horrible man I would never have guessed things would turn out so well."

"Aye, sir. I swear I would be dead by now if you hadn't interceded for me. It was the darkest day of my life. I feel very blessed."

They looked at each other with warm smiles. Then Mrs. Inglis gave herself a little shake. "Well, I'll get you some more hot water for your tea, Mrs. Robertson." And she was gone.

William and his hostess continued to chat about each of Mary Adelia's children and their families until it was time for William to return to his lodging for the night.

The following day, William reached the terminus of his journey —Bay View, at Digby Gut. Robert and William Turnbull were thrilled to see their old friend and minister.

William held Robert and William in the highest regard as well as their wives, especially William's wife, Ann. He frequently stayed with William and Ann, and so he knew them the best. Ann was born on the brig *Ann* on her parents' voyage from New York to Digby in 1789. She and her husband were sincere and dedicated Christians, holding prayer services every Sunday and catechizing the children, as well as collecting funds to build a church at Bay View.

The old friends sat in the kitchen so Ann could be included in the conversation as she put a roast on a spit over the fire and began to chop a turnip.

"Brethren," William sighed a great sigh of relief. "I am never so happy than when I am with you and the other Scotch families here. I feel I am finally at home. God bless you all!"

The Turnbulls smiled. "When you appear," Robert said, "our family seems more complete."

"How is George's family doing? It's been six years since he died, I think."

"Just so," William Turnbull nodded. "We all miss him. But he was not well for a long time and it was a relief when his suffering was over."

There was a long period of silence, each lost in his or her own thoughts of George. Finally, Robert cleared his throat. "We and others support his wife and children, and the children are almost grown now."

William nodded. "I'm glad to hear they are doing well."

Some of the children arrived at the table and they chatted about all the changes in the families in the area since his last visit. Finally,

Ann served roast pork with applesauce, along with potatoes and turnip. The chatting stopped for a while as they ate, then Ann removed the blueberry pie from the oven and served each of them a large slice, and again there was a comfortable silence as the friends savoured the pie.

Finally, William smiled at Ann, "My goodness, Mrs. Turnbull, your pies are so good! May I have another piece, please? I like it hot or cold, but hot is the best."

William dived into his second piece of pie. Everyone was always amused at how much William could eat and still be so 'slim'—the term they used behind his back was 'wiry'.

"I see you have a new horse, Mr. Forsyth."

"The Elders feel Blackie is too old for this trip. So Blackie is left for Will and John to ride."

"Indeed," Robert said, "that swim across Digby Gut would probably be too much for Blackie."

Everyone knew how much William cared for Blackie and, truth be told, it did seem strange to see William on another horse.

After a week of services, baptisms, and visiting, William started back. He often wished that he could move Mary and the children to Bay View, but he knew the congregation there could not yet support a minister.

On the way home, William stopped in Wilmot Township to visit the Bayard family. His student, Samuel, was now in Scotland to study medicine. Samuel and his older brother, Dr. Robert Bayard, were the sons of Lieutenant Colonel Bayard, a Major in the King's Orange Rangers during the American Revolution. Colonel Bayard sold off his land grant in Aylesford and bought five thousand acres in Wilmot Township.

The Lieutenant Colonel and his wife, Sarah, were happy to see William and invited him for lunch. Over the meal, William asked, "And what is the latest from Samuel? Is he enjoying his studies?"

"He is, indeed, Mr. Forsyth. You taught him well. His professors are all pleased and he had no trouble completing his studies. We want to thank you again for your care of him while he attended your school. His brother's practice in Horton Corner is flourishing.

Incidentally, we hear that the folk there plan to change the name of the community to Kentville, in honour of the Duke of Kent."

"Yes, I heard that rumour as well. The Duke of Kent spent a night there on a tour down the Valley, and I think they have been looking for a more auspicious name for some time."

Back home, William told Mary all about his visits to the Presbyterian families and the families of his students. Mary, in turn, filled him in on the goings-on in Cornwallis Township.

William also told Blackie all about his travels while he gave her an especially-good brushing and a special bucket of oats. Blackie seemed very content, so William relaxed his concern about his old friend.

But one morning in October, Will came running into the kitchen as William and Mary were eating their porridge at the kitchen table. William was just about to say, 'Shut the screen door,' when he saw the look in Will's eyes.

"Father, Blackie is down! She won't get up. You have to come!"

William dropped his spoon into the dish, splattering milk everywhere, and ran after Will to the barn. When he entered the stall and knelt down to touch Blackie, he knew she was dead.

"She must have died during the night, Will. She's gone!"

Mary arrived just in time to hear the pronouncement. They just all stood there. There was nothing to do or say.

William sat down beside Blackie and began to tell her what a good and faithful friend she had been from the beginning of his ministry. The others sat on a pile of hay, like mourners at a wake.

After a time, William said quietly to Will, "Go over to Mr. Newcomb's farm and ask him to come and see me."

When Mr. Newcomb arrived, he stepped into the barn without his normal loud greeting and gazed on the body of the horse. After a bit he said, "I collect your old horse has died, Mr. Forsyth. You'll want me to haul her away, I expect?"

"No, Mr. Newcomb, I would greatly appreciate it if you would help me dig a grave for her in the field near the ravine. And I'd like you to take her there."

Mr. Newcomb looked at William with disbelief. He had heard

that the minister was passing fond of his horse, and people often said that William talked as he rode along and they didn't know if he was talking to God or the horse!

He nodded slowly. "I'll send a couple of my farm hands to do as you ask, Mr. Forsyth."

Blackie had a 'decent Christian burial' with prayers and wild flowers. Later, William sent Will and John over to Elkanah's farm to bring Star over to the barn.

John Elkanah walked Peter, the old goat, back to the Barnaby farm, where there were other goats, and returned with a younger companion for Star, Reg.

It was the end of an era for William.

~

Not long after Blackie's death, William heard that the Kirk ministers in Pictou County were forming their own Presbytery and planning to try to close the Pictou Academy, which was for all non-Anglicans in the province, and turn it into a grammar school with a Presbyterian school board. *That's going to cause problems with the other denominations that send their children to the Pictou Academy*, William thought.

The strongest supporter of the Academy was the Reverend Thomas McCulloch, Moderator of the Synod and the appointed professor of divinity that year. William reported to the Elders, "It seems, brethren, that animosity is growing and everyone is taking sides—Kirk versus Dissenters, and Seminary-trained ministers versus those the Kirk sends from Scotland. I fear being drawn into this debate and having to choose sides."

"Cannot Nova Scotia use all the ministers that the Academy can train and all the ministers the Kirk can send?" Mr. Terry said. "Are we in Cornwallis Township, having been forced to share our minister with the folk in Horton Township since 1811, not proof of the great need?"

Other Elders nodded at Mr. Terry's words.

"You are right in all that you say, brother," William said. "There is no other way to discern this. Yet I feel a loyalty to the Kirk and we are mostly isolated from the troubles in Pictou County."

"I am not sure about the integrity of the Kirk," Mr. Terry said. "When I was in Halifax I heard a letter read about all the goings-on in Pictou County. A Mr. James Fraser, a school teacher who came from Scotland not long back, wrote it. I took some notes as I heard it."

"Will you share those notes?" William said, a little uneasily.

"I will try."

Mr. Terry stood up and produced a sheaf of papers from an inner pocket. William noted the Elders shifting in their seats as if settling in for a long sermon about an obscure text.

"This Mr. Fraser said that a minister or two from the Kirk came and preached boldly that the people had been stolen out of the Church of their fathers and made them seceders unknown to themselves. Some who heard this went to Dr. McGregor to ask, 'Why did you not tell us that you were a seceder?' He answered, 'Would it not be time enough when you would ask me of it?' Mr. Fraser said Dr. McGregor was playing on the simplicity of the people and that if he had honestly told them what was what from the first the matter would surely be better now, for the rancour of the division never settled."

"I am afraid that is true," William said.

Mr. Terry said, "Mr. Fraser went on to say that one of those new ministers, Mr. McRae, tried to get money from Mr. Fraser's congregation to support their divisive work. Here, this part is quite sharp, so let me read it out."

He cleared his throat and continued. "'Mr. McRae demanded that some of us speak to answer him. I arose immediately very near him and took out a quarter and told him, although this shilling would pay the whole sum you will not get it from me. Why destroy their college? Why don't you make a college of your own? If I have a barn would you burn it because you have none of your own?'"

Mr. Terry glanced up to make sure he had their attention. "Now listen to this. 'Under great astonishment, Mr. Fraser exclaims, 'I thought that you would be the last man to speak that way.' I told him I took the honour of being the first man. After that he had to dismiss the people without getting a copper to my knowledge.' So wrote Mr. Fraser."

"This is very harsh," one of the Elders said.

William said, "I have to admit that this does not show the Kirk in a very good light." *But I am not a Dissenter, so what should I do?*

After a general discussion that was mostly speculation, William said, "Brethren, I will keep you apprised as I hear of any developments. In the meantime, let us all pray for discernment."

As usually happens, no easy solutions presented themselves and all of William's worst fears came true. In 1822 the Kirk established their own presbytery in Pictou County.

"What will you do, William?" Mary asked.

"Well, I've had time to think about it—and I will probably be sorry in the end—but I feel I must support the Kirk now that they are in Nova Scotia. If they grow and expand into the Western part of the Province, they will need my support."

"What will you say to the Synod?"

"I think I will just not attend. They know I'm Kirk and that the Kirk ministers now have their own Presbytery."

"If the Kirk doesn't send any ministers to the western end of the Province, then you will be even more isolated than you are now. At least now you are part of the Presbyterian Church of Nova Scotia."

Mary was usually not so strong in her opinions, trusting William implicitly, but after a few minutes of silently peeling potatoes, she turned, hands on hips. "William, you know that those Kirk ministers are just a bunch of trouble-makers sowing contention over an issue that is not even relevant to us."

William nearly fell off his chair. "Mary, I don't think I've ever heard you be so, so firm in your opinions."

"I think the right word might be angry, William. Why would you join such mean-spirited and unchristian ministers, Kirk or no Kirk?"

"I felt that wasn't a question, Mary."

"Nay, I guess it was not. It's how I really feel about what I hear of their doings in Pictou County."

"I can certainly see why you're concerned. I concede you are probably right, but I feel I have to choose and it is a bitter decision. I will probably lose either way."

Mary turned and went back to preparing supper.

The night, in bed, Mary said quietly to William, "I think I'm becoming as contentious as those Kirk ministers. It is just so upsetting to see them tear the Presbyterian Church in Nova Scotia apart."

"You're right to be upset, my dear. I'm not very happy about what they're doing either, but let's not have it creep into our marriage."

They kissed each other good-night, but as Mary turned over, William could tell she still felt distressed over the Kirk and his decision.

As the time drew near for the annual meeting of the Synod, William was careful not to mention this fact, not wanting to have to defend his decision not to attend. Truth be told, he felt very unhappy about making this choice. Maybe he was afraid he could be talked into attending the Synod, despite his decision.

Finally he decided to go to Halifax to talk to the Reverend John Martin, the leader of the new Scotch Kirk Presbytery of Halifax and minister of St. Andrew's Church there.

"Are you sure we cannot join the Presbyterian Church in Nova Scotia and go into the future as one denomination, rather than competing with the Dissenters? I'm not sure I see the value of having two Presbyterian denominations in Nova Scotia."

"Mr. Forsyth, we are very pleased that you have decided to join your Kirk brethren and, no, we are representing the established Church of Scotland and not dissenters."

"But the split between Kirk and Dissenters in Scotland is only about the land owners appointing ministers to the churches on their land, a problem we don't have in Nova Scotia. There is no reason for them to dissent or for us to contend against them and take away all they have achieved over many decades in Pictou County."

"I'm afraid the rancour between the two groups in Scotland has caused a great rift that cannot be overcome, even though we are now in Nova Scotia."

"But why not provide ministers to all the townships that need ministers and leave the Dissenters to continue their good work in Pictou County?"

"The Church of Scotland needs to own all things Presbyterian—grammar schools, academies, and the distribution of grants received from the Legislative Council, as well as promoting a cordial relationship with His Majesty's Government. We do not want to compete with the Dissenters, we want to be *the* one and only Church."

They sat together in unhappy silence. William tried to pray, but his mind would not focus as he wanted it to.

Finally, Mr. Martin drew breath. "So, what's your decision, Mr. Forsyth? Are you going to join your Kirk brethren or no?"

"Aye, Mr. Martin, I'm loyal to the Kirk, but I do respect all the Dissenters have done in Pictou County."

Mr. Martin frowned and shook his head. "We'll be meeting soon to decide on our next steps. We'll send a message."

William nodded. He could see the conversation was going nowhere and he was sad that no attempt would be made to unite the groups and form one Presbyterian Church.

The two men had supper and by unspoken agreement talked of literature, the weather, and other neutral subjects. William left early the next morning, feeling quite uncertain about what benefit this situation would have for Nova Scotia.

A few days later, at home, William put down a letter he had been reading with a sigh. "Mary, have you ever heard the saying about the irresistible force meeting the immovable object?"

"Aye, William."

"Well, the word is that the latest Kirk minister to be sent to Pictou County, the Reverend Kenneth John McKenzie, is a match for our Mr. Thomas McCulloch and his Pictou Academy. They are both inflexible and determined personalities. I fear for what mischief this can create."

"Isn't McCulloch the chair of the Synod this year?"

"I'm afraid so. He is certainly the strongest defender of both the Presbyterian Church in Nova Scotia and the Academy, and nothing will deter him from protecting what he holds near and dear."

Where was this all heading and how would it end? William put his head in his hands and sat dejected for some time before going out to chop some firewood.

Despite the 'battle royale' going on between the Kirk and the Dissenters, there were breaks in the intensity in the form of some letters published anonymously in the *Acadian Recorder* newspaper. It was a badly-kept secret that the letters came from the pen of the Reverend Thomas McCulloch of Pictou County.

The purported author was one Mephibosheth Stepsure. The 'Stepsure Letters' satirized the indolence, restlessness and get-rich quick mentality of rural dwellers and town folk.

William and Mary read the letters in the newspaper themselves and laughed together about how true-to-life they sometimes seemed. When visiting his parishioners, William could often tell that they had received their newspaper upon hearing the uproarious laughter coming from within the house.

But surrounding the humour of the Letters was complete lack of humour or perspective by McCulloch and his supporters versus Fraser and McKenzie and their supporters. It was no laughing matter.

"William," Mary asked one day, "just what are the objections the Kirk has against the Pictou Academy?"

"As I understand it, the Kirk believes that Pictou County needs a grammar school, not an Academy. Dalhousie Academy in Halifax is the approved secondary school for Presbyterians—and, of course, the Pictou Academy is not just for Presbyterians but for all non-Anglican Nova Scotians. In addition, the Kirk objects to the very idea of Dissenters training men for the ministry—all training should be by the Kirk. So they have set out to destroy the Academy and its informal theology school that Mr. McCulloch leads."

It was true. Nova Scotians could follow the progress of the war in the newspapers as both sides tried to enlist the hearts and minds of Nova Scotians to their cause.

~

But all the attention in Cornwallis Township to the turmoil came to a standstill in 1824. William heard the news first from one of Elkanah's grandsons, who came riding up the lane to Salem Cottage, jumped down from his horse and announced to the family that Mr. Elkanah Morton had just died!

Elkanah had been much slowed down of late, missing Sunday services and meetings of the Elders, but he had been so much a part of Cornwallis Township for sixty-four years that no one seemed to expect that he would ever die. William went to visit his third wife, Elizabeth, who was, of course, very sad to lose such a fine man as her husband. She had always respected his dedication to his church and the community.

The funeral service was huge, filling the one-thousand-seat church. They brought Elkanah out the door of his beloved church one last time and carried his coffin over to the cemetery where they buried him next to his first wife, Rebecca, the mother of his children. Children and grandchildren and great-grandchildren led the mourners.

William was grieved at the loss of his great friend, who had been so loyal and supportive for his whole ministry. He still remembered vividly the November day he arrived in Cornwallis Township and met Elkanah just as he stepped out of the church door. If he closed his eyes, he could still see Elkanah's warm smile of greeting. Cornwallis Township wouldn't be the same without Elkanah.

Mary, Elkanah's granddaughter, comforted his great grandchildren and went back to Elkanah's farm where friends and other relatives had been busy preparing a luncheon for the mourners. Many of the Township women brought baked goods and the men promised to milk the cows and take care of the horses until the family were up to returning to these duties.

Elkanah was perhaps the last of the Planters of 1760. A new generation had taken over the farms and homesteads and now the third generation was well on its way to taking over in its turn. It was a time of reflection of how far these Planters had come and all that they had achieved in Nova Scotia in their bid for representative government and freedom of religion.

When Elkanah had made out his Last Will and Testament in 1819, he left some dykeland for the use of William and Mary during their lifetimes and to be used after to support building a church and school for the people in the west of Cornwallis Township. William was grateful for this land for his family's cows and sheep, as they were essential to his family's well being. He didn't say anything but he was rather sad that he was not deeded the land—it would have been something to give to his children. But he understood, as Elkanah wanted the people in the west of the Township to have their own church since they had always felt Chipman's Corner was too far for them to travel.

~

After some time, William and Mary went back to their usual routine. Elkanah would have understood. Planters were practical, plain-spoken people who had little time for sadness or crying. Life had to go on, and it did.

One day in 1825, when William returned from visiting parishioners, Mary looked up from her work. "William, I hear Mr. McCulloch has gone to Scotland?"

"Aye, my dear, gone to meet with the Reverend Robert Burns, Secretary of the Glasgow Colonial Society who have been sending Kirk ministers to Pictou County. I fear the worst from such a meeting."

"What is Mr. McCulloch's purpose for meeting with Mr. Burns, do you know?"

"Why, to persuade Mr. Burns to stop sending Scottish trained ministers to Nova Scotia. Mr. McCulloch wants to train all ministers at his so-far informal seminary."

"Can Mr. McCulloch really meet the demand?"

"Nay. Not in the short term, if ever. But no one can convince him otherwise, even his friends."

Soon news reached the Kirk ministers in Nova Scotia about the explosive meeting between McCulloch and Burns, turning the Kirk from McCulloch's cause. *What else could go wrong?* William wondered.

Apart from the high drama of Kirk vs Dissenters in Scotland, exciting things also happened in Cornwallis Township.

In 1825 Wellington Dyke, under construction since 1817, was completed with great celebration. Along with the previous Acadian dyke system, it held back the great tides of the Bay of Fundy and the Minas Basin from over 3,000 acres of land. The Dyke was named after the Duke of Wellington following his victory over the French at the Battle of Waterloo in 1815.

William, along with a goodly portion of the inhabitants of Cornwallis Township, had watched as the men of the Township laboured to build the dyke. They had to dig the earth and bring it by horse cart to the site and then shovel it into the retaining wall. The dyke was fitted with an *abiteau*, also known as a flap dam, which prevented the sea from surging up the rivers and covering the marsh at high tide but allowing the rivers to flow out to the sea at low tide.

In 1822, an especially high tide swept the whole dyke out to sea. After everyone got over the shock of this disaster, the men got together and re-constructed the dyke. So the celebration was especially happy.

That year, Will Forsyth left Cornwallis Township. He was to begin his medical studies at Glasgow University in October. There had been special prayers and a church picnic to see him off. He and his mother had a tearful good-bye. The younger children, although they would miss him, thought him off on a great adventure. He promised to write and write often.

As he and his father started off for Halifax, in the horse and cart William had borrowed from a parishioner, William's old trunk bounced and slid in the back. It was, of course, tied down but there was still enough space for it to move about.

On the way to Halifax, William gave Will all the advice he could muster. But he knew his son was a young man with 'his head on his shoulders', and a very devout Christian as well. It would take a lot for him to be led astray.

After a night in Halifax, father and son had breakfast at the inn and loaded the trunk back into the wagon for the short ride to the dock. William's pride in his son could not be overstated as he watched him ascend the gangplank and turn to wave from the deck of the ship. William waited until the ship was almost to the mouth of Halifax Harbour before he headed back to Cornwallis Township.

This is how my parents must have felt when they said good-bye to me all those years ago, he thought, as he imagined Mary dealing with similar feelings back home.

In 1826 McCulloch was still in Scotland trying to raise money for the Pictou Academy.

"Mr. Forsyth, Mr. Terry asked at a meeting of the Elders, "what is 'the Memorial' I hear about in the newspaper?"

William took in a deep breath and tried to decide where to begin. "Mr. Terry, Mr. McCulloch is accusing the Glasgow Colonial Society of interfering with the Presbyterian Church in Nova Scotia in a publication called a Memorial. Now the Scottish people are all embroiled in a controversy about the aims of the Society. There seems to be no end to the turmoil."

The next morning, Mary slapped the Acadian Recorder newspaper down in front of William before she put breakfast on the table. "Look at this!"

Just as William feared, the Scottish controversy had now appeared back in Nova Scotia as the Kirk ministers in Pictou County and in Halifax had sent their comments about the Reverend McCulloch to the Reverend Burns in Scotland, adding fuel to the fire.

After reading the article and pondering the contents for a while, William realized that Mary was furiously pounding, rather than kneading, the bread dough and that he had not received any breakfast. He hoped this was just an oversight.

"Mary, I'm wondering about my breakfast."

Mary looked confused for a moment and then plunked the plate of bacon and eggs—with the now congealing fat—down in front of him and returned to her very energetic kneading.

"Thank you, my dear. I won't ask how you feel about the latest news from Scotland as I fear what you might do with that dough." He smiled, hoping to bring a bit of levity into the situation, but Mary was still pounding away, so he ate in silence and went to haul some water.

When McCulloch returned to Nova Scotia in late 1826 he attacked the Kirk ministers in the newspapers

The fight soon extended into the Nova Scotia Legislature and the Legislative Council with members in these two bodies taking sides as well. This added to the animosity in Nova Scotia.

In 1828 Burns in Scotland published a 'Supplement' to rebut the charges against the Society, leading McCulloch to publish a 'Review of the Supplement', and then there was a further response from Burns.

"Mr. Forsyth," Mr. Webster said dejectedly, "what an embarrassing mess. Surely this is not what is to be expected by those who follow Jesus."

"I agree, Mr. Webster, I agree. We need the Glasgow Colonial Society to send us more ministers, but this whole turmoil has interfered with its intent and our need. Mr. McCulloch needs to stop attacking the Glasgow Colonial Society and the Kirk needs to stop trying to close down his Academy. I blame the Kirk for not sending ministers to where they are needed in the province, instead of to where there are plenty of ministers."

"I'm afraid I have a very dim view of the Kirk now, Mr. Forsyth, sad to say." Mr. Newcomb was standing at this point, waving his pointed finger in the direction of Scotland, William imagined.

Later, William heard that the Scottish Dissenters had formed a society to support McCulloch's Academy and the Presbyterian Church in Nova Scotia.

In the midst of these battles, the Townships needing ministers were left without ministers of the Kirk.

~

The Kirk and the Presbyterian Church in Nova Scotia might have been in the midst of a battle for the hearts and minds of the Presbyterians in the province, but such is life that there can be joy and happiness in the midst of contentious times.

In 1826 the Forsyths were invited to the home of John Elkanah Morton. He and Ann, his wife, had a lovely home in Upper Dyke Village and often invited friends and colleagues up from Halifax for the weekend, when they would throw a dinner party for them. John Elkanah Morton was Mary's first cousin, so the Forsyths were often invited...especially now that the Forsyth daughters were of marriageable age.

William always tried to make sure his daughters were well educated and able to dress and converse appropriately at these dinner parties and get-togethers. He hoped they would attract well-educated and industrious young men who would marry them. He often remarked to Mary that he would not be able to relax until his daughters were suitably married and his sons educated for a profession. Mary agreed wholeheartedly.

On that beautiful spring day, William and Mary, with six of their children and their nephew, Kerr Beckwith, set out along Middle Dyke Road towards Upper Dyke Village. Their four daughters were all dressed in their finery. The three boys were all neat and polished. The weather was warm and the dykeland fresh and green. They all chatted happily as they walked along. Ann, their hostess had arranged the seating just so. A servant poured wine and the conversation began.

William noticed that Jean, now twenty, was seated beside a nice young man who was introduced as Thomas Lydiard from Halifax. His father, Samuel, owned a brewery in Halifax and Thomas, the eldest son, worked for his father.

On the way home, Mary looked at Jean with a smile and said, "Who was that fine young man who attracted your attention all evening?"

"Oh, mother, he was just a boy from Halifax, Thomas was his name, I think."

No one was really surprised when Thomas came to call on William to ask him if he could court Jean.

"Mr. Forsyth, let me introduce myself and my family to you."

"Please do so," William said with an inner smile. He had already chatted with his wife's cousin about the young man.

"My name is Thomas Allister Lydiard. My grandparents, Thomas Lydiard and Sarah Worsley, came here from England in 1772. They settled in Sheet Harbour. My father, Samuel, came with them. He and his brother William went to Halifax and tried out several things before they became involved in the brewery business. I am the eldest son and will inherit the business."

"I hear," William said, "that in Halifax one half the population sells liquor and the other half drinks it."

"That's about right, Mr. Forsyth. That's why you can't go wrong with the brewery business. My uncle William died in 1811. I am looking forward to having a wife and children."

"But you have been married before?"

"Yes, my wife, Margaret, and I married in 1821. Margaret died giving birth to our son, who survived for only two weeks. They are both in the Old Burying Ground in Halifax."

"I am sorry to hear of your loss," William said, trying to imagine how he would feel.

"It has been the most painful thing in my life."

Thomas stared at his clasped hands on his knee, and they sat in silence for a time. Finally he gave a sigh and raised his head. "But I believe I am now ready to start again. Margaret would want that for me. May I have permission to court your daughter, Jean?"

"Of course, Mr. Lydiard, you may court Jean."

Jean, of course, had been listening at the door. She was so excited she ran to tell her sister Mary, who accompanied Jean back to the parlour emitting squeaks of joy.

The door now open, Jean and Mary entered the room. Mary overcame her happiness to play the role of hostess. She welcomed Thomas and asked what he would like to drink, and added, "Mother asks if you will stay for lunch."

"Most certainly," Thomas answered and Mary left to get them some cider and to let her mother know.

Thomas came up from Halifax quite often and wrote to Jean

every few days. After a time, he invited Jean to Halifax to meet his parents. William accompanied her, of course, and they spent a pleasant afternoon with the Lydiards.

After all the excitement about Jean and Thomas had died down, William realized that he needed to write to the Glasgow Colonial Society. He felt strongly that he must support the Society and try to encourage them to send a minister to Horton and to Digby. So he sat down and wrote to the Reverend Robert Burns.

> Having now spent thirty years in America, I must in some measure be acquainted with the difficulties which Ministers have to encounter. Congregations here have not the means of supporting Ministers as in Scotland if they trust to the subscriptions which may be put in their hands. Many poor people subscribe what they are never able to pay, hence the Minister is deceived if he trusts to them.
>
> But if they were sent out as Missionaries, they might, for some time, preach in several places as the ardour of the people would desire it, and in each place they might condition with the people to raise them a certain sum, for the time they might serve them. If they were acceptable preachers, they would kindle the emulation of the people in these societies who want to have them so that at length they might lay a sure foundation for their support for the remainder of their life.
>
> If I had known this when I came to America, I might have had a flourishing Church to my own satisfaction. From Vermont to Halifax, I might have been placed wherever I preached but I had to learn by sad experience. I sat down at length in Cornwallis, the most beautiful spot, but perhaps the most confounded, in all my travels, so that Lot's fate often penetrated me with sorrow.
>
> I pity the people of Horton for they had once a flourishing Church but not owing to themselves that Church was dispersed. One missionary to Horton and another to Digby might each of them I think found a foundation for a Church.

Word came in 1827 that Horton Township was to receive a minister. In fact, two ministers were coming—one to Dartmouth and the Reverend George Struthers to Horton Township. These were the first missionaries of the Glasgow Colonial Society not sent to Pictou County.

Deacon Elihu Woodworth and William travelled to Halifax by stage coach to meet Mr. Struthers in September, 1827. After a bit of a wait, two men in clerical garb appeared on the gangplank of the *Mercator*, with a woman beside them. William and Elihu met them as they stepped onto the dock.

"Welcome, gentlemen! Greetings!" William exclaimed.

"How was the voyage?" Elihu asked.

"Let us just say we are glad to be back on terra firma," the taller of the two said. "I am George Struthers and this is my friend and his wife, the Reverend James Morrison and Mrs. Morrison. Thank you for meeting us. What are the plans?"

"Mr. Woodworth and I will take you out to supper and then to your lodgings. Tomorrow we will introduce Reverend Morrison to the Reverend John Martin, the Kirk minister here in Halifax, and he will introduce you to the folks across the Harbour in Dartmouth, which is to be your parish. Then the following day, the Reverend Struthers will travel with us back to Horton Township, where he is to be settled."

Supper was a question-and-answer period as both new ministers peppered William and Elihu with their concerns. Elihu was so pleased that his congregation now had a minister that he willingly answered any and all questions.

William thought George seemed like a mature and sincere man, and invited him to stay at his home while the Horton folk figured out the arrangements for a manse. In the end, it was decided that George would stay with Elihu until further arrangements could be made.

Everyone knew that 'further arrangements' meant that George would be expected to find a wife and then move into the manse the congregation would supply.

But George was very frequently over to William's home for supper and to discuss Church business. William finally felt he was not alone as a minister of the Church of Scotland and he was happy to help George in any way he could.

William did notice that whenever George stayed for supper, his daughter Mary, now twenty-four, was very smartly dressed, with her hair tied up with ribbons. George apparently noticed as well.

Without any notice that Samuel Lydiard was unwell, William received a letter from Thomas saying that his father had died. William and Jean went to the funeral and, before they returned to Cornwallis Township, Thomas asked William if he and Jean could be married very soon as he had to take over the running of the brewery.

They settled on November 18, 1827 at St. Paul's Anglican Church in Halifax. William and Mary attended. Jean then moved into Thomas' home and William and Mary returned home.

With Will in medical school and Jean married, all was well in William's life. It was also exciting when Mary's cousin John Elkanah Morton was elected as the Member of the Legislative Assembly for Cornwallis Township.

The Reverend George Struthers was turning out to be a very sincere and dedicated man and the Horton folk were well pleased with their new minister. It was a great relief to William that he had some help and someone to talk to about Church affairs. Many an evening George and William spent together as George updated William on all the issues affecting the Church in Scotland. George also chatted about all William's fellow clergy back home. Since William knew all about Horton Township, he was able to inform George about the people and the issues so that George could get off to a good start.

Occasionally, William would see Mary, looking her prettiest, walking along the lane with George. It reminded him so much of his courtship of his pretty, vivacious wife in the early days. Mary, of course, would make an excellent minister's wife. She was well educated and devoted to the Church. She taught many of the little children in his grammar school. George would be very blessed to have such a wife.

Despite all the turmoil within the Presbyterian Church in Nova Scotia, life was good in Cornwallis Township. And 1828 would be yet another good year, for Will would be coming home from Scotland.

"We've got a lot to be thankful for, Mary."

Mary walked over to where William was sitting at the kitchen table and gave him a kiss on the cheek. William laughed at the unexpected response. He would have grabbed her hand, but both her hands were covered with wet feathers.

She skipped back to plucking the chicken. They both laughed.

9: Here we have no abiding city

In early 1828 George asked William for permission to court Mary. William thought to himself that George had already begun that process quite a while ago, but he happily agreed. George would be as excellent a son-in-law as he was a colleague in ministry.

"This is wonderful news, William," his wife said when he told her of the interview. "Our Mary will be such an excellent minister's wife. It's a match made in heaven."

"I couldn't agree more. Two daughters married well and a son just graduated from medical school. We are very lucky parents!"

Once the family announced the engagement, the Horton folk began the process of setting up a manse for their new minister and his wife.

Will would soon be coming home from Scotland as Dr. William Forsyth—the name had a wonderful ring to it. William's pride in his eldest son could not have been greater and the praise his son received from his professors once again confirmed William's ability to teach at the university preparatory level. The family and the whole Township awaited Will's return, for he was much loved by everyone that knew him.

Yes, 1828 would be a wonderful year.

In October, William took the new stage coach—up to this time the road had not been good enough for them, so this signalled great progress in the Province—to Halifax to meet Will as his ship arrived. The plan was to bring him home to a great celebration by the whole congregation. William entertained this dream all the way to Halifax—his son, his beloved eldest son, was a University of Glasgow trained doctor.

William had arranged with his wife's cousin, John Elkanah Morton, who had an apartment in Halifax, to stay with them until the next stage coach left for Horton Corner via Windsor in two days.

As soon as Will began to move down the gangplank, William could see something was wrong. Will didn't move with his usual energy and good-natured ease.

Running to meet him, William threw his arms around his son. After a long embrace, he held him by the shoulders and looked into his eyes. "Will, are you ill? Was it the sea voyage? Are you sea sick?"

"I am truly ill and have been for a while."

"Then let's take you to a doctor while we're here in Halifax. I'll get your cousin to arrange it."

"No, Father, I am a doctor." Will smiled wanly. "I know what is wrong and I have consulted the best doctors in Edinburgh. I have consumption."

Suddenly, all the joy and brightness of this long-awaited homecoming evaporated into thin air and a great pall descended. It covered everything with sadness and heavy darkness as it surrounded William and slowly invaded his heart and soul with despair.

"Nay, Will. Nay, my son!"

"I know, Father. I've tried to deny this verdict. I've begged and pleaded with the Lord that this not be true. But, of course, I know the signs and symptoms and it is hard to deny the truth for long. Can we go to Cousin John's now before I have no more energy left?"

"Of course, of course. The carriage is just over here. I'll send the driver back for your trunk."

They drove through the crowded streets of Halifax to John Elkanah Morton's Halifax home in silence. William's mouth was too dry to speak and Will seemed too tired to try.

As soon as they stepped in the door, the household's mood of celebration deflated into dejection and sad disbelief. The maid found both a nightgown and night socks for Will and William helped him to his room. After he was in bed, the maid brought him warm soup and bread. As soon as he had eaten he went to sleep.

William and the Mortons sat in the parlour in glum silence as they awaited their supper. Everyone knew that consumption was a death sentence. No one could believe that this bright and promising young man was going to die. Supper tasted like ashes.

The next day, Will stayed in bed while Cousin John arranged for a private carriage to take William and Will back to Cornwallis Township—and to even more dejection and sadness from his family and congregation.

After Will had been home for a few days, William and Mary sat at the foot of his bed and asked him to tell them about his illness—about consumption. That brought out the doctor in Will.

"Father, Mother, let me outline this disease for you. Its name since the time of Hippocrates has been phthisis. You would know what this term means, Father."

"Yes, Will, it means to waste away."

"Right. In *Book 1: Of Epidemics* that Hippocrates wrote over two thousand years ago, he describes phthisis as a 'weakness of the lungs with fever and cough. Most are affected by these diseases in the following manner: fevers accompanied with rigours…constant sweats, extremities very cold and warmed with difficulty, bowels disordered, sputa small and brought up rarely and with difficulty.' Hippocrates also noted the disease favoured young adults.'"

"Has there been no study of this disease since Hippocrates?" William asked incredulously.

"Oh, yes. Rene Laennec, a renowned French physician and medical researcher, studied this and other diseases of the chest such as bronchiectasis, pneumonia, pleurisy and emphysema. He developed a very useful tool, a stethoscope, which aids in hearing what is happening in the chest. Our professors asked each of us to purchase one for our medical bags as they are so useful. Before this stethoscope, we used to have to put our ear on the patient's bare chest—to the great embarrassment of the ladies."

"But this Laennec was not able to find a cure for phthisis?"

"He was not. He himself died of it in 1826. Part of the way he learned about consumption was to dissect the bodies of his patients after they died. In some European countries, like Italy, they believe that consumption is an infectious disease, and they won't dissect the bodies of those who died of consumption to protect themselves from the disease. But in England, Scotland and America, it is thought to be passed down through families. There are even areas of England and America that think it is caused by vampires, or that those who have the disease are themselves vampires!"

Mary interrupted the lecture. "Will, how can we best care for you? What will please you the best?"

"Mother, they say that fresh air, sunshine and good food are best."

Mary jumped up from the foot of the bed and exclaimed, "William, we have to take down these curtains and open the window immediately!"

William sprang to his feet. With one yank he pulled the curtains and rod to the floor. Mary scooped them up and moved them out of the room. Soon she was back to inquire what food Will liked the best.

"Soups and stews seem to help me keep warm and they don't upset my stomach. And beer or dark ale seems to suit me as well. And if I could have a warming pan for my feet I would be most comfortable."

The next day, after Will had had some rest, William asked him about the spread of this disease in Europe.

"It is a great epidemic sweeping through Europe. Millions are dying from it, many of them between the ages of fifteen to thirty-four."

"Does everyone so affected die?"

"Not one hundred per cent, but almost."

"And is there no cure?"

"No cure." Will lifted his hands in a gesture of helplessness. "We do not know if phthisis is infectious or hereditary or a cancer. So, not knowing the cause, we cannot come upon a cure."

"What do you think, Will? What is the cause?"

"I think it is infectious, but how it is spread I do not know. Having said this, I worry about my family but I have nowhere else to turn."

"My son, we could not bear to think of you so far from home, where we could not care for you. Get some rest and your mother will be up soon with some hot food."

Will's brothers and sisters came to visit him often. They did not talk about his illness, but about all their favourite things and all the happy times they had together as children. They brought him anything he asked for. The girls helped their mother with laundry and meals and the boys entertained Will with stories about their friends and the general happenings in the Township.

Very soon, Jean came up from Halifax. William and Mary told her what they could about how Will was doing, and then William led the way up the stairs to Will's room with Jean right behind him.

"Sister," Will said happily, "I am glad to see you."

"Will, I've heard the bad news and I had to come to see you. Father and mother say you are eating and sleeping well. You look very pale but much better than I thought you would."

She looked at him fondly, then suddenly glanced around the room. "Where are the curtains? Why is it so cold?"

"Sunlight and fresh air are advised," Will said. "Mother's quilts and a warming pan are keeping me quite warm. Do not fret. Tell me how you are doing? How is Mr. Lydiard?"

Jean sat down on the only chair in the room. She was just as beautiful as Will remembered her—pale skin, blue eyes and black hair. She was wearing a navy blue dress with lace cuffs and collar.

"Mr. Lydiard—Thomas—is quite well. His father died the year we were married and, as the eldest son, he is running the brewery. And, Will, good news! I will have my first baby in February. It will be our parent's first grandchild and you will be an uncle for the first time!"

"I greatly look forward to that," Will smiled.

Seeing Will's smile, just for a moment, Jean had a glimpse of the 'old' Will of her childhood—the Will full of energy and good-humour.

"Will, I am going to give you a hug."

"I'm not sure about that, Jean. I don't know if I'm infectious."

But before he had stopped speaking, Jean had hopped up on the side of the bed. She threw her arms around him and kissed his forehead before hopping off and running out of the room with a cheery, "Get some rest, Will!"

In the kitchen Jean found her sisters, Mary, Elizabeth Ann, and Margaret, and their parents. "He looks better than I thought, Mother! What do you all think? How does he seem to you?"

Elizabeth Ann said, "He is terribly weak—"

Margaret cut her off. "but we have hope. And we pray, of course. All the time."

"Sometimes, you know," sister Mary said, "I see glimpses of him the way he was before he went off to school. How he would tease us in those days!"

They avoided looking at their father and seeing the pain and sorrow etched on his face.

"How can I help while I am here?" Jean said.

"We are constantly making soups and stews," their mother said. "Oh, and doing his laundry. He frequently has bouts of 'the sweats', and then we must change his shirt and the bedding for dry things."

"Is he in bed all day long?"

"He has come down stairs several times," Margaret said, "and he wants to go out to the barn and walk down the lane, but it has been too cold to risk doing that."

"I will take him for walks, just short ones at first, as soon as he is able," Elizabeth Ann said. "Day or night, I am ready."

"Mostly," sister Mary said, "he sleeps, and sometimes he reads his Bible or one of his medical books. Father and John Elkanah put the trunk of books and medical things up in the attic. He told John Elkanah what to do to keep himself safe from getting consumption and other diseases."

"Now," her mother said, "Jean, my dear, how are you feeling? How is the first pregnancy?"

"I feel very well, Mother. We have a midwife lined up for February. Thomas is so excited about having children and being a father. The brewing business is going well. Thomas and his mother and many of his brothers and sisters work in the business. I have been helping out as well, but soon will have to stop until after the baby is born. Oh, and by the way, we will arrange for Will to have a supply of beer on a regular basis. We'll send it up on the stagecoach each week."

"We will all taste it for him," Margaret said, "to make sure it is good."

It was the first round of laughter the kitchen had heard in a long time.

~

On February 18, 1829, Jean delivered a healthy little girl, Margaret. When news reached her parents, there was subdued joy in the household.

"We are grandparents, my dear," William said quietly, with a smile at Mary.

Will's smile was ear-to-ear when he heard he was an uncle for the first time. Jean said in her letter that she would be up in the spring when the weather was a little better.

On March 23, Elizabeth Ann brought breakfast up to Will's room. Her cheery "Good-morning, Will!" was met with silence. Will had died during the night.

William sent Bezaleel for the doctor in Kentville, who, upon his arrival, confirmed the terrible reality. William, Mary and the girls were inconsolable.

Some neighbours came in to wash Will's body and wrap it in a clean sheet. The men then carried the body downstairs to the parlour and placed it in a wooden coffin that one of the men had brought over when he heard the news.

William and the family took turns sitting with Will's body until the next day, when an ox cart took the body to the church. Neighbours came and went bringing food, milking cows, feeding the animals, and sitting with the family for a time. Every family had been through many deaths of loved ones and everyone knew just what to do without having to be told.

The Reverend George Struthers led the funeral service and the sad procession across the road to the Chipman's Corner Cemetery

—a route William knew so well, having performed close to five hundred funerals in the time he had been in Cornwallis Township. He had thought that he knew how those mourners were feeling. Now he knew for certain he was wrong. He felt as though a cannon ball had gone right through his heart.

How does one continue when the pain is so great? he wondered. Although he hoped his behaviour was 'normal', inside he felt completely hollow and empty.

The rest of the family seemed to be sleep-walking. They made meals, did dishes and accepted the sympathy of all who came to give them condolences, but it was as if a gauze curtain hung between them and their visitors.

Finally, William found an outlet for his sorrow. He walked through the dry brown grass and patches of snow and the chill wind to Blackie's resting place. He told her what had happened to Will. Blackie had loved Will. She would want to know. She would understand.

Mary wished she had such an outlet for her grief, but hard work was the only activity that gave her any relief and so she just kept baking and cleaning and making quilts. The girls also kept busy all spring, preparing to plant their kitchen garden, milking the cows, making butter and cheese.

But after sunset, in the flicker of the candle light, there was no escape from the pain except for sleep at last.

One day, after evening prayers, William announced that he would take some money from the education fund to buy a gravestone for Will. "I will apply to the House of Assembly for a grant of £75 to start another grammar school so I can replace the funds."

The family all nodded in agreement. And so William had a very plain stone engraved and installed.

The family all went to the cemetery to see the stone after church the following Sunday. They stood in a solemn semicircle to admire its Latin inscription.

"Father," Bezaleel said after a time, "will you translate it for me? I can understand most but not all the words."

"Yes, my son," said William slowly. "Here is what it says:

> Sacred
> To the memory of
> That mortal
> William Forsyth
> Medical expert.
> The situation is:
> He with the highest grades
> Praised by his professors
> Worthy and beloved by everyone
> Devoted to his Saviour
> Died in
> His twenty-fifth year
> In the year of Our Lord 1829
> From this, what the reader finds suitable
> He should do.

"But *what* should we do, Father?" Bezaleel asked sorrowfully.

"Remember in all you do, my son, that here on this earth we have no abiding city. So choose your path carefully—choose the path that leads to the eternal city."

As they left the Cemetery, Elizabeth Ann pointed out the words on another gravestone:

> Stranger
> Pause as you pass by
> As you are now so
> Once was I.
> As I am now
> So you will be.
> Stranger
> Pause and think on me.

"Indeed," William said.

They walked up the road towards Salem Cottage in silence, each engrossed in his or her own thoughts. They spent the rest of the Sabbath day reading or writing letters to family and friends until the sun set and blessed sleep was possible.

It had not occurred to William that he had not heard from General Whitelaw of Vermont for some time, so when a letter appeared in the mail with a Vermont return address on it, he ripped it open eagerly. He learned, to his great dismay, that General Whitelaw had died. He tried to remember the last time he had written to his friend but realized it had been months ago.

William was distressed that he had not known about General Whitelaw's failing health. If he had, he would have written to express his great appreciation of General Whitelaw's friendship over all the years since they first met in Ryegate in 1798. He immediately wrote to General Whitelaw's family, letting them know how sad he was to lose his great, good friend.

~

One bright spot in all this dark sorrow was the courtship of the Reverend George Struthers and William's daughter, Mary. Mary would make a perfect wife for a minister. She was not beautiful like Jean, but she was well-educated, a good teacher, a wonderful housekeeper and very devoted to the Lord's service. George was old enough—at forty-seven years—and educated enough to see Mary's true spirit and her value to his ministry. It was 'a match made in heaven,' people said.

No one was surprised when George met with William to ask his blessing before he asked Mary to marry him. William smiled his approval. He was really happy for them.

The wedding was set for January 28, 1830. By luck, the Reverend John Martin of Halifax was going to be in Cornwallis Township around that time, and he agreed to marry George and Mary. In Horton Township, the congregation had found a manse for their minister and his new wife. Things were indeed looking up for a township that had gone without a full time minister for twenty-two years.

The whole Forsyth family helped prepare the manse for the newlyweds. As all young women did, Mary had prepared for her hoped-for future marriage by making potholders, tea towels, bath towels, nightshirts, sheets and pillowcases and all other necessary spun and woven materials. Relatives, friends and congregants supplied necessities as wooden spoons, a set of dishes and pewter ware—everything a new bride would need to set up her own household. The Horton folk provided a butter churn, a new broom, candles and candle holders. As well, they stocked the cellar with vegetables, salted beef and pork, smoked bacon and some barrels of cider. Donated furniture outfitted the manse, and would have to do for now. There was a new mattress and goose down coverlet, though.

When Mary's parents and siblings visited her a few weeks after the wedding, they found the whole house well-organized and cozy. She served them tea and cake. It felt so good to see Mary happy and content, they all agreed on the way home.

In September that year, John Elkanah left for Scotland. He would not be going to Glasgow University as the painful loss of his brother was still fresh in his mind. Instead, he would attend the University of Edinburgh. It was difficult for the whole family to see him go, knowing that nothing could really keep him safe from consumption. Still, John Elkanah very much wanted to become a doctor and so everyone put on a 'brave face' and wished him well.

"Don't forget to write." were his father's last words as he moved up the gangplank.

In November 1830, there was more good news from the Struthers family—Mary was pregnant with her first child. Although Will was never far from their thoughts, William and Mary could still rejoice over the happy news of their second grandchild on the way.

Jean and Thomas came up from Halifax for a few days at Christmas and brought little Margaret, whose first birthday would be in February. George and Mary came over after the Christmas Day service. Elizabeth Ann and Margaret had baked for days to be ready for the gathering.

William and Bezaleel had hung some spruce boughs over the

door frames and along the banister so the whole house smelled fresh and green. There was a letter from John Elkanah wishing everyone a Merry Christmas and saying how well his studies were going. All was happy and bright. They toasted not only the New Year, but the expectation of their second grandchild as well.

~

On January 18, 1831, William got up early because of the cold and went downstairs to make the fire in the parlour and dining room fireplaces. Mary would have already added firewood to the hot coals in the kitchen fireplace.

As he knelt to start the fire, he realized he wasn't hearing any noise from the kitchen, so he decided to check on Mary. As he opened the kitchen door, he could see her lying on the floor in front of the fireplace.

For a split second he paused, trying to make sense of the scene. She wasn't moving so he lifted her up and carried her the few steps to the daybed, then ran to the foot of the stairs and called Bezaleel. "Take Star and go get Dr. Webster. Your mother has fainted."

In his heart he knew she was dead, but he didn't want to know. He returned to the kitchen, put several logs on the hot embers and went back to sit by Mary and hold her hand.

Just before the girls came running into the kitchen in their night clothes, he looked up and saw through his tears a young woman in an apple-blossom-pink dress with white and green ribbons tying up her brown curls. She smiled at William and was gone.

William wanted to call her back but the words would not come out of his mouth, as his mouth was completely dry. "Good-bye, Mary," he whispered hoarsely.

The doctor confirmed the sad fact that Mary Morton Beckwith Forsyth had passed away suddenly, due to unknown causes. Some said she died of a broken heart because she and Will were so close as mother and son.

Once again a wake and funeral, once again William took money from the education fund to pay for Mary's grave stone, once again the emptiness—and, for the first time in thirty years, no Mary in his bed so that even rest and sleep were no solace.

William wrote to John Elkanah to tell him about his mother and also that he was short of funds for his tuition as well as for room and board. He told his son not to worry as he was starting another grammar school immediately.

On January 26, 1831 William posted an advertisement in the Nova Scotia *Gazette*:

> William Forsyth, minister in Cornwallis proposes, God willing, to commence his grammar school anew, the first day of February, proposes genteel Board to any gentlemen's children that may be committed to his care for tuition at twenty-six pounds per annum including Bed, Board, Washing and one pound per quarter for tuition and as he naturally expects this will be his last class he will teach, he intends to leave them as a memorial of his art of teaching as far as their capacities will admit. Scholars without boarding he will receive at twenty shilling per quarter and if any poor man has a child of distinguished talents, he will teach him gratis.

The Grammar School was soon up and running and William was kept busy, which he was thankful for. With a house full of students, Elizabeth Ann and Margaret were also very busy.

~

Mary's due date was August 4 and, right on time, she went into labour. After twelve hours she delivered a healthy baby girl—Mary Stewart Struthers.

William heard what happened next when he arrived a few hours later. As the midwife was waiting for the afterbirth to be delivered, she noticed a strange trickle of blood from the birth canal. As she examined Mary, the trickle increased in volume and the midwife began to knead Mary's stomach to get the womb to contract and stop bleeding, but all to no avail.

Mary knew something was wrong from the look on the midwife's face. "What is happening?" she asked anxiously.

Soon she was too concerned to hold the baby and she passed her back to the midwife's assistant.

The midwife met Mary's gaze. "I cannot stop the bleeding, Mrs. Struthers."

"But my baby," Mary said in a shocked voice.

The hemorrhage continued unabated and soon Mary was unconscious. She died a few hours later. The midwife and her assistant looked at each other in horror.

The baby began to cry.

Just then they heard George return home.

"Has the baby come?" he called up the stairs.

"Wait, sir. Wait as you are, please," the midwife called back.

The two women quickly covered Mary's body with a clean sheet. Then the midwife carried the baby down to her father.

George's smile of happiness disappeared as she told him the terrible news. He stared at the child for a second, then pushed past the midwife and ran up the stairs.

Mary looked calm and peaceful but as white as the sheet that she was wrapped in. George bent over and kissed her, then searched for a chair, looking as if he might faint.

"Leave me," he said to the midwife, who had followed him back into the room.

"Shall we take the baby to her family, Mr. Struthers?"

"Please do. Now leave me," he had said.

When William had absorbed this news, he spoke quietly to George. "I have made arrangements to bring Mary back home. I will do the funeral tomorrow. The baby is with Elizabeth Ann. Come back with me now, George. There is nothing more you can do here."

As in a dream, George followed William out to the barn. Deacon Elihu Woodworth had saddled his horse and led it out so George could mount it. All was done in silence.

William said to Elihu, "Thank you, Deacon."

Elihu could only nod.

They packed ice around the coffin for the journey to the church on a hot August day, and the funeral took place early the next morning. Another wake; another funeral; another walk to the cemetery; another time of deep mourning.

George moved in with the Forsyths for a time to be with his wife's family and his baby daughter. Elizabeth Ann and Margaret were learning to be mothers. They had hired a wet-nurse for the baby and she was staying in the house.

Everyone noticed that George took no interest in the baby and they were soon to find out why. A month after Mary's death, George announced that he was leaving Horton Township and travelling to Demerara in South America as a missionary.

"I have told Deacon Woodworth of my plans and I will leave within the month."

"But your daughter?" William said.

"I have asked Elizabeth Ann to take care of her. I will send back money for her care.

"But why not stay here? You can live with us and Elizabeth Ann can take care of Mary Stewart."

"I cannot stay. The pain is too great. I must leave."

"I have considered you as a son, George, and entrusted my beloved daughter to your care. She would not want you to leave this child bereft of both parents. Please reconsider."

"I will go to Demerara. I will not be persuaded otherwise!"

He did not see his daughter before he left.

With his wife, his eldest son, and eldest daughter gone, George in Demerara, a new baby in the house and the grammar school in full swing, life settled down to as normal a routine as could be expected under the circumstances. William was soon able to replace the money in the education fund. He wrote to John Elkanah to tell him about the death of his sister, and not to worry but to focus on his education.

In the midst of it all, they received news that Jean had given birth to a son, Samuel William Lydiard, on October 27. Within a few weeks, Jean and Thomas arrived by stage coach with little

Margaret and the new baby.

Everyone took turns holding the baby and making a fuss over him. But when they asked Margaret how she felt about her new baby brother, she frowned and they all realized that Margaret needed more attention, which they soon provided. Elizabeth Ann made her a little doll out of the left-overs from a quilt. Margaret Elliot baked her some cakes.

Soon little Margaret was all smiles—her happiness was in stark contrast to the mood of the rest of the family.

1831 finally ended and no one was sad about that.

~

In January, 1832, another event which should have been a happy experience for the family turned into one of great sorrow. Jean gave birth to her third child, little Jean Lydiard—a sister to Margaret and Samuel William. But a few months before she was due, Jean received a diagnosis of consumption.

The delivery went well and they named little Jean after her mother. The Anglican minister came to the home to baptize the baby and to pray with the family for Jean to overcome this terrible disease. One of Thomas' sisters, and his mother, cared for Jean and the baby.

Jean continued to be affected by the ravages of the disease. William went to visit Jean and the baby on several occasions and learned that the baby was not thriving. The doctors did not know why.

William sensed the news was coming but that didn't make it any less of a shock. On April 23 his beloved Jean died—taken away by that hateful epidemic.

William went to Halifax for the funeral at St. Paul's Church on the Grand Parade. The burial was in the Old Burying Ground nearby.

William arrived home the next day, exhausted in body, mind and spirit. Elizabeth Ann and Margaret had supper ready for him. Bezaleel had split the wood for the fireplaces and hauled water for the barn and the house.

"Have you noticed that Margaret Elliot has been acting a bit strange lately?" William inquired of his other children when she was out of the room.

"Aye, Father, for some time now," Elizabeth Ann said.

"Why didn't you say so? Does she not help with the chores?"

"Most of the time, Father, but we have to double-check to make sure they are done well."

"Well," William said after a thoughtful pause, "I dare say we are all behaving a little strangely, considering what has happened to our family lately."

The others nodded in sympathy with his assessment.

"I will have Dr. Webster take a look at her just to be sure," he said.

The family then waited for another 'shoe to drop'. It did on May 20, when little Jean Lydiard, who had struggled so hard to survive after her mother's death, followed her mother to the grave. Thomas now had two wives and two children buried in the Old Burying Ground, and Margaret and Samuel William to raise on his own.

"What will you do now?" William asked his son-in-law.

"Just keep working at the brewery, Mr. Forsyth. I have to support my mother and brothers and sisters, as well as raise my own children. My beautiful Jean is gone and once again I am on my own in life."

"I hope we will keep in touch, Thomas, so that I can see my grandchildren. I will drop in to see you any time I am in Halifax, and you are always welcome in my home. May God bless you. You were a very good husband to my beloved Jean and saw that she had good care right to the end. For that, I am truly grateful."

The two grieving men took leave of each other, still joined together by great sorrow.

~

That summer, the summer of 1832, William had his first 'spell'.

He had arrived at the Church that Sunday feeling a little strange but decided to go ahead with the service anyhow. In the midst of the sermon, while he was standing in the high pulpit, the congregation watched while their minister stopped speaking and just... stood there. They thought he might be going to fall.

Two elders rushed to his aid and helped him to his seat. Dr. Webster ran to the front of the church to see if he could help.

While Dr. Webster examined him, the whole congregation watched in silence.

After a short while, William became alert and asked Dr. Webster what was happening.

"You had a brief 'spell', Reverend, while you were preaching. How do you feel now?"

"My dear sir, I feel quite myself now. I will continue."

And he did—completing the sermon from the very point he had left off.

The benefit from having this 'spell' in public was all the concern and care the congregation expressed. For the first time, William came to understand that the Cornwallis people really did love him and were concerned for his well-being.

Soon after, William learned from Deacon Elihu Woodworth that the leaders of the Cornwallis and Horton Townships had formed a committee.

"What is the purpose of the committee?"

"Its first concern is how to support you better. This recent tragedy in your family has taken a toll on you, and we want to relieve your stress as much as we can."

William bowed his head. He could not deny the burdens on his spirit.

"You have been with us thirty-two years now and have tried to look after two congregations as well as teach at your grammar school and continue your missionary visits. It is too much."

"It is what I felt called to do."

"No one is called to do it all. We dearly wish your son-in-law had been able to continue serving at Horton," the deacon said.

"Mr. Struthers could not be prevailed upon."

"And that brings us to the present situation."

William looked hard at his friend. "And what has the committee determined?"

"It was a long discussion, and a hard one, but in the end we agreed to approach Mr. Sommerville."

"The Reverend William Sommerville had been visiting the region. He was recently from Northern Ireland and, if the rumours were true, was a Covenanter—a very strict sect of Presbyterianism.

"Ah," William said.

"We want no other minister," Elihu said, "but we are concerned for your health."

"So am I," William said with a wry smile. "And, beyond that, for the security of my family. John Elkanah will be at university until 1833. Elizabeth Ann is tasked with the care of Mary Stewart Struthers. Margaret Elliot is taking care of many of the household responsibilities and Bezaleel, only fourteen and needing an education, is caring for the animals, splitting wood, and doing much more. And I have sent my nephew James to university as well."

"We know this well. And our committee will do all we can to address your distress."

"My dear friend," William said, "thank you for your kind concern. Of course, I see I need some support. Please assure the Committee that I am quite willing to work in harmony with the Reverend Mr. Sommerville or any other pious Presbyterian minister who holds to the central doctrine of the faith and practice of the Church of Scotland."

Mr. Sommerville arrived in Cornwallis-Horton Townships to preach for a call. It was a communion Sunday and the Cornwallis Congregation had prepared the sacrament.

Mr. Sommerville gave a fiery sermon, outside the realm of careful and respectful argumentation that the congregation had learned to expect from Mr. Forsyth. Some eyebrows went up, some eyes narrowed, and some hands clutched the backs of the pews in front of them as if the congregants were facing a stiff wind.

Then, as William and the Elders moved to begin the communion service, Mr. Sommerville said, "I must say one more thing."

Everyone froze in their place.

"My conscience will not permit me to take part in a sacrament with a congregation that does not subscribe to the doctrines of the Covenanter Oath."

The Elders looked at each other, then back to Mr. Sommerville. Finally, Deacon Elihu said, "Sir, you knew our situation before you agreed to be here this day."

"If you have not yet subscribed, then you have work to do before we can break bread together," Mr. Sommerville said.

"Let me be clear, sir," Deacon Elihu said, as William and the elders of both congregations listened. "We do expect you to commune with us today."

"My dear sir, that can never happen."

"Mr. Forsyth, Elders, please begin the communion service. The congregation is waiting."

Mr. Sommerville took a seat next to Mr. Beckwith near the front of the church. As the congregation watched he received the communion plate and passed it on to Mr. Beckwith without taking any bread.

"But, Mr. Sommerville, you are to take communion with us." Mr. Beckwith said with confusion in his voice.

"Indeed, sir, I will take neither the bread nor the cup until everyone has taken the Covenanters Oath and tossed out this abomination called *Watt's Hymns*!" His voice carried to the walls of the building, so that no one was at a loss as to his meaning.

The Elders quickly put their heads together in a whispered consultation, but there was nothing to be done.

After the communion service, the Elders met with William.

"Brethren, I cannot work with Mr. Sommerville," William said. "He is quite determined to turn us all into Covenanters. This seems to be the case of the tail wagging the dog. He is invited here to preach for a call and instead he demands that we conform to his… his sect."

Elihu fumed, "I am quite aware that our Mr. Sommerville's sentiments are not in keeping with the central doctrine of faith and practice of the Church of Scotland, nor are they in keeping with the theology of Congregational churches."

Perhaps if we speak to him sternly he will relent," Dr. Webster suggested.

"Do you really think someone so bold will become amenable to our traditions and customs?" Mr. Newcomb asked through his teeth.

Back in Horton Township, Elihu attended the service Mr. Sommerville presided at the Presbyterian Meeting House on Kirk Hill near Grand-Pré. After the service, and Mr. Sommerville's departure, he met with the congregation to let them know what had transpired in Cornwallis Township.

After serious deliberation, in 1833 the Horton Township congregation issued a call to the Reverend Mr. Sommerville, and he accepted. Shortly after his installation, he preached in a most vehement way against *Watt's Hymns* as used in Congregational churches.

As Elihu reported to William on his next visit, Mr. Sommerville insisted that the only singing be from the Psalms of David in a patriarchal—Presbyterian—version, as he said the works of Isaac Watts were uninspired.

"My dear people," Elihu quoted him as saying, "it causes me pain to know that you are suffering from a most serious form of delusion if you hold that this hymnbook of yours, this *Watt's Hymns*, is pleasing to God and worthy of his worship. Nay, such a book deserves to be burned along with the most heretical writings of olden times. But, here is the good news, we are able to procure for ourselves a book most pleasing to God and worthy of his worship, the Scottish Psalter. I will be speaking to you about this matter in the days to come so that we might restore the purity of your worship."

"'Purity of worship' is not what he may think it is," William said as mildly as he could.

"There is more," Elihu said. "Our wilderness prophet has decided to publish a book."

"That is a bad thing?" William asked.

"In this case, it is. He has addressed it to 'the Presbyterians of Horton', to 'promote your spiritual well-being and the purity of worship in your public meetings.'"

"In a book he published for all to read? Not in a letter or an address to the congregation directly?"

"Aye. It seems very high of the young man to call our services impure."

"How is the congregation?"

"They are very dismayed. He has utterly trampled our *Watts Hymns*, Mr. Forsyth," Elihu said, "and he has no appreciation for our history as Congregationalists. But even so, the people seem to be unable to stand up to him. He is a most forceful and determined young man. The fact that it has taken them twenty-two years to get their own minister seems to override what he had done to us in just a few weeks."

Elihu and William were old friends and shared their thoughts freely. William thought about it carefully, not wanting to interfere in the relationship between the Horton Congregationalists and their Presbyterian Covenanter minister.

Finally, he said, "My dear friend, I can understand why your people are loath to disappoint Mr. Sommerville. But you have made a bad deal with this young man, who holds himself so high and the traditions of your people so low. I do not think that time or experience will change his ideas or behaviours in the least, as he appears to be most inflexible and does not even recognize this in himself. I believe you must take him as he is, or let him go if you are not able to reconcile yourselves to his ideas."

Elihu nodded. "I am sorry to say that your words fit my own judgment of the situation."

They sat in silence for a while, then Deacon Elihu attempted to change the subject. "And how are you and your family doing, Mr. Forsyth?"

"As well as can be expected. The baby is thriving with Elizabeth Ann's care. She is an excellent mother. With some help from the Beckwith family, I have been able to pay for Kerr's education to date. I have some concerns about Margaret, but most of the time she seems to be herself, and we can find no cause for her sometimes strange behaviours. Perhaps we have rather gotten used to them. John Elkanah will be back this fall and he will be a great help. Bezaleel seems to have taken over as 'the man of the house'."

William gazed fondly at his old friend. "And what about you, Mr. Woodward? How is your family? Quite a few to keep track of with four sons and five daughters."

"Well, as you know, one of our sons entered into a marriage that my wife and I disapproved of. But, despite our reservations, he seems to be happy and doing well. Perhaps that is all we should dwell on."

"Indeed," said William. And the two friends sipped their tea in silence for a while.

In 1833 William and Bezaleel went to Halifax to meet the ship from Scotland carrying his second son, now *Dr*. John Elkanah Forsyth, back to them. Despite his best efforts, William kept having flashbacks to Will's disastrous return. He both desired and dreaded the appearance of John Elkanah on the gangplank.

Bezaleel made a path through the crowd gathered to meet the ship so William could watch as the gangplank was lowered to the dock. Soon they saw a hale and hearty John Elkanah striding down towards them and they began to wave and move forward to meet him.

William had to work hard to stifle his tears, as he gave his second son a big hug and then held him at arm's length to examine him. There were not many words exchanged but lots of smiles and pats on the back.

When they reached the carriage, John Elkanah helped his father to his seat while Bezaleel ran back to get John's trunk. A porter brought it on a cart and loaded it on the back of the carriage. Then they set off to the Mortons' Halifax residence to let John Elkanah's cousins greet him with applause and warm wishes. It was in stark contrast to Will's arrival four years before.

One particular admirer was John Morton's daughter, Martha Ann. She smiled sweetly at John Elkanah as she handed him a glass of sherry. "What a wonderful accomplishment, Dr. Forsyth. You are to be greatly commended on your achievement."

John Elkanah glowed in this praise and the others looked on and laughed. A family guest asked innocently, "Aren't John and Martha Ann second cousins?"

"Indeed they are," John Morton replied with a sharp look.

Nobody dared pursue the matter.

The next day, the three men paid a visit to Thomas Lydiard so they could see for themselves how he was doing and visit with William's grandchildren. They found that Thomas was as busy as ever and that the children were thriving. William hoped that Thomas would stop working so hard and take some time to find a new wife —he was still a young man and needed the love and support of a good woman.

After this they went to the Old Burying Ground on Barrington Street in Halifax to visit the graves of Jean and little Jean. On the way back home, no one said much for a while.

Back in Cornwallis Township, John Elkanah received the grand welcome that he deserved. But for many, it brought back all the memories of Will's sombre homecoming a few years earlier.

~

William had not yet told John of his problem with the 'spells', for these had continued to happen from time to time. He was trying to decide if he could continue his missionary trips down the Annapolis Valley to Digby. Perhaps John Elkanah would go with him so he could have one last visit with his much-loved friends there.

As soon as all the celebrations were over, he told his son of his plight. John promised to write to his professors back in Scotland to ask for an opinion.

"But, Father," he said, "you cannot risk another trip down the Valley. Write to your friends and let them know your circumstances. Perhaps, Mr. Sommerville will go down this year."

William looked at his son with a wry smile at the mention of Mr. Sommerville's name. But later that day, put pen to paper.

My dear friends

It causes me much distress to tell you that I cannot visit you this fall. My health has become quite precarious and my son, now a doctor, advises me against this travel. To be able to see you all one last time and commune together would be my dearest desire, so I will pray that my health be restored. But it may be that we shall only meet again in the eternal realm, and what a joy that shall be.

As swiftly as possible, I will try to arrange for another minister to provide you with an annual visit.

My love and blessings to all.

John Elkanah took the letter to the Kentville post office, leaving William feeling rather forlorn.

The following Sunday, after the service, they all went across the road to the Chipman's Corner Cemetery to visit the graves of John Elkanah's mother, brother and sister.

"It seems so strange to have gone away for a few years and to return and realize that half your family has died," John Elkanah said.

"At least you were in Scotland and didn't have to live through it," Bezaleel said with some anger in his voice.

"Aye," John Elkanah said with sadness for his brother, indeed, for the remainder of his family. "I felt quite helpless and without support so far away from home, and you felt quite helpless and had to see everything first hand."

Bezaleel was taken aback. "Sorry, brother. I am sure it was very difficult for you as well. I am just angry because I loved them all and now we'll never see them again.'"

"I know," said John Elkanah, "I feel the same way."

William didn't speak. He felt quite angry as well, but felt he could not express it in front of the children.

"How could George run off to Demerara and leave everyone in the lurch, including his little daughter?" John Elkanah asked angrily.

"My sons, some days I think I understand and some days I don't. I do believe he loved Mary very much and perhaps he blamed the baby for her death. Grief is not a logical process and we all grieve in our own way and time—this much I have learned in the last five years. He may have regretted his precipitous decision by now. He sends some money for his daughter from time to time, and sometimes asks about her welfare."

They walked back to Salem Cottage together in silence.

Before Christmas, as soon as Martha Ann's family returned from Halifax, Dr. John Elkanah paid a visit with an eye to seeing the pretty young lady who had been so appreciative of his achievements. As he related to his father later, before he could see Martha Ann, her father made his position clear, in a relaxed meeting before the fireplace as they sipped sherry.

"My daughter is only sixteen and in the midst of her education. She cannot be courted until she is eighteen. If you must marry right away, then choose another, Dr. Forsyth."

Seeing John Elkanah's stricken look, he added, "You know you are always welcome here as a member of the family, so establish your practice and we will see how the next few years unfold."

And that is what Dr. John Elkanah Forsyth did, although it was not easy as there were other doctors in the area. He continued to build his relationship with Martha Ann at each and every family get-together.

At the end of 1834, William had finished his last grammar school. At the request of the Horton folk, he still preached there every sixth week and Mr. Sommerville occasionally preached in Cornwallis Township. William's 'spells' continued but he was always able to return to his ministerial work after some rest and sleep.

~

In early 1835 the Elders met to consider their circumstances and decided to write to the Reverend George Struthers in Demerara and ask him to return as Assistant Minister in Cornwallis Township. Dr. Isaac Webster wrote the letter. Surely, they all thought, he will want to return to see his child.

On January 15th Deacon Elihu Woodworth visited William.

"There's your favourite chair, and I think the tea is almost ready," William said as they got settled in the parlour. "Aye, there it comes now. Thank you Margaret, my dear."

"How are you feeling, my friend?" Elihu asked.

"My spells are, of course, of great concern to those who try to care for me. Happily, I don't remember a thing, but I do have to watch the worry in the eyes of my family."

"I can see that your family must be very concerned about you."

"Well, since there's nothing I can do about my situation, let's talk about anything else. How's Mr. Sommerville doing? Still trying to change you into good Scottish Presbyterians?"

"I'm afraid he has other concerns to worry about. We're having trouble paying his salary."

"Well, I know something about that situation, having never yet got my own promised salary." William said.

"I wasn't aware how bad the situation was until he 'begged for alms' during the Sunday service."

"I never had to do that, but I did think about it a few times," William said.

"I must say it's rather embarrassing for the congregation."

"What will they do?" William asked.

"I've called a meeting so we can consider our options."

They sipped their tea and nibbled the oatcakes Margaret had baked before turning the conversation to Elihu's family concerns.

~

In May 1835, due to William's declining health, the Cornwallis people contracted with Mr. Sommerville to preach one-quarter time. He agreed on condition that they use the Scottish psalter. Mr. Sommerville had now separated another Congregational church from its roots.

The benefit to William was that he had time to rest and relax for the first time in thirty-five years. He enjoyed the time with his family and especially his little granddaughter, Margaret Stewart

Struthers, now four years old. She so reminded him of his beloved daughter, Mary, at that age. His son-in-law, Thomas Lydiard often brought his two grandchildren, Margaret and Samuel William up for a visit. They looked happy and healthy.

One reason Thomas came to Cornwallis Township more often was his interest in Luanne Webster, Dr. Isaac Webster's daughter. Everyone was happy for them.

On May 5, the Church of Scotland, Halifax Presbytery, met at Horton. The Reverend Mr. Alexander Clark, a Covenanter from Northern Ireland, preached the sermon. William attended. He noticed the rather shocked responses of his fellow ministers when they first encountered him, followed by whispered conversations with glances in his direction.

Up to that point, he hadn't considered whether his appearance had changed. It rather rattled him.

On July 18 Elihu went to Cornwallis and dined at William's along with the Reverend Mr. Martin of Halifax. The next day, the Reverend Mr. Martin preached. This was an annual visit on behalf of the Church of Scotland Presbytery.

On August 10th William rode over to Elihu's house. The Reverend George Struthers was due to arrive in Halifax on August 12th, so the next day William and Elihu went to Halifax in Elihu's horse and cart. They returned the following day with George and all his belongings.

George had been gone for four years and William wondered how he had fared in Demerara—the answer was clear as they chatted—George was older and a little greyer but none the worse for wear.

"It felt a little strange," George said, "to stand on that dock again —the same dock where I had arrived in Halifax in 1827 along with James Morrison and his wife. How is James, or do you know?"

"As you'll remember, James was given a large parish. They built a new church in Dartmouth that held four to five hundred people. But in 1829 he took charge of the Royal Acadian School in Halifax. They accept middle-class students as well as poor children, Black children and Indian children. Many of the well-to-do in Halifax contribute to the cost of educating the poor. I think James still preaches in some of the Townships—other than Dartmouth—on a rotating basis."

"Well," George said, "I will have to get settled and then take a journey back to Halifax to see how he and his wife are doing."

George also wondered how his little daughter would receive him.

"She is four years old now," William said, "and we have talked to her about her father and tried to keep your memory alive so that she might one day be glad to see you. I imagine she will be thrilled to have a father and I hope you have brought her a small toy or doll."

"Oh, indeed, I have a small doll, the kind they make in Demerara. And some candy for her!"

"She will be very happy with that, I am sure."

"And how are you, Mr. Forsyth? You seem quite well to my eyes."

"Thank you, George, but I'm quite aware I'm looking a little older and a bit worse for wear. I am usually well, but from time to time I have 'spells' when I am no longer conscious of my surroundings. I have little to no warning that one is coming and do not know how long any given 'spell' will last—the most recent one lasted for a whole day. The doctors don't have any idea what is happening. It does make it worrisome to travel on horseback, but I can walk in good weather to the Church and visit those within walking distance. I have had to give up on my grammar school and doing services in Horton Township unless I can find someone with a horse and cart to take me there."

"Well, I am here to assist you, Mr. Forsyth."

"I am glad for your daughter's sake that you are back, although I must tell you that Elizabeth Ann has turned out to be a most devoted and capable mother and the child seems to be thriving."

As soon as they reached Salem Cottage, George jumped down from the cart and ran up the lane to the house. William tied up the horse and followed.

The Forsyths were waiting. Mary Stewart Struthers had on a pretty flowered dress with a matching bow in her long brown hair, which had been plaited in the back. George opened the back door and ran in, thinking the family was in the kitchen. He found them in the parlour.

Little Mary said, "Are you my father?"

George nodded and she ran to hug him. He picked her up and she snuggled into his shoulder.

"How are you, Elizabeth Ann, John Elkanah—Dr. John, I should say—and Bazaleel? And where are Margaret and Kerr Beckwith?"

"Margaret is not here at the moment. I suspect she is strolling along the road somewhere. She has not been well, shall we say," Elizabeth Ann said. "Kerr is in university. The rest of us are well, George, and we are glad to have you returned. Come, let us have tea and hear your stories about Demerara."

And so, with Mary Stewart on his lap, George told them what had happened since he last saw them. William and Elihu dragged his trunk into the kitchen and joined the family for tea.

Later that day, William, George and Mary Stewart went to visit her mother's grave at the Chipman's Corner Cemetery.

"Father cried," Mary Stewart said to William as Elizabeth Ann readied the little girl for bed.

Elizabeth Ann said, "We all loved your mother and miss her very much. I'll tell you some stories about her when she was a little girl after you're tucked into bed."

George settled in to the family once again, and he and William worked to provide ministry to the Cornwallis folk. George always deferred to William as the senior minister and William was careful to involve George in all decisions. The Elders all agreed that this arrangement was the best thing for the congregation.

In October 1835 there was a meeting of the Church of Scotland in Saint John, New Brunswick. Elihu attended and came back to share his impressions with William. "It was a good meeting, William. Everyone sends their best wishes for your speedy recovery."

William sincerely hoped it would be able to attend the next meeting and hoped it would be held closer to Cornwallis Township.

On November 8th, the Lord's Day, William preached in Horton.

The Lecture was on the 23rd Psalm and the text was the Letter of Jude, verses 20 and 21:

> But you, beloved, build yourselves up in your most holy faith; pray in the Holy Spirit; keep yourselves in the love of God; wait for the mercy of our Lord Jesus Christ unto eternal life.

On February 28th, 1836, the Lord's Day, William preached at the Horton Meeting House. His text was Peter's first letter, Chapter 2, Verse 24:

> He himself bore our sins in his body on the tree that we might die to sin and live to righteousness. By his wounds you have been healed.

On April 10, 1836 William preached at Horton and spent the night at Elihu's. The next day, William and Elihu went to visit the Averys before William returned to Cornwallis Township.

~

1836 ended quietly, but 1837 would not be a good year.

William received a letter from Thomas Lydiard reporting that little Samuel William had died April 13th. It was sudden and the result of one of the childhood diseases. William's only grandson was gone.

William took a stage coach to Halifax to visit Thomas and to see Samuel William's grave. Thomas was completely heart-broken. Poor little Margaret, now nine years old, was very sad but tried to comfort her father. It was a desperate state of affairs.

Shortly after he returned home, William had another 'spell'. This one seemed to last much longer than the others and William didn't seem to recover as well as he had in the past. Everyone waited to see if he would return to his former self. Gradually, he regained his strength but was soon prostrated by several more 'spells'. In October 1837, he was concerned enough about his health that he decided to make out his Last Will and Testament.

Bezaleel went to visit the office of the Judge of Probate to see what was required in terms of witnesses. On the 6th day of October the witnesses gathered. One wrote down what William said and they all signed the document. Elizabeth Ann was too busy with looking after little Margaret Stewart to handle such matters, so William made Margaret his executrix and his nephew, Dr. James Kerr Beckwith, his executor.

There wasn't much to leave to the children. John Elkanah—who had his education paid for—got all William's clothes. The other three were to divide the proceeds from selling the one hundred acres on the North Mountain near Baxter's Harbour. They were to divide among themselves anything else that was owed to William or could be sold—including the horse and foal, and the cows and sheep. The girls were to share the kitchen and household furniture. That was it.

After the witnesses were gone, William spoke privately to John Elkanah. "I want you to promise to look after your sisters. What I have left them is not sufficient to sustain them. They are both well-educated and can teach or tutor, but I fear for their welfare."

"Father, I promise that I will do all within my power to care for my sisters and make the best use possible of the education you have given me."

"Thank you, my son. That makes me feel much better. Look after Bezaleel as well. I cannot afford to send him to Scotland for an education and he does not seem to care about that. He is trying to become a merchant and that would be a good occupation, as it suits his abilities."

"I'll do my best for him, as well, Father."

"I hope you know that I am very proud of you. I see you have your heart set on Miss Martha Ann Morton."

"I do, and her father approves. I just have to have a well-paying practice and I may have Miss Morton's hand in marriage."

"You have my blessing as well," William said.

William then called his four children to his side and spoke plainly, as was his habit. "My children, I have done my best to care for you but my illness has prevented me from having another grammar school to raise more money for Bezaleel's education and perhaps to put away towards your futures, girls, in case you do not marry. John Elkanah and Bezaleel, I expect you to look out for your sisters' well-being. They have always been there to help and support you as part of the grammar school and looking after the boarders. They were essential to the success of my grammar schools and thus to raising money for your education. Elizabeth Ann has raised little Mary and thus was not available to suitors. Margaret has some condition which may prevent her from marrying or from working. I think George will marry again soon as he has been courting Miss Eliza Davidson. Oh, and Kerr is about to graduate with his medical degree and will, of course, be looking for a good situation and finding a wife."

"We will do our best for our sisters," John Elkanah said. Elizabeth Ann tried to speak, but buried her face in her handkerchief instead.

Margaret, whose gaze had been wandering all around the room, lingered after the others had left. She drew close to her father, who raised a hand to hold hers.

"I don't understand me," Margaret said slowly. "Do you?"

"I am afraid I do not," William said softly.

"But you love me anyway. You always love me." She squeezed his hand. "Thank you."

The congregation could see how William's health had failed. Although he tried his best, George had to take on much of what had been William's duties.

William spent more and more time thinking about eternal life. Every time he tried to imagine what Heaven would be like, it ended up looking a lot like his childhood in Scotland. He dreamed about running and playing with his friends in the summertime at that place in the river where they could swim, and about a brook where they played with their toy boats. There were sheep to count and lazy days spent looking up at the clouds. And then there were the rainbows after the rain—sometimes there were even double rainbows. It was fun to try to figure out where they began and where they ended. At tea time, their mothers would call them all home to have oatcakes and biscuits with the rest of the family.

More and more William spent a good part of each day back home in Scotland. If, finally, he regretted his decision to come to America or to Cornwallis Township, he did not say so. It was satisfying that his family, his students, his friends 'down the Valley', and his congregation loved him. He hoped the Lord would consider that he had been a good and faithful servant. That was all that mattered in the end.

On the Sabbath Day, February 9, 1840, William went home to the Eternal City.

End

Acknowledgements

This book came into being after years of researching my third great-grandfather, the Reverend William Forsyth, and my Kings County, Nova Scotia, New England Planter ancestors. I had only the slightest inkling about the Forsyth family when I started my research, and none about the Planters who had settled in Cornwallis Township in 1760. I remember finding a book about New England Planters on my mother's bookshelf after her death and wondering why she would have bought a book on this topic. Even after I had found out about the Planters, it took more years of research about their history in New England as the part of the Puritan Great Migration from England to New England, starting in 1620.

Having most of my questions about my Planter ancestors answered, an even greater matter arose: what was I going to do with all this material stuffed into many three-ring binders? I didn't know.

On my summer vacations with my three sisters, we went to many museums and graveyards, looking for ancestors. Many of them are buried in the Chipman's Corner Cemetery, near the site of the now-demolished Congregational-Presbyterian Church where Mr. Forsyth preached for forty years.

There was no gravestone for Mr. Forsyth, although I did discover that there had been one which had long-since crumbled into dust. That didn't seem right.

Gradually, the idea formed in my mind that I should write a book and use the proceeds to buy Mr. Forsyth a new gravestone. And so, I got busy. Never having written a book, but having read many, I thought, *how hard can it be?* Well, that's another whole story.

There are so many people whom I need to thank and acknowledge for helping this book come into being: First and foremost, the authors of the histories of Kings, Annapolis, and Digby counties. I owe all the background to the story to them. Second, the Kings County Museum and Genealogy Centre gathered a great deal of material on the Planter families and made it readily available to me with much generosity of spirit. I also made visits to the Mac-Donald Museum in Middleton and the Admiral Digby Museum in Digby. They made every effort to be of assistance.

Fourth, the Public Archives of Nova Scotia were always a great source of background material and their patience with my modest ability to use microfilm readers always amazed me. Fifth, the Genealogy Section of the Halifax Library on Spring Garden Road was always ready to help search for—and find—extremely helpful material.

The State of Vermont Historical Society had two of Mr. Forsyth's printed sermons, for which I will be forever grateful as they seemed the closest I could get to who he was as a person. Then the Public Archives found three of his letters and a proposal for a book by the Reverend George Patterson, which gave more details about Mr. Forsyth.

This scanty collection was the sole source of my knowledge about my forebear, I knew my book would have to be fiction, but fiction that was as close to the known facts as I could make it.

I would like also to acknowledge my three sisters, Elizabeth, Joan, and Janice, who for many years spent their vacations poring over ancient records in museums and tramping through graveyards all down the Annapolis Valley in search of our ancestors. It became rather like a treasure hunt for the graves of people I had found mentioned in histories and genealogies.

My greatest thanks must be to Moose House Publications for agreeing to publish my book. As my naiveté about writing books and what was involved in getting them published gradually wore off, I realized getting published was by no means certain and my 'masterpiece' might well end up being photocopied for my relatives and given to them as a Christmas gift. So, I am entirely grateful to Brenda Thompson, publisher, and Andrew Wetmore, editor, for their willingness to edit my book and publish it.

I so hope it will find readers who will enjoy the story of William Forsyth as he discovers whether Nova Scotia is his land of hopes and dreams.

Carolyn Jean Nicholson
Halifax, Nova Scotia
2021

Carolyn Nicholson

Select bibliography

Betts, E. A. *Bishop Black and His Preachers.* Sackville, New Brunswick: The Tribune Press for the Maritime Conference Archives, 1976.

Calkin, J. B. *Old Time Customs: Memories and Traditions and Other Essays.* Halifax, Nova Scotia: A. & W. MacKinlay, 1918.

Calnek, W. A. *History of the County of Annapolis including Old Port Royal and Acadia.* London: Phillimore & Co., 1897.

Coward, E. R. *Bridgetown, Nova Scotia: Its History to 1900.* Bridgetown, NS: Bridgetown and Area Historical Society, 1950.

Crawford, D. S. "Canadians Who Graduated With an MD from the University of Edinburgh 1809-1840" in *Osler Library Newsletter 118*, pp. 5-10, Spring 2013.

Davidson, J. D. *Handley Chipman: Kings County Planter 1717-1799.* Kings County, NS: distributed by the author, no date.

Davison, J. D. *Eliza of Pleasant Valley.* Hantsport, NS: Lancelot Press, 1983.

Eaton, A. W. *The History of Kings County Nova Scotia: Heart of the Acadian Land.* Salem, Massachusetts: The Salem Press Company, 1910.

Eaton, E. L. "The Survey Plan of Cornwallis Township, Kings County" in *The Nova Scotia Historical Review*, 18, no date.

Forsyth, W. "Sermon preached at Danville, Vermont, before the fraternity of Free and Accepted Masons of Harmony Lodge at the celebration of the festival of St. John the Baptist, June 25, 1798". Danville, Vermont, USA: Farley & Gose, 1798.

Forsyth, W. "A Sermon Preached at Windsor, Oct. 10, 1799 before his excellency the governor, the lieut. Gov. and the Council, and the House of Representatives of the State of Vermont". Windsor, Vermont, USA: The Vermont Historical Society, 1799.

Frith, J. "History of Tuberculosis, Part 1, Phthisis, Consumption and the While Plague" in *Journal of Military and Veterans' Health*, 22-2, 2018.

Fry, J. *Sketch of Chipman Corner, Kings County, Nova Scotia c.1670-1985*. Kentville, Kings County, Nova Scotia, Canada: Community History Group of Kings Historical Society. No date

Haliburton, T. C. *History of Nova Scotia*. Halifax, NS: Joseph Howe, 1829.

Hay, E. "Sommerville at Horton and Cornwallis" in *Covenanters in Canada: Reformed Presbyterianism from 1820-2012*, pp. 47-57. Montreal: McGill-Queen's University Press, 2012.

Hendy, M. G. *Where They Rest in Peace*. Kings County, Nova Scotia: Gaspereau Press, 2001.

Hill, R. A. *Some Chapters in the History of Digby County and Its Early Settlers*. Halifax, NS: McAlpine Publishing Company, 1901.

Jameson, E. O. *The Cogswells in America*. Copyright 1884 by E. O. Jameson.

Jones, J. G. *The War of 1812: a guide to the battlefields and historic sites*. Western New York Public Broadcasting Association, 2011.

Lee, R. H. *Project Canterbury: An Historical Sketch of the Church of England in New Brunswick*. Saint John, New Brunswick: Sun Publishing, 1880.

Longley, R. S. "The Coming of the New England Planters to the Annapolis Valley" in *They Planted Well: New England Planters in Maritime Canada* (pp. 14-35). Fredericton, New Brunswick: Acadiensis Press, 1988.

Madison Hamilton, T. M. *The Forgotten Immigrants: The Journey of the New England Planters to Nova Scotia 1759-1768*. Published on the Canadian Museum of Immigration at Pier 21 website, 2019.

Perkins, C. I. *The Romance of Old Annapolis Royal*. Annapolis Royal, Nova Scotia: Historical Association of Annapolis Royal, 1925.

Rand, E. *Canard Street: Cornwallis Township, Kings County, Nova Scotia*. Kentville, NS: The Kings Historical Society Community

History Committee, 1997.

Rothbard, M. N. *Excerpted from An Austrian Perspective on the History of Economic Thought Before Adam Smith, 1995*. Retrieved from the Mises Institute: https://mises.org

Savary, A. W. *Supplement to the History of Annapolis County*. Toronto: William Briggs, 1913.

Stevens, M. G. *Where They Rest in Peace: a Guided Tour of Seven Historic Cemeteries in Kings County, NS*. Wolfville: Gaspereau Press, 2000.

Truro Presbytery History Committee. *A Tale of Two Centuries: Truro Presbytery - Oldest in Canada*. Sackville, NB: The Tribune Press Ltd., 1993.

Wells, E. M. *History of Ryegate, Vermont*. St. Johnsbury, VT: The Caledonian Company, 1913.

William S. Bartlett, A. *The Frontier Missionary: a memoir of the life of Rev. Jacob Bailey, A.M. missionary at Pownalborough, Maine, Cornwallis and Annapolis, NS*. Boston: Ide and Dutton, 1853.

Wilson, I. W. *A Geography and History of the County of Digby, Nova Scotia*. Halifax: Holloway Brothers Printers, 1900.

Wood, A. "The Significance of Evangelical Presbyterian Politics in the Construction of State Schooling: A Case Study of the Pictou District, 1817-1866" in *Acadiensis*, 2-210, 1991.

Woodworth, Elihu. *The Diary of Deacon Elihu Woodworth 1835-1836*. Transcribed by F. I. Woodworth. Wolfville, Nova Scotia: Wolfville Historical Society, 1972.

Wright, E. C. *Planters and Pioneers: Nova Scotia, 1749 to 1775, revised edition*. Hantsport, NS: Lancelot Press, 1982.

Other resources

- A Parks Canada statement about the Bloody Creek Historic Site: pc.gc.ca/en/nhs/ns/bloodycreek/info
- A Loyalist claim for reparations after the American Revolution: royalprovincial.com/military/mems/pa/clmmagee.htm

- The unpublished autobiography of James Fraser, completed in1867.
- Various entries in the online version of *The Canadian Encyclopedia.*
- Various entries in the *Dictionary of Canadian Biography.*
- Various historical records and maps made available online by P. Landry.
- Genealogical records held by the Annapolis Royal Historical Society.
- The longislandsurnames.com website.
- Materials retrieved from the Disability History Museum website, disabilitymuseum.org.
- Materials on missionary movements retrieved from roxborogh.com.
- *The Huntington Family in America: a genealogical memoire of the known descendants of Simon Huntington from 1633-1915..* Hartford, Connecticut: Huntington Family Association, 1915
- The Committee on Church Worship and Ritual in the General Council of the United Church of Canada. *Forms of Service: Second Order for the Ordination of Ministers from the Book of Congregational Worship.* Toronto, Ontario, Canada: The United Church of Canada House, 1926.
- Material made available online by the Canadian Museum of Immigration at Pier 21.
- Material from the Provincial Archives of Nova Scotia, including
  - An unpublished prospectus by R. G. Patterson, around 1870, on Presbyterianism in the Maritime Provinces of Canada.
  - "School Orders" from 1800.
  - *What's Cooking: Food, Drink, and the Pleasures of Eating in Old-Time Nova Scotia.*
  - William's 1831 advertisement for his grammar school.
  - Unpublished personal letters and papers.

About the author

Carolyn Nicholson was born and raised in Nova Scotia, but it wasn't until she began years of research into her Nova Scotia ancestors that she discovered how deep her roots were there. This led to her decision to write her first book.

She is a graduate of Mount St. Vincent University and the Atlantic School of Theology, as well as the Halifax Infirmary School of Health Information Management, and has worked in both  these fields as well as teaching at the post-secondary level. She is currently retired and has completed her second book about her ancestors, with the working title of: *Traitors, Cannibals, Highlanders, and Vikings.*

Carolyn lives in Halifax and continues to research her Nova Scotia roots, in the company of her three sisters, who are always happy to go with her on her research adventures.

Carolyn Nicholson

Book club discussion questions

1   Do you remember leaving home as a young adult? What were your hopes and dreams for your life? What are your thoughts about William's decision to leave Ryegate, Vermont, and take a new position? (Chapter One)

2   Have you ever moved to a new community and been involved in the process of getting to know the people and the place? What are your impressions of Cornwallis Township: the place and the people? (Chapter Two)

3   Discuss the roles of women and men in this society. Would you like to be a woman or a man in 19th century Nova Scotia? Why? (See: Chapter Three: Mary Beckwith and Chapter Four: Salem Cottage)

4   What did you know about New England Planters and Loyalists in Nova Scotia before you read the book? Are you descended from either group?

5   Were you surprised to learn that some Planters and many well-to-do Loyalists had black slaves?

6   What stands out for you about William's trip 'down the Valley' as a missionary? For instance, the state of the roads, the people he met and their occupations, the stories told by the Loyalists and others, the state of government, religion, and education? (See: Chapter Five: The missionary)

7   Have you ever put off getting 'to the bottom of things'? What do think about William not getting paid and having to open a grammar school to support the family? What would you have done? (See: Chapter Six: The educator)

8   What are your impressions of William from his ad in the Nova Scotia *Gazette* regarding the opening of his grammar

school? (See: Chapter Seven: Land of hopes and dreams)

9   Has there ever been a moment in time when you felt that everything—while not perfect—was very happy and satisfying? What is in William's situation that he feels this way? (See: Chapter Seven: Land of Hopes and Dreams)

10   How is William feeling as he explains to his friend, Deacon Elihu Woodworth, about the decision of the Cornwallis Township Elders about the Horton Township church arrangements? (See: Chapter Seven: Land of hopes and dreams)

11   Have you ever felt it necessary to choose between options when you don't know which in the end will be the better decision? What do you think of William's choice in Chapter Eight: The Bitter Decision? Was Mary right?

12   Have you ever lived through an epidemic? Did you know that consumption (tuberculosis) was once epidemic in Nova Scotia? Can you relate to William's shock when he learns that his beloved son, Will, has consumption? (See: Chapter Nine: Here we have no abiding city)

13   William suffers through a lot of loss, as does his family. Do you think his final illness is a grief reaction?

14   Did William's story end in a satisfactory way? Discuss.

15   Sum up how you feel about William, his family, his life, the Township, and the people of Nova Scotia. Did you learn anything about yourself or present life in Nova Scotia?

www.ingramcontent.com/pod-product-compliance
Lightning Source LLC
Chambersburg PA
CBHW060859210726
48293CB00006B/1874